CRONICA ACADIA

Bend Sinister

C. J. Deering

ISBN: 069289991X
ISBN 13: 9780692899915
Library of Congress Control Number: 2017909095
CRONICA ACADIA : BEND SINISTER, Los Angeles, CA

cronicaacadia.com

Cover by Bukovero

Go I know not whither and fetch I know not what.
                                                —from a Russian fairy tale

I put on my robe and wizard hat.

—*bloodninja*

The dwarves recount their history in drunken song that owes more to melody than to fidelity. But this is a human history, and we will tell it faithfully.

The elves begin their stories in the middle and meander back and forth before coming out at the end. But this is a human story, and we will tell it in the human tradition, from the beginning.
—*Cronica Acadia*

If Dangalf had known it was his last ever commute home from work, it might not have seemed so bad. But he didn't know that, and so as he sat in traffic waiting to get home to the game, it felt interminable. It's not important from what job Dangalf was driving home; he was like millions in the modern world spending too many of their waking hours doing something that gave them no satisfaction and barely paid the bills, which included ever-increasing student-loan payments for a degree that had no bearing whatsoever on his present occupation. Still he had a photocopy of that degree displayed in his cubicle to remind himself that he was better than his circumstances, even if it was a source of amusement for his less educated but equally paid coworkers. And though the nature of his particular unrewarding method of making a living is unimportant, he in fact worked for the state employment office.

Don't ask him how he had gone from a prestigious program at an expensive university to being a government employee. He was not sure himself. He could only recall the speed bumps of the descent: professional rejection, unemployment, a broken heart, more professional rejection, more unemployment, financial difficulties. During one bout of unemployment, he began testing for government jobs, which fulfilled the required work search for his unemployment benefits. He was subsequently hired by the same agency that administered these benefits and had since remained gainfully employed. Unemployment, after all, was a booming industry.

But this full-time employment only met his basic needs and at a dreadful cost. His hope and confidence withered. It seemed apparent he would not escape his lower-middle-class existence. He would not be celebrated or successful. His father, who had worked his way up from the working poor into the lower middle class, had summed up his son's aspirations perfectly: Dangalf had expected the unexpected, and the expected had happened.

Life was cruel. *Real life* was cruel, he corrected himself. There was still the game.

Dangalf felt that if there were a meter on his desk, showing how much he was earning, after taxes, after gasoline and time spent commuting, if there were such a meter on his desk slowly turning over a penny at a time, showing how little he was earning, it would be all he needed to quit. Life was too precious. Work bought his life from him for a pittance. It gave him no creative outlet and robbed him of his individuality. It forced him to be with people he didn't like and took him away from those he did like. All his current existence proved to him was that not everyone whose life went tragically wrong ended up on the street. Or on the ledge.

If there was a plus side to his menial, unchallenging job, it was that he could practically do it on autopilot. Even most of the conversations he had during the workday were by rote. And that meant he could devote the higher functions of his brain to thinking about the game. He would plan new strategy to overcome present challenges, and he would even crack a rare smile when he thought back to recent triumphs. Thinking about the game was almost as good as playing it.

He wanted to quit his job before he was too old to do something else—but perhaps he was too old already? Talking to a steady stream of unemployed people each day sapped his desire to join their ranks. What could he do that would provide him accomplishment and a paycheck? Hero, seeker, mercenary, and adventurer were viable occupations only in the game.

Dangalf made it home after it was already dark. In his too-small apartment were two mismatched desks, back to back, each laden with overclocked CPUs and dual monitors with a tangle of peripheral devices. It was a gross violation of feng shui and probably several fire codes. His gangly roommate, Doppelganger, was already playing the game on one of the computers. (Dangalf and Doppelganger were not their birth names, of course, but are the names most fitting for this story. These are the names of their avatars in the game, the names they chose for themselves.)

Doppelganger was his oldest and dearest friend, and Dangalf was learning to despise him. He resented that Doppelganger could play the game all day while Dangalf went to work. He knew that Doppelganger's continued unemployment, his use of credit cards and other people's money to finance himself, and his protracted absence from the job market were hurting Doppelganger most of all, and Dangalf only incidentally, but Dangalf still decided to take it personally.

Doppelganger barely left his computer, and too few of those excursions were into the shower. Dangalf was certain the reason that none of his sexy, female neighbors ever showed up at his door with a bottle of wine and asked him if he wanted to hang out was because of Doppelganger. Dangalf had wanted Doppelganger to move out for months now, and tonight he was determined to speak his mind.

Dangalf did not rush to join his friend at the opposite computer. He instead took care of only the most rudimentary of housekeeping and hygiene so that he could devote the rest of the night to the game.

Doppelganger played at the computer with the History Channel on TV and with music playing on his iPod speakers. Multitasking, he called it. Dangalf turned the music and TV off.

"How'd the job search go?"

"Great. I didn't find anything."

"Did you look?"

"And it's your business how?"

"Because," Dangalf said, "you're committed to paying half the rent. Just how much more unemployment do you have?"

If you can lie a question, that's what Dangalf had done. He had quite illegally looked up his friend's status in the state's computers and knew Doppelganger had just gotten an extension for six months more of unemployment compensation. That was bad news for Dangalf. He wanted Doppelganger to become gainfully employed so that he could kick him out with a clear conscience. He knew Doppelganger would never get a job as long as he was being paid to play the game.

Doppelganger shouted with excitement because of something that happened in the game or because he didn't want to answer Dangalf.

Dangalf sat down to the game with a bottle of beer and a can of chili and popped the top off of both. The chili looked like dog food. He stuck a plastic spoon into its solid, greasy mass. Cooking and dishwashing took precious game time, and the chili would only be minimally improved by warmth. Dangalf slipped on his earphones and mic as he logged on. The insults and drudgery of the day faded as the game loaded. The developer's bouncy cinematic finished, the screen darkened, and the orchestral music rose. The words faded in and out on screen: *Hearken back to a simpler time...when all your problems could be solved with an axe.*

The game was *Cronica,* a massive multiplayer online role-playing game, or MMORPG. There were millions of paying subscribers who logged on to the Internet to play with and against other subscribers in a medieval world of swords and sorcery based on a pulp-fiction novel.

The loading screen featured a map of the game world Acadia. There were the free northern kingdoms of Vinlandia, Hybernia, and Albinia (human, dwarf, and elf lands, respectively) and to the south, Palusia, Sylvania, and Brimstone (orc, troll, and goblin lands, respectively). At the center of all the lands was the neutral Nemetia, home of the sprites, gnomes, and other magical creatures.

Dangalf was a human mage and Doppelganger, a human warrior. The other founding members of their group had been Regicide, another human warrior, and Elftrap the she-elf druid. Though Elftrap was male, he played a beautiful she-elf. Regicide had been the best player of them all, maybe the best player in the entire virtual world. But about six months ago, it seemed he had dropped off the face of the earth. (That description would be more accurate than any of them could imagine.)

Game dynamics required that players form complimentary groups to complete many of the quests. And these groups took names that were usually pretentious or vulgar. They had gone the pretentious route and called themselves the Keepers of the Broken Blade—Dangalf had spontaneously come up with the name, and it was agreed by the other founding members that it was a nice mixture of the mystical and the martial. Or to use game terminology, it was of the White School and of the Red School.

After Regicide had disappeared, the remaining Keepers had to replace him, and the dwarf blackguard Nerdraaage replied to their online post. Elftrap had a problem with Nerdraaage. First and foremost, he was playing against type. Dwarves were not the best blackguards, a class that required stealth and agility. Second, Elftrap thought that the name Nerdraaage showed a complete lack of creativity as he should have gone a different direction when he found the names Nerdrage and Nerdraage already taken by other players. Nerdraaage countered that his name was better than the other versions because it "Sounded angrier." His spunky defense of his name won over Dangalf and Doppelganger and, with Elftrap's grudging consent, the dwarf became the fourth member of the Keepers. It was a good grouping, and they had become like family even though none of them, save Dangalf and Doppelganger, had ever met in person. But they spent almost every night and weekend in the virtual world together. Even their arguments were familial in nature. When the smart and sarcastic Elftrap would cut down the naïve Nerdraaage, he would respond angrily, "Shut up, girl!" or some other gender-based insult for their only member with a female avatar.

She-elf avatars all had beautiful faces and gravity-defying bodies. And they wore the skimpiest of outfits. Clearly the game makers realized that the vast majority of their players were horny men and boys desperate to get a glimpse of even avatar cleavage.

The Keepers' races dictated that they play for the Acadian Alliance of Righteous Races (AARR), the alliance of humans, elves, and dwarves. They were the good guys (or "puritans" or "vanilla" as the AARR was flamed on message boards by opposing players). Their adversary was the Legion Pangaea, or just Legion, comprised of orcs, goblins, and trolls, and the players of these races reveled in their role as the bad guys. They were the "uglies" or "RGB" (for the red, green, and blue skin colors of the orcs, goblins, and trolls respectively) as Alliance posters flamed back.

Cronica provided a fully realized virtual world that offered camaraderie, discovery, conquest, and honor. All elements that Dangalf, and he suspected most players, found lacking IRL. The rewards were only virtual, but there was no denying the rush players felt when victorious. With victory came gold and reputation gains, and, unlike IRL, reputation meant everything.

Dangalf sometimes wondered if he was addicted to the game, but if so he was a functional addict. Doppelganger had told him stories about the Far East where *Cronica* players were sent to boot camps to break their addiction. Some players were reported to have committed suicide over setbacks in the game.

Though the Keepers were separated by thousands of virtual miles, it was only a matter of tossing a coin into a nearby water well and instantly teleporting from that one to any other well in Acadia. (Usually to the well to which you had intended to teleport.) Tonight that destination well was at the Temple of the Red Rose, where the Keepers gathered in preparation for an attack on the Witchfinder General. He had defeated them several times before, but they had been close to defeating him during their last attempt, and now they were convinced that they had the gear and the strategy to finally dispatch him.

The Witchfinder General was an NPC, or nonplayer character. More than that he was a boss, an especially powerful NPC designed to defeat all but the best groups of players playing their best game. Game lore explained that he was once one of the greatest enemies of the Legion until his zealotry turned him against all forms of magic and ultimately led to his corruption by black magic. Now holed up in his temple fortress, he was the most difficult and rewarding quest for only the most advanced players. Sadly, he also represented the endgame, the last and greatest quest available to players and the literal end of the game according to game lore.

An expansion of *Cronica*, adding new lands, quests, and (most exciting of all!) flying mounts, was already announced. Doppelganger was especially eager as the expansion meant he would be able to promote to Dragoon, a dragon-riding warrior. Though the expansion was promoted vigorously by Journeyman, the makers of *Cronica*, the release date was still not set. Veteran players like the Keepers were running desperately short of new experiences in the game. There were very few blank spots left on Dangalf's virtual world map.

The Witchfinder General did not disappoint. It was a glorious battle that required all of the skill and teamwork honed over their years of play. Doppelganger, the tank, with his metal armor, engaged the general at close range and took the brunt of the damage as his class was intended to do. Dangalf, the damage dealer, stood on a balcony and blasted the general with high-damage fireballs and frost bolts. Nerdraaage, the other damage dealer, would stab the general in the back with poisoned daggers, only to disappear when the general turned his rage toward him.

Blackguards were expert at evasion, even to the point of turning invisible (*unappear* they called it unapologetically), which was a necessity. Nerdraaage in his leather armor could not survive even one direct blow from the general. And if he died, he would have to buy back his soul from the ferryman, and by the time he returned to the battle, the other Keepers would probably be dead as well.

Elftrap used his druid powers to heal Doppelganger, who, even with his armor and warrior resilience, would have died a dozen times while battling the general.

Everyone knew their roles so well it was as if the team-chat feature was unnecessary. They slew the Witchfinder General in under twenty minutes, and he gave a dying soliloquy that lasted half that long, but they were too busy celebrating to pay attention. Dangalf and Elftrap even *danced.* (Their avatars appeared to dance with each other after they each typed the dance command.) They all took part in some cheering and bragging, and so the team-chat feature had not gone to waste after all.

Dangalf did not have to work the next day (or later today since it was already past midnight) but he knew he had to go to bed at some point. As his computer powered down, he still felt good from the play tonight. Was it possible that *Cronica* could actually lead to the release of endorphins? He only knew that the game made him feel good when nothing else did.

In his good spirits, he looked upon Doppelganger with pity. He wasn't such a bad sort. Yes, his hygiene wasn't great. He didn't wash his dishes and left dirty clothes all about. But Dangalf was suddenly overcome with a great sympathy for the fragile human being sitting at the desk across from him. Doppelganger had nowhere else and more importantly no one else. How could he ask him to leave?

"I was watching the military channel earlier today," said Doppelganger excitedly. "And they were saying that paratroopers yell, 'Geronimo!' because the guy who started it saw the movie *Geronimo* the night before he jumped. And that had me thinking, what if he had seen a different movie from 1939? Paratroopers could be jumping out of planes yelling, 'Gunga Din!' Or 'The Wizard of Oz!' Or 'Beau Geste!' It could have changed the course of the war if, when they jumped, our paratroopers yelled 'Goodbye, Mr. Chips!'"

"You have to leave," said Dangalf.

II

Dangalf fell asleep thinking about the game as he usually did. And though they had reached endgame, there was still content worth exploring in the game, and there was always PVP (player versus player). They had looted the Witchfinder General and each taken away some of the most powerful pieces available in the game. And the Keepers planned to meet in Acadia tomorrow with their new weapons and gear and put some hurt on the RGB.

For the Keepers, Saturday meant marathon gaming. Hours spent challenging and crushing villainy. Hours spent collecting a wealth of gold and jewels. Total immersion in the mythical land of Acadia. And this Saturday would be the same. Only different.

III

Dangalf's sleep was disturbed by a thumping against his bedroom window. He tried to visualize the cause of the annoying sound. It was too protracted to be incidental and not violent enough to be a crime. He was pretty sure it wasn't human at all. It was windy outside, and his imagination pictured that a wind-whipped flag was violently slapping against his window. But that wasn't it. Who flew flags in the city? Only government buildings. (He had seen the security guard outside his workplace bunch up a flag at the end of the day and stuff it under his sweaty armpit.) He would ruminate on the source of the noise a bit longer as he resisted getting out of bed.

His mind began to race with all of the memories that he didn't want to remember. Hell was a having a perfect memory. It was a swirl of unpleasantness that unfolded in his mind—a swirl of betrayal, personal failings, missed opportunities, and unrequited love. His heart began to thump in agitation, and the coursing blood raised him unpleasantly from his bed.

He kicked his legs onto the floor and stood. He released the ancient shade that wound itself angrily into a coil. He saw what caused the curious commotion, and it neither surprised him nor made sense. It was an agitated pigeon fluttering excitedly against the window. He reached up and lowered the shade again.

Doppelganger was already at the kitchen table eating cereal.

"What are you doing up?"

"Fucking bird," grunted Doppelganger.

Dangalf was trying to understand why Doppelganger was calling him a "fucking bird" when he noticed the same flapping sound from his bedroom was in the kitchen.

He stepped to the kitchen window where a pigeon refused to come to grips with the notion of glass.

"That bird was crashing into my window, too."

But it was not his bird. He remembered that his bird was whiter just as the whiter bird appeared next to the darker one and began his own futile dance against the glass.

"Storm coming. It messes up their radar."

"Pigeon radar?" asked Dangalf. And then, for no good reason, and despite many reasons not to, he opened the window, and both birds flew into the kitchen.

"They're gonna shite in my cornflakes," Doppelganger protested. *Cronica* players used the British spelling of shit to evade the game's profanity filters, and many had also taken to using the British pronunciation IRL in an attempt to sound worldly.

Dangalf retrieved a broom from behind the refrigerator, and it showered a large quantity of lint and debris in a sunlit arc. Why even have a broom, he thought, if it is only going to shower the room with more filth?

"Easy," cautioned Doppelganger. "They're more afraid of us than we are of them."

"Why would I be afraid of pigeons?"

"Don't hurt them."

"I'm just going to guide them back out the window." Before Dangalf could test his theory, both birds settled calmly on the breakfast table.

"That's odd."

"A message," added Doppelganger.

"What message?"

"They have messages on their legs." Doppelganger reached out cautiously to one of the birds, but it hopped delicately out of reach. The other pigeon moved closer to him. He took the message from the closer pigeon. "That other one must be for you."

Dangalf was a little afraid of the pigeons now. "Read it," he said.

Doppelganger looked at Dangalf as if to say, *You're not going to believe this* before he read aloud: "Heroes, seekers, mercenaries, and adventurers, a quest awaits you!"

A chill ran through Dangalf's flesh. He leaned the broom against the refrigerator and moved toward the other pigeon, which willingly gave up its message. Yes, that's what it said all right. *Heroes, seekers, mercenaries, and adventurers.* The same salutation used in *Cronica. A quest awaits you!* Delivered by carrier pigeon just as messages are delivered in the game. And just as in the game, these pigeons seemed to know the exact person for whom their messages were intended.

The pigeons fluttered back out of the open window. Dangalf and Doppelganger were silent as they read the quest over and over to themselves.

IV

D angalf and Doppelganger drove along silently in
Doppelganger's car. Dangalf did not even know what
Doppelganger's car was. All the identifying badges had been
torn off by vandals, or perhaps it had been such a disappointment coming off the assembly line that no badges had ever
been attached. Doppelganger had christened it the "Gray
Ghost" after its coating of primer. He never knew its original
paint color. Perhaps the factory that didn't bother to put badges on it also didn't bother to paint it. The floor was a shiny
collage of fast-food wrappers. Mercifully, in deference to the
occasion, Doppelganger had turned off his usually blaring ra-
dio immediately after starting his car. Why were they taking
Doppelganger's piece of shite anyway? Dangalf usually drove,
but he felt now as though most of his actions were on autopilot
since such a large portion of his brain was devoted to dealing
with the mystery of their quest messages. An ominous black
sky followed them, stopped when they stopped for gas, and
then followed them again.

After many miles Doppelganger offered, "Maybe it's a game promotion. They have a new expansion pack coming out soon."

"Greatest game promotion ever if it is. Why us?"

"Why not us?"

"Because it doesn't make sense. Those pigeons knew where to find us and wouldn't give up until we let them in. Even then, one pigeon let you take his message while the other one let me take his. As if they knew us individually."

The quest directions sent them to a town up north. From there it became more specific about roads and directions to take from the town. Dangalf hadn't eaten today and he had been up for hours. Even Doppelganger, who was always hungry, didn't suggest they turn into one of the many clown-colored fast-food restaurants that they passed. Hours later, in a strange new world, a new universe even, cold and hungry, they would wish that they had taken their last-ever chance to eat McNuggets. As they approached their destination, they turned off onto a dirt road.

"I don't like this," said Doppelganger.

"What?"

"This road going to nowhere. What if this is just the complicated scheme of some ass-molesting serial killer?"

"An ass-molesting serial killer and world-class pigeon trainer? Him I've got to meet."

They drove on, deep into the woods, sheltered from the intrusion of modern civilization except for the sickly sounds of the Gray Ghost. The ominous sky followed at a polite distance.

"No more directions."

"It's got to be close. Unless there isn't anything."

They slowed as they approached a clearing, and the shape of a building beyond the trees began to form. As the building appeared in full, Dangalf felt a chill run down his spine for the second time that day. He looked, mouth agape, at Doppelganger, who was also mouth agape.

To a *Cronica* player, the building was an icon. It was an inn. A human inn, to be exact. It was a two-story building about fifty feet long with a singular turret at the center where a staircase would be. The same generic structure, digitally rendered, stood in hundreds of places across Acadia. To a player it meant food, drink, shelter, rest, companionship, and more. The best inns provided NPCs such as trainers, quest givers, and sellers of rare items. But even the most modest inn provided sanctuary from the threats outside. The site of an inn held special meaning to a player. And now these two obsessive players approached one in real life.

They exited and stood by their respective doors. Their apprehension did not prevent expansive grins from covering their faces. Unique to each inn was an ornate sign depicting the name of the inn in a throwback to more illiterate times. This inn featured a black-and-gold shield adorned with a stripe running from upper left to lower right. It was an unfamiliar sign, and they could not name the inn. (In the game, they could have moved a cursor over the sign, and the name would appear as a tool tip.)

"It is some sort of game promotion," offered Doppelganger.

"That's impossible."

"What then?"

"Let's go in."

Doppelganger pointed to an ultracompact rental car parked nearby. It had an Acme Rent-a-Car license plate frame. "Who do you suppose that belongs to?"

"Wile E. Coyote?"

A small set of shoeprints led the way. They walked through the open oak door, their way lit by wall-mounted lamps. They walked past the stairs, which, if true to the game, would lead up to bedrooms. They entered the dining room where tables with benches were set about. Against the back wall was the bar. Near the back, a door to what would be the kitchen.

Dangalf's grin continued to test the elasticity of his face. It was a grin that was sure to give him sore face muscles, a condition he had not suffered from since he was a child and there was so much less reality to weigh down his enjoyment of a moment.

"Dangalf? Doppelganger?"

Both turned quickly to the voice on the stairs. It belonged to a small human male of indeterminate age. He could have been anywhere from fifteen to twenty-five. But the voice was familiar. Doppelganger got it first.

"Nerdraaage?"

"Yeah!"

Another Keeper was here. Now things were really getting spooky. "What are you doing here?"

"I got a quest to come here."

"Is there anyone else here?"

"Not on the first or second floor. I haven't made it down into the cellar. I—"

Nerdraaage didn't finish. The other two understood. Even the warmest, busiest inn wasn't immune from having a ghost or other creature in the cellar.

"Do you know what this is all about?" asked Dangalf.

"No. A carrier pigeon brought a quest to me."

"Me too," said a new voice. The others turned to the entrance, where a handsome male stood. The voice was familiar, but the others did not immediately make the connection. "I'm Elftrap. Who's who here?"

Elftrap the she-elf! But he wasn't a stereotypical geek like the childlike Nerdraaage, the pudgy and bespectacled Dangalf, or the gangly Doppelganger. In game jargon he was a classic mesomorph: athletic and good looking. (Though technically good looking was not a requirement of being a mesomorph.)

"Dangalf," said Dangalf weakly, finally meeting the male persona of the female avatar he had so often flirted and danced with.

"I'm Doppelganger."

"The Keepers of the Broken Blade," said Nerdraaage reverently. "All together in the same room for the first time."

"You must be Nerdraaage," scoffed Elftrap. "You look like you're twelve years old."

"I'm eighteen!"

"I want to see some ID." Elftrap stepped toward Nerdraaage and held out his hand. Nerdraaage blinked and reached into his back pocket and took out his wallet. "Look! He's got Velcro on his wallet!" said Elftrap.

"It's waterproof, you douche!"

"Waterproof!" laughed Elftrap. "Did you kayak here?"

"Shut your elf trap, Elftrap!"

"Worst retort ever," sighed Elftrap. He began to examine the room from floor to ceiling, with the same blissful enthusiasm that Doppelganger and Dangalf had shown.

"Wait," said Dangalf. "We all received messages by carrier pigeon coordinated to bring us here within minutes of each other. That would require organization and execution that cannot be explained except by—"

"Magic," said Nerdraaage.

"So you're saying it can't be explained," said Doppelganger.

"No one else has noticed that this setup defies explanation?" asked Elftrap.

"No," said Dangalf. "I think we've all noticed that."

"Why don't we call Journeyman?" asked Elftrap.

"That's a good idea," said Doppelganger. "I have the number on speed dial."

"That's the only number he has on speed dial."

Doppelganger squinted at his phone before putting it away. "No bars."

"The answers we're looking for must be right here," said Dangalf. "Why else would we be summoned here?"

"And here it is," answered Elftrap, now behind the bar. The others approached. "A quest continuation." Elftrap picked up a scroll, and four gold coins jingled onto the bar top.

The others gathered around, and Nerdraaage snatched one of the coins as if he was afraid someone would take two and he would be without. Dangalf and Doppelganger also took coins and examined them. It was a profile of a human named Steward Dukenfield on the obverse, and the Great Lighthouse, the symbol of the human Capitol of Vinland, on the reverse.

Elftrap read from the scroll, "You have done well to reach this point, but your quest is only beginning. Take these four sovereigns, one each for humans, dwarf, and she-elf, and throw them into the adjacent well. Throw them together, for only then will the summon group be completed. When you reach your next destination, your quest continues."

The well! In *Cronica*, the well would be behind the inn. And it was.

The ominous sky hovered impatiently overhead as the Keepers circled the well. A thick fog moved in quickly.

The well was round and stone and encircled with runes. Dangalf peered in. It was empty and black as far as he could see. He found a stone nearby and dropped it into the well. He and the others listened for about six seconds before they realized they would not hear it hit bottom.

"Who wants to go first?" asked Elftrap.

"First to do what?" asked Doppelganger.

"First to throw his coin in the well."

"And what do you think is going to happen?"

"Only one way to find out," said Dangalf.

Surprising the others, Nerdraaage tossed in his coin without a word. "Nothing," he said, disappointed.

"The scroll said to throw them in together," said Elftrap. "Good going Nerd."

"It didn't say we had to throw them in at the same time," said Dangalf as he tossed in his coin. "Anyone else have plans for tonight?"

"I was just going to play *Cronica*," said Elftrap.

"I think we're already playing," said Dangalf.

Elftrap tossed in his coin. The others looked expectantly at Doppelganger.

"I think this is real gold," he said.

"What do you want to do," asked Dangalf. "Sell it?"

"What do you think it would bring?" asked Doppelganger.

"Come on!" said Nerdraaage.

"Relax," said Doppelganger. "What do you think it will do? Magically transport us to another world?" He smiled at the rest of the Keepers. They did not share his good humor. With a shrug he tossed in the final gold coin. "Just like I—"

Dangalf didn't remember going to sleep, but he found himself waking up just the same. Curiously, he was standing as he awoke. More curiously, but as of yet unrecognized, he was standing in the supposedly fictional land of Acadia. And things only got more curious from there.

Dangalf stood on what felt like dirt, but there was a fog so thick that he could not see his own feet. But he did see some other things that were frighteningly unexpected. His long gray beard to begin with. He lifted up his shirt and pulled aside the beard. What had once been burgeoning man breasts were gone. And for the first time in his life, he had abs. He had abs not so much because the muscles were thick but because his skin was so taught against them.

The mist began to dissipate, and he saw that it was a dirt road, an intersection of dirt roads to be more precise, barely removed from the thick surrounding forest. At the center of the intersection was a well like the one they found outside the inn in that other world they occupied no longer, and beside that a directional sign for each of the three directions the roads led.

Doppelganger was experiencing the same awakening but it in a slower and duller fashion. Besides the seemingly instantaneous change in location, something even less explicable had happened. The feeling of his body had changed. His point of view was, he guessed, at least six inches higher than it was before. He felt the added weight of massive muscles in his chest, arms, and legs. But unlike the burden of weight, it actually made him feel explosive, like a coiled spring. These muscles held a lot more speed and strength than that to which he was accustomed. His thin clothing barely contained his rippling arms and legs. He could feel his hard, flat stomach under his shirt, but his expansive chest made it difficult to see his own belly.

Dangalf was the first of the others he saw in the receding mist. Dangalf's eyes widened as he took in the new Doppelganger. Even though the physical change was astounding, they each recognized each other. It was the eyes.

"Doppelganger?"

"What the fuck is going on?"

"What happened!" called out Nerdraaage. Nerdraaage was now thick with muscles. He sported a full red beard that must have weighed ten pounds alone. Dangalf could feel his weight in the ground as he moved toward them.

"What happened to you guys!" yelled Nerdraaage.

"We apparently became our characters from *Cronica*," said Dangalf.

"You're so tall!" replied Nerdraaage.

"In case you hadn't noticed," said Doppelganger, "you're a dwarf."

Shocked, Nerdraaage began looking at his own body and limbs. He quickly took hold of his red beard, more violently than he should have, and he let out a sharp, "Ah! It's real!"

"So are these!" said Elftrap as he appeared from the mist—or, more accurately, as *she* appeared from the mist. The "these" that she referred to were her breasts, which she cupped with hands under her shirt. She was now a slender but strong she-elf dressed like the others but only less so. Her garments left little to the imagination, which was just as well, as the Keepers' minds were reeling enough without the additional burden of imagining.

Elftrap was a stunning female with only the slightest points at the ears and eyes to differentiate her from a waifish human beauty. She-elves were some of the most eroticized creatures in fantasy art, and here was one in the flesh, stunning beyond the works of even the best, horniest fan art.

"Somehow I have become an anatomically correct she-elf," she said. "Look at you!" she said of Doppelganger. "You're built like a brick shitehouse."

"Right back atcha."

She surveyed her other companions as they surveyed her in return. She nodded her approval at Dangalf, who could only swallow in response. She looked Nerdraaage up and down. "Nice choice with the bright red hair by the way." Nerdraaage smiled sarcastically. Things were already returning to normal. A new normal. "So where are we?" she asked.

"Acadia," answered Dangalf pointing to a road sign that stood at the intersection of three dirt roads. "There's a sign for Hempshire, and I would assume the other two are for Hammersmith and Templa Taur."

"That says Hammersmith," said Nerdraaage. "But the third one is gibberish."

"You're gibberish," said Elftrap. "It clearly says Templa Taur. The Magic Wood." Elftrap said the last part as if a bit surprised herself that she knew it.

"You can read those signs?" said Dangalf.

The dwarf and elf nodded. "Why?"

"Because I cannot. I believe they are written in Dwarvish and Elvish respectively."

"I can speak Dwarvish," marveled Nerdraaage.

"And Acadish," said Dangalf. "If you notice the Hempshire sign, it is similar to English but it is not English."

"He's right!" said Elftrap. "I read it so naturally I just assumed it was English. But if I'm an elf, why can I also read human words?"

"According to game lore, human language or Acadish is the lingua franca of the righteous races," said Dangalf. "Just as Trollish is the tongue of the RGB."

"Does it bother anybody else that that is impossible?" asked Elftrap.

"If we stop suggesting that our new reality is impossible, we can probably cut down on a lot of unnecessary conversation," said Dangalf.

Nerdraaage started to say something and stopped. So they stood and talked about the situation, but the conversation kept coming back to the impossibility of the situation, and that resulted in a lot of unnecessary conversation, and finally they had to sit on the dirt road out of fatigue. All but Doppelganger, who would not fatigue and sat down only out of boredom.

They agreed on some key points, which was immaterial because the situation was what it was whether there was agreement or not. But for the record, they agreed that they were in Acadia at a point that in the game was called the crossroads or "noob central." (Noob being a variation on newbie, or a person new to the game.) Noob central was the place where all new Alliance players began and from where they would embark to their race's nearest town.

They agreed that they had all taken on the physical characteristics of their avatars from *Cronica*, right down to race, physique, and gender. To use the game terms, Doppelganger was the mesomorphic warrior, Dangalf was the ectomorphic mage, and Nerdraaage the endomorphic dwarf. Elftrap was a hybrid mesomorph/ectomorph befitting her druid class.

They agreed that each seemed to keep some of their original traits. Voices were the same or similar. (Elftrap's seemed to be a few octaves higher but still recognizable.) Speech patterns were the same. Dangalf and Doppelganger, knowing each other the best, agreed that their mannerism and posture remained the same, though it was hard to tell because the physical transformations were so striking. Their memories and personalities were intact. They also looked into each other's eyes and agreed that the eyes had not changed.

"The windows of the soul," said Elftrap more tellingly than any of them knew at the time.

"My eyes might look the same, but I am seeing better than I have ever seen," said Dangalf. "I don't need glasses."

"My vision is astonishing," agreed Elftrap. "And the sounds I can hear and the smells." She stopped to look accusingly at Nerdraaage. "These senses are going to take some getting used to."

Finally, they wore noob clothing, plain cloth garments and boots that offered little protection from the elements let alone the dangerous creatures they had to believe inhabited this land. Dangalf looked at the clothing that adorned them instantly on their entrance to this world and recognized something odd about it. But he would end up burning his magical clothes before he figured out their worth.

They had no money and no gear. It appeared to be the beginning of a long road to provide themselves with basic necessities in a strange and dangerous world. The conversation drifted back to the impossibility of the situation.

"I must be dreaming this whole thing," said Elftrap, looking at her long, slender legs stretching out before her.

"That's a pretty conceited way to look at it," said Dangalf, also looking at her legs. "You could say the same thing about the world we came from. This is as real as that world."

"It's impossible," said Nerdraaage.

"Not necessarily," responded Dangalf. "There's a school of thought that believes that there is an infinity of realities. If this is true, one of those realities would be a duplicate of Acadia."

"If there's an infinity of universes, wouldn't there have to be also an infinity of Acadias?" asked Elftrap.

"Infinity is a difficult concept."

"What do we do now?" asked Nerdraaage.

"We play the game," answered Dangalf. "We were summoned here. In time, maybe we'll find out why. But right now we have basic needs to take care of, like food, shelter—weapons." Doppelganger, who had been digging in the dirt with a stick, looked up, finally interested. "And we need to address those issues before we can afford the luxury of discovering our purpose. Hopefully the game concepts we know, that we're expert at, apply to this world."

"I'm hungry," said Nerdraaage.

"Hunger is not a game concept," said Elftrap.

"It is," corrected Dangalf. "You might not feel hunger, but it affects your stamina, how well your character plays. Remember the Triangle of Achievement when you first began the game? At the bottom was Preservation. That's where we are. We need food, shelter, and defense."

"We need money," said Nerdraaage. "Gold."

"So, according to the rules of the game, we need to head to town to pick up some quests for money," said Dangalf.

"Which town?" asked Elftrap.

"We should each go to our racial home towns," said Nerdraaage. "That's the way it is in the game."

"No," countered Dangalf. "We should stick together. We'll be safer that way. The Keepers of the Broken Blade is a good group. In that respect we've already achieved an advanced phase of the triangle: bonding. It will make the Preservation step that much easier."

"Where then?" asked Elftrap.

"Hempshire," said Doppelganger.

"Of course you want to go there," said Nerdraaage. "You two are humans."

"It just makes sense," said Dangalf. "We are two humans but only one each dwarf and elf. You can only begin your training in your own racial land. This will allow two of us to train before we venture to elven and dwarven lands. We're stronger if we stay together. If we die in the game, we can be resurrected. But there's no reason to believe that's true here."

"But Hammersmith is a dwarven town!" insisted Nerdraaage. "They'll have the best food, the best gear, great stone-wrought buildings, and dwarven hospitality!" His enthusiasm startled the others.

"How do you know that?" asked Dangalf.

"I don't know," said Nerdraaage. "I just know."

"The rest of you can go anywhere you like," said Doppelganger finally and with finality. "I'm going to Hempshire." Doppelganger leapt up and started down the road toward Hempshire without looking back. Elftrap followed leisurely. Dangalf stood with Nerdraaage.

"Come on, Nerd." Nerdraaage finally sighed and walked past Dangalf toward Hempshire. Dangalf slapped him on the back affectionately and was startled by the solid mass that met his arm. He was a knot of muscle over thick bones.

Doppelganger walked purposefully and found himself stopping repeatedly and impatiently for the rest of the Keepers. Dangalf and Elftrap both seemed to revel in the simple communion with nature brought on by walking down a deserted dirt road. They walked casually and not especially quietly because they did not notice they were being followed by well-armed and bloodthirsty foes.

Elftrap stopped. "There's a man on a wagon coming."

"How do you know?" asked Dangalf.

"I can smell him."

"Do you smell the wagon too?" scoffed Nerdraaage.

"The wheels need grease."

"Should we hide?" asked Nerdraaage.

"No," said Doppelganger.

"We have to meet with the people here eventually," said Dangalf. "A lone traveler seems like a safe introduction."

The man looked at them suspiciously as he approached. Dangalf walked to him with a broad smile, and the man stopped his horse and leveled a pitchfork at Dangalf. Dangalf raised his hands nervously.

"Hey, it's cool!" said Dangalf.

"Excuse us," said Elftrap. "We were just wondering if you could tell us where we are?"

"What kind of question is that?" answered the man.

"We're kind of lost," said Dangalf. "We were just wondering where we are."

"Well, right now you're no place. You're between places. But you are on your way to Hempshire."

"And this," said Dangalf motioning about. "This is the mythical land of Acadia."

"Mythical land of Acadia?" asked the man. "Are you daft? It's Acadia."

"Sorry. Poor choice of words."

Nerdraaage walked around the wagon, excitedly examining its authenticity. Suddenly he reached into the back and grabbed a large, folded, leathery item from under a covering.

"A dragon wing!" he shouted. The man stood quickly, and Nerdraaage had to fall to the ground not to be speared by the man's pitchfork.

"Bandits!" yelled the man. He leapt from the wagon and raised his pitchfork to impale Nerdraaage. Instinctively Doppelganger grabbed the pitchfork and took it from the man. He and the man were both surprised by the ease in which he did so. The others watched quietly.

Doppelganger's mind flashed with possibilities. He could snap the pitchfork in half. He somehow knew he was strong enough to do that even though it was hard wood. Or should he impale the man on the pitchfork for daring to attack one of his friends? No, he decided, that would be an overreaction, and he was surprised it even presented itself as an option. He decided to hand the pitchfork back to the man as a sign of goodwill. The man took it hesitantly.

"You ask odd questions. And I care not for the company you keep," said the man looking between the dwarf and she-elf. "I bid you farewell." He returned to his wagon and rode on.

"Godspeed," said Dangalf. Turning to his friends, he explained, "That's what people used to say." They watched as the man went the way they had come.

"That wing would have paid for everything we need," said Nerdraaage.

"You think?" said Dangalf.

Nerdraaage nodded. Blackguards were not allowed to wear any armor heavier than leather, and dragonwing was the lightest and strongest and rarest of leathers.

"It's very expensive," agreed Elftrap, whose druid avatar was also restricted to leather armor. "In the game at least."

"Oh my gods," said Dangalf. "If there are dragon wings, then there are dragons." Suddenly they all found themselves scanning the sky nervously. Only Doppelganger took any satisfaction in thinking of a sky full of dragons. If there were dragons, then there were dragon riders. He might become a dragoon after all.

Suddenly, Elftrap cried out, "No!"

"What?" asked Dangalf. Before she could answer, a group of black-clad figures rushed from the woods and ambushed the man in the wagon. He fought valiantly with his pitchfork, but he was outnumbered and outclassed.

Doppelganger's warrior blood began to boil, and he charged down the road. Dangalf grabbed his arm and was pulled for several yards before he could sway Doppelganger with one sentence: "What are you going to do without a sword?"

Nerdraaage and Elftrap joined them at the spot where Doppelganger had dragged Dangalf. Fortunately they were still a good distance from the carnage up ahead. The man in the wagon was ultimately overpowered, and his death cry echoed back to the four watching.

"Trolls?" asked Doppelganger.

"Humans," answered Elftrap.

"Human-on-human violence?" asked Nerdraaage.

"The Temple," said Dangalf, and the others believed him to be right. The Temple of the Red Rose. The deadly and merciless fanatics led by the Witchfinder General. The four had just defeated the general in the game, but apparently he was still a threat in this world. Or at least his followers were.

The killers took the horse and the dragon wing into the woods. One dallied to savagely remove the corpse's head. He raised the bloody head and his sword in taunt at the Keepers and howled a blood-curdling scream.

Seeing that they would not respond, the assassin sauntered into the woods with his trophy, his laughter echoing back to them. The four, the once-mighty Keepers of the Broken Blade, were humbled by their new reality. Doppelganger was red faced with anger and shame.

After waiting a good amount of time, the three males slowly and carefully walked to the wagon and confirmed what they had seen. Elftrap remained behind. The murder had overpowered her senses even from a distance, and she did not need closeness to it. Dangalf thought the victim might have letters or some other identification, but he had none.

Nerdraaage didn't look at the victim. His ruddy complexion was pale, and he seemed uncharacteristically nervous, at least for a dwarf (or what they knew of dwarves from game lore). Nerdraaage was terrified and sickened by the whole experience. He only followed the others to the wagon so as not to be shamed by staying back with the she-elf.

The four of them had all at various times and to varying degrees wanted to live in the world of Acadia as if it were real. Now that fantasy turned reality had become nightmarish. "We could die here," said Elftrap when they walked back to her.

"If there's a way into this world, there's a way back," said Dangalf.

"If I had my axe, things would have ended differently," said Doppelganger.

"You could have gotten us all killed," said Dangalf. "What possessed you to charge, unarmed, toward those guys?"

Doppelganger didn't answer immediately. He couldn't answer. Words and concepts swirled about his head, but he couldn't articulate them. In fact, even the word "articulate" was no longer part of his vocabulary. He grew frustrated as the others watched him for a response. What had possessed him? "Blood," he finally grunted before turning and again leading the way toward Hempshire.

Dangalf suddenly feared that geography and anatomy might not be the only changes that they had experienced in coming here. He worried that his smart, funny, gentle friend might no longer be any of those things.

V

They walked for hours. Doppelganger felt as though he could walk to the end of the world on these new legs, but the others lagged behind. Dangalf thought back to the game and how the walk from noob central to Hempshire was only about two minutes for his character to make at full trot. That short journey seemed annoying enough when he was impatient to play. Now he wondered if Hempshire was just a name painted on the sign and did not really exist.

"It doesn't take this long to walk to Hempshire in the game," said Nerdraaage.

"So they shortened it for the game," said Elftrap.

"You say that as if the game makers knew of this world," laughed Dangalf.

"They got the idea from somewhere," said Elftrap.

"*Cronica Acadia*," said Dangalf with sudden realization. "They based the game on a pulp fantasy." Maybe not so much fantasy after all, he thought.

"Finally." She smiled and nodded down the road. The others understood that they were near.

Hempshire might have disappointed someone who expected gleaming white castles and princesses riding in gold-leaf carriages, but to the Keepers, it was like coming home. They had all visited it many times over the years and were astounded to see it in reality and not entirely different than that envisioned by the game makers.

The first noticeable feature was a high wooden wall that seemed to run for hundreds of yards on both sides of an open gate. Guards stood by the main gate with long spears and shields with the Great Lighthouse on it.

"Their shields are red, white, and blue, like America," said Nerdraaage.

"Actually, red, white, and blue like the ancient divisions of our old world," said Dangalf. "Divisions that still exist in this world. Red for the warrior, white for magical classes, and blue for the craftsmen."

"So what's the plan?" asked Elftrap. "Should we tell them about the guy that got killed?"

"What if they blame us?" demanded Nerdraaage.

"Why would they blame us?"

"I'm always getting blamed for things I didn't do."

"We have to tell them," said Dangalf. "What if that was an advance party for a raid? The whole town could be in jeopardy."

The Keepers slowed as they approached the gate. The guards eyed them lazily but did not speak. One guard seemed very young. The other guard was big like Doppelganger but with a layer of fat over his muscles and a pockmarked face.

Dangalf, who hadn't yet realized how drastically his brain connections had improved and would continue to improve, was surprised by how strongly he was repelled by the ugly guard.

He realized he was tapping into some long-buried evolutionary marker that recognized disease and deformity as threats. How fortunate, he thought, that his comrades were all attractive and symmetrical. "I wish to report a murder," said Dangalf.

The guards' demeanors turned serious, and they stood upright. "What do you mean?" said the ugly one. "Who is murdered?"

"We don't know his name. He was on a wagon maybe five miles down the road."

"Ah. We heard about that."

"How did you hear?" asked Dangalf. "No one passed us."

"Hunters found him," answered the young guard. "They sent message."

Dangalf looked to the sky as a pigeon flew overhead, and he realized just how quickly news could travel in this world.

"He found a dragon wing in the woods and thought he had a buyer for it," continued the young guard. "Let your buyer come here, we says, but the buyer offered more gold to bring it to him."

"Fool he was," said the ugly guard. "Giving up a horse and a dragon wing to the general."

"He gave up his life, too," said Dangalf.

"Fools we have enough of," said the ugly guard. "But the town has only a dozen horses."

"May we enter?" asked Dangalf.

"Are ye beggars?"

"No," said Dangalf. "We're adventurers."

The two guards laughed boisterously and without fear of offending the Keepers of the Broken Blade. "Adventurers are always welcome," said the ugly guard. "Even ones that dress like beggars. The dwarf and elf, however, will need to find their own towns."

Dangalf asked, "Even if we vouch for them?" The ugly guard made an obviously dismissive sound.

"And who is going to vouch for you?" said the young guard.

"I thought you said I could go in," said Dangalf.

"You can go in," answered the young guard. "Doesn't mean you can go about vouching willy nilly."

"The she-elf can enter for the price of a kiss," offered the ugly guard.

"Ewww!" answered Elftrap.

Dangalf bowed slightly to the guards, and the others followed his lead back down the road several paces. "It's just like the game," said Dangalf. "Dwarves and elves can't enter human towns until they have a positive reputation with the human race."

"And how are we supposed to do that?" asked Elftrap.

"Through questing," answered Dangalf. "The same way we earn money."

"What are the early human quests?" asked Nerdraaage.

Doppelganger and Dangalf looked at each other while they independently thought back to the very beginning of the game so many years ago.

"Dire wolves," said Doppelganger.

The others blinked and swallowed. "That sounds just a little bit dangerous," said Elftrap.

"Pfft," Doppelganger said dismissively (which is the best way to say pfft).

"Who gives that quest?" asked Nerdraaage.

"The Sheriff of Hempshire."

"Where is he?"

"In the town," said Dangalf dejectedly.

"So we're right back where we started," said Elftrap.

"Well, Doppelganger and I can get the quest. At least we'll pick up some copper. You can stay in the woods, and we'll bring you out some food and drink. Blankets."

"No," answered Doppelganger. "We'll all get the quest and do it together. There's a secret way into Hempshire, if this world really does match the game."

As unpleasant as it was traversing the reverse of the drainage ditch, the Keepers did it on hands and knees with little complaint. It would be dark soon, colder, and they knew that the hunger gnawing at their bellies would only get worse. Whatever feelings of entitlement to comfort they had had in the other world were forgotten. They were in a new world, a new universe even, with new rules, and they understood if they did not do everything necessary to take care of themselves, they could die.

The guards paid little heed to, and in fact, unless otherwise required, kept their distance from the shitehouses that lined the inside of the back wall of Hempshire.

Doppelganger and Dangalf appeared first from the shitehouses, pulling the more obvious pieces of muck from their filthy clothes. With no guards close by, they signaled for Elftrap and Nerdraaage to follow them up and out.

Dangalf assisted Elftrap, who seemed to have avoided becoming as foul as the others. She rubbed her hands in the dirt by way of washing them. "You know, you two could have entered the front gate and met us here," she said.

Doppelganger and Dangalf looked at each other angrily.

"Why didn't you think of that, wizard?" snarled Doppelganger.

"It was your plan," started Dangalf, but he stopped short when the reaction of the others told him he was being too loud.

It was dusk, and the guards carried lamps or torches, but most of the lamps around town were not yet lit. The Keepers took advantage of the darkness and crept past mostly shuttered wooden buildings to what they hoped was the direction of the sheriff's office. When they did not find it, they circled around a cluster of official-looking buildings without success. They all knew Nerdraaage and Elftrap could be discovered at any moment, and they feared what the punishment might be. "Why don't you two wait under this building," said Dangalf. "We'll come and get you when we've found the office."

"Look," said Elftrap. "It's got to be right around here."

"It should be that building," whispered Dangalf pointing. "What does that sign say?"

Her eyes could still see the faded sign in the growing darkness. "Shire-reeve."

"Reeve?"

"Yes, R E E V E. Reeve"

"Reeve," contemplated Dangalf. "Shire-reeve. Sheriff?"

"It must be," said Elftrap.

The office was open and unguarded. Doppelganger and Dangalf entered. The halls and first rooms were dark, and they were concerned that the shire-reeve had left. They were startled when a commanding voice called out from a room in the back, "Who brings that smell of shite into my station!"

The shire-reeve, they were sure of it, appeared silhouetted in the doorway fastening his belt. It held a short sword to his left side. He was no donut-eating sheriff. He was built like a bull with a full head of gold and silver hair and a perfect scar on his cheek.

"We are adventurers," said Doppelganger.

"Sire," added Dangalf.

"Sire," said Doppelganger.

"Come no further, you filthy bastards!" The shire-reeve retreated and then reappeared with a lamp and approached them. He looked them up and down before relaxing his guard. "What's all this, then?" he demanded.

"We seek to prove ourselves," said Dangalf. "And make some honest coin as well."

"Prove yourselves how?"

"Is there a wolf bounty?" asked Doppelganger.

"There is always a wolf bounty," said the shire-reeve. He sat at the closest desk and began writing on a scroll. "Names?"

"Doppelganger."

"Dangalf."

The shire-reeve looked further irritated as he asked them to spell their names. The shire-reeve finished the scrolls and handed them over.

"Four dire wolves' tails may be turned in for one crown and another twenty-five farthing for each tail over four," said the shire-reeve. Dangalf recognized the denominations from the game, where the farthing was a copper coin, a crown was silver, and gold coins were sovereigns. "And they must be fresh kills. There is only tar and feathers for those who would cheat the treasury." They each thanked the shire-reeve as he presented them their warrants. Dangalf bowed awkwardly. And then, looking sympathetically, the shire-reeve asked, "Where are your weapons?"

"We have none."

"And how would you slay a dire wolf without a weapon?" When the shire-reeve saw there was no answer, he went into another room and returned with two swords and shields. Doppelganger and Dangalf took the equipment and thanked him excessively. Dangalf was near tears at the gesture. The shire-reeve was obviously a hard man, and he owed them nothing, but still he had seen something in the two wretches and taken pity on them.

"These are Hempshire property. Do not compound your lowly state by purloining them. I do not ask the nature of your foulness as that will only delay your departure. You will kindly leave following your original footsteps as carefully as possible."

"We are two others," Dangalf nervously interjected. "They await outside."

"If they are as foul as you, it is just as well."

The shire-reeve took two more scrolls and followed them out the front door. He stopped angrily when he saw Elftrap and Nerdraaage. "You bring to my town a beggar dwarf and an elven whore!"

"Whore!" said Elftrap.

"Guards!" Several guards from different directions charged in the direction of the shire-reeve's cry.

"Prithee, sire," pleaded Dangalf. "They seek only to aid us humans." The guards arrived and took Nerdraaage and Elftrap at spear point.

"I do not watch over a border town with all matter of foreign refuse loitering and beguiling."

"They are our friends," said Dangalf.

"Are you so low as not to know this world judges you by the company you keep?" asked the shire-reeve. After considering the foreigners a moment, he signed the two scrolls and tossed the warrants before Nerdraaage and Elftrap. "Put your names upon those orders, if you can write, and be gone. Do not return until you have proven your worth."

The guards marched the Keepers out of the front gate, cursing them and their foul smell along the way. "Prithee, sire," Elftrap said, gently mocking Dangalf.

"It worked, didn't it?" he answered.

They fell under the glare of curious townspeople. Dangalf couldn't help but think that being covered in waste and marched out of town at spear point would not help their reputations.

When they were outside the main gate, the guards retreated, and Doppelganger headed south into the woods. "I hope he knows where he's going," said Dangalf.

"He does," replied Elftrap.

"How do you know?"

"I smell wolves."

Dangalf looked up at the impossibly large full moon. A godsend. A new moon would mean they were also blind on this dangerous quest. How long were they gone from their home world? Less than twelve hours, he estimated. Less than twelve hours ago, the greatest threat he could conceive of was a power outage that meant he couldn't play *Cronica* or even watch TV. Now his very life hinged on a full moon and a borrowed sword and shield.

After a few miles, Elftrap shushed their quiet talking and clumsy branch breaking. "Wolves," she said.

"All I can smell is shite," said Nerdraaage, glancing down at his soiled garments.

"What does a wolf smell like?" asked Dangalf.

"These ones smell like lambs' blood." She took the lead from Doppelganger.

Dangalf handed his sword and shield to Nerdraaage. "You'll do better with this than I will." The dwarf took the gear apprehensively. Dangalf picked up a sturdy branch and swung it about to get its feel.

The next mile was slow going as Elftrap waved off the slightest crunching misstep and even Nerdraaage's labored breathing.

"Stop!" she ordered Nerdraaage.

"I have to breathe!"

"Don't you see that?"

"What?"

Elftrap picked up a femur-sized branch and stepped lightly to Nerdraaage. She placed the branch into a black area on the ground right before Nerdraaage and a ferocious metal trap severed the branch with sparking metal teeth. Nerdraaage swallowed hard.

"Follow in my footsteps," she said quietly.

Nerdraaage hopscotched after her. "Stupid long-legged elf," he muttered before she shushed him again.

Yes, she was long-legged, thought Dangalf. Watching her move stealthily through the moonlit woods was the most beautiful sight he had ever beheld.

The slow going frustrated Doppelganger. Now he also could smell the blood of their fresh kills, and he was eager to have at them. He thought of starving humans as the wolves ravaged their livestock and small human children being carried away by especially rapacious wolves. His blood began to boil. They needed to kill sixteen wolves for each to complete his quest and earn honor with Hempshire and the humans. Doppelganger wanted to kill sixteen hundred.

Doppelganger had always liked animals and never hunted. He had not so much as a fistfight in their home world, but his new bloodlust did not surprise or shame him. He knew intuitively that he had become different and not only in physique. He had a warrior's mentality now. Carnage is what warriors do, and to do it well it needed to be done without the complication of over-thinking. As Dangalf's mind had expanded, and would continue to expand, Doppelganger's brain sealed off parts that were not necessary or helpful for a warrior to access. Contemplation was a vanity. He was now of single-minded purpose. He would become a wolf-killing machine. He grit his teeth as images of foul wolves crushing human infants in their massive jaws assaulted his mind.

They caught up to Elftrap at the lead, where she had stopped. "There's a bunch up ahead," she said. "I don't know if I can do this. They look like dogs."

"I don't think I can do it either," said a terrified Nerdraaage.

"I'll kill them all," Doppelganger offered coolly.

"Okay, we can do without the macho attitude," said Elftrap.

Dangalf suddenly recalled a school trip to the museum where he had seen bones of dire wolves. In his mind he could clearly see the displays and read signs that described how these skeletons represented canines that in life weighed 150, 180 even 200 pounds! Hypercarnivores they were called. So successful that it was thought that they died off after eating all the prey that could not outrun them. Which was fortunate for early man, who appeared just about the time dire wolves became extinct.

The memory of a trip from so long ago in such detail startled Dangalf. He had not yet figured out the physical changes in his brain, the ectomorphic rewiring that had taken place, but he was recognizing that he was learning to instantly reconnect to every memory he had stored in photographic detail. Even the shape of his brain had changed, though he was not yet aware of it. The cleave of the two hemispheres was virtually gone. Dangalf would be henceforth thinking outside the box because the boxes of his brain were no more. Right brain and left brain, all the parts combined in one seamless, brilliant, instant thinking machine. But he sensed also danger in a brain that did not compartmentalize. A brain with near-unlimited recall could be a hindrance when survival required a simple and instant fight-or-flight response. But now, coolly and intellectually, he made the determination it was time to fight.

"We're all in this together," said Dangalf trying to sound inspiring. "The rules have changed, boys and girls. Remember how that traveler was butchered earlier today? That's what's going to happen to us if we don't progress in this world. And the way to progress is by questing, and questing means killing. What do you think the dire wolves would do to us if they ambushed us?"

And suddenly the dire wolves ambushed them. Three giant, snarling dire wolves with glowing red eyes to be exact—180-pound canine monsters long extinct from the other world. Elftrap leapt six feet up into a tree, but the circumstances did not allow anyone to stop and marvel at this feat.

Nerdraaage backed off, suddenly feeling that a sword and a shield offered little protection against three quick, strong, bloodthirsty brutes. Dangalf steeled himself for attack with his branch held defensively across his chest. The three snarling wolves approached him first. Doppelganger let out a ferocious scream that caused the slightest startle in the wolves. All three turned their glowing red eyes on Doppelganger and stalked him.

Nerdraaage dropped his shield and sword and fled back toward the road. Dangalf quickly picked them up, discarding the branch that he now realized was no better than a twig against a hypercarnivore.

Doppelganger brought his sword down and severed the spine of the first charging wolf. He grabbed the second in his big hands as it pounced on him. He strangled it while the beast's ferocious, gnashing maw plunged within inches of his face. The third wolf went low to Doppelganger's legs and tore into the flesh. Dangalf stabbed the third wolf from behind, terrified that the killer would turn on him. And it did.

Dangalf backed up uneasily, crouching behind his shield. In a flash the wolf had the shield in his jaws and tore it out of Dangalf's hands. The wolf gave Dangalf the slightest respite as he chewed the metal shield a bit before tossing it aside. Dangalf knew his bones were next on the wolf's plate.

Doppelganger tossed the second wolf aside and charged to Dangalf's aid. He brought his sword crushing down on the third wolf's head. Dangalf shuddered at the doglike cry it uttered as Doppelganger continued to hack and stab it to death. Doppelganger went back to the first wolf, dragging itself across the ground by its forepaws, and killed it. He went to each of the carcasses and removed their tails. He tossed the tails to Dangalf. He laughed as he splattered Dangalf with another bloody tail.

Elftrap lowered herself to the ground and looked at Doppelganger with big round eyes. "Where's Nerdraaage?" asked Dangalf.

"He ran away," said Elftrap.

"We should get him."

"No," said Doppelganger. "Let's finish the quest while I'm in the zone."

"He might be hurt."

"I'll go to him," said Elftrap. "If you don't need me." Please don't need me, she begged silently.

43

Dangalf looked at Doppelganger before answering. "We'll meet you back at the road," he said.

Doppelganger moved ahead roughly through the brush. Three down and thirteen to go, thought Doppelganger. Dangalf nodded solemnly to Elftrap before following.

"Good luck," she said.

VI

Nerdraaage sat on the road, and Elftrap stood about ten paces from him. She had known for a few minutes that Dangalf and Doppelganger were on their way back but hadn't bothered to tell Nerdraaage. They had not said anything to each other.

Dangalf appeared from the tree line first. He was carrying a pile of wolf tails in the bowl of his shield. Elftrap thought he looked a little tired and a lot blood splattered but otherwise fine.

"We got enough tails for all of us," shouted Dangalf.

Doppelganger followed. His clothes were shredded and remained only on his body because they were pasted there by blood. His arms, legs, and face were stained crimson. Elftrap was sure that not all of the blood could be wolf blood, but Doppelganger looked triumphant nonetheless. He carried a locked chest in front of him.

"What is that?" asked Elftrap.

"A treasure chest," said Doppelganger. "Just like in the game." Up close she noticed how pale he looked and saw that he had gashes all over his body that seeped blood when he moved. She looked at Dangalf, who shared her concern.

Nerdraaage peeked at them between the fingers that covered his face. He did not want to see them or be seen by them in his shame. Why had he been so fearful compared to the others? What was the point of being in a sturdy, strong dwarf body if he was going to be the same fearful, weak man-child he was in the old world? The skinny wizard and elf girl took to combat better than him.

"Is that sixteen?" Elftrap asked of the tails.

"Eighteen," answered Dangalf.

"Why so many?"

"They just kept coming."

"It appears the wolves killed a couple of trappers," said Doppelganger. "We found this chest on a broken-down wagon."

"Too bad we don't have a lock-picker to open the chest," said Elftrap. Treasure chests in the game required keys or skilled lock-pickers to open them. Doppelganger smashed the chest upon the ground, and it cracked open.

"Another game concept bites the dust," said Dangalf.

The lock held, but the hinges were broken. Doppelganger tore the top from the chest. The contents were modest but might as well have been gold and jewels to the Keepers. There were animal pelts. There was a handful of copper coins, which Doppelganger said he would hold for all of them. "The bank of tank," he assured them.

A carrier pigeon fluttered out of a broken cage, and Elftrap gently retrieved it. It took immediately to her shoulder. "Now we can send messages!" she smiled.

"Who are we going to send messages to?" asked Doppelganger with a laugh.

"In time," she said. "Things will not always be as desperate as they are now."

Dangalf took out a small, unmarked bottle. "Healing potion?" he suggested.

"If they were trappers, it could be some kind of poison," said Elftrap.

"The bottle is too ornate for poison I would think."

"Only one way to find out," said Doppelganger as he took and drank the bottle.

"Are you crazy!" yelled Dangalf.

The taste was terrible, but the effects were almost immediate. They all watched in horrified fascination as the lacerations and avulsions on his arms and legs mended themselves with new, pink skin. The color returned to his skin as if his body had suddenly replaced his lost blood.

"What this world lacks in indoor plumbing it more than makes up for in magic," said Dangalf.

Doppelganger removed a plain but functional dagger from the chest. "This will look good on my belt," he said. "When I get a belt."

"This is a dagger, and our blackguard should carry it," answered Dangalf. They all looked to Nerdraaage, who slowly lifted himself off the ground and walked to the others. He took the dagger but even this didn't feel right. He couldn't imagine anything more terrible than stabbing something.

Elftrap sat on the ground writing something. Dangalf peered at her work, and she turned it away from him, which he found to be very odd. "What are you writing?"

"I'm putting my name on the shire-reeve's warrant so we can turn in the quest. Give me your scroll, Nerd." He dropped the scroll next to her.

On the journey back to town, a dejected Nerdraaage brought up the rear. Elftrap looked at Doppelganger with the same foreboding that Dangalf had already felt. She tried to put a positive spin on it. "You've certainly adjusted to our new circumstances," she said.

"And what about you leaping ten feet into a tree?" said Doppelganger.

"I was just as surprised by that as you were," she said. "And it was only about six feet."

"We have changed more than we even know yet," said Dangalf. "Physically and mentally. There has been some vestigial awakening in us. Like a race memory. I think we are tapping into the knowledge of ancient ancestors—ancestors who were warriors and wizards and maybe even elves and dwarves. We might adjust to this new world better than we had hoped."

"What about..." said Doppelganger subtly referring to Nerdraaage. "He was not very dwarf-like. If the lore about dwarves is correct."

"I don't know," said Dangalf. "There's a piece of the puzzle that's still missing for him."

VII

I t was sunrise when they returned to Hempshire. They were dirty and tired, and they had great gnawing holes in their bellies, except for Elftrap, who said she "could eat." Dangalf wasn't sure which was more important, eating or sleeping. "Eating," insisted Doppelganger.

Doppelganger and Dangalf entered through the front gate, but the guards were disinterested in Nerdraaage's and Elftrap's warrants and wouldn't let them pass. The dwarf and elf were again forced to enter through the toilet.

Nerdraaage mistimed his entrance and unseated an occupant of the facilities. He and Elftrap ran to the shire-reeve's office as Nerdraaage's victim called for aid.

Doppelganger and Dangalf picked up their pace to intercept their comrades just as Nerdraaage fell face first just outside the shire-reeve's office.

Elftrap hid behind Dangalf, who did his best to look brave as they became again surrounded by the unforgiving ends of multiple spears. The shire-reeve exited his station at the sound of the commotion.

"Sire, my comrades and I have completed your quest!" shouted Dangalf.

Doppelganger walked to the shire-reeve, bowed slightly, and dumped the wolf tails before him. The shire-reeve nodded to a young scrivener who had followed him out the door. The scrivener counted the tails.

"Eighteen," he reported.

The shire-reeve held out his hand, and Dangalf deposited the warrants in it. The shire-reeve waved for the guards to stand down, and the spear points withdrew. He examined the warrants.

"Bartleby," said the shire-reeve, and the scrivener took quill to paper. "Let it be known that the humans," he paused to read the warrants, "Doppelganger and Dangalf have proved themselves in the service of Hempshire. Also the she-elf Ashlyn has with her service proved herself a friend of humans."

"Who is Ashlyn?" whispered Dangalf. Elftrap, henceforth to be referred to as Ashlyn, smiled shyly.

The shire-reeve continued: "As well as the dwarf Nerdraaage." The shire-reeve took a coin purse from his belt. "Payment from the treasury made to each of them. Notify Vinland."

Notify Vinland! The Keepers of the Broken Blade sighed collectively as they took their first step to respectability in their new world. The shire-reeve turned his attention back to the Keepers.

"Might I suggest that you spend some of your reward on hot water and soap?" The shire-reeve nodded, and the males bowed. Ashlyn curtsied for the first time and hoped she did it right.

Dangalf turned in his sword and crushed shield to the scrivener. With a look from Dangalf, Doppelganger also reluctantly surrendered his arms.

"Let's go to the inn," suggested Dangalf after the shire-reeve departed. "Maybe we can get a bath there."

They walked down the main road of Hempshire and attracted as much fascination as they displayed. The town was bigger than in the game, but they recognized the iconic businesses that were found in all the game's major towns: the butcher, the baker, and the...chandler. Well, it might not have been very poetic, but the result was the same. They made a quick stop at the chandler for some soap.

They passed the village smithy under a spreading chestnut tree. There was also the ubiquitous cheese shop. The pungent odor signified that it was not uncontaminated by cheese as was the *Homage Fromage* cheese shop in the virtual Hempshire.

The population of the real Hempshire was different from that of the virtual Hempshire as well. Where this time of day the virtual Hempshire was teeming with warriors and wizards, druids and blackguards, the real Hempshire was teeming with merchants and craftsmen, farmers and guards. In the game world, these people were the NPCs. The Keepers were the only heroes he could see, and a sad lot of heroes they were at this point. But that lack of heroes made sense to Dangalf. Wasn't their old world populated overwhelmingly by NPCs? Very few people in that world could be called hero, seeker, mercenary, or adventurer. What a revelation! He had had to travel to another universe to figure out what was wrong with his old life in his home world. He had allowed himself to be a Non-Player Character! He was confident, though, that he wouldn't make that mistake in this universe.

Dangalf spotted a building with a wizard-hat-shaped sign. The Wizened Wizard! "That's where you go for wizard training!" The others nodded, not nearly as excited as he thought they should be. He decided it would be best to introduce himself after he bathed. Even Nerdraaaage cheered up looking at the sights of the bright, busy town.

"Ashlyn?" Dangalf finally asked.

"Yeah. What's that all about?" added Doppelganger.

"Elftrap was fine for the game. But we're in a real world now, and I thought it would be better to have a real name."

"Yeah, thanks for not telling me I could get a new name," grumbled Nerdraaage.

"I have another concern," she said. "We're supposed to be lawful-good aligned. How right is it that Doppelganger killed the wolves and we all took credit for it?"

"O M Gs," said Nerdraaage.

"And I don't think we should have looted that chest either," she said. "That was human property, not spoils of war. I mean, if we're going to play the game properly..." She trailed off.

"I came into this world with about five percent body fat," pleaded Dangalf. "And I've burned through most of that. I would like to get one meal in my belly before I worry about what is lawful and good." Ashlyn sulked quietly. Dangalf continued, "The wolf bounty was a group quest, and they, in the game at least, never measured individual contribution to the completion of a group quest. Everyone got credit for it. We were all there. We all took risks. And bottom line, it was just to get you and Nerd some rep so we could get you into the front gate. There will be many more quests, and we'll all contribute. And in the game, trapping is illegal. What little we got from the trappers' chest falls under spoils of war."

"I guess that makes sense," she said.

"But you're right," he added. "The Alliance is lawful-good aligned, and I believe the Keepers must follow that path as well if we're going to be successful." Ashlyn appreciated the acknowledgement and smiled.

And there it was. Hempshire's celebrated inn, The Silent Woman. The promise of food and drink and rest brought them to new heights of joy.

The Silent Woman signage featured a headless woman. Ashlyn, still settling in to her new gender, suddenly found the joke behind the sign to be a little creepy.

They had only gotten to the open front door when Master Tolliver, the burly innkeeper, intercepted them. He bellowed something about the four not fouling up his premises when he was arrested by Mistress Tolliver, who took him by the arm and spun him back into the inn.

Mistress Tolliver was an ample woman with pendulous breasts barely contained in her low-cut dress. Nerdraaage was immediately enamored of her, which he did not understand because he had never before liked zaftig women (or fat chicks, as he called them).

Mistress Tolliver looked Ashlyn up and down sympathetically. Two of her brutish boys stood behind her and looked Ashlyn up and down not so sympathetically.

Ashlyn vaguely described their predicament to Mistress Tolliver, who made all those sympathetic feminine facial gestures and sounds. "We will get you some new clothes. But first, a hot bath."

"Can I help!" offered the oldest of the boys. Mistress Tolliver smacked him with the back of her hand so violently that it startled the Keepers despite the violence they had already witnessed in this world. Without missing a beat, she turned again to nurturing mother and made some more sympathetic sounds at the Keepers. She collected some copper from the bank of tank and said she would have one of the boys pick up some new clothes for them. She told the male Keepers that they could get a bath at the stables and ushered Ashlyn into the inn.

At the stables, Dangalf and Nerdraaage stripped quickly to be first to bathe. Dangalf won. The stable master fed their soiled clothes into his fire with a pitchfork.

"You're covered in that red hair," Dangalf said from the tub to an especially naked Nerdraaage. Nerdraaage only laughed in response. "You know you could stand behind a post or something. Someone could come by." Nerdraaage just laughed again and made no effort to conceal himself.

When Nerdraaage finished bathing, Doppelganger stripped. "Dude, you are built like a brick shitehouse," said Dangalf with awe.

"Regretting your decision to go full ectomorph?" asked Doppelganger. When first creating a *Cronica* character, players were prompted to pick what percent they wanted to be of two different qualities: mesomorph and ectomorph. Simply put, mesomorph dealt with size and strength and primarily benefited classes of the Red School (the weapons classes), and ectomorph dealt with intellect, which primarily benefited classes of the White School (the magic classes). Intellect was at the expense of size and strength, and the reverse held true as well. A third quality was endomorphism, but that quality was not selected but fixed according to race, with the dwarves being most endomorphic and the elves least.

When Dangalf designed his avatar, he moved the slider to 100 percent ectomorph. This maximized his intellect, but the trade off was the frail body he now inhabited.

Doppelganger had designed his character hastily and before he fully understood the game concepts, resulting in his having chosen a 90 percent mesomorphic character. Most warriors went 100 percent mesomorph, with blackguards and hunters usually going somewhat ectomorph since their success depended on more than sheer brute strength. Intellect was such a wasted ability for warriors that Doppelganger contemplated deleting his character and starting from scratch at full mesomorph. It was only the months of intense game play he had already invested in his character that prevented him from doing that. So he compensated for his weakness with the best strategy, gear, and enchantments the game provided. He easily vanquished most of his opponents regardless. In fact only former Keeper Regicide ever regularly beat him.

Doppelganger wondered if the slider error he had made years ago in the old world would come back to haunt him in this world. Would that 10 percent ectomorphism frustrate his efforts to be a truly great warrior? Could he be another 10 percent bigger and stronger than he was?

That worry vanished as he found himself hard-pressed to fit into the washtub. He squeezed his ass and ankles to the bottom of the tub and washed as best as he could. "Help me bathe!" he barked at his friends. "I can hardly move."

"You're sure you can't move?" asked Dangalf before he and Nerdraaage alternated by dumping buckets of hot and cold water on him. He had to make an extreme effort to control his anger as they laughed hysterically. After all it was pretty funny, and he was getting clean.

Young Tolliver arrived with their clothes and joined in the water torture. Doppelganger understood why Mistress Tolliver had slapped him so violently. The frolics finally ended when a frustrated Doppelganger broke through the tub, and the water spilled everywhere.

Dangalf and Nerdraaage got dressed and were soon complaining that their new clothes were ill fitting and unfinished. Tolliver rolled his eyes and asked how they expected their clothes to fit before they saw the tailor. Dangalf loved it! Tailored clothes on a pauper's budget!

After visiting the tailor, the trio headed to the cobbler, where they were able to trade their looted furs for nice footwear and some silver coins to boot.

They headed again for the Silent Woman, where Master Tolliver allowed them to enter after a cursory exam at the front door.

Inside was a magnificent painting of a regal-looking William Dukenfield wearing a sash of red, white, and blue. When Dangalf mentioned the portrait, Tolliver shook his head at their ignorance and told them it was a great source of pride that Dukenfield should be the first-ever commander of combined human, dwarf, and elf armies. And for now, the supreme allied commander was the closest thing the humans had to a king, he added.

They sat in the dining room, where there were a dozen male customers. Most of them sat alone. Some ate. All of them drank.

Doppelganger and Nerdraaage sat as Dangalf headed to the bar. A friendly, busty serving wench approached. Too skinny, thought Nerdraaage, but he would still do her.

"You gents be having wine?"

"Ah, sure," answered Doppelganger. He smiled confidently at her, and she was not unreceptive.

"Aged Vinlandian?"

"For three," said Doppelganger.

"Be right back."

Dangalf took a seat with them. "Well, I asked Master Tolliver if he had any other strangers come in here. People who said they were from a distant land, maybe even another world."

"What did he say?"

"No. I also asked if death were permanent in this land or if for a small fee you could buy your soul back."

"What did he say?"

"He asked me to stop talking to him."

The wench set down wine in three cups and placed a hand on Dangalf's shoulder.

"Sorry, love. Master Tolliver says you pay for your drink in advance." Dangalf looked over to Tolliver, who looked at him suspiciously.

"How much?"

"Eight copper. Each."

"Twenty-four copper for wine!" said Dangalf. "Better enjoy it."

Nerdraaage looked at the wine and pushed it away. "Could I just get some water?"

"Are you having a laugh?" she said. "I suppose if you don't mind the company of horses you can drink all the water you like." The wench took their payment and went away laughing.

"We need to try to make an effort to blend in," said Dangalf. He tipped his cup to Doppelganger and they drank. "Not too bad," he said of the wine.

"Wine for breakfast," said Doppelganger. "I could get used to this."

"Not at these prices. We'll all be drinking with the horses."

A buzz ran through the bar as a dozen necks craned toward the stairs leading to the second floor. Doppelganger, Dangalf, and Nerdraaage looked also, Nerdraaage standing for a better view. "Oh, shite!" he said as he sat back down.

Ashlyn stepped delicately downstairs, trying to remain unaffected by the commotion and the eyes fixated on her. She scrubbed up very well, and her hair was up. She wore simple hemp clothes, but they were in the she-elf fashion and provided minimal coverage. Bare shoulders, bare stomach, bare legs—bare long legs that glided down the stairs as gracefully as they'd bounded through the dense woods last night. Dangalf did not think it possible for her to be more beautiful. But then she smiled and became so.

Ashlyn found this attention embarrassing but not unpleasant. She went to their table and sat down almost on Dangalf even though the empty side of the bench was next to Nerdraaage. She put her arm around Dangalf to steady herself on the fraction of bench she occupied.

"You look…nice," offered Dangalf.

"So do you guys in your new clothes!"

"Not like you," said Doppelganger.

"I'm so embarrassed," she protested. "Mistress Tolliver went to all this trouble to make this for me from an actual she-elf pattern. I didn't see how I could refuse."

"How much did that cost!" demanded Nerdraaage.

"This?" she replied. "Nothing. It was a gift. It's amazing the skill people can have without machines."

"Want some wine?" asked Dangalf as he slid Nerdraaage's cup to her.

"Yes!" she said taking a drink.

Dangalf was becoming intoxicated by more than the wine. "Are you wearing perfume?" he asked.

"Oh!" she protested again. "Mistress Tolliver dabbed this plant extract on me. Spritewillow. Do you like it?"

Awkward silence all around.

"Well," she backtracked. "Not do you like it, but does it bother you? 'Cause I can go wash it off. See, Mistress Tolliver only has those four boys, who she says are as rough as her husband, and she never had a daughter to spoil, and spritewillow is very expensive, and I didn't want to insult her, and does anyone else think I'm talking too much?"

"No," said Dangalf as coolly as he could. Her breath was warm and wine flavored.

Doppelganger and Nerdraaage looked at each other so as not to have to look at Dangalf and Ashlyn. Ashlyn finished the rest of the wine.

"So I asked Mistress Tolliver, in kind of a roundabout way, if she had met any other strangers like us. The short answer is no."

"I asked Master Tolliver the same thing."

"You're so smart," she said.

Dangalf blushed. He was falling for Ashlyn and made himself think of the man he had met that had turned into Elftrap and renamed herself Ashlyn. But the image of that man was fading fast as it was replaced by the incarnate sexy she-elf whose warm, wine-flavored breath tickled his whiskers.

"Anybody else hungry?" interjected Doppelganger.

"More wine!" said Ashlyn.

The serving wench approached, her demeanor now quite reserved. Dangalf noticed it and couldn't help but wonder if it was spite directed at Ashlyn, who had joined them since the wench's last appearance.

"I don't think we can do anymore wine," said Doppelganger weighing the change purse.

"We have our own hemp wine. Only a copper a cup. Not as tasty as the Vinlandian, but it'll make you loose," and then out of the side of her mouth, "or looser for some of you." Ashlyn got the inference and shot a look at the wench. Ah! Thought Dangalf, clearly it was spite!

The serving wench brought them venison roast and a platter of boiled potatoes, corn, turnips, and cabbages. Ashlyn ate only of the vegetables. Dangalf had some of everything. He had never had turnip and cabbage before, and he could not understand how he had missed out on something that tasted so good. Doppelganger and Nerdraaage started eating the vegetables only after the meat was gone.

Between bites, Nerdraaage asked, "Why did she tell us to save the corn cobs?"

"Because they don't have toilet paper," answered Dangalf. But Nerdraaage was certain he was answering a completely different question.

Even though they were on the precipice of bankruptcy, they kept the wine flowing. Finally the wench took pity on Nerdraaage and brought him a cup of water. He promptly spit it out. "It tastes like dirt!"

"It's probably from a well," said Dangalf.

Nerdraaage was done eating and didn't like the taste of the water, so he sat and watched his friends' happiness increase proportional to their drunkenness. He lowered his head and softly cried.

"What's wrong?" said Dangalf.

"I want to go home."

"Well, we can't right now."

"I don't belong here."

"That's because you're not smart," Ashlyn said.

"Leave me alone."

"Seriously," she said. "A dwarf that doesn't drink. Why do you think you sucked last night?"

"I don't remember you doing so great last night!" he said.

"I'm a ninety-pound elf!"

"Of course!" said Dangalf. "Alcohol!"

God how Nerdraaage hated Elftrap! Or whatever he was calling himself now! Especially now because she was probably right. In the game, dwarves needed to maintain a 0.1 to 0.3 percent blood alcohol content for peak performance. Maybe that was true in this world. He would need to try it. He couldn't again bear the humiliation of his cowardice last night. He would have thought by now that he was accustomed to humiliation with all of his experience with it in the old universe, but it had become more painful than ever. Maybe this was the race memory that Dangalf was talking about and his new dwarf brain had very little tolerance for cowardice.

Dangalf pushed his wine before Nerdraaage, who smelled it. Nerdraaage had only been offered a drink before from an older cousin—some brutal liquor that smelled like poison before he could even taste it. He choked it down to please his cousin only to vomit it up seconds later. He smelled the hemp wine. It had a nutty, earthy, creamy smell. He did not know how his brain recognized those characteristics, but it did smell good. He took a sip, and it tasted even better. He downed the rest of his glass and smiled broadly. Doppelganger and Ashlyn pushed their cups to him.

And the drinking began in earnest.

Soon they were all shite faced. Ashlyn leaned heavily on Dangalf. Nerdraaage was red faced partly from drunkenness and partly from getting slapped by the serving wench. And now he broke into song:

Tell her to make me a cambric shirt
Everyone someday drinks the gravewhisper wine
Without a seam or needlework
Then she'll be a true love of mine

Tell her to enter the profundity
Everyone someday drinks the gravewhisper wine
And follow it down to the forgotten city
Then she'll be a true love of mine

The handful of patrons cheered his music. The silence left after Nerdraaage's ditty was filled in another corner where a patron played a fiddle softly.

"Where the hell did you learn that?" laughed Doppelganger.

"I don't know," Nerdraaage shrugged.

"I think pub songs are a race-memory for dwarves," said Dangalf. "Where did you get those lyrics?"

"I don't know."

"He just changed the words," said Ashlyn. "That's a Simon and Garfunkel song."

"No it isn't," said Dangalf.

"It totally is!"

"I mean, I know they did it, but the song goes back at least as far as an ancient ballad called "The Elfin Knight." He sang about gravewhisper. That's not something that exists in our old world."

"You saying they stole our song?" asked Doppelganger.

"Maybe we stole theirs. Well, stolen might be a little harsh. Bards played that song all over. Maybe an ancient bard brought it from one world to the other."

"When did you get so smart?" asked Ashlyn.

"I've always been smart," said Dangalf. "But yes, my brain has changed. All my memories are much more accessible."

"I think my brange has chained too," slurred Nerdraaage.

"How would bards get from one world to the other?"

"How did we get here?" asked Dangalf.

"So do you think we'll ever be able to leave this place?" asked Ashlyn.

"Who wants to leave?" demanded Nerdraaage.

"I don't know," said Ashlyn. "Still it would be nice to know if we can."

"I agree," said Dangalf. "But we have to take care of our basic needs first. Doppel and I can get our training here, and then we can move on to Hammersmith and Templa Taur for your training."

"Yes! Hammersmith next," demanded Nerdraaage.

"It is on the way."

Ashlyn shrugged. Nerdraaage pumped his fist in the air.

Doppelganger moved some silver and copper coins around on the tabletop. "Things are going to be tight for a while," he said.

"I've got an idea," said Nerdraaage, drunkenly stepping back up on his chair.

"Is there a human here who will arm wrestle me for a crown!" he challenged.

"I will," said Doppelganger.

"Not you. Anyone else?"

"I will!"

The voice came from a sturdy farm boy in the corner. He was a foot higher than Nerdraaage but not quite as wide. They met at the empty table between the two parties. Another man, perhaps the boy's father, held the contestants' clasped hands in a neutral position before announcing, "Ready, steady, go!"

The farm boy slowly and steadily worked Nerdraaage's fist toward the table until he was only an inch from defeat. Nerdraaage looked warily back toward the other Keepers, who watched anxiously. Suddenly Nerdraaage's look of consternation turned to a broad smile. "Psyche!" said Nerdraaage, and he twisted the boy's arm back until it cracked the tabletop. The older patron set a silver coin on the table, and he and the boy, rubbing his hand, went back to their table.

"I owned him!" Nerdraaage announced to the bar. He returned to his friends, who were cheering him, and slapped a silver coin next to their other money. Tolliver stepped to the table and scooped two silver coins from their small stash.

"That's for the table you broke," he said to Nerdraaage.

Dangalf didn't like Nerdraaage's lack of sportsmanship, especially since he was introducing foreign terms such as "psyche" and "owned," and he told him so. Dangalf said all the Keepers should be careful not to contaminate this world with language and concepts from their own world. He was met with a skeptical look from Nerdraaage.

"It's like *Star Trek*," said Dangalf. "The prime directive says you can't interfere with or contaminate the normal development of another civilization."

"Starfleet General Order Number One," added Ashlyn.

"This is a new world for us, and you're Captain Kirk," said Dangalf.

"I'm Captain Kirk," said Nerdraaage nodding.

They could barely keep their eyes open and agreed it was time to seek lodgings. "If we're going to be paying for training and gear, looks like we'll be sleeping in the stable," said Doppelganger. He slid some coins to Dangalf. "For your training and gear," he explained.

"We need to budget for wine, too," insisted Nerdraaage.

"Mistress Tolliver said I could take a room here without charge," said Ashlyn. "But just me." She grimaced by way of an apology.

"That's fine," said Dangalf.

"I'm gonna head for the stables," said Doppelganger.

Nerdraaage and Dangalf rose to join him, but Ashlyn covertly held onto Dangalf's sleeve. Doppelganger and Nerdraaage shuffled toward the door and turned back to Dangalf.

"I'll be there in a few," said Dangalf. He sat back down next to Ashlyn.

"I'm in the corner room in the back. Maybe you can sneak in. If you want."

A kettledrum pounded in his chest. He was sure her elf ears could hear it.

"Yeah, okay," said Mr. Nonchalant.

VIII

Ashlyn waved to Dangalf from her window situated above a latticework. He climbed easily, fueled by liquor and lust. He was glad to be a pure ectomorph on this occasion, as the lattice supported him without a sound.

Ashlyn pulled him into the small room, laughing quietly. "Do you mind sleeping on the floor?" she asked.

"No."

"I figured it had to be better than sleeping in the stable."

"Oh, yeah," he said with a chuckle.

"I'm so tired," she said. "Goodnight." And she laid down with her back to Dangalf. He didn't mind. Her body was as attractive from that angle as from the front.

"Goodnight."

Dangalf did not fall immediately to sleep. His mind raced as he played back all that had transpired in their first twenty-four hours in this new universe. He decided that what was most astounding was the mind's capacity to accept the impossible when no other choice presented itself.

IX

Doppelganger was not surprised or displeased to wake up covered in hay on the dirt floor of a barn in what he had previously thought to be an imaginary land. He judged it was afternoon based on the angle of the sun.

He heard Nerdraaage before he saw him. He leaned up on his shoulders and saw him in the corner of the stable, snoring loudly.

Doppelganger rose, dusted off the more prominent pieces of hay, and took the main street back toward the Silent Woman. The narrow street was bustling with townspeople, and a flock of children ran out of the schoolhouse as a school bell sounded—a real clanging bell, not one of those shrill alarms he remembered from school.

He was overcome by the smells of fresh food. He smelled smoked pork as he walked past the butcher and baking bread as he passed the baker. His stomach rumbled angrily, which was unusual. His old self had only ever wanted caffeine for breakfast.

He saw Dangalf and Ashlyn at a back table of the Silent Woman. They greeted him exuberantly, and he noticed Dangalf fiddling with a deck of oversized cards as he joined them. Ashlyn fed seeds to their pigeon.

"We have come to the conclusion that we are not dreaming and we are truly in this magical world," said Dangalf by way of greeting.

"I'm thinking that might not be so bad," said Doppelganger as he sat. Ashlyn brushed some straw from his back. "Not that we have any choice at this point."

Ashlyn whispered to the pigeon and held it out to Doppelganger. "Take Clay. Introduce yourself so that he can find you anywhere."

"Trust her," said Dangalf.

Doppelganger took the bird awkwardly and asked, "Why Clay?"

"Clay pigeon," answered Dangalf. Doppelganger only shook his head slightly, to which Dangalf replied, "I know, right?"

"Shut up," said Ashlyn.

"Heroes, seekers, mercenaries, and adventurers, good morning!" bellowed Nerdraaage upon entering the inn. He marched over to his friends. "Innkeeper! Wine all around!" Nerdraaage sat down roughly on the bench, and Doppelganger handed him the pigeon. "Can I at least get him cooked?"

"No!" shouted Ashlyn as she took the bird back. She whispered to it while glaring at Nerdraaage.

"What are you saying?" demanded Nerdraaage. "What is she saying?"

"I don't know," said Dangalf. "But you might want to start wearing a hat."

"Sweet deck," Nerdraaage said grabbing Dangalf's cards.

"No!" shouted Dangalf as he grabbed the deck back. "Page one of the instructions, and I quote, 'Do not let others touch the cards until they are fully attuned to you.'"

"A divination deck," said Nerdraaage solemnly. Tolliver brought over the wine, and they ordered food.

"So what did that deck cost?" asked Doppelganger.

"Eighty farthing."

"Eighty farthing! That was for training and gear!"

"This is gear for a mage."

"You never had a divinity deck in the game."

"There was only one time in the game that I came across the traveling salesman who sold divinity decks, and I always regretted not buying it when I had the chance. I didn't want to make that mistake in this world. This could save our lives. And since we only seem to get one life here, it might be worth eighty measly farthing."

"It could have waited. You don't even have a wand yet."

"The guy was a traveling salesman. Who knew when we'd see him again? Or if we'd see him again?"

"There's a reason they have to keep traveling," said Doppelganger.

"I know what I'm doing. This is an investment. I'm not spending money frivolously."

Nerdraaage noticed a ring that Ashlyn sported. It was a silver spider with a great black stone abdomen. "Cool ring!"

"It's an amulet," she said holding it up proudly. "Dangalf bought it for me."

"Dude!" shouted Doppelganger. Dangalf did his best to hide behind the deck's tiny instruction booklet.

Tolliver delivered their food, and they ate. Dangalf and Ashlyn ate just a little. But they watched Doppelganger consume mountains of food. And Nerdraaage seemed to match him bite for bite, and they both washed it down with wine. It was clear that they were hemorrhaging coin.

A bedraggled, white-haired human in a pirate shirt and a wooden leg clopped into the inn. Nerdraaage leapt up excitedly.

"Salty! Hey, look, it's Salty!" The others were surprised themselves to see *Cronica*'s infamous seadog beggar.

"Do I know you, sire?"

"Not really," Nerdraaaage said slapping him on the back. "But we've known you for some time."

Like most beggars Salty wasn't too interested in conversation that wasn't addressing who was going to pay for his next drink. Nerdraaaage might as well have said, "We are four men from an alternate universe where you exist as an annoying character in a computer game," and Salty's next line would have been the same: "Can you help an old sea dog buy a cup of grog?"

"Oh, that's classic!" shouted Nerdraaaage slapping the bony beggar on the back. "That's great!"

"Can you?" repeated Salty his hand trembling.

"Huh? Oh, I don't have any money," said Nerdraaaage.

Master Tolliver entered from the kitchen and charged directly at Salty. He picked him up roughly and dragged him to the door. Dangalf handed a couple of farthing to Nerdraaaage, who caught up to Salty and gave it to him.

"I will not forget your kindness," said Salty as he was bum-rushed out the door.

Nerdraaaage returned to the table triumphantly. "That was great!" he insisted.

"Look at you covered in dirt and hay," said Ashlyn. "Salty should have been giving you coins."

X

"You've been reading that booklet for an hour," Ashlyn chided Dangalf.

"Yeah, do a magic trick or something already," added Nerdraaage.

"I think I can tell everyone's future. At least a significant event in the not-too-distant future."

Dangalf fanned the cards out and set them on the table.

"Do we pick a card?" asked Ashlyn.

"No. If I do this right, the card should pick you." He waved his hands over the card and whispered some magic words.

"What?" sniggered Doppelganger.

And then suddenly a card rose from the deck and placed itself in front of Doppelganger. One card each placed themselves in front of Ashlyn, Nerdraaage, and Dangalf.

"No way!" said Ashlyn.

"Shite!" said Nerdraaage.

"Shite is right," said a startled Dangalf.

"What now?" asked Ashlyn.

"I don't know," stuttered Dangalf. He returned to the instruction manual. "Turn them over," he said after a moment.

They looked to Doppelganger as they silently decided to reveal the cards in the order they left the deck. He turned over a depiction of a road that forked into two roads forming a *Y* shape in the middle of the card. One road passed a windmill and the other a tower.

"Crossroads," said Dangalf, looking back and forth between the card and the manual.

"What does it mean?"

"A decision."

"What does it mean to me?"

"You will have to make a decision about something."

"At some point in the future, I will have to make a decision about something," said Doppelganger. "That's amazing! Where can I get one of those decks? Oh, that's right. They guy left town right after he sold you that one."

"Not just a decision, a crossroads!" said Dangalf. "Next."

"Me," said Ashlyn.

They silently watched her turn over a card depicting a nude man and woman entwined by a serpent. He held a sword with a broken shield at their feet.

"The lovers," said Dangalf clearing his throat.

"What does that mean?" asked Nerdraaage.

"How old are you?" answered Ashlyn.

"There's an uncommon element," said Dangalf, feverishly thumbing through his booklet. "The broken shield. It indicates a contest."

"What's an uncommon element?" asked Ashlyn.

"There are fixed cards in the deck that have traditional meanings. But the cards have the ability to introduce uncommon elements with each use that can change or add to the traditional meaning. For example—"

"My turn," interrupted Nerdraaage. They watched as Nerdraaage turned over a depiction of a skeleton upon a pale horse.

"Death."

"Death!" said Nerdraaage.

"Don't worry," assured Dangalf. "It is representative of change. It could mean—"

"That you die," said Ashlyn.

"Well, that would be a change," agreed Doppelganger.

"But I see an uncommon element as well," said Dangalf.

"What's an uncommon element?" asked Nerdraaage.

"I'm just going to turn my card over," Dangalf said in exasperation. His card depicted a rose in full bloom. The stem was covered with thorns, and a single red blood drop hung from the stem.

"What does that mean?" asked Doppelganger.

"Well, a rose means different things. A rose in full bloom means love. But the thorns indicate problems or pain."

It was then agreed that Dangalf needed more schooling on the use of the divination deck. As Dangalf carefully returned his deck to its box, they discussed what they each needed to do next. It was agreed that today was shot for the Keepers. Hempshire bustled from sunup to sundown, and it was nearly the latter now. But grand plans were made for the next day. Doppelganger and Dangalf would each inquire about their respective training. Nerdraaage would take a job already offered him to clean the stables. He was less than enthusiastic, but it was agreed the group could no longer finance his newfound love of drink. Ashlyn, who ate very little and was so far provided free room by Mistress Tolliver, would assist the innkeeper's wife for her own spare copper.

XI

Early the next morning, Dangalf crept out of Ashlyn's window and down the latticework and made his way to the Wizened Wizard. It was a small, round, two-story building and outside the front door flew a plain white banner. Dangalf knocked on the solid wood door. A series of clanks and scrapes indicated that a key was turning and a bar was being removed from the back of the door. It opened, and when no person made himself known, Dangalf stepped inside.

As Dangalf's eyes adjusted to the darkness, he observed the door closing, locking and barring itself. He was unthreatened by the self-locking door and grinned excitedly.

The circular walls were covered with bookshelves. And each shelf was full of books with colorful but worn covers in sizes ranging from a yard high to only a few inches and placed upon the shelves in a loving disorder that would take a team of theme park imagineers weeks to replicate.

On tables near the back were jars of smoking and bubbling and oozing and hissing liquids. Next to these were jars of powders that weren't doing much of anything at all. And next to these were more books, some of them brazenly splayed.

And at the back of all this was the eponymous Wizened Wizard. He read from a book that was half as tall as the room, and he used a giant magnifying glass to do that. He wore a black robe and pointed hat, both inscribed with moons and stars and other celestial objects. The images did not reflect light so much as they seemed to generate their own eerie glow.

"Magic apprenticeship is two crown and twenty farthing," said the wizard. "Place the fee on the silver tray if that be your intention."

Dangalf walked to the tray and set down his payment. A white cat on the table sauntered over to his coins and moved them around with its paws as if to count them. No, thought Dangalf, it must just be playing with them. The cat looked up expectantly at Dangalf and he suddenly noticed he was one farthing short. He dug into his pocket and placed another coin on the table.

"Sorry," he said to the cat.

"Whom are you talking to?"

"The cat," said Dangalf.

"Wendell does not understand Acadish."

"Of course. It's just for a moment, I thought…"

"He understands Elvish if you speak that tongue."

"Uh, no."

"Then you will have to restrict your conversation to me. Your fee provides for a rudimentary wand, an apprentice robe, and loan of the books you will need."

"Do I get a hat?"

The wizard looked away from his text for the first time and looked at Dangalf. "You have to buy your own hat."

The wizard stood and went into a back room through a white door. Dangalf recognized the door as meaning the room was restricted to only members of the White School, of which he was not yet. The wizard returned with a black robe and wand.

"I am Weyd Salint. I was apprentice to Archmage Ozymandias."

"The great and powerful Ozymandias. The greatest of the human wizards."

"You know of a greater wizard?"

"Me? No. It's just that the troll necromancers are supposed to be quite powerful. They're well regarded in the, uh, where I come from."

"Rubbish." Weyd was a classic ectomorph and slightly smaller than Dangalf. "Necromancers are the most wretched of creatures. Since you know nothing of magic, and will have to unlearn what you think you know, I will illustrate it for you thusly: It is far easier to burn down a house than it is to build a house. But that does not mean the vandal is superior to the carpenter."

"I did not mean to insult you or Ozymandias. I can only aspire to that greatness."

"I hope for your sake you do not even approach greatness."

"Why?"

"Ozymandias remains locked in his tower, always peering at the furthest stars or pouring over ancient texts to unlock the secrets of the arcane, unable to bear even for a moment the distraction of mere mortals. Even the humble presence of a former apprentice. And he has lived thusly for over sixty years."

"Sixty years! How old are you?"

"I am old."

"How old?"

"Very old."

"Oh. I mean, 'cause you look great!"

"Thank you. Go ahead and put on your robe"

Dangalf felt wizardly as he put on his new robe, but he couldn't help thinking that it was no protection against arrows or daggers.

"Say, why do we wear cloth robes?" asked Dangalf. In the game magic classes were restricted from wearing metal armor, but he did not know why that would apply here. "It seems to me if we wore adamantine, we would be virtually immune to physical attacks while we cast our spells."

"Articulated magic comes from the channeling of the body's electroplasm," explained Weyd. *Cronica* players knew about electroplasm. It was proportional to a character's intellect and was needed to cast spells. Real-world descriptions of this essence included mana, mojo, od, and kundalini. But it is correctly called electroplasm. "Metals interfere with that channeling," continued Weyd. "Leather to a lesser extent. Even cloth inhibits this channeling to a slight degree."

"So what you're saying is it would most benefit the wizard class to be completely naked," said Dangalf.

"Yes, but then where would we carry our coins? A loose-fitting robe is fine for our purposes."

"Druids wear leather though," Dangalf ventured based on game dynamics.

"Druidic magic draws mostly from external life forces and is not impaired by flesh and bone," said Weyd.

"So why can't a blackguard or ranger wear metal? They're not magic classes."

"They could wear metal," answered Weyd. "But metal armor is loud and those classes succeed or fail according to their stealth."

Dangalf silently rebuked himself. He could have figured that last part out himself.

"And you will find even our Red School friends borrow some magic from this world," continued Weyd. "And what path of the Wizard Class have you chosen?" On Dangalf's look, Weyd explained that the wizard class was divided into two branches, the pacifist Sages and the combat Mages.

"Combat," said Dangalf.

"Ah," nodded Weyd in his first, and even then only slight, appearance of satisfaction with Dangalf. He picked up a well-worn tome from his shelf and returned to Dangalf.

"And are you ready to begin your training?"

Dangalf straightened himself out in preparation. "I'm ready. What will you do? Say an incantation over me? Tap me with your wand?"

Weyd presented the book he had picked out. Dangalf took the book and looked at its cover. *Elemental Elementalism: Fire and Ice.*

"How does this work?" asked Dangalf.

"How does a book work?"

"Yes," said Dangalf. "When I open it, does a bright light shine out that imbues me with all the wisdom of the book?"

"No. You read it."

Dangalf flipped through the book. "I have a divination deck," he volunteered.

"Why?"

"For divination."

"Where did you get it?"

"From a travelling salesman."

"There are many travelers, not all of those well intentioned. Divination is sometimes classified as a black magic."

"Oh. I didn't know that. Why?"

"The Templars have a saying. You must step into the abyss to see beyond—"

"Today's illumination," finished Dangalf. "The Witchfinder General said that before we killed him."

"You killed the Witchfinder General?"

"Uh, no," said Dangalf awkwardly. He made some awkward hand gestures but no more words availed themselves.

"I think I would have heard of it if you had," said Weyd. He went to another shelf and carefully picked out three dusty tomes. "These books will help explain your divination deck."

"I don't need those," said Dangalf. "The deck came with an instruction booklet." Dangalf held out the palm-sized booklet, and Weyd took it.

"What is your name?"

"Dangalf."

"Dangalf," said Weyd, balancing the dusty tomes in one hand and the small booklet in the other as if offering Dangalf a choice. "You have to decide just what kind of mage you wish to be."

Dangalf sheepishly took the tomes and looked around at the walls of books surrounding him. He wondered if it was too late for him to become a warrior.

It was about this time, in a field outside the Hempshire compound, that Doppelganger was wondering if it was too late for him to become a wizard.

He had just been knocked to the ground from a vicious blow of a wooden sword across his neck. Now, still dazed on the ground, the angry face of Alfred the Merciless screamed at him.

"And now you're dead! And your head is hanging on some orc's belt! And do you know why!"

"Because I let my guard down?"

"Because you let your guard down! Get off the ground and get into combat stance!"

Doppelganger stood and towered over the little, angry warrior trainer. He crouched forward with his wooden sword raised for striking and his wooden shield raised for blocking. Alfred charged Doppelganger, who backed away from the spinning fury of the wooden weapons.

"You fight like shite! You can't always back up! A warrior needs to use aggression! Attack me! Attack me!"

Suddenly Doppelganger overpowered Alfred's blows and charged him. Alfred stepped aside and struck hard blows to Doppelganger's back and head, again sending him painfully to the ground.

"If I'd known you would do whatever your enemy command- ed, I would have told you to fall on your sword," screamed Alfred.

Alfred screamed everything, but the guards spoke of him in hushed and reverent tones. They described in detail the inju- ries he had received and the battles in which he received them. Doppelganger, when he had a moment of rest, would try to match Alfred's scars with the stories he had heard. And wher- ever there was not a scar, and sometimes overlapping, was a rune tattoo, each of them a ward against a different magical spell. But most impressive of his bodily modifications was "C" on the side of his neck. It identified those few heroes, the Merciless, who had killed at least a hundred each of goblin, orc, and troll. Few pre- tenders would appropriate this decoration because when it was discovered to be false, among other penalties, the disingenuous tattoo was cut or burned off. Doppelganger wanted that tattoo.

Doppelganger had gotten off on the wrong foot with Alfred with his answer to Alfred's first question: why did he want to join the warrior class? Doppelganger said he wanted to be a Dragoon, and this inflamed the flammable Alfred. Dragoons were the greatest of all warriors. And here was this hymen that had not one day of training aspiring to be one of those elite.

How was Doppelganger to know that Alfred himself aspired to be a dragoon and, despite having the requisite Merciless title, he had thus far been overlooked? Overlooked literally, he was sure. Alfred resented that the towering Doppelganger would ap- peal to that bias of the Dragoon command where humans aver- aged well over six feet in height. Even dwarf dragoons averaged as tall as Alfred.

Both Doppelganger and Dangalf were now candidates in their chosen classes. Whereas Dangalf was called an apprentice and had no responsibility beyond his studies, Doppelganger was called guard and was expected to do service in that respect. The upside to guard duty was free training and a pittance of a per diem.

XII

Dangalf felt very magical in his robe but couldn't help but feel naked without a wizard's hat. Holding the wand would help, but so far Weyd refused to release it to him.

A wand was not a requirement of casting spells. (This was another example of his magic knowledge that Dangalf would have to unlearn due to the misinformation of the home world's fiction.) But a wand helped with aiming, boosted the power of spells, and, as a visible weapon, had a certain intimidation factor. It acted as a battery storing electroplasmic energy in excess of the caster's bodily pool. This was especially helpful when the caster was depleted of his natural electroplasm and could use the wand to continue casting spells until it also was depleted. As he continued to develop his pool of electroplasm, Dangalf would eventually carry a staff, which was a more powerful version of a wand.

Weyd was only slightly stern with Dangalf when he discussed wand etiquette. Otherwise he was a grandfatherly figure, and Dangalf thought it safe to bring up the Keepers' predicament.

"Have you known of people from other worlds?" he asked.

"Oceania?"

"No. No place on this world. But from a different world entirely. Maybe a different universe."

"It is said that the ancients traveled to another world freely. But that is only a mythology from what we know today."

"How did they do it?"

"Lost ceremonies performed at a magical site."

"Where is this site?"

"In Nemetia at the axis mundi."

"Actual beings could move between worlds?"

"Yes. In the ancient time."

Dangalf smiled. Is it possible? Elves and Dwarves visiting ancient Earth and shaping our own mythology?

"But that portal was closed during the Schism. And now Nemetia has fallen to Axis aggression. If any ceremonies are performed there now, they are the dark dealings of witches and necromancers."

"Nemetia has fallen?" Dangalf asked quietly. In the game these sacred groves were neutral, incorruptible.

"Yes." Weyd approached a large vase that held not flowers but scrolls, and he selected one.

"This is the world you have entered," he said unrolling the map. It was Acadia not unlike that of the *Cronica* startup screen. But this map showed both the neutral lands of Nemetia and half of the elf kingdom shaded to show Legion occupation. He could see that the Alliance was on the precipice of defeat. He would need to tell the other Keepers.

"May I borrow this map?" he asked. Weyd nodded. "And what is this schism that you mentioned?"

Weyd ventured back beyond a white arch and returned with a volume that was kept separate from the front library. "A knowledge of magic is but an artifice without a knowledge of the world. This book is a history of this world but much more than that." He handed the small, heavy volume to Dangalf. It was beautifully bound but undecorated on the outside. Inside, it was a magnificent example of an illuminated novel handwritten and illustrated with vibrant and metallic colors. He was astonished to see the title: *Cronica Acadia.* "On a superficial level it is a history of this world," continued Weyd. "On its deepest level it is the key to ultimate knowledge. For that you will need to read what is not written in words. The *Cronica* is the abstruse entwined with the arcane and disguised as enigma. Glean what you can from this book first."

Dangalf scanned ahead through the multitude of pages with illustrations and maps and many tiny words. "But it will take me a year, months at least, to read this."

"You need only look at each page and capture it. Understanding will come later. Sometimes much later. Once it is in your memory, you will be able to access it for reference or comprehension later. I found it helpful many years ago to set aside part of my mind and to visualize a library, not unlike this one..." Weyd looked about and wrinkled his nose. "Only perhaps a little cleaner, to visualize a library where I placed my mind's copy of each book I had looked upon. It is when I slumber that I read these books. And so will you."

"You want me to read while I sleep?"

"No, dear apprentice. I'm afraid you won't be sleeping for several weeks."

XIII

The Keepers met for dinner after Doppelganger and Dangalf's first day of training. The others had already taken a table at the Silent Woman when Dangalf showed up with his map. He unrolled the map, and he was not disappointed by the cries of shock and concern by the others at the precarious state of the Righteous Races. Any enthusiast of the board game Risk could see that the Legion's advantage put the Alliance in grave jeopardy. And they were all enthusiasts of the board game Risk.

Dangalf hadn't even let them digest the map when he told them of the book he had just been given. *Cronica Acadia*. It was a revelation to them all. Wasn't the game *Cronica* based on a pulp novel called *Cronica Acadia*? Were these books the same? Dangalf had another shocking revelation. A portal long since closed had existed between the two worlds. Dwarves and elves may have visited ancient Earth!

None was more keen to hear about the *Cronica Acadia* than Ashlyn, for she had designed her own avatar to be generously ectomorphic, and her intellect was yearning. Dangalf continued solemnly, "The *Cronica Acadia* is the abstruse, entwined with the arcane, surrounding—"

"Creamy nougat?" said the not-so-ectomorphic Nerdraaage.

"This is deadly serious," said Dangalf. "Nemetia is in enemy hands. Weyd said if we were summoned here from the axis mundi, it was likely done by a powerful witch." The others were flattered and terrified to varying degrees.

XIV

After his two weeks of basic training, Doppelganger earned the distinction as the first guard of the shitehouse. Alfred explained a weakness was recently discovered when unfriendly dwarf and elf forces breached the compound by climbing through the drainage ditch. Doppelganger nodded as he feigned ignorance about the incursion. He was given a shield and a spear and a helmet with leather lining that smelled of other men's sweat. He didn't want Alfred to criticize him as delicate, so he put on the helmet with the smelly, wet lining. He did dare to ask for an axe—after all, his weapon could mean the difference between life and death, and he already knew the axe was his weapon of choice. Alfred screamed that Doppelganger was a piece of shite who was in no position to suggest what weapon he needed, and he further screamed that it wasn't a spear but it was a glaive and that it was more useful to a guard than an axe as he could plant the butt in the ground and leverage the weapon to dismount a rider. Doppelganger did not bother to argue over the likelihood of an attacker charging out of the shitehouse on horseback.

Alfred lead Doppelganger to a miserable spot barely farting distance from the shitehouses and ordered him to stand there until relieved. Doppelganger feared that his most difficult task would be to stay awake, and he had asked his friends to come by and visit him. Nerdraaage cheerfully responded that he would come and see him each time he needed to take a shite. But it was only a few minutes into his shift that his friends came bounding down the dirt path toward him. Just seeing them made him smile. Even Dangalf had taken a break from his studies to visit poor Doppelganger. But he brought a book with him. He was had become one of *those* people.

They were excited to see Doppelganger, but his friends' company did come at a price. "You finally found a job suitable for your talents!"

"You should set up a table with mints and a tip jar."

"You should carry a plunger instead of a spear."

"This gives new meaning to the expression 'Halt! Who goes there!'"

"Do you have to stand so close to the shitehouses, or do you just like the smell?"

"I told you guys to come by one at a time," Doppelganger interrupted. "That way, I would have company over a longer period of time instead of you just all coming and going together."

"Yeah," answered Ashlyn. "But we decided that would be boring for us."

"And you," he turned on Dangalf. "You had to bring a book with you? You thought there might be a lull in the conversation and you could sneak in a few chapters?"

"What?"

"I'm out here all night, and I don't have a book."

"Would you like to borrow it?" Dangalf asked doing a terrible job of not sounding patronizing.

"What is it?"

"Evenson's *Black Tongue Primer.*"

Doppelganger shook his head. "You know what I've been doing this last thirty minutes? I've been watching that anthill. Better than any TV show I've ever seen. Better than any movie. And I'll be watching it all night."

"Do they do anything at night?"

"I guess that'll be one of the things I learn."

"Well, I'll expect your report in the morning."

Now Doppelganger knew that Dangalf was mocking him, and he began to simmer. "You go around with your nose in a book all the time and you could miss out on a lot of things."

"I'm not a naturalist, dude. I can't be gazing at ants all day. This is my time to read and read as much as I can."

"And you don't think you could learn anything by watching these ants?"

"Like what? How to lift forty-two times my own weight?"

"Please," interjected Ashlyn. "Can we not have another epeen contest about which is better, the White School or Red School!"

"Red School," said Nerdraaage.

"Doppelganger," said Ashlyn. "How's your training going?"

After a moment getting over his anger, Doppelganger told them about his introduction to shields and swords and spears and the emphasis on defensive tactics. Offensive tactics would come as he proved himself. He told them that he was taught who and how to salute and showed them. Dangalf, who had always been a know-it-all and would only become more so, told them that the salute had evolved from the practice of helmeted guards lifting up their face shields for inspection.

Dangalf was pressed to discuss his training, but he dodged the subject. He explained it was wizard code not to discuss the training. "Who are you, David Copperfield?" demanded Nerdraaage.

"It's not like that. It's just considered poor form to discuss what you're learning until you've learned it. For example, you don't tell someone you're learning to conjure fire. You show them that you can conjure fire after you can do it."

"You're learning to conjure fire?" asked Nerdraaage.

"Yes."

"Was that so difficult?"

"It is if every day you ask if I can conjure fire yet and I can't. That puts a lot of pressure on me. Conjuring fire is my foundation skill. If I learn it, I become a conjurer, a scroll-carrying member of the White School. If I don't, I might be shoveling shite too." Each of the classes had a foundation skill that was unique to their class and was of an exceptional nature.

"That is pretty heavy," agreed Ashlyn. "Do you think you can do it?"

"I actually think I can," answered Dangalf. "I mean this world, I can just sense it being filled with magic as if I could pull it right out of the air. I can almost smell it."

"That's just the shitehouse," said Nerdraaage.

"My foundation skill is shapeshifting," said Ashlyn. "It's still inconceivable to me that it would be possible."

A guard on patrol approached from a distance. "Is that the guard that wanted to kiss Elftrap?" asked Nerdraaage.

"Yes," said Dangalf. "And it's Ashlyn."

"William," said Doppelganger of the guard. "He's an ass."

William stopped at the group at looked at them contemptuously until finally setting his gaze on Ashlyn. "Darling, you don't have to hang out at the shite-hole if you're desperate for a man's comfort."

"Excuse me?" said Ashlyn.

"Sire, I ask you to be respectful of our lady friend," said Dangalf.

"Lady!" laughed William.

"That's enough of that," said Dangalf.

"We don't want any trouble," said Ashlyn.

"And what will you do about it, skinny?" he challenged Dangalf.

"Why don't you ask me what I'm going to do about it?" said Doppelganger.

William turned on Doppelganger furiously. "You noob!" The Keepers were all startled to hear that online insult uttered in this universe. "You hold a glaive for one day and think you can stand up to me! I challenge you to a duel!"

"I accept!" Doppelganger said quickly.

"In front of the shire-reeve's office tomorrow during the changing of the guard. All will witness your humbling." William marched angrily away in the direction that he came.

"I don't want you guys getting in fights over me," said Ashlyn.

"This is a chivalrous world. Men don't just stand there while their women are being attacked," said Doppelganger.

"She's not even a real woman!" said Nerdraaage.

"You shouldn't have gotten involved," said Dangalf. "I was handling it."

"I'm a warrior," said Doppelganger. "I need to duel. That's what we do."

"He could kill you!" protested Ashlyn.

"He's not gonna kill me."

"How do you know?"

"If he's beating me, I'll just concede."

"In the game!" said Ashlyn. "You don't know that that applies here." They were all silent for a moment.

"If he kills you, then he'll have me to deal with," said Dangalf.

"And what are you going to do?" asked Doppelganger. "You can't even conjure fire."

XV

The morning of the duel Doppelganger went to his training as usual. Alfred greeted Doppelganger by calling him
"worthless and weak." He then went on to say that Doppelganger
still smelled of shite from his assignment the night before. Or
maybe that was just his normal smell, he added. "I'm dueling
today," said Doppelganger.

"With who?" Alfred said without screaming.

"William."

Alfred paused. "It should be a good duel."

A kind word from Alfred! Suddenly Doppelganger was
buoyed with confidence. But it was only momentary. He began
to think that Alfred was taking pity on him, and that concerned
him. Alfred remained unusually quiet. Doppelganger took up
his wooden sword and shield without being told. He felt today's
training was especially important and was eager to begin.

"Hold on a moment," said Alfred. He went to the back of his
wagon and returned to Doppelganger. He handed Doppelganger
a metal shield and axe. "I normally don't introduce real weapons

this early in training but you won't be dueling with wooden swords," said Alfred. Alfred took up his own metal shield and sword.

"Dueling is not combat," he explained. "Combat is about killing your enemy. Dueling is about honor. It goes without saying that you do not want to be killed in a duel. However, it is almost as important that you do not lose honor."

"If you kill someone in a duel, you could be charged with murder?" Doppelganger asked hopefully. Dangalf had researched the subject and told Doppelganger as much.

"Only if one refused a surrender. Or if one was to kill another of much lower rank. You two are of equal rank."

The lesson was relatively easy. Doppelganger believed that Alfred did not want to overly tax him prior to the duel. He was, however, disappointed when Alfred sent him on his way at the end of the training day. He hoped that he would walk with him to the duel.

As Doppelganger approached the shire-reeve's office, he saw what a spectacle the duel had become. The changing of the guard meant that nearly every guard in Hempshire was present. The guards stood watching Doppelganger, clearly aware of and waiting for the duel. Even the shire-reeve had stepped from his office and waited. The gathered guards had also attracted a hundred or so curious townspeople to the site. Doppelganger felt his nerves turn to anger as he observed the crowd, especially the townsfolk, who for all he knew had never picked up a weapon in combat. Damn NPCs!

There was Master Tolliver laughing and chatting with the smithy. He hated Tolliver's ruddy, smiling face. He would get to sate his bloodlust without a hint of threat to himself. Doppelganger wished he were a spectator. How much easier this would be if he could have at least seen a duel before participating in one.

He saw his opponent finally and decided that William looked disappointed that Doppelganger had shown up. William's grave look was some comfort.

The other Keepers arrived, and he smiled confidently for their benefit. Nerdraaage bumped fists with him. Dangalf smiled weakly. Ashlyn hugged him. Regardless of her previous incarnation, she certainly felt like a real woman pressed against him.

Nerdraaage had a wineskin bag slung over his shoulder. He held it to Doppelganger, who took a drink. "You're going to kick his ass," said Nerdraaage.

"How long has he been a guard?" asked Dangalf.

"Eight years," said Doppelganger.

"That's a long time," worried Dangalf.

"That's great!" said Nerdraaage.

"That he has eight more years experience than me?"

"Eight years and he's still a guard," explained Nerdraaage. "He's just an NPC. Eight years from now you're going to be a Dragoon, and he'll still be a guard."

Doppelganger nodded, wanting to believe Nerdraaage. It gave him some confidence where his weapons did not. He still carried the small, dull metal axe and shield he had just used in training.

The shire-reeve stepped into an empty spot between the two combatants, and Doppelganger knew it was time. He stepped forward as did William. He noticed the fine longsword and shield that William sported. The shire-reeve looked at him curiously.

"Doppelganger is it not?" asked the shire-reeve.

"Yes, sire."

"How long have you been a guard?"

"Two days today, sire."

The shire-reeve turned toward William. "So there won't be much honor for you even in victory?" he asked. William looked chagrined. "Do you wish to call this off?" asked the shire-reeve. Dangalf and Ashlyn brightened.

"He paid me great insult. But if he would care to ap—"

"No," said Doppelganger before William could finish.

The dye was cast. If Doppelganger were to be a warrior in this world, he would need to duel. And this was as good a time to start as any. The dire wolves had not killed him, and an overweight, pockmarked guard would not either.

"Very well," said the shire-reeve. "Step back three paces each of you."

The shire-reeve held a piece of red fabric in his outstretched hand. "When this cloth hits the ground, the duel will commence."

"Stop!" Only one man in all of Hempshire could make such a command at this juncture. The crowd turned and made way as Alfred approached Doppelganger. "Get rid of that trash," he said.

Doppelganger nodded quickly to Nerdraaage, who ran over and collected the lesser shield, axe, and helmet.

"You will use mine," Alfred announced. Doppelganger thought that he saw William's eyes momentarily roll back into his head as if he would faint right there.

Alfred handed Doppelganger a battleaxe that was so well balanced that it seemed to turn feather-light as he held it up in striking position. He handed Doppelganger his Merciless commemorative shield. It was round and had vicious-looking spikes on the front. Ringing the shield were words in Acadish, Dwarvish, and Elvish. In the center it said *Alfred the Merciless.*

Doppelganger slipped his left arm through the heavy leather straps of the shield. Alfred attempted to put his helmet on Doppelganger, but clearly it wouldn't fit. "Your head's too damn big." Alfred took the old helmet from Nerdraaage and stuck it back on Doppelganger's head.

Doppelganger looked down at the magnificent shield and wondered how long it would take him to kill one hundred each of orc, goblin, and troll. But he was getting ahead of himself. Did he not now have a human opponent six paces in front of him who would like nothing more than to end Doppelganger's warrior ambition right then and there?

"Ready," said the shire-reeve. It was more command than question, so neither party answered. They raised their shields and weapons. The red cloth was dropped and a second later hit the ground.

For another second after the duel began, they just stood in place. Suddenly William made his move and charged with a series of three overhand blows that clanged harmlessly on Doppelganger's shield. The ineffectiveness of the attack emboldened Doppelganger, and the physical jarring of combat dispensed with whatever nerves had plagued him.

Doppelganger retaliated with his own overhead blows that crashed monstrously against William's shield. He raised his shield so high against the withering blows that Doppelganger saw William's unprotected belly. But an axe strike there would likely eviscerate William, so he kicked him instead. William doubled over, and his labored breathing stopped altogether for a few seconds.

It was a very lopsided duel, Doppelganger bashing forward and William retreating hopelessly. The crowd jostled around behind them as the spectators attempted to keep the duel in view. William's retreat was halted when he found himself back to the shire-reeve's office and unable to move further. Doppelganger rained blows down upon the splintering shield until the shield itself cracked in half and William slid down to the ground. Doppelganger smashed the sword with his axe and it too was dropped, leaving William with his bare arms outstretched defensively. Doppelganger raised his axe for the killing blow and paused ever so slightly. His look of ferocity must have said he was willing and able to deliver that killing blow. "I concede!" shouted William.

A cheer rose up from the crowd. Doppelganger took his weapon in his shield hand and lowered his right hand to assist William off the ground. That struck him as the noble thing to do, and though he wasn't feeling particularly kind at the moment, he knew that others were watching. William did not say anything or even look him in the eye.

The shire-reeve congratulated Doppelganger. "Well done," he said. And then the crowd, led first by the guards, pressed in around him. Tolliver could not reach Doppelganger but shouted a promise of the best dinner Doppelganger had ever had. He wasn't such a bad sort, thought Doppelganger.

When the crowd thinned, Doppelganger walked to his friends, who had kept their distance. They all smiled in joy and relief. "You won your first duel!" said Dangalf.

"And you won it so easily!" added Ashlyn.

"You didn't think I could do it!" he chided them. "You had faith in me," he said to Nerdraaage.

"Yeah," said Nerdraaage. "But I'm drunk."

Doppelganger remembered his borrowed gear and searched out Alfred. He saw him chatting with the Captain of the guard. Beaming with pride, Doppelganger approached Alfred, who turned to face him. He stood before Alfred no longer as a lowly guard but as a comrade in arms. A victorious combatant. An equal. "You forgot everything I taught you, you hymen!" screamed Alfred as he roughly pulled his gear from Doppelganger.

XVI

Tolliver kept his promise and served roast pork to the Keepers. He also opened a bottle of Aged Vinlandian for the table.

With his duel victory, Doppelganger was suddenly enjoying the warrior prerogative, or at least the prerogative of victorious warriors. There were congratulations from the town's most prominent citizens, the adoring compliments of children, the flirtations of lovely maidens, and now even the skinflint Tolliver was gifting the most expensive items on his menu.

The pork was an especially nice change for Nerdraaage, who had taken to ordering the roast beast, the cheapest item on the menu, for every meal so that he had more drinking money. "Roast beast?" Doppelganger had asked him the first time. "You never did the Chef's Surprise quest, did you?"

"No," Nerdraaage had replied.

"So you don't know what roast beast is?" Dangalf had asked.

"No, and I don't want to know," Nerdraaage had said quickly. "It's cheap and it tastes good. That's all I want to know." But tonight at least he knew he ate pork.

"Good company, good food, good wine," said Dangalf. "What more could you ask for?"

"That," said Nerdraaage, looking to a table of men who puffed on long pipes. Dangalf nodded sympathetically, but their funds were not yet liquid enough for smoke.

Dangalf shared with the others his newfound knowledge of this world from the *Cronica Acadia* in a greatly abbreviated form: "First there was God. The uncreated God they call him. The transcendent God, and he plays very little part in the legends other than getting the ball rolling. He had some children. Gods also. The immanence they call them. And he took them and hid them in the world. Not to punish them or because he feared them but because he wanted to test them. This is the Before Time. Now on top of the world God put all sorts of monsters or daevas, so he puts the daevas there and gives them free reign over the surface. Well eventually the gods have had enough of living in the dark, and they create the Inversion, where they turn the world inside out and they take their rightful place on the outside and all the daevas are trapped under the surface. This is called the classical age, and everything was great, but like the uncreated God before them, these gods bring their own children into this world, and those were the three righteous races of elf, dwarf, and man. And that went on for a really long time, eons or so, but then the unrighteous races show up. And the legends conflict on whether that was because the gods put them there to test the righteous races or because they were put there by the daevas still underground. And there was an unrighteous image of each of the righteous ones, and that was the troll, goblin, and orc. And for a while after that, righteous and unrighteous lived together until a troll king killed an elf princess and ruined everything. And that was the first murder. And Woden was so angry that he sundered the world so that each of the races should remain forever separate and distinct."

"Who's Woden?" asked Nerdraaage.

"He's from game lore," said Ashlyn. "Woden was the leader of the pantheon of the gods."

"Never heard of him."

"Sure you did," said Dangalf. "Our home world had a day named after him. Woden's Day."

"Never heard of that either."

"Wednesday!" said Ashlyn. "I always wondered why that day had such a funky spelling."

Dangalf continued. "And the Sundering was followed by the three hundred days of darkness, and pieces of the cracked world floated away such as Oceania, only recently rediscovered. And though the three hundred days of darkness was rough, after it came the Golden Age, when sapiens—both righteous and un-righteous races are called sapiens—they became independent of the gods, and the great schools were formed. And in time a portal was opened to another world and travelers went back and forth between them."

"The portal to our world?" asked Ashlyn.

"It would seem," said Dangalf. "And there was a great con-flict between the two worlds about the future of the White and Blue Schools, and a civil war almost erupted between the righteous races. The solution was the Schism, which saw the closure of the portals between the worlds and ushered in the present age."

"What age are we in now?" asked Doppelganger.

"The ages are usually named in retrospect," said Dangalf somberly. "But the End Times has been suggested."

He told them that the last Great War between the Alliance and the Legion was finally ended due to what the dwarves call the Three Pillars of Victory, but only after significant advantage had been gained by the unrighteous as illustrated by Weyd's map. The question remained, when was the next Great War?

On to more mundane but nonetheless important topics, he described to them that this world had twenty-four-hour days (for the most part) and twelve-month years (for the most part). "For the most part?" asked Ashlyn.

"These are imperfect measurements like our home world," explained Dangalf. "And they sometimes play catch-up as we did with leap year."

Time was measured by sundials and candles and hourglasses, though these hourglasses were often designed to measure times much greater than or less than an actual hour.

Coinage was the copper farthing, the silver crown, and the gold sovereign. Bars of gold and even rarer metals were used as higher denominations of currency but were so far beyond their means at this time as not to warrant further discussion.

Dangalf told them that because of the stubbornness of their home country in not switching to the metric system, they were all familiar with the measurements used in Acadia, such as miles for distance, pounds for weight, and pints for volume. Only occasionally did he think they might encounter a term such as league that they might not immediately recognize, but he reminded them that he was there to keep them informed about such things, and for the record, a league is three miles. And as a side note, he told them dwarves, the first great builders of this world, created measurement. But Nerdraaage was not as nearly impressed by this achievement as Dangalf wanted him to be.

Finally he explained the base-twelve numbering system that was sometimes used in spells or ceremony. "What does that mean?" said a slightly inebriated Nerdraaage.

"Duodecimal," he said. "They have two more numerals than us. A number that looks like X represents the decimal ten, and a backward three represents the decimal eleven." He wrote on a parchment as he described the following: "In duodecimal one-zero is what we know as twelve and one-zero-zero is what we know as one-hundred and forty-four."

"That's confusing as hell," said Ashlyn.

"Confusing is October being the tenth month," insisted Dangalf. "Duodecimal is preferable to decimal in many ways. And a dozen coins is still a dozen coins regardless of how it is represented. New numerals. Same old numbers. Math is universal."

"I thought we were in a new universe," said Nerdraaage. And that is where Dangalf decided he had educated the other Keepers about their new world enough for one day and returned to his drinking.

XVII

The scrivener entered the inn and approached their table. Doppelganger beamed at the expectation of more congratulations, but that was not the scrivener's motive.

"Ah, Doppelganger and Dangalf," said the scrivener. He might have been as young as twelve, but he sounded like a thirty-year-old accountant. "We have a problem."

"Vinland, we have a problem," said Nerdraaage.

"Would you have a seat, Master Scrivener?" said Dangalf.

"Thank you," said the scrivener. "And you may call me Bartleby. We have sent record to Vinland of your deeds, and now we hear back from the sages that they have no record of any of you."

"Is that a problem?" asked Doppelganger.

"It is if you want acknowledgement for any of your deeds. Were your births not registered?"

The four looked at each other blankly. "No they're not," said Dangalf.

"Well, it's never too late," said Bartleby, and he placed some scrolls and other tools on the table. "You first, Doppelganger. Your place of birth?"

"That's difficult to say."

"We were born between towns," added Dangalf.

"Then what town were you born nearest to?"

"This one."

Bartleby wrote on a scroll with great flourishes, and then he held the tip of the quill pen in the candlelight. He took Doppelganger's thumb and jabbed the end of the pen into it.

Doppelganger stood up angrily, pulling Bartleby up with him. Even William hadn't spilled his blood.

"Oh dear," said Bartleby.

Dangalf and Nerdraaage each took one of Doppelganger's big arms, and he released Bartleby. He sat back down, still flush. Bartleby carefully placed the scroll before Doppelganger.

"I suppose I should have warned you about that. If I could just get you to place some of your blood next to my signature." Doppelganger did so.

"What is the point of the blood?" asked Dangalf.

"The sages want it. They have magic that will show your character and also if you have records already with them. There are plenty of rapscallions who would like to start over with a new identity, but nothing gets past the sages."

When it was Dangalf's turn, he started to expound on the potential invasion of privacy poised by the sages maintaining a giant database of everyone's blood.

"Prime directive," Ashlyn said, and Dangalf's own words shamed him into surrendering his blood to Bartleby.

The process was repeated for Ashlyn. "You realize we all have the same birthday now," she said.

"Happy birthday," said Dangalf. "Maybe Tolliver will bring us another bottle of wine."

"As for you, Master Dwarf," said Bartleby. "This will serve only as a record of your service to the humans. You will have to register with your own people. The dwarves are very particular about their clan affiliations and are not ready to turn over those responsibilities to the sages. But rest assured, when your lore-keepers create a record of your birth, they will have our record of your good deeds. Good day to you all." They thanked Bartleby as he departed.

"I have guard duty," said Doppelganger, rising to leave.

"Hey," said Dangalf. "I took tonight off from studying for you."

"You can still study."

"No I can't! I'm drunk!"

"You can come visit me at the front gate if you get bored."

"The front gate?" asked Ashlyn. "A promotion?"

"You could say that. If any of you have to take a shite tonight, you might want to say hi to William. That's his new post."

"Great," she said. "Now I can't use the bathroom anymore."

Doppelganger did not want to leave his friends, but he was excited about being on the front gate. He expected the shift to pass quickly as he would have another guard to talk to and maybe even some townspeople or visitors passing through the gate. And there was always the possibility of a raid or a bandit trying to run the gate.

After a full day of physical punishment, Doppelganger had to pull guard duty for four to six hours. Ashlyn and Nerdraaage were employed as well, Ashlyn at the Silent Woman and Nerdraaage working at both the stables and the smithy as needed.

Only Dangalf avoided any actual employment. His reading requirements were significant even when away from his instructor, and additionally there were few occupations suited for an apprentice mage. (Ashlyn had suggested he could hire himself out for children's birthday parties.)

Of greater irritation to Doppelganger and Nerdraaage was that it appeared that Dangalf got a full night's sleep and then could often be found sleeping during the day. Dangalf explained to them that during the day, when he was lying down with eyes closed and sometimes snoring, he was not actually sleeping but was in fact slumbering. The distinction was lost on them.

XVIII

Slumber as practiced in the White School was the process that allowed the body to rest and regenerate electroplasm while the mind remained fully awake. Dangalf had taken Weyd's advice and constructed in his mind a magnificent library that he had seen in a movie with green leather furniture and bookshelves so high he needed to use a ladder to get to the top shelves. Already he had about two dozen books on the shelves and none more prominent or convenient than the *Cronica Acadia*. As he took down any of these books during his slumber, he could open them and see them as clearly as if he was looking at the original. Now they were in his psychic library permanently, to be perused as he needed or wanted, complete in every facet as he had captured them during his waking hours down to dog-ears, wine stains, and scribbled notes in the margin. And slumber reading was faster and more intuitive than conscious reading.

Dangalf added to his imaginary but fully realized library a window overlooking a green forest with lighting that would change according to the real time in Acadia. He then put in a great red door leading to the outside. He thought for a moment and decided to put a lock on the door, and there it was.

Each time he entered the slumber state, he appeared in a library filled with more books. Once he entered to find a gross of new titles on the shelves. Every book he had read in the other world was now replicated here in his library: *The Maltese Falcon. Catch 22. Animal Farm.* The Hardy Boys! There they were a bunch of them from his youth: *The Tower Treasure, The Secret of the Old Mill, The Clue of the Broken Blade!* (With some chagrin Dangalf realized that he had unconsciously named the Keepers of the Broken Blade after an old Hardy Boys mystery and not by spontaneous brilliance.)

Each mystery was wrapped in cellophane and with their Dewey decimal number on the binding. He excitedly picked up *The House on the Cliff* and opened it. There it was as true as the day he looked at it as a boy. He turned past the title page and was shocked to see that the following pages were blank. The same with *What Happened at Midnight* and *While the Clock Ticked.* And then his memory struck twelve. When he turned to the back of each book, there he saw the final pages. In his youthful impatience and ignorance, he had skipped most of the stories only to read the dénouements. He only wanted to find out the secret of the old mill or what happened at midnight. He hadn't wanted to actually read the books. His youthful indiscretion now forever deprived him of these books in their entirety in his psychic library.

Finally he took one of his newly captured books from the shelf and sat down to read it. *Medicinal Applications of Slumber.* It was a dreadful title, but Weyd had suggested it should be among his earliest studies. It proved to be a fascinating lesson on the consciously directed repair of the physical body during slumber. It demonstrated that with sufficient intellect a human could apply the life-extending regeneration that was natural to the immortal elves and dwarves. After finishing the book, he ruminated on it a bit. He marveled at the idea that his intellect would allow him that kind of control over his body's healing functions. But how to proceed? Suddenly a knock came at his door. He got up nervously and then relaxed. This library, and whatever world existed outside were all in his mind. His doing. There was nothing out there to be alarmed about. Or was there? He made a peephole in the door, slid the peephole cover aside, and looked out. All he could see was a burning candle. Curious, he opened the door, and there stood seven dwarves in mining helmets with little candles attached to them.

"We're here about the repairs," said the dwarf foreman. They carried tools and barrels and wheelbarrows of electroplasm, protoplasm, blood, and white bile. (The White School had little use for the Red School biles of yellow and black.) Dangalf stepped aside, and the dwarves marched into his library and looked about.

"Should I make you a—a doorway?" asked Dangalf.

"Would be better than us tunneling through these fancy walls," said the foreman.

"Ooh velvet," said another dwarf, rubbing his hand on the upholstered walls.

And Dangalf added a lovely wood door, which he made blue in honor of the dwarven craftsmen who would be using it. The foreman opened the door, and it led down a fleshy, veiny tunnel that shimmied with respiration and circulation. "We'll work as quietly as possible," the velvet-loving dwarf promised, and they squished down the fleshy tunnel until the lights of their bobbing candles disappeared in the dark.

And with that Dangalf began the process of consciously repairing the damage done to his body by injury and age. In fact he became so proficient that he awoke one time to Ashlyn staring at his beard and asking him if he was dying his hair. After that he took the dwarves off of follicle duty. They had serious work to do after all.

XIX

After six weeks of training, Doppelganger was finally given one day a week off from training and guard duty as was customary for students and workers. Doppelganger was both, but he still only got one day off.

On their first day off together since arriving in Hempshire, Doppelganger and Nerdraaage met up with Dangalf and Ashlyn in her room. Neither Doppelganger nor Nerdraaage thought anything about Dangalf spending so much time in Ashlyn's room. The stables were no place to store all the books he was surrounded by (even outside his imaginary library), and her room had a small desk and a lamp. And she had a comfortable bed for all the time Dangalf spent lying down with his eyes closed and snoring but not sleeping.

Dangalf asked the others for a moment to finish reading. "I thought you didn't read books anymore!" charged Nerdraaage, who was still unclear on the concept of the library Dangalf had built in his mind.

"He reads while he's asleep," Ashlyn corrected, incorrectly. They started going through his piles of books that Doppelganger and Nerdraaage were certain that he didn't need and could never hope to read. There were grimoires, language books, divination deck instruction, and at least one book of poetry: *Mayhap the Rain.* (Mayhap the third-worst poetry in this universe.) Dangalf bought the book because he had become one of those book lovers who not only enjoyed books for their content but for their actual appearance. It was a slight but well-bound book, and, at only two farthings at the Hempshire library's equivalent of a bargain bin, he could not resist it.

His friends started making up titles for the books as they pretend-catalogued them: "*The Big Book of Sorcery.*"

"*The Necronomicon,* Cliff's Notes edition."

"*Magic For Dummies.*"

"*Everything You Always Wanted to Know about Hex but Were Afraid to Ask.*"

"*I Should Have Been a Warrior* by Merlin the Magician." Even the increasingly humorless Doppelganger was getting in on the action. What magic there is in a day off from work, thought Dangalf.

The three laughed harder which each new title they imagined. Clearly they were not going to let Dangalf finish the book he was capturing, and he only had about sixty pages left. "So you guys started drinking early I see," he said.

"*Black Magic Voo Doos and Voo Don'ts.*"

XX

They had a big, leisurely brunch, and Dangalf chided Ashlyn for introducing the word "brunch" to a befuddled Mistress Tolliver. "So what do we want to do?" asked Ashlyn.

"How about a quest?" suggested Nerdraaage.

"Why not? It would give Doppelganger and me a chance to use our training in a practical situation," said Dangalf.

"Practical situation?" countered Doppelganger. "Just what do you think I'm doing each night for six hours?"

"Guarding the toilet?"

"You know I'm at the front gate now!"

They strolled over to the shire-reeve's office to see what quests were posted. There was another presumptive adventurer perusing the board as well. He wore green tights and a feather in his cap and carried a modest bow and quiver over his shoulder. Ashlyn wondered if he knew how much he looked like Robin Hood and if he also knew that it wasn't a good look for him. It wasn't even a good look for Robin Hood. For his part, the stranger looked upon the Keepers with obvious bemusement.

"Mayhap this," suggested Dangalf of a posted quest.

"What is mayhap?" asked Doppelganger.

"It means perhaps."

"So why not say perhaps."

"Come on," protested Dangalf. "We've all begun to speak more formally, more traditionally since we've been here."

"Not 'mayhap,' we haven't."

"You don't want me to say mayhap?"

"No."

"I vote no," said Ashlyn.

"We're voting?" asked Dangalf.

"Ten thousand gold pieces for the head of the Witchfinder General!" said Nerdraaage breathlessly over the largest and most sun-faded posting. "That's like a million gold pieces here."

Robin Hood laughed out loud. "I can just imagine you four marching your way through the Temple of the Red Rose to slay the Witchfinder General," he said.

"We did it before," said Ashlyn.

"Take that back," demanded Doppelganger.

"What do you mean?"

"You have insulted me and my friends. Apologize for your comment unless you will face me in a duel."

Robin looked Doppelganger up and down. Doppelganger was still poorly clothed and geared but for some reason the dandy adventurer did not take up the towering brute's offer to duel. He smiled generously, removed his hat and bowed. "Mistress Elf, Master Dwarf, honored fellow humans, forgive this humble vagabond for speaking out loud of your wretched appearance." Robin returned his hat to his head and left them cheerily.

Nerdraaage fist-bumped Doppelganger. Doppelganger boasted about how no one would speak to his friends that way, and they certainly wouldn't speak to him that way and certainly not anyone wearing tights.

"Did that guy insult us with his apology?" whispered Ashlyn.

"I believe he did," Dangalf whispered back.

They came upon this faded quest: "Heroes, Seekers, Mercenaries, and Adventurers, a quest awaits you! Daughters of Arachne continue to harass travelers on the road to Vinland and other points south. It is believed that they are responsible for the murder of several children and many more sheep. Bring their carcasses to the office of the shire-reeve of Hempshire for a reward of five copper each."

"Daughters of Aratch-nee," said Nerdraaage. "They want us to kill women?"

"Spiders," explained Dangalf.

It was agreed that this quest would be good for their reputations and the reward was fair. It would also take them down the southern road, which none of them had taken except for Doppelganger, who had patrolled it for only a few miles. And they all agreed killing spiders would be far less distasteful than killing dire wolves.

They separated to gather their gear, what little they had, and met again at the front gate. Dangalf and Ashlyn arrived together at the gate first. They sat on the ground in the shade of a guard tower. Nerdraaage appeared next and carried a small hemp bag in his hand.

"What is the bag for?" asked Ashlyn.

"For the spiders," said Nerdraaage.

Dangalf and Ashlyn shook their heads at him. He turned to see Doppelganger approaching them and pulling a wagon behind him. He turned back to the others.

"Big spiders," said Nerdraaage. Dangalf and Ashlyn nodded.

Doppelganger walked past them. "Come on," he said. Dangalf and Ashlyn spontaneously jumped on the back of the wagon. Doppelganger barely noticed their weight. "You want a free ride?" he asked and then he suddenly began running all out. His powerful legs propelled them quickly, and Dangalf had to grab the side of the wagon to keep from tumbling out backward. Nerdraaage ran after them, his little legs unable to keep up. He caught the back of the wagon as he fell and was dragged for many yards before Dangalf and Ashlyn could help him into the wagon.

And this is how they traveled for about ten miles. Dangalf marveled at Doppelganger's strength and endurance. But it was a melancholy feeling. Doppelganger was the one least like he was in the other world, personality wise, and he missed how his dear friend used to be.

The elf eyes saw it first. "There," she said pointing into the woods. Doppelganger stopped and pulled the wagon to the side of the road.

"What?"

"Webbing." Doppelganger pulled the wagon into the woods with them. He had borrowed it, and it was important to hide it from thieves.

The canopy of the woods blotted out most of the noonday sun, and the color of the leaves and bark gave the woods a gray, monochromatic look. It felt ten degrees cooler in the woods than it had on the road.

The others saw what Ashlyn had seen from the road: trees decorated with white spider webbing. The webbing became thicker and more expansive deeper into the woods until the trees became coated in whiteness, giving a wintry look to the cool darkness.

Dangalf brought out his wand. Doppelganger strapped on his borrowed shield and axe. Nerdraaage armed himself with his dagger and sucked some wine from his bag. So far he felt none of the apprehension that he had when they faced the dire wolves.

Ashlyn was unarmed, but it was agreed she was capable of taking care herself with her heightened senses and gazelle-like swiftness. Still, Dangalf took the opportunity to tell her to "stay close."

Ashlyn went to a small white mass. She peeled the sticky web back, and the others were surprised to see the mass begin moving. She revealed a fawn, barely higher than her knee. It bounded away from the spider-infested woods. A spider with a body the size of a softball scurried toward Ashlyn. "Whoa," gasped Nerdraaage.

Doppelganger was first to the spider and raised his axe, but before he could strike, Dangalf shot a bolt from his wand that killed the spider instantly. The others stood over the smoking carcass.

"Very nice," Ashlyn said.

"Are you okay?" Dangalf asked.

"Of course she is, dumbass," said Doppelganger. "Spider didn't come anywhere near her." And he pressed on into the woods.

Ashlyn did not have an issue with killing the spiders. The Legion planted broodmothers, first-generation daughters of Arachne, around Acadia as part of their ecological warfare. Even an untrained naturalist such as Ashlyn recognized these spiders as harmful invaders of the Vinlandian ecosystem. Dangalf had told them the legend that Arachne, the Spider Queen, was a daeva escaped from the center of the world. What was undisputed was that she now resided deep in the Palusian swamps, where she was worshipped and feared, and fruitfully multiplied.

The Keepers stopped short of a cluster of spiders resting on their webs. Doppelganger suggested that he and Dangalf, as the trained members of the group, would kill the spiders while Nerdraaage and Ashlyn would do carcass runs back to the wagon. Dangalf and Ashlyn agreed that was a good idea.

Nerdraaage, however, took a swig from his bag, raised his dagger, shouted, "For Hybernia!" and charged into the cluster.

His vibrations on the webbing brought a dozen spiders descending on him. He stomped the first one, and it cracked and oozed under his foot. But others followed. He stomped and stabbed at them, but they were too numerous, and he felt one scurry up his back and onto his neck. Doppelganger punched the spider from Nerdraaage and chopped it neatly in half before it hit the ground.

Dangalf wanded bolts of fire as other spiders attacked. After less than a minute, there were a dozen spider carcasses. Webbing ran all through the trees, some of it nearly invisible, and each plucked strand summoned more spiders.

Nerdraaage smiled with great satisfaction. The wine had done its trick. He had fought well and fearlessly as a dwarf should. And he still hadn't had a day of training.

"Did you get bitten?" Dangalf asked.

"No," said Nerdraaage. "It will take more than a big bug to bite through this hide."

They ventured on, careful to not rouse more spiders than they could handle. Ashlyn ran the spider carcasses back to the wagon. After several trips, she returned to find the others covered in spider goo and resting. The smell of burnt spider was sickening, and it was almost as dark as night under the tall trees. She stopped over one dead spider with a body the size of a basketball. Its long legs still twitched. "They're getting bigger," she said.

"The deeper we go," said Dangalf approaching the carcass. "Maybe it's time to pack it in."

"How many carcasses do we have?" asked Doppelganger.

"Five or six dozen," she said.

"I think we're getting close to the broodmother," said Dangalf. "I don't know if all of us together could kill her."

"We could," said Doppelganger.

"Even if we killed her," said Ashlyn, "someone might get hurt. Let me get my healer training before we test our limits like this."

It was agreed that they should call it a night, and they rose to collect the remaining carcasses. Ashlyn turned suddenly toward the unexplored woods.

"What?" asked Dangalf.

"Someone called for help," she said.

"In there?" asked Nerdraaage. "With the broodmother? Good luck to him!"

"It's a dwarf," she said.

"We could go get help," said Dangalf.

"And if he's dead when we return?" asked Doppelganger.

"We're a not ready for the broodmother," said Dangalf. "We're two apprentices and two noobs. There's no dishonor in going for more help."

"I would feel dishonor," said Doppelganger.

"That's just your blood and bile talking," said Dangalf.

"I say we help him," said Doppelganger.

"Well I say we go for help," said Dangalf. They looked to Ashlyn.

"I won't be of any help, so I abstain." They looked to Nerdraaage for the deciding vote.

"You heard the she-elf," he said. "There's a dwarf that needs help." And he took another swig of wine.

Dangalf made torches from bark and branches and spider silk and lit them with his wand. Ashlyn took the lead and moved stealthily through the traps of web. The three pressed on with limited spider contact. Those that did approach them mostly retreated in the face of the torches. A few aggressive ones were quickly killed.

Finally they lost sight of Ashlyn. They looked about in panic. Dangalf was about to yell out when she dropped from the trees behind him. "It's me," she said gently but not without spooking him. "I've found him. Wrapped up like a mummy and attached to a web that reaches sixty feet into the air. To the top of the tallest tree. And on that web..."

"Let me guess," said Dangalf. "Broodmother?" She nodded solemnly.

"How big?" asked Doppelganger looking at the edge of his blade.

"Smaller than a car. Barely."

Ashlyn returned to the lead, and they followed her to the dwarf's cocoon. The space was crisscrossed with fine white silk leading up into the darkness above. The others could not see the broodmother up in the darkness, but Ashlyn assured them that she was there. "Would our torches hold her off?" asked Dangalf.

"I doubt it," she answered. "Her legs are longer than your arms even with torches."

"The way I see it, we have two choices," said Dangalf. "We grab the dwarf and try to make a quick escape, or we attack her and have a fight that we might not need to have and may not win."

"I say we attack her," said Doppelganger.

"Of course," said Dangalf.

"What is the best spell you can cast?" asked Doppelganger.

"I have a pretty decent fireball."

"What is the casting time?"

"About three to five seconds usually. Depends on how big it is."

"How long would it take the broodmother to get down here if we attacked her?"

"That's hard to say," said Ashlyn. "Maybe four or five seconds."

"So you could hit her twice with your most powerful spell before she even reached us," said Doppelganger. "Then I step in and finish her off."

"*We* step in to finish her off," added Nerdraaage.

"I can't hit her from here. I can't even see her!"

"Maybe if you go to the top of this tree," said Doppelganger looking up. "After you cast your spells, climb down the tree while we chop her up."

Dangalf put his face into his palms and shook his head. "It might work," he finally replied. Ashlyn helped Dangalf to the highest branch that would support his weight. She stood next to him, holding his torch and helping him balance. "I don't see her," he said.

"She's not at the center of the web," she answered. "You see that black spot at about one o'clock?"

Dangalf looked about with a frown on his face. The frown turned to terror when he spotted the broodmother. "Oh, shite!" he said.

She tilted the torch to him, and he took some flame from it. (He had not yet learned to conjure fire.) The flame grew as he cultivated it, but it did not burn him because he had learned to ward himself against fire before he learned any other spells.

Doppelganger and Nerdraaage watched breathlessly from below as the ball of fire grew. "Oh my gods," said Doppelganger, verbalizing the amazement of the other Keepers.

The ball grew to about a foot in diameter, and it grew no more. "Here goes," said Dangalf. He cast the fireball at the black spot on the web. Two seconds later it exploded on the brood-mother and tore one of her legs off. She let out an animalistic scream that shook them all. None had expected a screaming spider!

"Again!" shouted Doppelganger to the stunned Dangalf. Dangalf began casting another fireball.

The broodmother was slowed by her missing leg but still crawled quickly toward her attacker in the tree. Doppelganger and Nerdraaage dodged the broodmother's severed leg as it hit the ground like a tree trunk.

Dangalf nurtured a new fireball between his hands—six inches, one foot, one and a half feet in diameter. "Look at that," whispered Nerdraaage in awe. Dangalf cultivated the fireball even bigger. Ashlyn smiled excitedly. Doppelganger pounded excitedly on Nerdraaage's shoulder.

The broodmother continued her descent to where the web met the tree where Dangalf stood. His fireball had grown to two feet in diameter. "This is the biggest I've ever made," said Dangalf focused on his fiery creation.

"I love you!" said Ashlyn.

And with those words, Dangalf turned instantly to Ashlyn, and his fireball snuffed out. "Get down!" shouted Doppelganger.

Ashlyn pulled Dangalf toward her and tried to help him down the trunk. The broodmother leapt from the web and landed in the tree. Her long legs stabbed violently at Dangalf and Ashlyn. "Get down," ordered Ashlyn.

"You first," said Dangalf.

"I can get down easier than you! Get down before I kick you down."

Doppelganger and Nerdraaage could only watch. "Be ready," said Doppelganger.

Ashlyn dodged the broodmother's legs. Dangalf climbed down as quickly as he could. The broodmother lashed at him with her legs. One of her serrated legs caught Dangalf's robe. She pulled him toward her giant gnashing mandibles. Ashlyn stuck a branch between the mandibles before she could bite Dangalf. The broodmother released Dangalf, who fell down through several layers of branches before hitting the ground hard.

The broodmother's mandibles crushed through the branch, and she turned on Ashlyn. Ashlyn scampered up to the top of the tree, and the broodmother leapt to the top right behind her. Just before she could impale Ashlyn with a leg, Ashlyn leapt to an adjoining tree. The brood mother leapt after her. This tree was barren, however, and there were no branches to shield Ashlyn. The broodmother pinned her against the trunk of the tree. The giant spider was too fast. As the gnashing mandibles closed in on Ashlyn, she raised her hands defensively. And she saw it. Her spider ring was glowing black. But since things can't "glow black," she must have been mistaken. She also thought she heard the ring begin speaking a spider language, but since she was wrong about the glowing black, she could also have been wrong about the spider language. Her friends never saw the glowing black or heard the spider language. But the broodmother did. She released Ashlyn and leapt to the next tree and scampered down it toward the others.

Dangalf lay prone on the ground. Everything hurt, and the fall had knocked the breath from his lungs. He worried that it would be weeks before he could walk again. And then the broodmother landed on the ground before him, and he scurried behind the nearest tree like a monkey. Her legs darted around the trunk after him, tearing and stabbing him.

Doppelganger charged the spider's flank and removed another leg with his axe. She pivoted toward him instantly. Doppelganger took refuge behind his shield, and her legs rained down upon it. It felt as if each leg was a battering ram driven by a team of men. His axe cold not come anywhere near the spider body, and he hacked at her legs, always a split second too late. Oh Alfred, you were right! How he wished he had a good eight-foot glaive now! Or a spear even!

The broodmother's strength was overpowering, and Doppelganger was pushed backward quicker than he could retreat. His retreat disturbed smaller spiders that stung at his legs. Nerdraaage ran to his aid and protected Doppelganger's flank with his torch, but the damage was done. Doppelganger's legs became paralyzed, and he crumpled to his knees as the broodmother rained blows on his shield. His arm strength waned, and the shield battered his head and shoulder under the spider's weight. Is this how he would die? Squashed by a bug? The humiliation was almost as painful as the pain.

The next sound he heard was an explosion, and he collapsed to the ground under the full weight of the broodmother. He could smell burning spider, and he knew it was dead. Dangalf had gotten off another fireball, and it had been a good one.

Nerdraaage and Ashlyn pulled Doppelganger out from under the spider. "How do you feel?" she asked.

"Good," he said. "Considering." He lifted himself into a sitting position.

The others cut free and unwrapped the dwarf. He had a thick mane of black hair and a long braided beard. "Drink," he said faintly. Nerdraaage tipped his wine bag into the dwarf's mouth, but the dwarf turned and let it stain his cheek. "Beer!" Nerdraaage found the dwarf's beerskin and lifted it to his mouth. He drank for several seconds.

When he was done, Nerdraaage smelled the liquid and took a swig himself. Dwarven beer! He had never tasted anything so good in his life. It would be hard to go back to wine.

"I am of Clan Stonefist," said the dwarf. "They call me Angus the Young." The Keepers introduced themselves. Dangalf made Angus a torch, and there was an awkward moment when he handed it to him only to realize Angus had only one arm that was already holding his beerskin. So Dangalf carried two torches.

They walked Angus to his nearby camp, where he collected his things. Then they walked back to their wagon of spider carcasses. There were still remnants of daylight away from the heaviest canopy of trees. The small spiders gave them a wide berth but did not flee. A thousand octuplets of eyes watched the Keepers who had just killed their great broodmother. "The ring you gave me saved my life," said Ashlyn to Dangalf. She showed him, and the stone of the spider's abdomen that had been black was now blood red.

"One-time use only, I guess," said Dangalf, regretting he had not bought, could not have afforded to buy, all the wards and charms and trinkets and artifacts that the mysterious salesman offered. "I'm sure the metal must be worth something."

"No," she said pulling her hand away. "I want to keep it."

Angus looked suspiciously on all of them as if there had been some nefarious purpose in their rescue of him. "You have not said your name, lad," said Angus to Nerdraaage.

"I said it. It's Nerdraaage."

"That's only half a name. What is your clan?"

"I don't have one."

"You're not strange are you!" Angus suddenly said to Nerdraaage. Ashlyn found this to be hilarious.

"No," said Nerdraaage defensively. "At least I don't think so."

Angus relaxed and continued walking. "Aye, well you would know if you were. And I suppose I would too. Why no clan then? Orphaned were ye?"

"We were all pretty much orphaned in this land," said Dangalf.

"Shame, though, when it happens to a dwarf," said Angus. "You grow up without knowing your people or your ways."

"Does he think that we don't have people and ways?" Ashlyn whispered to Dangalf.

Angus picked silk off the trees as he walked. The others listened while he told his story to Nerdraaage. "I knew there were spiders in these woods, not so close mind ye, but it was either camp here or travel on to Hempshire and sleep with the humans," said Angus. He turned back to Dangalf and Doppelganger quickly. "No offense intended."

Angus explained he camped off the road not only too deep into the woods but also after drinking too much. He did not awake until he was entombed in the spider silk. He told Nerdraaage that he would make everyone aware of his heroism in rescuing him. Then he turned to the others following, "All of you. The dwarves will know of your friendship!" This was very good news as, if he was sincere, it meant the humans and Ashlyn would not be barred from dwarven towns as Ashlyn and Nerdraaage were barred from Hempshire.

Angus presented the collection of silk to Ashlyn and said it was enough to make her some nice clothes. "Thank you," she said, smiling and thinking that she had misjudged the coarse dwarf.

"Then you won't have to go about half dressed," he added.

"Good haul," said Angus when they reached the wagon. Dangalf spotted something in one of the larger carcasses. He pulled open its mandibles and tugged on some leather. He struggled a bit but finally pulled out the mystery item that unrolled into tall leather boots bound to each other by twine. They looked good despite the spider's digestive process or maybe even better because of it.

"You never know what these spiders might eat," said Angus. "Always gut them before you sell them."

For Dangalf it was a revelation. It had always bothered him when he had killed some monster in *Cronica* and it dropped loot, such as clothing or a weapon, that the monster had no business carrying. The spider with the leather boots now provided a logical explanation. "Leather," Dangalf said of the boots. "I can't wear them."

"I can wear leather," said Nerdraaage.

"So can I," said Ashlyn.

Dangalf looked back and forth between his two leather-loving friends. "Oh, I wonder who he'll pick," said Nerdraaage.

Doppelganger picked up the wagon and started it toward Hempshire with the others following. Ashlyn stepped lively in her new, thigh-high leather boots. "If they fit her so well," Dangalf explained to Nerdraaage, "they would not fit you at all." And even Nerdraaage had to admit the boots would not look as good on him.

XXI

Angus's obvious preference for the Keepers was with Nerdraaage first, Doppelganger second, Dangalf third, and Ashlyn last. He spoke almost exclusively to Nerdraaage, but what he had to say was of interest to them all. He had trained in the Red School, as was tradition for his clan, up through the soldier rank. But since losing his arm in battle, he had trained in the Blue School and was now a weaponsmith. He insisted with pride that his loss of arm affected only the speed of his smithing, not the quality. He also promised them all fine weapons made by his own hand if they would visit him in Hammersmith. "We're going there next!" said Nerdraaage.

"Your friendship is our honor," said Dangalf. "I know of your clan. One of the six founding clans of dwarven civilization." And Angus was greatly impressed and pleased that a human should know something of dwarven history, especially history that reflected well on his clan, and for the remainder of the journey, it was so that Dangalf temporarily replaced Doppelganger as his second-favorite member of the Keepers.

XXII

The ancient humans and elves were already fast friends when they came upon the mysterious dwarves. For where the humans had gone outward from their racial home, the dwarves had gone inward, under-ground and ultimately into the depths of their sacred mountains. One elven joke of particular resentment to the dwarves was that the elves and humans did not even know the first dwarves they met were alive until they dusted one off and he sneezed. The earliest dwarf town, then still outside the mountain, was comprised of the so-called beard clans: Blackbeard, Bluebeard, Brownbeard, Redbeard, and Yellowbeard. When a later group of dwarves appeared and sought to join the town, Bran, the legendary first king of the dwarves, consented. But they would be different from the founding five in that they could not, nor would any future clan, be able to name themselves for their beards. And since they were not of the origi-nal five, none of their clan would ever be able to be king. But as the first outsiders to join, they were likewise elevated over the latter clans because all of the royal guards would come from them. And it was thought very wise that the king should be guarded only by those who could not be king themselves. And so this sixth clan was named Stonefist, and it was agreed that they should otherwise be honored with the five royal clans because six is a better number than five. Because as the first builders of this world, the dwarves knew what a perfect number three was and had a likewise affinity for numbers evenly divisible by three. And were there not six peaks of their sacred mountain range? And didn't these ancient dwarves also believe that the world itself set upon three pillars? Even today a dwarf will say that a foolish or false person sits upon a two-legged stool.

Cronica Acadia

XXIII

Back at Hempshire the town was closed, and Dangalf cast an ice spell over the spider carcasses so as to preserve them. Angus awoke Tolliver, who forgot his anger when Angus took out his fat coin purse. (He wore it in the dwarven style on leather strap around his neck, inside his shirt, safely behind his heavy beard.)

Angus treated the four to dinner. They ate and drank well, and then Angus introduced them to the pleasures of the pipe and Hempshire's renowned leaf. "The best thing to ever come from human lands." He puffed and puffed and passed.

When Angus learned that his rescuers, save Ashlyn, were still sleeping at the stables, Angus ordered two double rooms. Nerdraaage bunked in Angus's room, and Dangalf and Doppelganger shared the other.

Dangalf liked not having to enter this room through the window, but he missed the late-night conversation he would normally have with Ashlyn until one of them, usually her, finally fell asleep. He instead had to settle for reciting from the *Cronica*

Acadia to Doppelganger (who didn't look interested but didn't object either):

"An estranged dwarf, or strange dwarf, is a dwarf who has been disenfranchised from his clan and by extension the entire dwarven race for acts ranging from great crimes like cowardice to multiple crimes of a lesser nature such as thievery. They are not permitted to enter any dwarven town and as such must live in border towns or the wilderness. Any dwarf unsuitable to keep the company of other dwarves is even more unsuitable companionship for humans. Some strange dwarves have even been known to ally with our enemies and as such should be killed on sight as you would kill an orc, and that killing will be considered lawful."

Doppelganger closed his eyes as Dangalf read. He had gotten the best sleep of his life on the floor of the stable, but sleeping in a bed again, even an undersized one, was a pleasant respite, especially for his spider-bitten legs. He drifted off to sleep pleasantly, to tales of a fantastic world of swords and sorcery, dungeons and dragons, demons and damsels, begettings and beheadings—all the more fantastic because it was real.

XXIV

Angus had the Keepers up early the next morning, and they collected their spider bounty, and Bartleby dutifully recorded their latest deed. But Angus insisted on speaking to the shire-reeve in a tone that embarrassed and worried the Keepers.

When the shire-reeve appeared, Angus presented his own papers by way of introduction, and it showed that he had an honored reputation with the humans as well as membership in the Red and Blue Schools. He then passionately, almost belligerently, lobbied the shire-reeve to reward the Keepers for not only saving his life but also for eliminating the scourge of the broodmother. Though no such reward had been authorized, the shire-reeve on his own authority ordered that the paymaster pay to the Keepers two sovereigns each in addition to their honor and reward for disposing of so many of her despised children. And the Keepers were giddy, even Doppelganger almost, as they received eight shiny gold coins with their silver and copper reward. The gold was deposited with the bank of tank, but each kept a handsome bounty for his or her private purposes. And they weren't done yet.

They took the carcasses to the tanner, who paid them for the bodies, from which he harvested the venom sacks and silk glands. It was then that Nerdraaage realized that the beerskin he had bought from the tanner was formerly a venom sack.

The tanner also slit the bellies open for them, but there was no more loot to be had. Dangalf, hearkening back to the game, thought that was an especially bad drop rate.

Finally, with only a cartload of spider legs left, they rolled to the back door of The Silent Woman. "What are we doing here?" asked Nerdraaage.

Master Tolliver came out, cracked open one of the legs, and smelled it. "Still fresh!" said he as he pulled out his purse.

They helped him carry the legs into the inn's cellar, and never again did Nerdraaage order the roast beast.

They said good-bye to Angus, who promised them that a marvelous welcome was awaiting them at Hammersmith, Bran Keep, or wherever Clan Stonefist could be found, and he boasted that Clan Stonefist could be found at the three corners of the world.

XXV

Things progressed uneventfully over the next few weeks. Doppelganger's training was winding down, and Alfred was not as draconian as he had been in the beginning. He had even taken on two brothers from a local farm who wanted to be warriors. He had promised their father that he would keep the best one of the two and the other would be returned in time for the harvest. After all, the Alliance needed food as well as warriors.

Alfred even entrusted Doppelganger to handle rudimentary elements of the boys' training. Doppelganger liked them both and was glad he didn't have to send one back to the farm. They both idolized Doppelganger, which annoyed Alfred. He was nowhere near the warrior that Alfred was, but he figured, as did Alfred, that they were impressed because he was so tall.

Dangalf's training was also nearing an end, but not before one more significant blunder. He absent-mindedly spoke aloud a spell as he waved his wand and cast Weyd in a giant block of ice. Wendell jumped on the top of the block and cried at his master.

Dangalf went to the block and rapped on the top with his knuckles. It was a nice solid block. Weyd would have been impressed if he were not inside it.

Frozen inside the block, Weyd still managed to roll his eyes at Dangalf who held up his index finger, which he hoped meant "just a minute" here as it did in his old universe. He closed his eyes and entered his virtual library, where he hurriedly thumbed through his copy of *Elemental Elements: Fire and Ice* for the counterspell.

He opened his eyes and looked to Wendell—he wasn't sure why—and the cat seemed to be looking at Dangalf as if to say, "What an idiot!" And the clever cat jumped off just before the ice cracked as Weyd freed himself.

XXVI

Doppelganger was sparring with both farm boys at once as Alfred approached with a small wagon. "You hymens go practice your parry," screamed Alfred at the farm boys. "Orcbait, come over here." Doppelganger had come far in his training. He had been promoted from hymen to orcbait. "Set down your shield and sword." Alfred went to the back of his wagon as Doppelganger unequipped himself. "You fight well enough with shield. You could be the best guard in all of Hempshire." Doppelganger understood the insult, and it burned in him. "But dragoons don't carry shields. They carry this." Alfred tossed him a massive battleaxe. It was so heavy that Doppelganger took a step back when he caught it. Doppelganger had been weight training with anvils to the point where ordinary things no longer seemed to have a weight. But this was no ordinary thing. It was a two-handed weapon. He would not, could not, sport a shield when he wielded this monster.

"All right, orcbait," ordered Alfred. "Have at me!"

Doppelganger roared and brought the mighty axe down on Alfred's ceremonial shield. It made a horrible metal on metal sound as it skittered violently against it before being deflected off.

"Now let's try that again," said Alfred. "And this time, don't hold back."

Again Doppelganger swung the massive axe onto the shield. It screeched again but Alfred moved brilliantly around Doppelganger, who seemed off balance. The sparring continued, and Alfred gave Doppelganger a wicked blow to the gut with a mace when Doppelganger was exposed either because he held the axe for too long over his head or he left it lowered too long after a strike.

"Overhead is your most powerful strike, but it is also the one that leaves you most vulnerable! Save it for the finishing blow!" The violent sparring and lecturing continued. "Without a shield, your weapon provides your defense! A sweeping strike keeps your enemies at bay and can strike multiple targets!"

Doppelganger noticed that the two farm boys had stopped their own practice to watch him spar. Alfred must have noticed his inattention because he smashed Doppelganger in the face with the mace. It was a brutal blow, the hardest Alfred had ever hit him. He had hit Doppelganger a lot, but it had always been on an armored part of his body or a fleshy area that would not break. Warm blood ran down his face and onto the ground.

But Doppelganger was not worried about his injury. He was not embarrassed by his inattention. He was not nauseated by the sight and smell of his own blood or the sound it made as it slopped onto the ground. No, Doppelganger was not any of those things. He was only angry. And suddenly Doppelganger changed.

His skin flushed red. Thick veins appeared all over his body dark in color as they now carried superoxygenated blood as well as biles yellow and black. The martial humors fed the warrior's strength, anger, and recklessness respectively and flowed to his heart and lungs and brain. Only the most essential and primitive thoughts were now being processed by that brain. His muscles and bones took on increased size and strength, and his britches strained at the seam. The leather straps of his armor creaked in protest against his engorging physique. His cheeks and brow pressed forward, a bony shield around his eyes. Doppelganger was no longer capable of pain or fear or fatigue. He felt only rage. Alfred might as well have been an orc rapemonger at that moment. He could not have wanted to kill him more. And with one massive blow, he brought the axe down through Alfred's heavy metal shield and everything unfortunate enough to be behind that shield.

Unconsciously he unleashed a battle shout that blended seamlessly into the unworldly scream of the axe cutting through the shield. Metal sparks illuminated the scene, and the farm boys did not recognize Doppelganger's face. It was so contorted as to be unrecognizable by even his next of kin. Doppelganger drove down with his axe until it buried in the ground.

Alfred had sidestepped the destruction and now shook the remnant of his shield from his arm as he backed up from Doppelganger. Doppelganger pulled his axe from the ground and pursued Alfred, still intending to kill him. He swung the massive axe in a large arc where Alfred was standing, but Alfred was no longer there when the axe arrived. He stepped aside with only inches between his face and Doppelganger's axe. Doppelganger's exaggerated swing exposed his back to Alfred, and Alfred stepped into it, put his arms around Doppelganger's head and neck, and put him to sleep.

Doppelganger regained consciousness to the sound of one of the farm boys asking if he was dead. He blinked his eyes open in answer. The farm boys watched him nervously. "Each class has a foundation skill that makes it special," said Alfred. "For the warrior, it is the *bloodwarp*. More than a rage, it is a change in the very structure of your body and brain. Your size and strength, your skill, and your weapons mean nothing without it. It is what will allow you to fight when others are cold and scared and fatigued. When your bones are broken and your dearest friends have fallen, when you face an overwhelming enemy, the bloodwarp is what will allow you to triumph when others flee. Or perish."

Doppelganger did not speak. He felt strange. Almost unclean. He had been taken by pure murderous rage that would have spared no one in his path. He did not think often of the old world. What was the point? But he did in this moment think back to the game that they used to play. *Cronica*, he recalled. He remembered the bloodwarp he would call upon in the game to give his avatar superpowers. Back then all he had to do was push a key on a keyboard.

The two farm boys looked at each other and turned around. They walked away without saying a word. Alfred saw them too and knew that they would not return. He did not regret seeing them leave. Better they find out early that they were not meant to be warriors. Hempshire had enough guards.

Doppelganger stood uneasily. He picked up Alfred's shattered shield, but "sorry" was an inadequate response. He had sundered an artifact, a shield presented to Alfred by the Supreme Allied Commander. "It can be repaired," said Alfred. "So can your nose." And then he stepped to Doppelganger and popped his broken nose back into position.

Alfred went back to his wagon and lit a red candle. He scribbled on a hemp scroll and then dripped candle wax on it. He embossed the wet wax with his seal. "Your bloodwarp came late in training," he continued. "But it did come, and so you are promoted. You are no longer a guard. Your new rank is mercenary. You will be paid for each day of service to the Alliance and for each enemy kill. And you must do so in prescribed numbers before you are able to train for the next level."

Doppelganger understood his charge. Enemy kill did not refer to wolves or spiders. It meant sapiens. Orcs, goblins, and trolls. He had wondered if he could kill a sapien, but the blood-warp had answered that unequivocally.

Alfred finished the parchment and held it across his chest. "This is your commission. I will notify Bartleby of your promotion, but you would be advised to keep the sages informed of your progress so your commission can be recreated if lost." Doppelganger took ten crown from his purse and handed it to Alfred, who in exchange handed him his commission. "Mercenary is a low rank, but you must conduct yourself honorably nonetheless. You are now a sponsored member of the Red School, Doppelganger." It was the first time Alfred had used his name. "I am your sponsor, and I expect that you will not disappoint me." Alfred turned back to his wagon and made some notes. "Do you still want to be a dragoon?"

"Yes, sire." Doppelganger smiled.

"A dragon is not faithful like a gryphon. He will eat his own master if given half a chance."

XXVII

D angalf stood nervously before Weyd, who was going down a scroll as if it were a checklist, which it was. "And there is only one last thing," said Weyd, looking at Dangalf.

Dangalf held out the palm of his hand, and they both looked at it expectantly. Dangalf cupped his hand and concentrated. A bead of sweat ran down his face. It all came down to this.

Suddenly a spark lit in his hand and turned into a small ball of flame. He had conjured fire, flame created without tinder or wand, the foundation skill of the mage class. He smiled in relief and passed the small ball playfully between his two hands before handing it off to Weyd. He had actually been conjuring fire consistently for several days, but still it was necessary to do it now under examination.

Weyd looked at the small flame before blowing it out and checking the item on his checklist. Weyd prepared for Dangalf a certificate similar to Doppelganger's. However, instead of mercenary he had been appointed to the rank of conjurer, and his commission was sealed with white wax.

Dangalf could not have been more thrilled (or relieved after learning earlier in the day that Doppelganger had been promoted), yet it was bittersweet saying good-bye to the old man. "You have learned all that you can," said Weyd. "You must go forth and put your knowledge to practical use. You must also learn to connect to parts of your mind that are so far unknown to you. For there is much more to learn when you have the capacity to learn it."

"Well," said Dangalf, stumbling. "It's been nice studying with you. I just want to say, you know, thanks for everything. I think I learned a lot. Sorry again for freezing you in that block of ice."

"I said we would not discuss that further."

"Right. Sorry. Do you think I could return to you when I need further training?"

"There are many gifted magical trainers in this land."

"I know, but I like you."

Weyd seemed touched by Dangalf's friendship. "I will train you further if that is your wish. I hope you are successful in your pursuit of the arcane and the abstruse."

"Thanks again," said Dangalf, and he turned to leave.

"Meow!" cried Wendell.

"Well good-bye to you too, Wendell," said Dangalf playfully. He tried to pet him, but the cat dodged his hand and tapped his paw quickly on the table. Strange, he thought, and then he remembered. He reached into his pocket and retrieved ten crown, which he set before the cat. Wendell played with the coins almost as if he was counting them.

XXVIII

That night the four celebrated at the Silent Woman with expensive food and drink. Congratulations were given by Nerdraaage and Ashlyn and exchanged between Doppelganger and Dangalf for their promotion and inductions, albeit sponsored inductions, into the Red and White Schools respectively. It represented not only a substantial inroad to the bonding step of the Triangle of Achievement but also provided a clear path to the next level: Recognition.

After the formality of the congratulations, Doppelganger was mocked for his broken nose and Dangalf for being a "conjurer." "Pull a rabbit out of your hat," demanded Nerdraaage.

"No hat," apologized Dangalf.

And the drinking began in earnest.

Nerdraaage had picked up yet another expensive habit from Angus, who had given him his own pipe when they departed. Already red faced from drink, he lit up and passed the town's celebrated leaf product to Dangalf. Dangalf inhaled deeply and smiled with satisfaction. He had never had smoke like that in his lungs before. He passed the pipe to Doppelganger, who refused it. The mellowing effects of the smoke were poison to a warrior. Unlike drink, smoke could retard the bloodwarp.

"Come on, pussy," challenged Nerdraaage.

"Do you know what they call a warrior who smokes?" asked Doppelganger.

"What?"

"A guard."

Ashlyn took the pipe. She was especially attractive tonight as for the first time she wore a diaphanous garment crafted by Mistress Tolliver and made from the spider silk given to her by Angus. Ashlyn smoked deeply but gracefully.

"Elves don't smoke," said Nerdraaage.

"You don't tell me how to be an elf and I won't tell you how to be a dwarf," she exhaled.

Nerdraaage was very excited that tomorrow they would depart for Hammersmith, the dwarven town where he would begin his own training. He bragged ceaselessly about the superiority of Hammersmith over Hempshire: the quality of food and drink, the friendliness of the people…

Dangalf gently reminded him that he was not born a dwarf and all that he knew of Hammersmith was from a computer game and a few conversations with Angus. "And we have an Odeon!" said Nerdraaage. "You two have been training. You don't know how boring this place has been for us. But you'll get to go to the Odeon!"

"A whole town filled with dwarves," she said. "Just shoot me now."

"The Odeon at Hammersmith is one of the great landmarks of Acadia," continued Nerdraaage.

"Yes," answered Dangalf. "And so is the Great Library at Hempshire."

"Hempshire has a library?" asked Nerdraaage.

Dangalf recited from the *Cronica Acadia* as he was wont to do: "After the great darkness had lifted, it was determined by Acadian governors that each town begin the construction of a landmark that would make each town special and desirable and help to alleviate overcrowding at the capital cities. So as to expedite the return of persons to their respective towns, it was ordered that each improvement be advertised as being a landmark no matter how modest or unfortunate it be. The Hot Springs of Bad Manor are so hot as to boil the skin from an elephant. The Port at Mount Albin features a handsome and sturdy dock but is unfortunately situated in a landlocked mountain town," and, finished reciting, he said, "I would add to that list the Great Library at Hempshire."

"So," said Nerdraaage. "It doesn't say anything about the Odeon at Hammersmith."

XXIX

They awoke early the next day and ordered hearty breakfasts. The others dug in, but Ashlyn dawdled over her boiled vegetables. "I order raw vegetables, and she always peels and boils them. 'Vegetables are dirty,' she says."

"Plenty of dirt outside if you're still hungry," said Nerdraaage between bites.

Doppelganger and Dangalf laughed. When Nerdraaage saw he had made his friends laugh, he laughed the loudest. Ashlyn smiled in bemusement, but she wouldn't give Nerdraaage the satisfaction of laughing.

Despite the boiling of the vegetables, Ashlyn had a tearful farewell with Mistress Tolliver, who called her "my sweet elf" and loaded her down with so much food, wine, and clothing that Dangalf and Nerdraaage had to share the load. (They were careful not to let Nerdraaage carry the extra wine.) And for the omnivores, a dozen nomble pies. Om nom nom.

Nerdraaage bid farewell to his bosses at the smithy and the stables. The stables master promised Nerdraaage that whenever he got tired of adventuring, he would always have a job "shoveling shite." Nerdraaage didn't know what to say.

Dangalf returned all of Weyd's books, even regrettably some he was unable to capture for his mental library. Dangalf bid final farewell to Weyd. He also said good-bye to Wendell, who seemed disinterested.

Against Nerdraaage's wishes, Doppelganger got a shave. Then he went on a shopping spree for the first time since arriving. He bought himself a plain but solid battleaxe and sharpening stone from the smithy. From the tanner he bought an axe scabbard and good boots for the long journey ahead. He visited the fletcher for a bow and arrows. (And then he went back to the tanner for a quiver.) Finally he visited the armorsmith and sprang for some mail shirt and leggings—the first two modest pieces of armor in what he hoped would someday be a full suit of plate armor.

Doppelganger debated saying farewell to Alfred. He didn't expect a tearful farewell with him, but he didn't want the little warrior to mock him either for being a "sentimental lass." He walked to the training field, where Alfred was heaping abuse on a new recruit. Alfred saw his approach and turned to face Doppelganger with a look that seemed to say, *Are you still here?* Doppelganger stopped, still about twenty yards away, and raised his hand in salute. Alfred returned the gesture, and Doppelganger turned back to the front gate. That went better than he expected.

Doppelganger said good-bye to the shire-reeve and thanked him. The shire-reeve wished him the best of luck and gave him a used Vinlandian shield for his service. Doppelganger said good-bye to some of the guards he had befriended and was flattered by their words. "Wish I could go with you," was the most common sentiment. He did not ask them why they couldn't. Finally he was out the gate and sitting on the grass waiting for the others. Nerdraaage was next.

"Nice gear," he said upon seeing Doppelganger.

They all had some disposable income, but Nerdraaage had spent almost none. He still wore his same hemp shirt and pants from their first day in Hempshire. When it was suggested he spend his coin on something other than smoke and wine, he said he would wait until Hammersmith because he wanted to buy "dwarven-quality" items. He had not even bought a scabbard for his dagger, which he carried around in a pocket where it occasionally stabbed him. Nerdraaage took a swig from his wine bag and offered it to Doppelganger. Nerdraaage sat next to him and had a smoke.

Ashlyn was next. The long-legged she-elf looked stunning in yet another new outfit.

Dangalf arrived five minutes later. He looked at Doppelganger in his new gear. "I'll be right back," Dangalf said as he retreated back into the front gate. Eighteen minutes later he walked back out the front gate sporting a large smile and a pointy black wizard hat. Doppelganger looked at him sternly. "What?"

"What did that cost?" asked Doppelganger.

"Oh," said Dangalf. "About three silver. I guarantee that's less than you spent on that new armor."

"This is an investment. You're just pissing away money. Or are you going to tell me that that pointy hat helps you channel electroplasm?"

"Not exactly," said Dangalf. "So Nerd wants to smoke his money, and I want to wear mine."

"You've been smoking Nerd's money right with him," said Doppelganger. "It would just be nice if everyone made purchases that would benefit all of us."

Nerdraaage looked between his two friends with concern. Ashlyn draped an arm over him sympathetically. "It's always the children who get hurt when parents argue," she said. Nerdraaage shrugged her arm off.

"We're not all warriors! We don't get off on sharpening axes and beheading people! The rest of us want to enjoy some comfort!"

"Okay, Harry Potter."

"Oh, okay, Conan."

"Okay, Gandalf."

"Okay, Hercules."

"Okay, Merlin."

"Okay, body dysmorphia."

"I don't know what that means."

"I know. It's sad."

"Let's just go," said Doppelganger, and the others followed him.

"Why don't we just drop some coins in the Hempshire well and teleport to Hammersmith?" asked Nerdraaage.

"Can you do that spell?" asked Dangalf.

"No."

"Well neither can I."

Master Tolliver had prepared for them a crude, hand-drawn map with distances measured in time. It was four hours' walk back to the crossroads. It was fortuitous that they had decided to go to Hempshire when they first arrived because Hammersmith was two days' journey. If they had headed for Hammersmith first, they probably would have died along the way. Templa Taur was even further.

Doppelganger walked first, his long, powerful strides taking him well ahead of the others. When he was far enough ahead, he would stop and wait for them. He tried to let his countenance display his impatience with them, but if they understood his countenance, they chose to ignore it.

Dangalf and Ashlyn walked lazily behind, chatting away as they had so many nights in her room before they fell asleep. They were still talking about the hat. "If one highwaymen sees this hat and says, 'Oh, a mage; I'll find an easier target,' and saves one of our lives in the process, I think that's a damn good investment."

"Totally," agreed Ashlyn. "And I think it will make you a better wizard. You need to dress the part to play the part."

"I think I'm going to lose the beard though."

"No!" said Ashlyn. "You look great."

"Really?"

"Yeah. I would have no faith in a clean-shaven wizard. You look so distinguished." Nerdraaage sighed loudly.

There was some sentimentality attached to reaching the crossroads again, and they stopped momentarily to reflect on how far they had come. Then they took the road south to Hammersmith. Ashlyn lingered looking at the road that lead to Templa Taur. As the others stopped, Dangalf returned to her. "We'll go there next," he said. "I promise." Ashlyn smiled, and they caught up to their friends on the road to Hammersmith.

After an hour they came to a large chasm spanned by a rope bridge. On the other side was Hybernia. None of them had ever taken a rope bridge before, but they could not see another way across. Doppelganger gamely charged out, followed closely by Nerdraaage. It looked sturdy enough, but Dangalf felt it was silly to test it with the two heaviest Keepers at the same time and let them finish crossing before he and Ashlyn attempted it.

On the other side, a giant boulder with an iron rune cut into it announced their arrival in the dwarven land.

They continued walking well into the darkness when they found a nice camping spot close to the road but hidden. They ate well before going to sleep. Dangalf was surprised how cold the ground was at night because it was very warm during the day. He shivered his way through the night and vowed he would not sleep outdoors again without a fire.

The next day they ate breakfast, and Ashlyn released Clay with a message for Mistress Tolliver letting her know they had survived the first night. Doppelganger criticized Ashlyn for dispatching their only pigeon on such a trivial mission. Dangalf interjected that if the pigeon was worth anything, it would return to them.

Once on the road, they passed a dwarf soldier heading in the opposite direction who challenged Doppelganger to a duel. Despite his lack of experience and inferior equipment, he defeated the dwarf easily. His opponent never overcame Doppelganger's reach advantage. The dwarf was gracious in defeat. He suggested that Doppelganger make side wagers when he dueled. He felt Doppelganger's skill was much greater than his reputation or appearance would indicate and that Doppelganger could make some good silver, maybe even gold. He departed by saying that Doppelganger had all the makings of a future dragoon. "And you thought he was difficult before," Ashlyn whispered to Dangalf.

Doppelganger waxed poetically about how he was "in the zone" and described the two-minute duel, which they had all seen, for the next two hours of the journey.

The road became bereft of other travelers, cottages, signs, or other comforting features, and the Keepers decided to camp early and well off the road for their final night before Hammersmith. Dangalf lit a campfire, but it was still cold, and they all slept under the same blankets, and because it was so cold nobody found anything wrong with the extreme cuddling, the two shivering ectomorphs bookended by the mesomorph and endomorph.

They woke at dawn the next day and had a breakfast of most of the last of their food before splitting up to attend to personal business. Dangalf lingered at the campfire, still not defrosted from the previous night.

Nerdraaage ran up breathlessly, and Dangalf immediately feared someone had been kidnapped by highwaymen or trampled by a battlepig.

"Dude," said Nerdraaage in his loud whisper. "I just saw Elftrap bathing! Completely naked!"

"Oh, I don't want to hear that," said Dangalf. And then, thinking better of it, he asked, "What did you see?"

"I never wanted to take a screenshot so much in my life!" he said. And then in a more conspiratorial whisper, "She's completely hairless down there!"

"I'd read elves were hairless but for their heads," said Dangalf. But it was too vulgar for him to run after her and try to get a peek himself. Still he asked, "Is she still naked?"

"Would I be up here?" answered Nerdraaage.

So Ashlyn had been bathing. Dangalf should have seen it, metaphorically speaking. Two days on the road and the males were filthy and rank while she remained clean as a cat. He pulled a small leafy twig out of his beard and wondered how long it had been there.

Ashlyn joined them and dried her dampness by the fire. Dangalf couldn't help but look at her and see that she was full of…grace. Yes, she was graceful. When was the last time he used that word? Had he ever used it in the old universe? Words like graceful and chivalrous and wicked were almost expunged from modern conversation in the old world, as if they described qualities that no longer mattered.

As they approached Hammersmith, they came across their first farm. It was large and seemed to be growing some sort of grain that was attended to by dozens of dwarves. They passed more farms and began to pass some isolated cottages. The road traffic increased inversely proportional to their distance from Hammersmith. They had not seen any horses or other mounts on the road since the farmer who was murdered. In the game mounts were restricted to players who had reached a certain rank and could afford the expense. Here the shortage of mounts was due to centuries of war, but the result was similar: mounts were almost exclusive to military units or the very wealthy, with others being communal property of various towns and entities.

They felt the chill before they saw the snow. They were at high altitude now, but it was difficult to tell how high as the road was winding and the woods were thick. Doppelganger charged forward like the thin air had no effect on him. Likewise, Nerdraaage trod excitedly forward as if he was in his element, and he was.

"I wish I had a jacket to give you," said Dangalf.

"I'm fine," smiled Ashlyn.

Any passing party that contained a military-age male was subject to a duel challenge from Doppelganger. Most declined but a few accepted and even agreed to wagers. Doppelganger won three contests handily and made some silver before they were in sight of Hammersmith.

They arrived at Hammersmith with enough daylight to marvel at the mountain city. It was built on an enormous ledge about halfway up one of the peaks in the Purple Mountains range.

Nerdraaage had no problem entering the front gate. The dwarven guards took only cursory glances at Doppelganger's and Dangalf's commissions.

"Halt, she-elf!" ordered a guard as he and another blocked her progress with spears.

Doppelganger and Dangalf came to her defense quickly, and their actions brought more guards with spear points. Doppelganger reacted instinctively, and he disarmed the first guard to approach him. This action was of great concern to the other guards.

"Alarm!" shouted different guards.

"No!" shouted Nerdraaage.

"Stop!" shouted Ashlyn.

A guard jabbed Doppelganger with the blunt end of his spear to back him off, but it had the opposite effect. Doppelganger began to undergo the bloodwarp. He removed his massive axe from his back. It looked for certain that there would be combat as more guards arrived and surrounded him. Dangalf knew he was looking at the ruination of their budding reputations with the dwarves and maybe his friend's death, so he raised his wand.

"Wand!" shouted another guard. All the dwarves looked on as Dangalf cast his spell. But it was Doppelganger who was the target, and he was suddenly cast in a block of ice. This had the immediate effect of confusing the hell out of the guards. Dangalf made an exaggerated motion of putting his wand away and raising his hands.

The sergeant of the guard arrived. "What's going on!" he demanded. Nerdraaage introduced himself and his friends and Dangalf presented his commission. The sergeant knew them by reputation.

"Angus the Young has spoken of you," said the sergeant to the Keepers. "But what happened here?" The other three explained as well as they could while Doppelganger remained encased in ice. "He has the rage of a dragoon," said the sergeant. "But he is no dragoon. He will banned from the town if there are any more disruptions."

"Thank you, sire," said Dangalf. The sergeant and the extra guards returned inside the gate. The Keepers walked to their frozen friend. "Is he all right?" asked Nerdraaage.

"It's purely a defensive spell," said Dangalf. "It won't harm him."

"How do you get him out," asked Ashlyn.

"I don't know if I want to be around when he gets out," said Dangalf. He paused before casting the counterspell. With a great cracking of ice, Doppelganger was freed and stumbled slightly. To everyone's relief, he placed his axe back on his back.

"That's a good spell," said Doppelganger.

"Yeah," agreed Ashlyn.

"That was the first time I ever used it," said Dangalf. First time intentionally, he thought.

They entered the town. It bustled with activity, mostly the activity of she-dwarves. Ashlyn noticed each she-dwarf they passed checking out Nerdraaage, but he was oblivious.

There were merchants on the main street—the butcher, the baker, and the chandler—and private cottages beyond those. Dwarves were defensively minded, and all of the buildings, public or private, were stone and none had ground-floor entrances. The entrances were on the second floor with wooden steps or rope ladders leading up. Not even a brick shitehouse was good enough for the dwarves. They were all stone wrought also, with second-story entrances so that a dwarf could make a last stand even if he was sitting.

The larger merchants and government buildings were built right into the side of the mountain with intricately carved facades.

Once inside they looked for Angus. His home was conveniently located close to A Farthing Away, the inn, fondly known to the Keepers from the game, with its colorful sign depicting a hand holding a copper coin. Angus met them in front of his home. He was excited to see Nerdraaage and polite to the others. His wife, a blond dwarf with a protruding belly, joined them.

"And you must be the one who saved my Angus," she said to Nerdraaage.

"Well, I had some help," he answered.

"I'm so grateful," she continued. "I'm in no condition to be a widow, as you can see." She spread her dress fabric tight across her pregnant belly.

"Wife," said Angus. "Let's not get all maudlin. Your Angus would have found a way to get himself out if these strangers had not happened by." Angus introduced his wife as Rhona. She smiled genuinely to the humans but smiled awkwardly at the she-elf.

"Nerdraaage," said Rhona. "I don't believe I've heard that name afore. What does it mean?"

"Uh," Nerdraaage stumbled.

"It means wise and warlike," said **Dangalf** quickly.

"I like it," said Rhona. She rubbed her belly and looked down at it. "Looks like you finally have a name, little Nerdraaage!" The Keepers were too polite to laugh and too astonished to say anything.

"We're all Angused out," said Angus. "Time to go in a new direction."

Rhona went in their cottage, and Angus led the Keepers behind it, where he made his weapons, and asked them what they wanted. Nerdraaage received a dagger, which was the clear choice for a presumptive blackguard. It was far superior to the blade that he had carried since they arrived in this world and was even decorated with a dwarven rune on the pommel. Doppelganger showed Angus the axe he had just bought in Hempshire. Angus took it and said it would "melt down nicely" before handing Doppelganger one of his own creations. Doppelganger knew immediately upon touching the dwarven axe that it was superior to the one he had just purchased two days ago. Ashlyn graciously accepted a dagger even though she could not carry metal when she became a druid. Dangalf asked if Angus had any staffs, to which Angus replied weaponsmiths don't make staffs, "trees do." Dangalf accepted a dagger to be polite even though he knew as a pure ectomorph he was more likely to be disarmed of his dagger than to successfully stab an enemy with it.

Angus caught Doppelganger looking at large decorated blades on display. "Some of my handiwork," said Angus. "You don't want those blades, lad. They will hang over the mantle of a rich merchant or farmer who has had no adventures. These plain blades will do for you until you take a better one from your dead enemy or are gifted one for doing some great deed."

XXX

A Farthing Away was a great convivial atmosphere, and they passed by parties drinking and laughing and of such familiarity and good spirits that one of the party would only have to say to another of the party, "I suppose you would know something about that!" and it would elicit great gales of laughter with none laughing harder than the one accused of knowing something about that.

Angus and the Keepers were seated and served house beers so they would have something to drink while they looked over the drink menu, which was painted on an entire wall of the inn. And it wasn't long before they were drinking and in good spirits, with Dangalf saying to Nerdraaage, "I suppose you would know something about that!" And they all laughed with none laughing harder than Nerdraaage.

Angus lit up and so did Nerdraaage. He took a drag and passed the pipe to his friends. Doppelganger declined and passed the pipe on to Dangalf, but Dangalf pushed it back in his direction. "No," said Dangalf. "You really need it."

Doppelganger took a drag and passed it on. Dangalf smiled and took his own drag. They all enjoyed the warm tavern heated by a great fireplace nine feet long and extending six feet into the tavern. It was good just to be sitting on something other than cold ground, especially for Dangalf who had "gone wizard" and did not wear anything under his robe. He imagined that the svelte and barely clothed Ashlyn also enjoyed being in the warmth, but she had not made one complaint about the temperature during the entire trip. Dangalf for one had already made mental notes of what comfort items to bring on their next trip of any great distance.

The inn was packed with dwarves, and though the town was predominantly female, the inn was mostly male. Some of the imbibers were young enough to still sit on fathers' laps.

They had never seen the Silent Woman this crowded in all the nights they had spent there. And they had arrived just in time. A few minutes after they got their table, it was standing room only. "So where is the Odeon?" asked Ashlyn.

"Right there," said Angus pointing to a raised wooden stage against the wall.

"That's it?" asked Ashlyn.

"It might not look like much, but we've had some world-class acts perform here," said Angus. What a shock it must have been for a world-class act to finally see the celebrated Odeon, thought Dangalf. "Clan Wintergreen Dancers," continued Angus. "Alfred Hawthorn Hill's Poetry Festival," he said with a nod to the humans. "Six-Fingered Mungan. Back when he still had eight fingers. Clan Millstone Precision Goat Riders."

"Precision goat riders!" said Dangalf.

"Well," said Angus. "After seeing the Odeon, they decided it would be best to have the performance outside."

The *Cronica* programmers must not have known of, or intentionally ignored, the modest nature of the real Odeon at

Hammersmith as they had created a massive and architectur-ally grand Odeon in the virtual Hammersmith. As the game had gained in popularity and become more culturally signifi-cant, top-name music and comedy acts performed digitally in the Odeon before an audience of player avatars. It didn't matter how anachronistic the particular act was to the *Cronica* world as long as they were well known. Celebrity was the corrupting force of everything in the old world.

Ashlyn rolled her eyes at Dangalf. The Odeon might not be as pleasant a diversion as she had hoped. Dangalf could only smile sympathetically. A man took to the stage and began play-ing a hurdy gurdy. They smoked and drank, and soon the under-whelming Odeon was something else to laugh about even as they enjoyed the dwarven musicians who rotated through it.

Angus patted Nerdraaage on the back affectionately. "Good news, lad," he said loudly over the hurdy gurdy. "Your blood tested as pure as the driven snow. As I knew it would." Nerdraaage had stained some of his blood on a scroll for Angus while they were still in Hempshire when Angus had promised to send it to lorekeepers, the dwarven sages, for cataloguing. "But unsullied blood is just one facet of the gem. Another is your clan. I don't have to tell you that you won't get far in this world without a clan. It's unnatural. I mean, look at how you're dressed and who you associate with. No offense intended," he offered to the other Keepers.

Doppelganger giggled at this and Ashlyn touched his hand. "A baked warrior," she said. "I like you better this way."

"God you're so fucking hot," said Doppelganger, leaning into Ashlyn. She took her hand from his, but it was not for displea-sure that she recoiled.

"Yeah, she is," agreed Dangalf, who was too stoned to be jealous.

"And," continued Angus. "If you don't belong to a good clan..." and he finished that sentence in Old Dwarvish.

"That makes sense," said Nerdraaage when actually he was still trying to make sense of what Angus had said as he was not used to this strong dwarven beer and was baked on top of that and not fluent in Old Dwarvish and not especially clever to begin with.

"Well," continued Angus, now turning to his other table-mates. "I don't have to tell any of you the long, storied history of Clan Stonefist."

"No, you don't!" said Ashlyn as more plea than agreement. Her friends giggled.

"Of course not," agreed Angus. "Our reputation is as good as adamantine. So what I'm getting around to is this: how would you like to join Clan Stonefist?"

"Yeah, okay," said a totally inebriated Nerdraaage, and they pounded each other's chest three times to seal the deal.

Angus stepped onto the table and, with a voice that was actually able to quiet the noisy inn, announced: "Listen up, dwarves. Many of you know that Clan Stonefist is expanding along with my wife's belly. And we look forward to that blessed day in another eighty-four months." The crowd cheered loudly except for those that were not inclined to Clan Stonefist, but they dared protest only silently with folded arms. "But before that time, I am pleased to announce that there is to be a joining ceremony in which we welcome this lad who is to be orphaned no more. Cheers for my new brother, Nerdraaage!" The crowed cheered, and his friends congratulated and patted Nerdraaage. He looked up at them bleary eyed. "The newest member of a clan that goes back thirty thousand years!" added Angus.

Dangalf had noticed this about dates in the *Cronica Acadia*. Many major events were recorded as happening "ten thousand years ago." And he had come to the conclusion that "ten thousand years ago" was shorthand for "a really, really long time ago and too far back to say with any accuracy." And "twenty thousand years ago" was twice that long. But "thirty thousand years ago" was a particularly dwarven claim and should be taken with a grain of salt.

"What?" said Nerdraaage of the hoopla.

"You're joining Clan Stonefist," said Dangalf. "That's one of the best clans in the game." Then he turned to Angus to try to explain his remark. "I mean in this world. I mean, in any world."

"The best!" said Angus leaning into Dangalf. "The royal clans take turns on the throne, but the Praetorian Guard is never unemployed!"

And the five of them clashed cups together. "Clan Stonefist!" they toasted. Nerdraaage smiled proudly. "Well that sucks," whispered Ashlyn.

"What do you mean it sucks?" slurred Nerdraaage.

"You can never be king of the dwarves."

But the Keepers' excitement over the joining ceremony may have been tempered, or quashed altogether, if they knew that there were only two ways to join a clan. And one of those ways, being born into it, was no longer an option for Nerdraaage.

XXXI

Hammersmith had gone to sleep. The only noise outside was the sound of drunken dwarves tumbling into and out of second-story shitehouses before heading off to bed. The Keepers got one large room in the inn and shared it. Nerdraaage was passed out when they brought him up, so he got to sleep on the floor. Dangalf also got onto the floor, perhaps out of habit, and fell asleep. Doppelganger took a bed. It was dwarven, which means it was plenty sturdy for him but only accommodated his frame down to his knees. Nonetheless he passed out quickly. Ashlyn knew she would pass out soon, but first she allowed herself a liberty she had never allowed before. She looked over at Doppelganger's broad, bare chest and unshaven face and thought about what he had said to her earlier that night. In the few seconds before she passed out, she acknowledged to her shame and dismay that Doppelganger too was "so fucking hot."

XXXII

Doppelganger awoke to his friends chatting softly and Nerdraaage dressing. "Do you have enough money?" asked Dangalf.

"I think so. I was trying to think about what kind of supplies I'll need to buy," answered Nerdraaage. "Burglary tools. Poisons. Some poisons are supposed to be really expensive."

"Well, you won't need everything your first day," said Dangalf.

"I hope I don't have to buy a lot of books," said Nerdraaage.

"I'm sure you'll get some books," said Dangalf.

"I hope not as much as you," said Nerdraaage.

"No class needs as many books as the wizard class."

"Is Ashlyn awake?" Doppelganger asked.

"No," said Dangalf.

"Yes," said Ashlyn as she rolled over in the direction of her friends. She even looked beautiful just waking up after a night of drinking and smoking. Dangalf wanted to tell her how he felt, but he knew that those words would not win her heart. And Doppelganger and Nerdraaage would make fun of him. Or they would be so scandalized that they would be unable to mock him, and that would be even worse.

"First day of school?" she asked Nerdraaage.

"Yes," he smiled.

"Our little dwarf is growing up," she said.

"Metaphorically speaking," added Dangalf.

Angus knocked and entered when called. "Angus," said Nerdraaage. "Thanks again for inviting me to the clan."

"My pleasure, lad," answered Angus. "Course we won't have the ceremony until after you're done school." Nerdraaage's friends wished him luck as Angus took him away for the start of his blackguard training. Unlike the other classes, blackguards did not have an official apprentice status. Blackguards engaged in a lot of illegal activity, but they would not have any protection of the law until they were commissioned. A blackguard trainer would disavow any aspirant who was caught stealing or spying, and the flogging or other penalty would be the aspirant's to bear. And apprehension meant that the aspirant's training that officially didn't exist would be officially ended.

Angus led Nerdraaage through Hammersmith proper. "There aren't a lot of dwarf blackguards," said Angus. "It's considered somewhat unseemly. Most dwarves have the opinion that sneaking around and poisoning people is better left to the humans. Have you thought about the other Red School professions?"

"Like what?"

"You could be a warrior. Or a ranger. Both have proud dwarven histories."

"Well, we already have a warrior in our group. And as for a ranger, well, the she-elf plans to be a druid, so we don't need another naturalist."

"Yes, your friends," sighed Angus. "A motley group it is. How did you come to associate so closely with two humans and a, the other one."

"Well, we sort of came into this world together."

"But still, that was in the past. You're among your people now. There are other young lads in Stonefist seeking adventure." Angus continued in Dwarvish with another ancient saying, "There are no weak links in a dwarven chain."

"I couldn't leave my friends."

"Loyalty is a master trait. But should your friends not share it, just remember your own kind will always have a place for you."

"I will," said Nerdraaage. They exited the front gate. "Isn't the trainer in town?"

"Lad," said Angus stopping for emphasis. "The blackguard trainer is a human."

Angus led Nerdraaage about a mile down the road and pointed off into the woods.

"He's supposed to be down that way in a wooden house," said Angus. "I will let you find it on your own. Sometimes the battlepigs make it up into these woods. You have a weapon?" Nerdraaage displayed his daggers. "You have coin for lessons?"

"Yes."

"I'll see you later at the inn." Angus turned back toward Hammersmith. Nerdraaage looked into the snowy, deep woods.

"Is there a path to his place?" he yelled after Angus.

"Not if he's a good blackguard, there won't be."

XXXIII

D oppelganger introduced himself to the captain of the guard and offered his services in the defense of Hammersmith. This offer of service to ally towns was a necessary and documented part of his progression to the next level of training. It was also one of the ways that the per diem rank could earn some coin. The captain introduced himself as Donald of Clan Bluebeard. Doppelganger recognized Bluebeard as one of the royal clans—in fact, the royal clan of the present king of the dwarves.

"You may call me Captain," said Donald. "Do not concern yourself that I am the royal so and so." Donald examined Doppelganger's commission and added him to the rolls.

The guards had forgiven Doppelganger's excesses at the front gate when he first arrived. The dwarves admired other members of the Red School, especially big ones. They told him of the dwarven Red School tradition, second only in favor to the dwarves' beloved Blue School. But the Red School had gained even more prestige since the subjugation of the Blue School during the Schism, which we will discuss in more detail later.

The guards all wanted to duel the big human, but he could no longer sucker his opponents into monetary wagers. His reputation as a duelist had reached Hammersmith ahead of him.

Donald took an immediate liking to Doppelganger, having spent many years in Vinland as a military attaché, where he developed an undwarven fondness for wine and humans, in that order. He was never considered kingly material, but his clan affiliation meant he could otherwise pick the assignments that pleased him. But during the Great War, when dwarven numbers were made a third and then a third again, most attaché positions became luxuries the dwarves could no longer afford, and Donald took the unglamorous role of Captain of the Guard at Hammersmith.

Back at his cottage, Donald offered Doppelganger Aged Vinlandian and drank with him. He gave Doppelganger a belt with an oversized crest of Hammersmith as a buckle. It offered solid protection for his belly. But Doppelganger liked it mostly because he felt as though his appearance was taking on that of a seasoned fighter (even if he had not yet earned this trophy).

XXXIV

Dangalf and Ashlyn found a small and isolated magic library. The selection was modest even by the standards of the Great Library at Hempshire, but it had comfortable chairs and was well lit. Sunshine poured through stained-glass windows projecting the constellations of their new world onto the floor. Those blue dwarves would not shoddily build even a white library.

They had the library all to themselves, and Dangalf began his rapid capture of the books, careful not to miss a page. There were no druid texts for Ashlyn to study, but she was fascinated to read about counterspells to druidic magic. She thought it would be helpful to know what sorcerers and witches could and could not do against what would be her own magic set. She enjoyed reading, but Dangalf pressed her to capture the books instead. He insisted the book would be there in its entirety in her virtual library when she learned to slumber, and now it was important to record as many books into her mind as possible as opposed to reading them for comprehension. But elf slumber differed from human slumber, and he had only limited success in teaching her his method. He told her how he had perfect recollection of his trip to the tar pits museum with its sights and sounds and smells, and she understood what he meant. But she countered that he was pure ectomorph and she was not. She could not hope to have the eidetic recall that he had, and he finally gave up his argument when it looked like she was getting angry.

XXXV

After an hour of wandering hopelessly in the woods, and worrying about battlepigs, Nerdraaage decided it would be best to see if he could find his way back to the road. Only after giving up did he find a structure that he must have passed a dozen times, camouflaged by color, trees, and an unwillingness to be seen that was downright inexplicable for a house. He made his way to the front door. He knocked several times without response, so he began to knock louder and call out, "Hello" repeatedly. The door finally opened, and when no one appeared, he walked in still knocking and crying, "Hello!"

A ghostly voice that alternately came from behind him, from another room, and whispering into his left ear said, "You stomp around these grounds like an elephant. I've been smelling your pipe since you first came into my woods."

"I haven't smoked all day," said Nerdraaage.

"You carry a pipe, and that is what I smell! And now that you have entered my home, I can smell your sweat, your breath; I can smell your arse!"

"Is there anyone else I can talk to? Someone who trains blackguards?"

The ghostly laughter sounded from several points around Nerdraaage, and he spun in a circle trying to face it.

"Blackguards are quick and precise and smart. Few dwarves possess all these traits. You have none! Do not come back!" And an unappeared hand spun Nerdraaage around and an unappeared foot pushed him out the door.

XXXVI

Nerdraaage and Angus were drinking in the inn when Dangalf and Ashlyn entered. Taking note of the earliness of the hour, Dangalf gently asked, "How'd training go?"

"Terrible. He said he wouldn't train me."

His friends were dismayed. This certainly wasn't a game dynamic, a trainer refusing to train. What would this mean for the future of the Keepers? "Why not?" asked Dangalf.

"He said dwarves don't make good blackguards."

"Human bastard," said Angus. "No offense intended."

"None taken," said Ashlyn.

"But they have some great dwarven trainers here. I could be a warrior..."

"What would Doppelganger say to that?" said Dangalf.

"Or a ranger..."

"No," said Ashlyn.

"You being a blackguard," said Dangalf. "I mean, that just makes the group complete. Without any redundancy."

Angus said in Old Dwarvish, "There is no weak link in a dwarven chain." Even though they didn't understand Old Dwarvish, Dangalf and Ashlyn suspected that Angus was undermining the Keepers.

Doppelganger and Donald entered the inn and made their way toward the others. Donald was intercepted at another table, but Doppelganger joined his friends. "I see you're making mighty friends, human," said Angus. "You see the captain of the guard there?" asked Angus of the others. "Royalty he is. Donald of Clan Bluebeard."

"But his beard is black!" said Nerdraaage, and Angus nearly fell off his chair. The others had never seen Angus so spooked, even when he was first released from the cocoon of spider silk. He pulled Nerdraaage close to him.

"Never tell a Bluebeard his beard is black!" Angus whispered urgently. "We don't have a warg in that fight."

They all nodded understanding. It was a mistake any of them could have made because in the game where they got their knowledge of this world, Clan Bluebeard dwarves all had bright blue beards.

XXXVII

A nd when the first five dwarven clans agreed to form a society and put an end to war between dwarves, it first became imperative for each of the clans to take a name, which was not before needed. (They had only names for the others, their rival clans—pejoratives, really—prior to this agreement.) The obvious choice for most was to be named after their beard color, and Clans Brownbeard, Redbeard, and Yellowbeard were easily decided. But two clans were black of beard and insisted that they alone should be Clan Blackbeard for having the blackest beards. Such was the controversy that one of the two black-haired clans met at midnight fully armed and prepared to murder the other clan, this being the ancient times after all, to claim the title of Clan Blackbeard. And that clan was lead by Bran, the greatest of all dwarves, who gives name to their home and highest peak and is also their first king. And just outside the enemy's camp, one of Bran's brothers whispered to him, "To think those other dwarves would lay claim to having the blackest beards of all. Why your beard is so black that here in the moonlight it looks blue!" And then Bran's clan snuck into their enemies' camp, each taking position over an adult male dwarf and raised their weapons to strike when Bran announced,

"Ye are all caught unawares in very undwarven repose! And ye should all be hacked and pummeled to death should it have been of our choosing! Know this then, that your petty lives and flimsy beards have been spared by the mercy of Clan Bluebeard!" And as terrible a story as this might appear to sapiens of a modern disposition, it is celebrated by all dwarves as the greatest-ever act of dwarven compromise.

Cronica Acadia

XXXVIII

Doppelganger was informed of the blackguard trainer's unwillingness to take on Nerdraaage. Doppelganger's blood boiled, but he said nothing. Only the reddening of his face showed that he was greatly aggrieved by this slight to his friend. "So," said Nerdraaage. "I was thinking I could train to be a warrior like you!"

"No," said Doppelganger firmly.

"Well," said Nerdraaage. "I've got to be something!"

"Let's go talk to your trainer," said Dangalf.

"Yes!" said Doppelganger a little too eagerly.

"You guys would do that for me?"

"Of course," said Dangalf. "We'll go now." Dangalf poured the rest of his beer into his mouth. He might need it.

"You guys are the best friends anyone's ever had," said Nerdraaage as he stood. "Elf, you can't come."

Ashlyn frowned. "We'll be back shortly," Dangalf reassured her.

Doppelganger led Dangalf and Nerdraaage as they marched into the woods where the blackguard trainer resided. "Why couldn't Ashlyn come?" asked Dangalf.

"I don't want her to make fun of me," said Nerdraaage.

"She wouldn't do that. She felt really bad that you couldn't get your training."

"This trainer might say some embarrassing things, and I don't want her to hear."

"Like what?"

"He said he could smell my arse."

Doppelganger stopped in his tracks. "Wow," he said. "And I thought my trainer sucked. Maybe you should become a ranger."

"Ashlyn is our naturalist," insisted Dangalf. "Look, animals and elves and trolls all have a heightened sense of smell. I'm sure that's what he meant. This blackguard is human. I suspect his arse smells too. Let's go see him."

"That's another problem," said Nerdraaage.

"What?"

"I didn't actually see him."

Nerdraaage found the hidden house quicker the second time. Dangalf stopped the others at the front door as he thought it was important to establish ground rules before they encountered the blackguard. "Now remember," said Dangalf, "we're here as advocates for Nerdraaage. Let's be diplomatic."

"Blackguard!" shouted Doppelganger, pounding on the door. "Show yourself!" The door swung slowly open. "There's no one there."

"That's what he did to me," said Nerdraaage.

Doppelganger pushed in first followed by Nerdraaage and Dangalf. The windows were blacked out, and red lamps lit the room. There were workbenches against each wall, some with colored bottles on them and others with locks and tools. A variety of weapons adorned the walls. There were books on a shelf. Beyond that first room, it was so black it looked like it might have been the edge of the universe. An impenetrable blackness. The door closed behind them.

The ghost voice spoke from around the room: "Why did you come back?"

Nerdraaage screamed and fell to the ground. "My knee," he yelled. Doppelganger armed himself with his axe and looked about for a target.

Truthfully, it was not a ghost. It was a master of the black-guard class, an assassin, using a skill that made him *unappeared*. If he were observed at all, it would be only briefly when he struck, and then most would only see shadow or smoke. It took signifi-cant skill to see his true form, and that's how Dangalf saw him, when he struck Nerdraaage. A black-clad figure with a wrinkled human face. And was he wearing sunglasses? "We just want to talk," pleaded Dangalf.

"Do you always bring your battleaxes for conversation?" said the ghost. And the shadow appeared behind Doppelganger. For less than a second, Dangalf saw the wrinkled human face wear-ing black goggles. No, not wrinkled, badly scarred.

The ghost hand waved across Doppelganger's face from be-hind, leaving a black raccoon mask across his eyes. Doppelganger turned and swung at the ghost, but it was gone. But Dangalf was ready for the blackguard when he appeared behind Doppelganger, and when he struck, Dangalf struck. He cast the blackguard in an ice block. "Shite!" yelled Doppelganger. "I'm blind."

"It's okay," he said. "I got him." Dangalf went to a blackened window and swung it open, filling the room with light. He ran to Doppelganger and helped him to a seat. He checked on Nerdraaage, who said he was all right. Dangalf went back to his block of ice and peered in at the empty cube. "I don't got him," he said weakly.

The ghost appeared behind Dangalf. Dangalf let out a cry and dropped instantly to the floor, minus his wand, which the ghost had taken.

The scarred ghost allowed himself to be fully visible. He was garbed from neck to toe in black dragon-wing leather—"blacks" the blackguards called this garb—and he wore goggles with black lenses. It seemed strange to Dangalf, since the room was so dark to begin with. Dangalf noticed daggers in each of the ghost's hands even though he hid the blades by pointing them up behind each arm. The black ghost stood over his quarry and chuckled wickedly. "What a motley crew," he said.

Dangalf saw Ashlyn enter quickly and silently through the window, and in a flash she had her dagger pressed against the black ghost's neck.

The ghost recognized his attacker as a she-elf and her weapon as a dagger even though he could not see either. "An elf," said the ghost smiling. "Now that I did not expect." In a move that seemed more magic than acrobatic, the ghost unappeared and reappeared behind Ashlyn. He held both daggers pressed up against her breast. She stood there holding her dagger where the black ghost had been. For a moment she half expected to die when he unexpectedly inhaled her neck and kissed it. She dropped the dagger at the shock of being kissed.

"What's happening!" asked the blind Doppelganger.

"You have unexpected allies, dwarf," the ghost said to Nerdraaage as he returned his daggers to their sheaths. "Perhaps I have underestimated you," And then to Ashlyn, "Close the window, she-elf."

"What about my friends?" she asked.

"They are unharmed," said the ghost. "It was only the suggestion of pain. I did not wish to spill their blood on my goblin carpet. Go on."

Nerdraaage and Dangalf got off the floor slowly. "If that was the suggestion of pain," said Dangalf, "I hope I never feel real pain." He checked on Doppelganger, who said that his vision was returning. Ashlyn closed the window, returning the room to near darkness.

The ghost took a chair and removed his goggles. "I have not seen the light of day in three years," said the ghost. "I would have looked on it unkindly if you had ruined the night vision I've cultivated over that time." He introduced himself as Icil and bid the others take seats. He poured and passed around glasses of wine to each of them. They looked at their glasses and each other suspiciously. "Please drink up. I have so few guests."

"Hard to believe," said Doppelganger, tears and blinding agent streaking his face black.

"An enraged warrior is a formidable opponent," said Icil. "But I have found blindness to be an antidote to the bloodwarp." He turned to Ashlyn. "You I could train to be a blackguard." Then to the others he said, "You have not fucked until you have fucked a she-elf blackguard. The combination of good girl and bad girl in one lithe package is otherworldly."

"I am definitely otherworldly," said Ashlyn.

"That you are," said Icil. "But alas, the she-elf blackguard is the greatest of rarities."

Dangalf smelled his wine for impurities. Not that he knew what an impurity smelled like.

"What happened to your face?" asked Nerdraaage.

"Not cool," said Ashlyn.

"I am proud of each of my scars," said Icil. "And I will gladly tell their stories, especially to one who presumes to be a blackguard. I was the third blackguard charged with killing a troll deathspeaker who had killed a hundred of our fighters. Bedka the Beguiler. The two before me had never returned. I waited in her slumber vault for thirteen hours before she arrived. Once there, her guards took position outside her door, and the door was closed. She began the unmasking, a process by which they use magic to uncover any blackguard that might be hidden. I was warded against her spells, but this witch had another method that the sages were unaware of. She sprayed an acid liberally around the room. She hit me directly in the face with it, but I did not move or make a sound. She settled into her bed, and I waited motionless for another hour while the acid ate my flesh. When she finally fell asleep, I struck. She took my good looks, but I took her head."

"You're an assassin?" asked Dangalf.

"Yes."

"A master class blackguard," said Nerdraaage in awe. The master classes did not exist in the game but were advertised to be part of the expansion pack along with flying mounts and the new world of Oceania.

"Do you bear the mark of the centurion?" asked Doppelganger.

"A warrior vanity," said Icil. "It impresses me not that some dragoon slew a hundred or even a thousand peons. I kill those who kill dragoons."

"Then why are you here?" asked Dangalf. "Training blackguards outside a dwarven town?"

"That is exactly why I am here. I am required to provide service to the Alliance. So I made myself a blackguard trainer to a town where there should be no blackguards. That was to allow me to pursue my vendetta."

"What vendetta?" asked Doppelganger.

After a moment Icil answered, "I lost something of great value."

"Your she-elf?" asked Ashlyn.

"Yes," said Icil looking far off. "She was killed by a troll necromancer and her undead knight. Betwixt her spells and his swordplay, they are formidable. And I say that as one who has been called formidable by the greatest enemies that we have. And now I spend my time studying them and planning my vengeance. I came here to get away from other distractions, and up until now I had been left alone." Icil spoke directly to Nerdraaage. "But I will train you, master dwarf. Persistence is a noble trait. And it will be a pleasant diversion from my other pursuit. I will make you into a mercenary suitable for my own signature upon his scroll. Or I will at least have a few laughs trying."

"Maybe both," said Ashlyn cheerfully.

Though it was late, Icil said there was time for half a lesson, so all but Nerdraaage left the hidden home.

XXXIX

Doppelganger, Dangalf, and Ashlyn went to dinner at the inn, and Angus beckoned them over to where Donald held court. Introductions of those not already introduced were made. And the Keepers explained that they had gotten Icil to take on Nerdraaage, which quite impressed Angus.

Donald said that he could see Doppelganger becoming one of the great warriors of the ages, and he hoped that when he was legendary he would come back to visit Hammersmith. "Did I not tell you how, when I was paralyzed by spider toxin, this lad single-handedly rescued me from a daughter of Arachne!" enthused Angus.

"I don't remember it that way," Dangalf said slyly to Ashlyn.

"I thought Nerdraaage single-handedly rescued him," she said more slyly.

The dwarves smoked their own pipes while Dangalf and Ashlyn shared his. Doppelganger refused a hit from Donald's pipe, to which the captain replied, "Smart lad!" and continued smoking.

Dangalf rocked out to the dulcimer sound coming from the Odeon. He was so buzzed that he was surprised when he finally recognized the musician as Angus. How perfectly dwarven, he thought. A musical instrument played with hammers! It took him another minute to remember that Angus only had one arm, and he played with both hammers in one hand.

A lute player had taken the stage when a comparatively sober, but not sober, Nerdraaage made his way through the crowd. Doppelganger shouted a drunken greeting to him.

Nerdraaage excitedly told his friends about his lessons, and they tried desperately to focus and comprehend. Nerdraaage emptied his rucksack onto the table. There were books on poisons, which Dangalf picked up. "I need to see these when you're done," he said.

"I have a better idea," said Nerdraaage. "Why don't you take them now and tell me what they say."

Dangalf nodded. "You have a book on unappear?" asked Dangalf. This was the blackguard's foundation skill as demonstrated earlier that day in its highest form by Icil.

"Those secrets have never been written down," said Nerdraaage solemnly. "And I have taken an oath to protect that secret with my own life if necessary." Dangalf could not be blamed for asking. Blackguards were considered the greatest threat to the wizard class.

"And look at this!" Nerdraaage said proudly. He showed them a small satchel in black leather that he draped over his shoulder.

"You're going to wear a purse?" asked Ashlyn.

"It's not a purse; it's a murder kit!"

"Sorry. I get those two confused."

"Oh, and he gave you this too," said Nerdraaage as he slid a small wrapped package to Ashlyn.

She unwrapped a small white flower and would have touched it had Dangalf not screamed, "Don't touch it!" He slid it away from her by the packaging and toward himself. "That's grave-whisper," he said.

"Great," she said. "I'm being stalked by an assassin." And then she giggled drunkenly at her own seriousness. Dangalf and Doppelganger looked at her dumbly. "He's not behind me right now, is he?" she asked.

"How would we know?" asked Doppelganger.

"He's not stalking you!" said Nerdraaage. "It's a gift."

"It is very expensive," said Dangalf. "He might have thought you knew how to handle it, being an elf and all."

"Apparently he didn't know how bad I am at being an elf," she said. And then picking up on Dangalf's first sentence she said, "Expensive! What could I get for it?"

"A sovereign gross," ventured Angus. A hundred and forty-four gold coins! That was more wealth than the Keepers could imagine. In all their time in this world, combined, they had earned maybe a dozen sovereigns. Ashlyn clapped excitedly for herself.

"I think we should hold onto it," said Dangalf.

"Why?" asked Ashlyn.

"Because if you need a gravewhisper extract, you might not be able to find one, even if you have a sovereign gross."

"Who needs gravewhisper extract?" she demanded.

"Mages use it," said Dangalf. "Blackguards use it. Druids might also have use for it."

"Yeah," she said. "But he gave it to me!" And then on Dangalf's disappointed look, she said, "Okay. I'll save it."

"Just be careful," he said. "If you touch it or inhale it, you could die."

"You die if you inhale it," said Doppelganger. "Maybe you should wrap it back up."

"It's perfectly safe as long as you don't antagonize the flower," Dangalf said. He slid the wrapped flower back to Ashlyn.

"Hey," she said. "Why don't we go get my training?"

"No," said Nerdraaage.

"I guess we could," said Dangalf to Doppelganger. "One of us could escort her to Templa Taur. Either you or me. I don't care which," he lied.

"No," insisted Nerdraaage.

"Break up the group?" asked Doppelganger. "There's still a lot of bad things outside these gates, and it's three, four days to Templa Taur."

"You could both escort me," said Ashlyn. "Nerdraaage will be safe in Hammersmith. When I'm done training, we can meet him back here."

"No!" shouted Nerdraaage.

"That might work," said Dangalf.

"Dangalf and I will just get rusty sitting here in town," said Doppelganger. "We need some adventure."

"No!" shouted Nerdraaage again. "I shoveled shite in Hempshire waiting for you guys. Now you can all wait for me as we agreed. And when I'm done, then we'll all go to Templa Taur and wait for Elftrap. But we're going to do it as the Keepers!" The others were chastened by Nerdraaage's conviction.

"Fine," she finally said. "I'll wait. And it's Ashlyn, by the way."

XL

Nerdraaage continued his training. He seemed ill after many of his lessons, and he blamed it on poisons that Icil administered for the stated purpose of building up his immunity. The other Keepers privately worried that Icil would kill Nerdraaage, for they were still not convinced that the assassin's purposes were pure. Moreover they suspected that if his purposes were pure, he wouldn't be an assassin. Finally they agreed that Icil was not killing Nerdraaage when Nerdraaage did in fact not die.

Nerdraaage's debriefing of his latest improvements and newest abilities grew shorter nightly, until finally, like a true blackguard, he did not speak of what he learned even when asked. The others missed the exuberance of the untrained, unsophisticated Nerdraaage but agreed he seemed happier and more confident with his newfound skills. And they took solace in the fact that he might now be trained, but he was still mostly unsophisticated.

Doppelganger and Dangalf received a per diem for patrolling the Greater Hammersmith area with the guards. The pay was slight, and the Keepers' finances withered as lodgings, food, drink, and leaf took their toll. Ashlyn didn't get a per diem, and she found the dwarf employers reluctant to employ a she-elf. That reluctance manifested itself in her continued unemployment. There was talk of selling the gravewhisper flower, but it still was hoped that this could be avoided. Nerdraaaage was inexact about when his training might be completed, and it was contemplated that they should switch lodgings back to the stables. And though Doppelganger still periodically boasted that the best sleep he ever had was in a stable, the high altitude meant that sleeping outside would be much colder in Hammersmith than it was in Hempshire.

Nerdraaaage's training was a significant expense. He began outfitting himself with his "blacks," a few pieces of cheap black leather that tended to stain his skin black when he sweated, which was most of the time. Instead of "blacks" Icil called Nerdraaaage's leather his "squeaks" because it was of low quality and squeaked whenever Nerdraaaage moved. It was a squeak that was only perceptible to the finest ears in the quietest environment, but stealth meant everything to blackguards. Icil had advised against black leather, as it was known to be the de facto blackguard uniform and might invite trouble that Nerdraaaage was not yet capable of defeating or escaping. But Nerdraaaage thought it looked cool, so he bought squeaky, cheap, black leather. He idolized Icil and wanted to look like him even if he did not idolize Icil enough to take his advice and not buy squeaky, cheap, black leather.

Doppelganger, Dangalf, and three dwarven guards walked down the main road from Hammersmith. The guards were happy to have Doppelganger with them on patrol. As for Dangalf, they viewed him as more of a curiosity. "Hey, wizard, can you turn this bloke into a chicken," said one guard about the second.

"No, sorry," said Dangalf. "I don't do metamorphism."

"What did he say," asked the third guard.

"He can't do it," said the first guard.

The third guard said something in Dwarvish that Dangalf was sure was an insult but he would not know without Nerdraaage to translate. (Dangalf was already learning the enemy language of Trollish. Dwarvish would have to wait.) *I should cast him in a block of ice*, thought Dangalf of the offending dwarf. *That would show him.* But that spell could not be cast often, so he saved it for now.

They stopped at a farmhouse that had lost two farmhands (one dead, one crippled) to a monstrous battlepig. With the ending of open hostilities between the Alliance and the Legion, the Legion had resorted to covert warfare. The trolls bred boars of preternatural size and strength and speed and fitted them with armor. They were twisted into hateful, destructive creatures by black magic. Then these boars were released into the wilds of Acadia to wreck havoc on wildlife, crops, and unfortunate sapiens.

Hammersmith's ranger would normally track and kill the beast, but he was away.

It was hoped that the Hammersmith guards with their human auxiliary could find and kill the battlepig.

They stopped at the farmhouse, where the surviving farmhand described the boar as at least eight hundred pounds. He had lost a leg, so the guards did not openly mock him, though they knew that no eight-hundred-pound armored pig could make it to the doorstep of Hammersmith. "Let's find the beastie," said the first guard, and they departed the farmhouse and headed into the wilderness.

"If we'd only brought a hunter instead of a wizard," said the third guard to dwarven laughter. He didn't even mask his insult in Dwarvish this time.

"Wizard is the class," said Dangalf. "I'm a conjurer." The dwarves were not impressed.

One of the guards located the bloody ground where the boar had struck. They gathered around and examined the animal's tracks. "That's a nine-hundred-pound boar!" said the first guard.

"A thousand," said the second.

"You're gonna need a bigger boat," said Dangalf.

The guards turned and squinted at Dangalf. "And why would we need a boat, wizard?"

"It's just…something I heard where we come from," said Dangalf laughing.

"You hunt boars by boat?"

"No," said Dangalf. "It's a joke. He gets it." Dangalf pointed at Doppelganger, who stood there looking like he didn't want to get dragged into the conversation.

"Maybe we should split up," said the first guard, looking directly at Dangalf.

They spread out as they went deeper in the woods. Dangalf angrily kicked at the dirt, silently cursing the stupid dwarves for making him feel stupid.

"Hey," whisper-shouted Ashlyn. Dangalf looked about in a circle before he remembered he was looking for an elf and should look up as well. He saw her in a tree above him.

"What are you doing here!" he demanded.

"You're walking right into the battlepig!"

"You can see him?"

"I can smell him."

"What does he smell like?" asked Dangalf sniffing at the air.

"Bacon."

"Very funny."

"It's not funny," insisted Ashlyn. "Those troll a-holes burn the armor into the pig's skin, so he smells like bacon. And he can smell you!"

"The pig smells me?"

"He's lying in wait behind that hill. I'm sure of it."

"Ah," said Dangalf. "I remember reading that pigs are used for hunting truffles because of their keen sense of smell."

The third guard walked over to Dangalf. "Who are you talking to, wizard?"

"The she-elf in the tree," said Dangalf, and he turned back to see that Ashlyn was gone. "Well, she was right there." The guard nodded suspiciously and walked away. Dangalf pressed on, toward the hill, softly calling for Ashlyn.

Suddenly a second hill appeared on top of the first hill. But this one was covered in metal plates, thick black hair, and snorting, steamy breath. The second hill wasn't a hill at all. The massive battlepig saw Dangalf, and all one thousand porcine pounds bore down on him with that preternatural speed. "Run, wizard!" shouted the guard.

"I've got him!" said Dangalf as he aimed his wand and cast the battlepig into a block of ice. He missed. The last two times he cast that spell, it was against a moving target, and both times he missed. Dangalf felt the instant and horrendous chill of impending death. He began casting his fireball, but almost as soon as he started, he calculated that he might not cast it before the battlepig struck him. Just like in the game, he had a split second to decide if he should continue with his spell casting or start a new, quicker spell from scratch. It was a simple calculation for him, yet the fear of imminent death had a chilling effect on his thought processes. *Fear is the mind killer.* Shite, Dangalf. Time for eluding not alluding!

"Run!" shouted Ashlyn.

Dangalf made the wrong decision. His fireball was still two seconds from casting, and the pig was just one second from pulverizing him. His great and expanding mind had so much information at instant recall, but he was unfocused by terror. *Fear is the little death. La petite mort.* The orgasm. Orgasm? A great unbisected brain, eidetic memory, a large and ever increasing virtual library of knowledge, and still his mind had flailed and failed spectacularly. And now he would die. The warrior's lizard brain would have served him better in this instance.

The dwarf pushed Dangalf out of the way, and the pig struck the guard full force and sent him flying into the air. It was as if the guard had been struck by a car going thirty miles per hour if the car had subsequently charged its prone victim and stomped and gnashed and gored him.

Doppelganger heard the commotion and saw the battlepig. He raised his bow and took aim. His first several arrows were deflected by the thick armor. Doppelganger's excitement had spoiled his precision. He finally got one into the battlepig's shoulder, but the beast did not even flinch. Doppelganger drew his axe and began the long charge.

The dwarf fought valiantly from his prone position. He had lost his boots and helmet and spear in the initial collision and now the battlepig violently gored through his armor and then flesh.

The pig produced this supernatural squealing that bade Dangalf to cover his ears and flee into the woods. But he stood his ground and cast his fireball. It was a good one, and when released it exploded against the squealing monster and knocked him sideways and to the ground. But to Dangalf's horror, the smoldering pig struggled back up on shaky legs and stumbled toward him. But even a stumbling, wounded battlepig moved quicker than a human. Dangalf saw the bloody tusks and teeth gnashing toward him as he retreated. He heard a blood-curdling scream and was glad when he realized it was not his own. Doppelganger was charging. The battlepig turned just in time to see the big mercenary with his axe over his head. Doppelganger smashed the axe onto the pig's armor cap, which popped free from its head. It tumbled to its side, and the earth shook. Its hooves still stuttered as Doppelganger and the two other dwarves chopped and stabbed at the fleshy seams around his armor, and the tortured life of the battlepig was finally ended.

Dangalf kneeled down by the dead guard and began crying. Doppelganger saw Ashlyn in the tree. He was surprised but motioned for her to depart.

The guards joined Dangalf over their dead comrade. "It's my fault," said Dangalf. A guard patted him on the shoulder. Dangalf would have preferred that the dwarf spat on him. He deserved it. He could not apologize to the dead dwarf for missing his spell or thank him for saving his life. Some conjurer he was. If Weyd Salint were here now, he would likely tear up Dangalf's commission and withdraw his sponsorship to the White School.

Perhaps Dangalf should tear up his own documents and go back to Hempshire to shovel shite for a living. That's what he deserved. Even now, he was selfishly engaging in self-loathing instead of mourning the dead hero before him. And that only filled him with more self-loathing. Maybe he would travel to Vinland and join the Guild of Sages and Seers. They were only NPCs in the game, but in the real Acadia they were an honored and respected magical body sworn to pacifism.

"We will avenge you, Earc," said the second guard. Earc, thought Dangalf. Hearing the dead dwarf's name brought on a fresh flood of tears. He hadn't even been good enough to introduce himself to the dwarf who would sacrifice his life for him.

"Aye," said the first guard. "We will avenge you with spit and fire." And then they put Earc back together, putting what they could of his flesh back into the gored cavity and then dressing him as much as possible in his torn clothes and armor. One of the guards retrieved a cart from the farmhouse, and they lifted Earc onto it.

Then with Doppelganger's help, they lifted the pig onto the cart as well. Dangalf thought it was disrespectful to lay Earc next to his killer, but he didn't say anything. He didn't deserve to say anything in the company of the others. He might not say anything ever again. He wondered if there was a magical order of pacifists that also took a vow of silence and shoveled shite. Doppelganger pulled the wagon back to Hempshire.

Dangalf looked at his strong friend and felt all the weaker. He wiped away his tears and snot and didn't allow himself to cry further. He needed to show at least that much strength.

A crowd had gathered at the gate to greet the heroes, but their celebration was tempered as they learned of Earc. And one woman was especially distraught, and Dangalf imagined it was Earc's wife, but he didn't inquire and kept his distance from the commotion.

He saw Ashlyn standing alone, as she always was in this dwarven town when her friends were not present. She smiled weakly at Dangalf, and he smiled back. Just seeing her was great comfort to him. She banished the deep blackness that he thought was permanent just a few hours ago. He went to her as the two bodies were removed from the wagon. "I'm so sorry," she said.

"It wasn't your fault."

"I should have stayed here. I will get my training before I join you on any more quests."

"You may have saved my life. You and Earc. I would have walked right up to that pig before I even noticed him. I can't smell anything."

Still at the cart, Doppelganger was the center of dwarven curiosity and congratulations. "Look at him," said Ashlyn smiling. "They're going to make him an honorary dwarf before we leave here."

"He deserves it," said Dangalf. "He just does everything right. He was born to this world."

"Like when he disarmed the gate guards and you had to freeze him before he got us all killed?" said Ashlyn.

191

"I guess that was pretty stupid of him," said Dangalf with a laugh, and he tried not to feel too bad about laughing now.

The dwarven praise did not go to Doppelganger's head. In fact, reliving the moment, he had grave concerns about his own performance. Yes, he had screamed mightily and run fast and planted his axe deep in the battlepig's skull, but those were affectations. Conscious decisions. He had not manifested the bloodwarp. Not even watching Earc brutally killed or his dearest friend in mortal jeopardy had brought about his all-important foundation skill. He had only experienced the bloodwarp once, and Alfred had had to beat it out of him. To promote to soldier, Doppelganger would need to be able to spontaneously generate the supernatural strength and toughness of the bloodwarp. Without the bloodwarp he would never be more than a big guy with an axe.

The armor was pried off of the dead boar, and he was cooked outside the inn on a giant spit that barely contained the behemoth. It seemed the entire town came out for the celebration and a meal.

Doppelganger, Dangalf, and Ashlyn met with Donald and Angus in the inn, where they sat with two guards. Doppelganger repeated not for the last time what had happened to Earc.

Nerdraaage returned from training and joined them. He inquired about the festivities, and Doppelganger told him about Earc's death, still not for the last time. A she-dwarf brought around a tray of roasted boar, and they all took some except for Ashlyn, who declined.

"Come, on," said the she-dwarf. "It's tradition."

"It seems so gruesome," said Ashlyn.

"It's tradition," insisted Nerdraaage even though he himself had only just now learned of this tradition.

Ashlyn took a small piece, and the she-dwarf waited until she tasted it. The she-dwarf smiled and sprinkled some red wetness on Ashlyn, who cringed. "What is that?" asked Dangalf as they were all anointed.

"That would be pig's blood," said Ashlyn wiping her face with a cloth soaked in beer. "It must be some kind of pagan ceremony."

"A pagan ceremony is what it would be in our home world," said Dangalf.

"What is it then?"

"A ceremony."

"Why aren't we at war right now?" demanded Doppelganger. "They kill us with their devious methods, and we don't do anything."

"There are no truces for blackguards," said a confident Nerdraaage. "Even now, we are behind their lines gathering information, assassinating leaders, striking at their war machine. Icil told me."

"Fine for you," said Doppelganger. "When do I get in on it?"

"You forget how depleted our forces were after the last war," said Donald. "We no longer had an army capable of aggression. But there will be open hostilities soon enough. We must take back lands that they now occupy—first and foremost Nemetia, before their witches can exploit its great magic. But as we grow stronger, they grow weaker. The Cult of Uroboros has turned troll against troll and all of the trolls against the orcs and gobbies."

The Keepers knew the Cult of Uroboros. In the artificial symmetry of the game world, Uroboros was the Legion version of the allies' Witchfinder General. They were both isolated compounds where only the most skilled players would venture to fight the murderous and powerful bosses. But in this world, the Uroboros was not isolated and despised like the Temple of the Red Rose but had in fact spread its apocalyptic influence throughout troll lands.

XLI

The Cult of Uroboros is an ancient troll apocalyptic death cult, vile and dangerous even by apocalyptic death cult standards. The Uroboros is unique in its desire to hasten the end of the world. It prophesies that the trolls with their allies will defeat and annihilate the Acadian Alliance of Righteous Races. Then, further, the trolls will turn next on the goblins, whom they shall destroy, and then finally on the orcs, whom they will also destroy. With all the other races of Acadia eliminated, troll house against troll house will do battle until only one house remains. Then that house will battle to the death until only one troll remains. He will be the Elemental Troll, the greatest and most powerful of all trolls. The Elemental Troll, after some preparation, will summon the devourer of this world and do battle with him. If the Elemental Troll is victorious, he will take the place of the defeated god and will raise up his troll brothers as masters of the world and again raise up all the other races to serve as slaves in a perpetual troll kingdom under a troll god. The cult, which has much to dissuade potential adherents, not the least of which is to summon the devourer of this world, has nonetheless gained favor among many modern trolls, even members of the royal family, which it seeks to displace as leaders of the Legion. Recent archeological finds returned from Oceania have been used by cult priests as evidence of the cult's infallibility. The Guild of Sages and Seers has dutifully disseminated Uroboros supremacy theory to the goblins and the few learned orcs to sew dissent among the Legion Pangaea.

Cronica Acadia

XLII

"Has anyone ever tried to talk to the trolls?" Dangalf asked. There was stunned silence at the table.

Angus barked something in Old Dwarvish, clearly more ancient wisdom, that the other dwarves found quite amusing. Donald didn't laugh. He tried to frown disapprovingly at Angus, but Angus was too drunk to notice. But the other dwarves around the table laughed heartily, none more so than Nerdraaage.

"What?" said Dangalf frantically. "What? What did he say?" Even Ashlyn covered her mouth to stifle her laughter. "What are you laughing at?" Dangalf demanded.

"I don't know," she said. "It's just infectious."

Dangalf shook Nerdraaage to get his attention. "What? What did he say?"

"Oh," said Nerdraaage wiping a tear from his eye. "He said, 'What is the point of conversation with one who will not agree that beer is wet?'"

Angus said, "Know this, human: Earc is dead, and he was killed by troll hand as sure if he died by dagger."

"We'll strike back at the Legion soon enough," said Donald. "And the humans will be right by our side. They're as ready as we are."

"And why wouldn't the humans be ready for war?" slurred Angus. "Removed they were from the worst of the conflict. They lost none of their lands. And they have more men scurrying about now than before the Great War."

"Theirs was one of the Three Pillars to the Legion's defeat," said Donald. "Ozymandias sunk the Trollish Armada. We would be overrun otherwise."

"Bah," sputtered Angus. "If this Ozymandias was so powerful, why does he no longer show himself? He's another human fraud!"

"He's not a fraud," said Dangalf. Angus turned on him angrily before waving dismissively to him with his one arm and storming out.

Dangalf had sensed a discontent about the reclusive Ozymandias whenever his name came up. He had sunk the Trollish Armada and saved Vinland and by extension the Acadian Alliance. But why had he vanished and where had he gone? If his powers were so great, why did he not take the battle to the heart of the Legion and smite their armies?

Dangalf was measured in his defense of Ozymandias because he had no personal knowledge of the great elementalist. But Weyd believed in Ozymandias, and Dangalf believed in Weyd.

Supreme Allied Commander Dukenfield further burdened the ancient wizard by promoting him to archmage, a title that didn't exist before it was bestowed on Ozymandias. He alone was promoted to a master class above all others of any school. And the other classes and schools soon established their own master classes in response. The Red School christened their best warriors, who were just learning to ride dragons brought back from Oceania, dragoons, after the Dwarvish word for dragon.

The deadliest blackguards became assassins. The White School christened their best druids as fenix, and other archmages were also promoted.

On the subject of Ozymandias, the Legion propagandists remained silent, which was unusual if you knew anything about Legion propagandists. It was likely that they were unsure of his powers themselves and decided not to provoke him, reasoning that it was better to have a fraud in a tower than an archmage on the battlefield.

"You'll have to forgive Angus," said Donald. "Sometimes he sips the beer of madness. Sometimes he chugs it. He blames a human for the loss of his arm. It was a human captain—a strong, brave warrior, a shining example of humanity—who through sheer force of will raised a raiding party of human and dwarves with the express purpose of killing the hated Necromancer Princess Gykoja. Angus was in this party. Bravely they did fight all the way to Gykoja's tower, losing many men, when the human captain came within striking distance of the depleted witch. To hear Angus tell it, instead of killing Gykoja, the young captain knelt before her and allowed himself to be killed by her. She in turn raised him as a lich and turned him against his own men. Angus was among a handful of the party who were able to escape and return. But he paid with his own arm. Angus swears that the human captain purposely sacrificed himself to the witch, but it is beyond belief that anyone would willingly become a lich. But Angus believes it, and sometimes he is not always fair to humans. And the loss of his arm may well have brought about the early stages of the wilding."

Dangalf knew of that condition from his studies. Aged and infirmed dwarves were often taken by the wilding. It was an ever-increasing belligerence and recklessness that helped insure that no dwarf lived beyond a respectable age. The dwarves had developed a culture in which their own immortality was viewed as unseemly. It was not believed that any dwarf could live a thousand years without finding an honorable time to die. Dangalf was reminded of something Weyd said as he discussed the life-extending benefits of slumber: "Immortality sounds like a good idea until it happens to you."

"Well, if you'll excuse me," said Donald rising. "I am due at Earc's wake."

"At this hour?" asked Dangalf.

"Well," said Donald. "I know humans like to send their honored dead out to sea, but we like our dead in the ground."

"I would like to go," said Dangalf.

"Good," said Donald. "The more the merrier. Three days we have at Earc's grave to make sure no witch sets his undead corpse upon us. And we don't want that, do we?"

"No," said Dangalf, sobering up quickly. He glanced at Ashlyn, who also seemed unnerved by the prospect.

"Are you going to finish that?" Nerdraaage asked Dangalf of the roast pork on his plate.

XLIII

Dangalf sat at Earc's gravesite with Donald. During the day, he was able to slumber a bit, but at night he remained cold and terrified by every unusual sound and dark movement. But nothing terrified him more than when Donald became alarmed and would reach for his weapon before eventually relaxing again.

Doppelganger, Ashlyn, Nerdraaage, and others came by, but only Dangalf and Donald were there for three days straight. Donald did it out of tradition for his fallen subordinate. Dangalf did it out of a sense of duty. Earc was dead because of him, and Dangalf felt an obligation to make sure Earc stayed dead. He felt this not so much because he feared zombie Earc would target him in particular, though that was a concern, but more because he wanted the fallen hero to rest in peace.

XLIV

Nerdraaage was nearing the completion of his training, and everyone was excited. Doppelganger and Dangalf continued to go out on patrols and other special assignments of varying interest for their per diem. At night they ate, drank, smoked, and played goat, a particularly dwarven card game with only one loser. It could get very expensive to be the goat, and it was a great irritation to Nerdraaage that, of the Keepers, Ashlyn was the best player of his race's game.

Doppelganger was walking past the front gate when he stopped at a commotion of dwarves. He watched as a dwarven patrol led a she-elf into the front gate. She was beautiful and glowing—literally glowing as if a beam of sun shined just upon her. But she also looked troubled and kept her gaze down. Donald was the first to make his way down to the delicate she-elf and, shockingly, bowed to her. She curtsied delicately in answer. She was stunning and also very sad. She brought up her head only once to make eye contact with Doppelganger as she passed him. Doppelganger's heart melted, and he feared that he must have looked very stupid as his mouth hung open in awe. He closed it, but it was too late. She had passed. The reeve of Hammersmith, who had not deigned to meet the Keepers, rushed out of his home to meet her, and they went inside. Of the crowd that surrounded her, only Donald was also permitted in. Doppelganger had to sit on the ground right where he had stood and relive the moment of her passing.

Doppelganger returned to the inn and began drinking more heavily than usual. He wanted to forget the she-elf who had left him breathless. No good could come from dwelling on her, but he knew dwell on her he would. Dangalf and Ashlyn joined him shortly, and he did not speak of the she-elf even though they could tell he was preoccupied.

Angus also joined them, and then Donald joined them. A crowd followed the captain and spread around the table as everyone was curious about their unexpected guest. Donald did not disappoint.

An elven princess had been ambushed by a troll assassin, he related. Her Templar bodyguard, outmatched by the blackguard, cast on the princess a shield of protection. It was a spell so powerful that it would protect her from all harm for three days and so powerful that it consumed the life of her Templar in the process. The troll tried all his assassin's tricks on her, but he could not harm her or even touch her, even when he spat at her in rage. Finally, he slew the royal unicorns and unappeared. Ashlyn gasped. She did not know why she knew it to be the gravest of crimes to kill a unicorn.

Donald told them that the princess then traveled by foot to the nearest allied town, Hammersmith, still protected by the Templar's spell. "That's why she was glowing!" Doppelganger said excitedly. "I saw her," he explained more quietly.

Nerdraaage joined them with a look of great self-satisfaction. "So you've all heard?" he said to the gathering.

"Heard what?" asked Dangalf.

"You are now looking at the Alliance's newest mercenary," he announced. There were congratulations all around, and a kilderkin of beer was placed heavily on the table. Like the third-class warrior, the third-class blackguard was called a mercenary.

Nerdraaage spread out his commission scroll on the table. He noticed with embarrassment that the commission was for Nerdraaage of Clan Stonefist even though he was not a member.

"I uh, well, I uh, uh," Nerdraaage explained to Angus.

"We have to make that document official," responded Angus. "We'll have the joining ceremony tomorrow!" And there were more cheers and congratulations.

"So you can unappear?" asked Dangalf after congratulations were done.

"Of course," answered Nerdraaage.

"This I've got to see," said Ashlyn.

"Oh all right," said Nerdraaage.

Nerdraaage stood perfectly still like a model in the dwarven version of the JCPenney catalog.

Ashlyn was the first one to burst out laughing. Nerdraaage remained perfectly motionless and completely visible. Finally, even Doppelganger and Dangalf could not contain themselves and laughed. "This is the funniest thing I've ever seen," said Doppelganger.

"Dude," laughed Dangalf. "We can still see you."

"Give the lad a chance," interjected Angus.

Still Nerdraaage did not move and remained completely visible. Suddenly he faded ever so slightly, and the crowd let out a spontaneous "Oooh!" He faded a little more until he was translucent. He broke his pose and returned to full opaqueness.

"Pretty cool, huh?" he asked excitedly.

"We could still see you," said Ashlyn.

"Here, in a bright inn," said Nerdraaage. "But at night or in the woods, you won't see me."

"But aren't you supposed to be able to unappear completely even in a bright room?" asked Dangalf.

"Look," said Nerdraaage. "The important thing is I am commissioned now. I'm going to get better with practice."

"When it is required, he will unappear completely," said Icil as he suddenly became fully appeared behind Ashlyn. She jerked when he put his gloved hands on her bare shoulders. "Or I would not have sponsored him." The entire inn was momentarily stunned by the sudden appearance of the black-clad human assassin. Even his face was masked.

"How are you tonight, my lovely she-elf," Icil asked as he leaned over her shoulder.

"Fine," she managed. She grabbed Dangalf's hand for support.

Angus stood on the bench with his fist on his hip reproachfully. "All this time just outside our gate and only now you enter our inn," announced Angus. "Do you find the company of dwarves distasteful?" The rest of the inn watched anxiously.

"What makes you think I have not before entered your inn?" asked the assassin.

"Let me rephrase that for one who sneaks about unseen," said Angus. "Why have you waited so long to show your face in our inn?"

Icil slowly removed his leather headgear, exposing his scarred face and deformed ears. "Mine is not a face that begs to be shown."

Angus thought for a moment and burst out laughing. The crowd exhaled and laughed with him. "And they won't soon be stamping any coins with my face either!" shouted Angus. "Will you drink beer with us, blackguard master, or do I need to buy you wine?"

"I will drink the finest drink in the land," said Icil. "Dwarven beer." The crowd cheered at the black-clad human.

"Then sit, my friend, and drink with us," said Angus. And Angus and Donald and the other dwarves pounded their fists respectfully on Icil's chest as they introduced themselves or were introduced.

Ashlyn turned quickly to Dangalf. "Please don't leave me," she whispered. "He really scares me."

"He really scares you?" quoted Dangalf. "Is that code for he turns you on?"

"No. It's code for he really scares me."

"I will get a chair," said Icil.

"There's plenty of room," insisted Nerdraaage. He slid over to leave a spot on the bench between himself and Ashlyn. She glared at him, but he didn't understand.

"Put your arm around me," she whispered to Dangalf.

"I don't know. I don't want to piss him off." She grabbed Dangalf's arm and put it around her shoulder as Icil sat next to her. Dangalf did a terrible job of looking nonchalant.

Various dwarves took to the Odeon stage and played music and sang. Angus went from table to table and even left the inn periodically while he made arrangements for the joining ceremony.

Doppelganger asked if Icil had heard about the attack on the princess. Icil had more than heard about it. He had just returned from the scene of the attack, and only footprints remained.

"I thought assassins didn't leave footprints," said Doppelganger.

"They leave footprints only for other assassins."

"Do you know his work?" asked Donald.

"It was not a he," said Icil.

"A female assassin?"

"Assassins."

"Two!"

"Two she-trolls," said Icil. "That is why the princess's Templar did not stand a chance. Two sisters that strike as one. Some believe that they are twins, so connected are they. They kill in such perfect unison that they are able to step in each other's footprints so as to leave only one almost imperceptible set of tracks. Only a handful of rangers could have spotted the deception. It was only luck that I spotted it myself. One blade of grass folded on top of the first sister's print by the second sister."

"You know them?"

"They are deadly adversaries, but they do not serve the Legion directly. They are in private service."

"Whose service are they in?"

"The Necromancer Princess Gykoja."

"Gykoja!" said Angus, slamming his one remaining fist on the table.

"I am aware that you have suffered a loss due to this witch. I as well. There are many families scarred by her evil. I came here to make plans to take her head and those of her minions. But now that they are unicorn killers, these she-trolls have turned an hourglass on their own lives."

"They tried to kill a princess," said Doppelganger. "You're saying that the greater crime was killing her unicorn?"

"There is no shortage of she-elf princesses," said Icil. "But once killed no unicorn is ever replaced. The mystery is why such a talented pair would target such a lowly elven princess."

"Maybe they were after the unicorn," said Ashlyn.

"They did steal its horn and its blood," said Icil. "But they also could have killed a wild unicorn for those. If I were to question the princess, I would ask her why she was so far from home." He looked to Donald.

"Dwarven law holds that no foreign king is above even the most common dwarf," said Donald. "But in practice there is great respect for elven royal blood."

"But you're of the king's blood yourself!" insisted Angus.

"Aye, but I am no prince. It is not my place to question a bona fide princess."

"Too bad that princess didn't have you with her instead of a Templar!" said Nerdraaage.

"No," said Icil. "I could have killed them both, I believe, but not before they killed the princess. That is why the royals use only Templars for bodyguards. Her Templar saved her life where no other could. Let us drink to this unnamed hero!" And they all raised their cups in salute.

"And to Earc," announced Dangalf, and all raised their cups again.

Icil finished his cup, wiped the foam from his face, and turned back to Ashlyn. "I think you will make an excellent druid," said Icil. "I can just imagine you with a big, fluffy tail."

"What about Nerdraaage's training?" she said, changing the subject. "Doesn't he need to know unappear better?"

"Some can unappear easily and completely at the mercenary level," said Icil. "They may have better stealth skills than Nerdraaage, but he has better blade skills than most. He will unappear when he has to."

Nerdraaage punctuated Icil's remarks by punching his dagger into the table. "Blade skills for the win!" he shouted.

"I would obliterate that dwarven rune from the pommel," said Icil.

"And why is that?" challenged Angus.

"It is additional information for the enemy should he drop his blade."

"And why would he drop it?"

"Because sometimes there is a lot of killing to do," said Icil. "And blood is slippery. And even the strongest hand can leave a blade behind. But I suppose it doesn't really matter. In time, when he has proved himself, the trolls will open a book on him."

"A book?" asked Nerdraaage.

"Just as our sages open books on our infamous enemies, so the trolls will open one on you. And then all their Legion will vie to be the one to close that book." No one needed it explained what was meant by having your book closed. "And when your trail of dead is grand enough, then they will even put a bounty on your head."

"Do you have a bounty on your head?" asked Nerdraaage.

"We have heard there is a one-thousand-sovereign bounty on your head," said Donald.

"I have heard that too," said Icil with a smile.

"A king's ransom," said Angus.

In time the conversation turned lighter. Icil unrelentingly and unsuccessfully hit on Ashlyn for almost an hour before he announced that he was leaving Hammersmith. The gathering hushed with concern, especially the dwarves just introduced to their mysterious human neighbor. He explained he must leave to further his vendetta against Gykoja, and that returned good cheer to the dwarves. What Icil did not tell them was that he had also taken the blood of the unicorn. To defile even a dead unicorn was on dubious legal and moral grounds, even when committed by one on so noble a quest. Nerdraaage interrupted the well-wishers to ask if he couldn't stay for his joining ceremony in the morning.

Icil seemed somewhat taken aback by the invitation. "You never told me," said Icil.

"Oh, sorry," said Nerdraaage. "We just decided today."

"I will of course be there." Icil said goodnight to the dwarves and the Keepers. Nerdraaage, who, even stoned, stood in respect as they bid good night to the master blackguard.

Finally Icil took Ashlyn's hand and kissed it. "Forgive my coarseness," he whispered. "It was only during the course of our conversation tonight that I realized you had not before lain with a man." Ashlyn looked wide-eyed at him. "I hope that we meet again when you are not such an innocent." He smiled and walked out of the inn. He waited until he was out the door before he unappeared. Ashlyn did not know how his words had made her feel, only that it was a very strong feeling.

XLV

The next morning the Keepers awoke early. They ate and discussed their plans. It was thought unlikely that the joining ceremony would be without a feast, and that meant they would need to stay one more day before they could head off for Templa Taur. One more day of drunken excess and room charges. But they all knew it was important for Nerdraaage to join a clan, especially now that it was embossed on his commission.

Doppelganger, Dangalf, and Ashlyn shopped, and due to the excitement of Nerdraaage's commissioning and clan joining, they overspent on gifts. They bought a buckskin jacket and pants for Nerdraaage to wear over his blacks and his own bow and quiver. He had told them how blackguards often played the part of hunters to avoid unwanted attention.

Benches had been set up in front of the reeve's office carved into the mountainside. With about thirty minutes to go before the ceremony, the seats were filling quickly, but the Keepers were ushered to seats of honor in the front row of the right bank of benches.

Ashlyn was careful to sit between Doppelganger and Dangalf so that Icil would not be directly next to her. Angus pulled Nerdraaage away from his friends to introduce him to the members of the clan that were able to arrive in time for the hastily arranged ceremony, including Angus the Elder, Angus the Red, Just Plain Angus, and Angus Junior (Angus the Young's father, first brother, first uncle, and first son, respectively), who with himself and his wife made up the six pillars of his family. Rhona said what a lovely day it was for a joining ceremony and sat behind the Keepers.

Doppelganger saw the glowing elf as she looked curiously on the proceedings from an upstairs window. His heart began to beat a little faster with the thought that she might come down to watch. He had the perfect excuse to talk to her as it was his friend who was the subject of the joining ceremony. Instead, she observed that Doppelganger was observing her and let the drapes fall shut. Doppelganger's heart sunk but at least he had the satisfaction of smiling at her which was a vast improvement over his previous interaction with her.

Dangalf's hat was taken in a gust of wind, and he pursued it. Donald greeted the Keepers and took a seat next to Rhona. Ashlyn thought Dangalf had returned and leaned into him to whisper and instead found that she had leaned into Icil. She recoiled.

"I didn't mean to scare you," said Icil. "But I saw an empty seat." He patted her bare knee and she jerked it away.

Ashlyn had felt the eyes of a hundred lusty males but none had dared touch her intimately. (Except for Dangalf, who had accidentally touched her breast one night and then turned beet red and apologized so profusely that she finally had to tell him to shut up.) Icil had her in a dither, and no one in the whole world (this or the other) had ever made her dither. Dangalf apologized silently to Ashlyn as he dusted off his hat and took a seat next to Icil.

The reeve appeared on the steps with a handsome leather tome, and Angus walked Nerdraaage over to him. "Congratulations, lad," said the reeve. "You're joining a fine clan."

"Thank you, Reeve," said Nerdraaage.

The musicians played a lively tune, and Nerdraaage looked back to his friends and smiled. He noticed a she-dwarf marching slowly toward the steps. She was gaily dressed, festooned even, and carried a firkin of beer under one arm and a gold-and-silver tankard with her free hand. "Who is that?" asked Nerdraaage.

"Your bride," said Angus. Nerdraaage doubted his ears. He looked back to his friends, who had also heard Angus. Ashlyn covered her mouth as she felt it would have been inappropriate to burst out laughing. Doppelganger and Dangalf were dumbstruck. They looked back and forth to each other and the encroaching bride. She was young, blond, and not unattractive.

"I thought this was a joining ceremony," said Nerdraaage.

"Aye," said Angus. "And what did you think we were going to join you to? A goat?"

Nerdraaage looked at his bride and Angus and the reeve and his friends and Icil and then back to Angus. "I thought I was joining the clan."

"What part of joining ceremony do you not understand?"

The bride reached the steps and smiled sweetly at Nerdraaage. He was too stunned to even smile back. The reeve began saying some sort of ancient and florid speech, but Nerdraaage didn't hear it. "Morna, do you find Nerdraaage fit for your clan, your family, and your hearth?" asked the reeve.

"Aye," said the bride.

Nerdraaage looked back to his friends for help, but they were none. That damned reeve was still blabbing about something. "And you, Nerdraaage, will you tap Morna's firkin?"

Angus held out a hammer and tap to Nerdraaage. He might as well have been holding a scorpion and a handful of warg shite.

None of it made sense to Nerdraaage, and he wasn't about to touch either one. "Nerdraaage?" said the reeve.

"Answer him, lad," said Angus. Nerdraaage looked at his bride and Angus and the reeve and his friends and Icil and back to his bride. He didn't know what to do. And then he did it. He unappeared.

The crowd went "ooh" and then all was quiet except for one low chuckle coming from the human assassin. He leaned into Ashlyn and whispered, "I told you he could unappear when he had to."

Angus walked over to Doppelganger and Dangalf. Dangalf squinted and leaned back as for some reason he thought Angus was going to slap him. "You're his seconds," said Angus. "Go get him."

Doppelganger and Dangalf rose and stood awkwardly, not sure how to proceed. Donald stood. "I'll go with you," he said.

Ashlyn tugged frantically on Dangalf's robes, but he pulled them away from her. "They'll find him," Icil reassured Ashlyn. "He hasn't learned *walk without footprints*." She smiled at his efforts to comfort her. "Well," he continued. "Looks like we have a joining ceremony and no couple. What will we do?" He patted her again on the knee, and she dithered a bit more.

XLVI

They found Nerdraaage in the best hiding place in Hammersmith: sitting behind the white library. As Donald and his friends approached, Nerdraaage looked tightly coiled, but he made no effort to spring. "I'm sorry," he said.

"Not to worry, lad," said Donald. "You just got a case of elf feet."

"I thought the joining ceremony was just to join the clan. I didn't know about the marriage."

"That's the problem when dwarves are reared outside the clan."

"I want to be an adventurer."

"She knows that."

"I just don't think I'm ready for marriage. I'm not that experienced with women. I mean she-dwarves."

"Neither was I my first time!"

"How many times have you been married?"

"All three times."

Dangalf thought that was an odd expression, and a second later he thought he had figured it out. "How many wives do you have?" he asked.

"Three," said Donald plainly. "Every dwarf must do his part. We don't breed like the humans do every nine months. Sometimes two or three like a sow." Of course, thought Dangalf. Three wives because the world itself sets upon three pillars!

"We wanted to leave tomorrow," said Nerdraaage.

"That's fine. Get married, get your tattoo, and tonight enjoy your wedding hearth. Tomorrow, you'll be on your way."

"Tattoo?" Nerdraaage brightened.

Donald rolled up his sleeve revealing the ornately inked names of his wives in three separate bands. "Come on, lad," said Donald. He said something in ancient Dwarvish, but then he repeated it in Acadish, "There comes a time when every dwarf must stop drinking beer from his boot." Dangalf started thinking that ancient dwarves couldn't describe a sunset without using beer. "There's something else that bears mentioning," said Donald. "The books for Stonefist are open now, but they won't always be. It is a fleeting opportunity for someone of unknown quality to be given a chance to have his name inscribed on such a fine roster."

"What do you guys think?" he asked of the humans.

"Well," said Dangalf. "There is a question of documents already sent to the lorekeepers identifying you as Clan Stonefist. Misrepresenting clan affiliation is a serious offense."

Nerdraaage pulled out his commission scroll to see if it had changed since he last looked at it. It read, "Nerdraaage" and below that, "Clan Stonefist." Still not convinced, Nerdraaage looked to Doppelganger for his wisdom.

"You could do worse," said Doppelganger with a shrug.

Nerdraaage, resigned, stood and faced Angus. "Do I send her coin when I'm gone?"

"She knows you don't have two farthing to rub together. She has her own house and garden. She's Clan Stonefist, and they take care of their own. Course, if you strike it rich during your adventuring, it wouldn't hurt to send some of it her way."

XLVII

Later that night, Nerdraaage crawled into his wife's bed and undressed under the covers. His smiled proudly at his new tattoo but his arm still hurt. Dwarven skin is thick, and the tattoo is inked very deep. Morna entered wearing a long, practical nightgown and got into the bed with him.

He found her very attractive in the firelight. She was more squat than females he had been attracted to previously, but his own squatness and his drunkenness made her more appealing.

They lay separately for a moment until she leaned over and kissed him. He leaned toward her, and she laid back. He climbed on top of her, and she pulled up her nightgown. She exhaled on him, and he found the beer smell and the softness of her flesh to be arousing. Things progressed quite naturally, and he found her hearth warm and pleasing. And Nerdraaage, who was a virgin in the other universe, lost his cherry to a she-dwarf.

XLVIII

Before first light the next day, Nerdraaage's friends waited for him outside his wife's cottage. They had been in Hammersmith, as Ashlyn had calculated it, "forever," and all were eager to get on the road.

"Goodbye, wife," said Nerdraaage as he headed out her front door and down her rope ladder. Walking away, he turned nervously to Doppelganger. "I've forgotten her name!"

"Isn't it tattooed on your arm?"

Nerdraaage slapped his big friend on the back, "We dwarves know what we're doing!"

Farewells were said at the gate to Angus, Rhona, Donald, and other acquaintances that they had met during their weeks in Hammersmith. Doppelganger looked back to the reeve's office for one last look at the princess, but it was not to be.

Angus told Nerdraaage to send him a bird on occasion, and Rhona tied a scarf of Stonefist tartan around his neck. "You probably won't wear this when you're out murdering and such, but you can wear it at other times," she said. The other Keepers had observed that he had also been given many gifts of coin after his joining service, but they did not know how much, and he had not told them.

The Keepers were loaded down with food and beer, but they knew for the long journey to Templa Taur, that they would probably have to hunt and gather their own food as well. They could conceivably carry enough food if they didn't bring beer, but that wasn't going to happen. And so they departed.

They passed the unmarked spot in the woods that led to Icil's abode, and they all turned respectfully even though they knew it to be abandoned.

"Your reading came true," Ashlyn suddenly said to Dangalf.

"About what?" he asked.

"The death card for Nerdraaage," she answered. Nerdraaage also listened at the sound of his name. "You told Nerdraaage that the death card signified change. And now he's married."

"That's right!" said Dangalf triumphantly.

"Maybe it would have been better just to die," said Doppelganger.

They had only walked a few hours when a pigeon fluttered down to Ashlyn and gave up its message. It bore the seal of the Reeve of Hammersmith and implored them to come back immediately on a matter of "Alliance security."

"Are you kidding me?" groaned Ashlyn. But they all realized they could not refuse.

XLIX

Donald came down the road with a patrol to intercept them and did so about an hour still outside of Hammersmith. They asked what was of such import, but he said it was better not to speak of such things in the open.

It was just past ten when they arrived at the town gate. Donald ushered them into the reeve's private office. Dangalf admired the reeve's library while the others sat in his overstuffed chairs. The reeve entered through another door and held it open with his back as the glowing elven princess entered. Those who were sitting knew to stand.

"Princess, these are the adventurers I spoke of," said the reeve.

Dangalf spontaneously bowed. Doppelganger and Nerdraaage followed with their own awkward bows. Ashlyn curtsied. "I'm sorry that I don't know their names. Except for this one I just joined yesterday," he said nodding at Nerdraaage. "What was your name again?"

"Nerdraaage."

"Yes, that's it. Nerdraaage and the rest of you, this is Princess Dymphna of the elven royal family. Fifteenth?" the reeve asked the princess.

"Eighteenth," she answered in a gentle, aristocratic voice.

"Eighteenth in line to the throne," continued the reeve's introduction.

Doppelganger noticed that she had made eye contact with each of the Keepers except for him. The princess and the reeve sat, and the Keepers followed suit. The reeve continued: "The princess was attacked in the western wood and was fortunate to make it here alive."

"Yeah, we heard," interrupted Nerdraaage excitedly. The reeve looked at him reproachfully. "Sir. I mean, sire. Master Reeve."

"And if you lot know about it, you can be sure the enemy knows about it too. The princess should have been out of here a day ago, but, pardon my human tongue, the princess is caught in a pissing contest."

The princess let slip the most delicate laughter that she quickly stifled. She looked down at her own lap with a wicked grin until she could compose herself. Doppelganger saw now that she was more than the stunning elven royalty he had admired from afar. If it was possible to fall in love with a woman, or in this case a she-elf, over something as trivial as stifled laughter at an indelicate comment, then he had just done so.

The reeve continued for the benefit of those who were not preoccupied with romantic daydreams: "The Legion or other wicked parties sent out two assassins to kill the princess. It was only through the heroic efforts of her Templar that she escaped. We are not concerned with why they wanted to kill her. We simply want to get her back to elven lands, where she'll be safe. A day ago a flight of dragoons was to arrive and transport her, but they were rerouted to the front at the last moment. Now we are looking at another day or longer before dragoons or elven guards will be able to arrive for her. But the princess does not want to wait another day, and honestly, I agree with her. We do not have the resources here to protect her. She has asked for escort immediately for the nearest elven town, Templa Taur. We became aware that you four also were embarked for that town. We, the princess and I, are agreed that the best defense is for her to leave immediately without fanfare and in the company of unassuming travelers. The Acadian Alliance of Righteous Races calls upon you to escort the princess and to lay down your lives if necessary in her defense."

Heroes, seekers, mercenaries, and adventurers! thought Dangalf. In the game this quest would be simple enough to accept and would offer great rewards. But here, in this real world, it posed great risks for their lowly group. Those two she-troll assassins could be unappeared just outside the gate for all they knew. They had already seen how effortlessly Icil had incapacitated the four of them. Two assassins with murderous intentions would kill them all in a few seconds, not to mention all the other threats they might face on unfamiliar roads with such a high-profile companion. They would have to consider this quest with great deliberation and accept it only with the informed and willing consent of all the Keepers.

Doppelganger stood up. "We accept," he said. The princess now made eye contact with him and nodded slightly.

L

The reeve and Donald walked the princess and the Keepers to the front gate. "An escort quest," said Nerdraaage. "This will be great for our reputations. Especially with the elves!"

"If we don't get killed," said Ashlyn.

"I am sorry that I can not spare any guards," said Donald. "We are at half strength as it is. But we leave you in very good hands, I believe."

"You have provided accommodation far above any obligation you had to me," said the princess. "Your deeds will be known to my family."

"Thank you, Your Highness," said Donald.

Doppelganger was smitten. It just seemed like she said everything right. He guessed that was the advantage of growing up in a royal family where you were schooled in the social graces from an early age. For the first time in this world, he was ashamed of his lowly status. If he were a dragoon, then she might look at him differently. The master classes were highly respected, the closest a commoner could come to being royalty.

A young she-dwarf from the stables brought over a pony. "There is only one pony in the stables, but you are welcome to it," said the reeve.

"How are we all supposed to ride on that?" exclaimed Nerdraaage.

"It's for the princess," said the reeve, scowling.

"I do not see the advantage of riding when my party travels by foot," she answered.

"It affords opportunity for escape, Your Highness!" answered the reeve.

"Your kindness is appreciated, but I will not leave these brave four to die in my place," she said. And then, smiling, to Ashlyn she said, "We walk together. My sister and her companions." There were a few more words of farewell, and the princess and the Keepers departed the front gates.

"I never liked escort quests," Nerdraaage said softly to Dangalf. "I never escorted an NPC that didn't want to walk right through the enemy camp."

"She has free will," said Dangalf. "Hopefully she'll go around the enemy camps."

"There are no enemy camps on the road to Templa Taur," said Dymphna reminding them all of how well elves could hear. "Only wild beasts and highwaymen and perhaps assassins." There was an embarrassed silence. "May I know your names?" she said.

Doppelganger almost blurted out his name—he wanted to, but then he thought better of it. He would not answer until she looked at him and addressed him directly. Then he would know if she had even a hint of interest in him. Only to her direct question and pleading eyes would he give up his name. Yes, it was a good plan.

"I'm Nerdraaage, and this is Doppelganger," said Nerdraaage. "Dangalf and Elftrap," he said, pointing to the others.

"Actually it's Ashlyn, Your Highness."

"Ashlyn," said the princess. To the others she explained: "If you did not know, it means 'dream' in our tongue. I used to wish that it was my name."

"What does your name mean, princess?" asked Nerdraaage.

"It has no such literal meaning. I was named for an elven princess who was flayed alive by a troll king."

"Well," said Nerdraaage confidently. "That probably won't happen to you with us here."

Dymphna again stifled a laugh as she had in the reeve's office. "You are very encouraging, Nerdraaage," said the Princess. "All of you please address me as Dymphna. At least while we are between towns." They nodded agreement. "Do you have a birthday, Doppelganger?" she asked.

"Of course," he answered. "Don't you have a birthday?"

"I suppose I do. But for elves they pass without notice. I am fascinated by the fanfare on the anniversary of a human birth. Such bravery in the face of your mortality."

"For us," said Dangalf. "It's more a celebration of life and not mortality."

"I don't see how you could separate one from the other," said Dymphna.

"I probably won't be able to after this," said Dangalf.

"When I was young, I asked my tutor why some humans had so much ambition. And he said it was because they lived such short lives. And then I asked him why so many more humans had no ambition at all. And he said it was because they lived such short lives."

"Sounds like your tutor needs to make up his mind," scoffed Nerdraaage.

Dymphna laughed. "That was not his only shortcoming. For he failed to tell me just how funny dwarves are!"

"I had not considered how these differences in lifespan are another chasm between our races," said Dangalf. "Between mortal and immortal."

"I never liked the word immortal. Elves are quite mortal. Some use the term immortal, but indefinite I believe is more suitable. I would be felled by an axe as quickly as a human. Probably much more so. But there is otherwise no limit on the span of our lives. But even human wizards learn to magically extend their lives."

"You're learning to be immortal?" Doppelganger asked Dangalf.

"Well, like the princess said," Dangalf explained. "More indefinite than immortal."

"You are all from far away," said Dymphna.

"How did you know that?" asked Doppelganger.

"I am a seer," she said.

"A seer," whispered Nerdraaage to Ashlyn. "A pacifist. She's going to be no help in a fight." Ashlyn shushed him.

"You are from no land that I have beheld," said Dymphna. "Not even on a map or in a dream. Beyond Oceania even."

"Yes," said Dangalf. "You see very well."

"It is my calling," said Dymphna. "My family is quite displeased that I do not heed it."

"Why don't you?" asked Dangalf.

"Because you see not only the good but the bad. I remember when I was little I had such a clear vision as if I was awake. And my room was full of butterflies. That was my father's name for me. Butterfly. And then my ancestor Dymphna came to me. And I saw what had been done to her, how the trolls had made her into a butterfly. She had come to warn me about something, but I would not listen to her. It was too terrible even to look upon her. I swore it to be true, but no guards saw anyone come or go. And I showed them all the blood in my room, but they said it was my own. I never took another lesson after that. I knew I could not bear to see some things." And three of the Keepers found this to be a very odd story, but Doppelganger became only more smitten.

LI

In time, Ashlyn was able to slow her pace so that Dymphna and Doppelganger were out of earshot. Dangalf and Nerdraaage lagged with her. "It would be a lot easier to protect her from the enemy if she wasn't glowing in the dark," said Ashlyn.

Dangalf and Nerdraaage chuckled. "That invincibility spell should wear off soon," said Dangalf. "Such a powerful spell," he marveled. "Too bad it kills you to use it." Death spells. He would learn some in time, though he dreaded the knowledge—dreaded the circumstances where he would have to consider using one.

"She's so pretty," said Ashlyn. "I wish I looked like that."

"You're beautiful," protested Dangalf. "Stunning even." Neither noticed Nerdraaage rolling his eyes as he decided to start lagging behind Dangalf and Ashlyn.

"Really?"

"You're much better looking than her," said Dangalf. "She's a wispy blonde. You're like Snow White."

"Snow White?" said Ashlyn.

"With your dark hair, your red lips, your alabaster skin," said Dangalf, finally allowing himself to speak aloud what he had only thought. "I've never seen a more beautiful creature in this or any other universe I've been in."

Ashlyn smiled briefly. "She is such an obvious princess, though. She's so delicate. She's fine boned," said Ashlyn.

"Fine boned!" said Nerdraaage with a chuckle.

"She's a seer," said Dangalf reassuringly. "A pure ectomorph. You're a druid. A hybrid class. Of course you're going to be thicker. Have a little more padding."

Ashlyn folded her arms across her chest and sped up her pace to leave Dangalf behind. "What?" asked Dangalf as Nerdraaage howled with laughter.

Doppelganger and Dymphna remained oblivious to the antics behind them. There was obviously a great deal of attraction between them, but for now it was light and fun. "I heard the dwarf talk about escorting me back to my homeland," said Dymphna. "What does ka-ching mean?"

"It means our blackguard has not learned the basic stealth technique of whispering," said Doppelganger.

"You do not want to tell me? It must be very bad."

"Ka-ching refers to a financially rewarding endeavor."

"The dwarves make me laugh," she said.

"I thought dwarves and elves were rivals?"

"That is mostly jealousy on the dwarven side. According to lore, the elves are the most beloved of Woden."

"The elves are the most beloved?"

"Well," said Dymphna smiling. "It is elven lore." She was so beautiful and refined. Doppelganger had to pick among a thousand different questions he wanted to ask her. He picked the one that seemed most pressing. "Why would two assassins be sent after you?" asked Doppelganger.

"It makes no sense," said Dymphna. "They say self-divination is an illusion, but from what I have seen, I play no direct role in any major event."

"Indirectly?"

"It is possible," she agreed. "That I am a catalyst or vessel for something greater that me. But that will be harder to divine."

"I wish we had waited for the dragoons," said Doppelganger. "I think it would have been safer to try to defend you within the walls of Hammersmith."

"I sensed it was the right time to leave," said Dymphna. "Are you not enjoying our time together?"

"Of course. But I won't be able to forgive myself if anything happens to you."

"Well," said Dymphna. "If it makes you feel any better, if anything does happen to me, I think it will happen to you also."

"Doesn't make me feel a lot better," said Doppelganger, and they both laughed. "At least you still have your protection. What does it feel like?" he said looking over her glowing magical shield.

"It is not unlike…" Dymphna struggled to explain. "Do you remember, when you were a child, and you ran as fast as you could, and you were able to run across the top of a lake or river?"

"No," said Doppelganger. "That's called drowning when human children do it. Unless the water is frozen. And that often leads to drowning as well."

"I'm sorry," she laughed. "I have become too heavy also to run across water. But you must tell me what this force feels like from the other side." She held out her robe to him.

"I did not think I was allowed to touch an elven princess," said Doppelganger.

"A human mercenary?" said Dymphna in mock horror. "You most certainly are not allowed! But the spell will prevent you from actually touching me."

"If I'm not going to touch you," said Doppelganger. "I might as well not touch your face."

She smiled at him and lowered her eyes as he reached his hand up to her face. The fine hairs on his hand stood up as it neared her protective aura. Suddenly the protection spell ended, and he touched the royal face.

Dymphna's eyes widened in shock, but she did not pull away. Instead she put her hand over his hand. But it was not an affectionate gesture. In fact, she looked right through him.

"He's not supposed to touch her," whispered Dangalf.

"Shite," said Nerdraaage. "Looks like we better get ready for another wedding."

Dymphna grew silent when she released from Doppelganger and began walking at a more determined pace. Doppelganger asked her what had happened. She begged for peace so that she could interpret the vision.

LII

They passed the last farmhouse and the presumptive safety of the greater Hammersmith area. Nerdraaage said he would "walk point" after a term he heard in a war movie. He marched ahead of the others, unappeared and visible to only the most sensitive creatures. He was to give a birdcall if any threat approached.

They had walked far, further then their travel plan had provided for, and it was dark. They were not tired, but finally it was hunger that made them stop. Dymphna led them to a fresh-water spring that was far enough from the road to allow them to build a small fire.

They sat and ate. Doppelganger and Nerdraaage did their customary amount of damage to the food supplies. "We made good time," said Doppelganger.

"At this rate, we will be in Templa Taur in three more days," agreed Dymphna.

Ashlyn took a large bite of bread and was chewing it when Dymphna sat next to her and smiled. She saw that all Dymphna ate was a leaf, and it took her three bites to eat that! Ashlyn prayed that the princess would not make her speak with her mouth stuffed with bread. She chewed as quickly and quietly as she could. She was disgusted with herself for her indelicacy. She was a she-elf after all. But she had been dining only with dwarves and human males.

They drank and laughed easily. Dangalf and Nerdraaage lit up their pipes. Dangalf took a hit and handed his pipe to Ashlyn, who waved him off. Nerdraaage stood up and half-stumbled the short distance to Dymphna and handed her his pipe.

"We do not smoke," said Ashlyn reproachfully.

Dymphna held the pipe excitedly. "I will try it if you will, sister," she said. Ashlyn held her hand out to Dangalf, and he turned his pipe over to her.

The two she-elves looked at each other and placed the pipes in their mouths. Dymphna inhaled. Ashlyn closed her eyes and inhaled. Her pipe crackled from the cold air being drawn over the burning leaf. Dymphna let out a tiny puff of smoke. Ashlyn held her smoke a long time before exhaling it luxuriously.

"You're very good!" cheered Dymphna.

"Thank you," said Ashlyn without opening her eyes.

Dymphna offered the pipe to Doppelganger. "No thank you," he smiled.

"May I go again?" Dymphna asked Nerdraaage.

"I should have brought another pipe," said Nerdraaage as he sat down heavily next to her.

They continued to smoke and drink and laugh. They even convinced Nerdraaage to sing a dwarven song without having to ask him:

In the shadow of
Our ancient redoubt
They paid the price

Of great renown
The Battle of Nemetia
The Battle of Nemetia

He sang of the eighteen thousand dwarves who died in just three days during their unsuccessful defense of Nemetia, but it was still a peppy little number and did not sour anyone's mood. "Who would have thought the company of humans and dwarves to be so pleasant?" said Dymphna. "Nerdraaage, you made the funniest face this morning."

"I did?"

"It's the only face he has," exhaled Ashlyn.

Dymphna did her best to relate the story through her laughter. "You asked how all five of us would ride one pony, and the reeve told you that the pony was for me alone, and you looked at him as if to say, 'Who is she to ride while I walk?' It was all I could do not to cry out with laughter. I cannot wait to tell my family."

"Well, we believe that dwarven royalty is no better than a common elf," Nerdraaage said proudly.

"You said that backward," said Dangalf.

"What?"

"Never mind." And they all laughed.

Dymphna eyed Ashlyn's technique in amazement. "You have smoked before," she finally said.

"You are a seer!" said Ashlyn, and they all laughed.

"You strangers have no idea how unusual you are in this land," said Dymphna.

"What do you mean?" asked Doppelganger.

"Elf with dwarf with human," said Dymphna. "Red School with White School. It is unprecedented. You ignore the natural antagonisms that exist between your races and classes as if they weren't there. Is this how things are where you come from? Elf, dwarf, and human living in harmony?"

"Not exactly," said Dangalf.

"We're the Keepers of the Broken Blade!" shouted Nerdraaage.

They hadn't really considered how unusual they were in this land. But it was true that they had not seen other mixed groups. After all, theirs was a bond formed in a digital world where they played divergent characters but they were all human. The class and race differences in the game were superficial. But here, races and classes had vastly different experiences and ambitions.

And now here they were, running all over the land together as each got his training while the others idled. Those who were already trained were coming to the realization that this was an inefficient imposition.

Dymphna raised her cup before them and, slurring slightly, said, "By royal proclamation it is called for that the Keepers of the Broken Blade endure forever." They all touched cups joyfully, but Dangalf couldn't help but feel a certain melancholy. He had not before considered that the Keepers might not endure forever.

LIII

They continued on to Templa Taur at first light the next day. They walked in the formation they had ended in last night: Nerdraaage on point, Doppelganger and Dymphna in the middle, and Dangalf and Ashlyn bringing up the rear. Dangalf and Ashlyn spoke easily again as Ashlyn had realized how she had overreacted to Dangalf's innocent and accurate body-type comparison. She had to, but hated to, admit her reaction was entirely female.

Suddenly Dymphna ran ahead of Doppelganger, and like an excited child she clasped a spinning feather as it drifted to earth. She took it to Ashlyn and asked, "May I?" And Ashlyn consented, but to what she was not sure. Dymphna wove the beautiful silver feather into Ashlyn's hair. To the others she explained, "The feather is a sacred symbol to our people. It is said you cannot move on to the next world if your soul is heavier than a feather."

They reached the crossroads for their third time in this world. Each time they were a little better off than the last. Dangalf had introduced the Triangle of Achievement on their arrival as a model for their survival in this new world. The first step, Preservation, and the second step, Comfort, were achieved. They were now decently clothed and they had weapons and skills and coin for food and lodgings. They had started with nothing, and that is the hardest place to start from. And the first improvements to their situation had come slowly. He smiled as he remembered an anecdote about Nerdraaage when he had been first paid for his work at the stables. He excitedly went to the tanner and bought a dwarven coin purse and after buying it realized he no longer had any coins to put into it. But now they had gold coins rubbing against their silver and copper. If they were to lose all their coin tomorrow, they could build fires and hunt. And they had skills to earn more coin. They were now well into the third step of the Triangle, Bonding. They had had an advantage in that step by coming to this world together, and they had made further improvements. Doppelganger, Dangalf, and Nerdraaage were all members of their particular schools. Nerdraaage had just married into one of the best clans. But even before then, when they had nothing and smelled of shite, they had worked hard and dealt honorably with the people they had met, and friendships had arisen in each town they visited. And now to top it all off, they were escorting—more than escorting, becoming simpatico with—an elven princess. If anything, they had overshot Bonding and leapt headfirst into the fourth step, Recognition!

Doppelganger was amazed to discover it was still thrilling to talk to Dymphna and believed that her give and take in the conversation was evidence of her own fascination. When he saw a flower by the side of the road, he spontaneously picked it and handed it to her. She thanked him and promptly ate it. Doppelganger smiled and nodded as if he had intended for her to eat the flower all along.

Their final night in the woods, an omega wolf, nearly starved, attempted to snatch Dymphna while the others collected firewood. She was able to leap into a tree until Doppelganger ran back and slew the beast. Dymphna returned to earth and thanked Doppelganger. "Poor beast," she lamented. Doppelganger asked Dangalf to cast a cold spell on the wolf so as to preserve it for another day.

"I will carry it to Templa Taur," Doppelganger told Dymphna. "I know the elves detest wasteful killing."

Dymphna looked at Doppelganger wide eyed. "You are enigma to me," she said. "You act more elven than human. Let alone a human warrior, the class burdened with the heaviest souls." Dangalf smiled hopefully. It was as if Dymphna was helping Doppelganger reconnect to the sweet man he was in the other world.

LIV

They began their journey early next morning with Dymphna promising them that they would reach Templa Taur with enough daylight to see the full majesty of the Town in the Trees.

Doppelganger alone was not celebratory. He couldn't help worry that arriving at the elven village would mean his parting from Dymphna. How could it be any other way? He wanted to tell her that he loved her, but he couldn't. She clearly appreciated his company on this journey, but what interest would she have in him when she was safe and among her own people? He hoisted the cold wolf over his shoulder. Dymphna, as if she sensed his regret, took him by the hand, and they touched for the first time since he accidentally put his hand to her cheek. "It is truly a magical town," she said to him, and he was replenished by her smile. What a crime he had committed against himself to spend so much of his life not in love.

Doppelganger and Dymphna walked on and spoke of everything without ever an uncomfortable pause. There were pauses to be sure, but they were the comfortable kind. Dymphna held Doppelganger's hand without shame.

They crossed a small bridge and entered Albinia. No sign announced the border of the elven lands. None was needed. Where dwarven forest had not differed greatly from human forest, the elven forest was teeming with flora and fauna. The colors were myriad, and the variety of life was astounding: flowers of every shape and size, toadstools the size of shrubbery, and trees towering over them all. The only break in the woods was the road, and even that was as green as grass. Great butterflies and lumbering bees decorated the very air. Dangalf could feel the land was teeming with the protoplasm that powered druidic magic. The usually guarded Ashlyn was giddy and peeled off her boots. She and Dymphna ran into an open field of grass and flowers and rolled around like cats.

"It has been too long." Dymphna sighed contentedly in the grass.

"Longer than you can imagine," added Ashlyn.

The men were slightly embarrassed and a bit jealous as they watched the two immortals frolic like children. And they were mighty curious when the two she-elves looked back to them while whispering and then proceeded to blow dandelion spores into each other's faces. After a few minutes, the she-elves rejoined them, and they continued on to Templa Taur with a bounce in their step. And that bounce was not just because of the springy quality of the mossy road.

Nerdraaage, still on stealth point, alerted them to the approach of two mounted elves. But Dymphna could already see that they were a Templa Taur patrol. Nerdraaage pulled on a horse's tail to spook the rider and got a good swift kick in the belly for it. It was all he could do to remain unappeared with the wind knocked out of him.

Before the patrol could locate the source of the invisible wheezing, they recognized the princess's approach and rode to her. The two riders dismounted and bowed. The guards were anxious to speak to her but waited until she spoke first.

"Would one of you guards take the wolf from this brave human?" she said.

"Yes, Your Highness," said the first guard.

"He has made a long journey," she continued. "Make sure he receives a proper ceremony and that his pelt goes to the tanner. I want him to make a suitable garment for our ragamuffin sister," she continued. Ashlyn cast an embarrassed glance down at her wardrobe. The guard laid the carcass across his steed.

"Your Highness, would you take my mount?" asked the other guard.

"You would deny me my boast that I walked from Hammersmith to Templa Taur when I am this close?" said Dymphna. "I will walk with my friends." One of the guards sent a quick message by bird, and then they both fell behind the others, walking beside their mounts, as the journey to Templa Taur continued.

Dymphna took Doppelganger's hand again. She did so without gentleness, as if she was entitled to grasp his hand as she pleased, with the presumption of a girlfriend or wife. Doppelganger did not mind. "We are so close now that I want to tell you something," she said smiling. "Something I have known for some time."

"Go on."

"Do you remember the moment we first saw each other?" she asked.

"Yes," said Doppelganger.

"When was it?" she asked as if she didn't believe him.

"At the front gate of Hammersmith. You were beautiful but so sad. I didn't know what to do."

"I remember too," she said. "I was heartbroken. Another had given his life to preserve me, and I don't know that I deserved it. And I looked over to you because you towered over the dwarves."

"So did you."

"But you much more so. And in that darkest hour I saw you. And more, I saw your brilliant aura, and I had a vision. And what I saw was that while I was with you, no harm would come to me."

"You knew that before we even left? You might have told us sooner."

"I pursued my studies long enough to know the first rule of prophecy," she answered. "If you want a vision to come true, tell no one. We made it safely because you all took the steps necessary to make it so."

"And your other vision?" asked Doppelganger. "When I touched your cheek?"

"Second rule," she said. "Refrain from sharing visions until you understand yourself what is seen. But I will say this: I see a time when we are parted. And during that time, look for me close to your heart."

"What does that mean?"

"That is all I can say for now." His mind was not sharp, not like he knew it used to be, but he repeated her words, hoping to remember them: *I see a time when we are parted. And during that time look for me close to your heart.*

And they reached a clearing. "Templa Taur," announced Dymphna to the group. She watched the faces of her new friends instead of looking at the town itself. Their amazement did not disappoint her.

The town of Templa Taur existed entirely in the giant trees before them. All the buildings, homes, merchants, and the inn were built as magnificent tree houses. Large branches served as walkways between buildings. Many were wide and sturdy enough to support horses and carts. Where branches were lacking, rope bridges and ladders made the connections between buildings and neighboring trees.

At the top of the trees great canopies collected water. They saw elves entering the town in large baskets pulled up from the ground.

"It's like the buildings grow from the trees themselves," said Ashlyn.

"Amazing," said Dangalf. "Is this an engineering feat or elven magic?"

"A little of both," said Dymphna. "The tree is consulted during each phase of construction so as not to burden it."

"The tree is consulted!" repeated Nerdraaage injecting the first tone of cynicism in the moment.

"Come, Nerdraaage," said Dymphna smiling. "Let me repay dwarven hospitality with elven."

The eyes of the elven guards observed the royal approach, and the reeve and other civilians and guards were lowered to the ground just as Dymphna and her escorts reached the basket. The reeve and the other greeters bowed.

"Thank you for greeting us, Master Reeve," said Dymphna. "If you would be so kind, we have had a long journey and wish to forgo any ceremony."

"Your Highness," said the reeve.

"Is the scrivener here?"

"Yes, Your Highness," said the reeve as the scrivener stepped forward and bowed.

"The elves have new allies who have paid a great service to the royal body," she said. "Doppelganger and Dangalf of Hempshire and Nerdraaage of Clan Stonefist are honored friends." The scrivener wrote furiously. "And our sister Ashlyn is also to be honored for her service. She is here for training, and I want that to be charged to me. All of their expenses while here shall be charged to my house."

"Yes, ma'am," said the reeve.

"Free room service," whispered Nerdraaage to Dangalf, who waved him quiet.

They entered the basket and were lifted up into Templa Taur. It was smooth like an elevator but slower. The town bustled similar to Hempshire and Hammersmith, only this one was about thirty-six feet in the air.

"Guard," said Dymphna. "Please take Ashlyn to Ciar."

"Yes, ma'am," said the guard.

"She is our druid trainer," Dymphna explained to Ashlyn. The guard bowed to Ashlyn before leading her off. Ashlyn followed and spun around quickly to smile anxiously at her friends.

"Are the royal quarters vacant?" asked Dymphna.

"Yes, ma'am," said the reeve. "They are being readied for you now. And a dispatch has been sent to the royal family advising them of your safe arrival."

"Very good," she answered. "Would you see to the quartering of our guests? I will find my own way to the royal house."

"Yes, ma'am," answered the reeve as he bowed. He then pointed the way for the Keepers with a flourish of his hand.

Well this is it, thought Doppelganger. It was fun while it lasted, but the princess was back in her own element and had already palmed them off on the reeve. He smiled politely at her as he fell in line behind Dangalf.

Dymphna stopped his progress by holding onto the back of his shirt. He stopped and turned to her, but Dymphna did not smile or even look at him. Dangalf and Nerdraaage turned from following the reeve.

"I'll catch up with you later," said Doppelganger.

"Oh," said Dangalf walking backward. "I see how it is."

"Should we wait up for you?" asked Nerdraaage mouth agape and tongue hanging out. Doppelganger dismissed them with a wave of the back of his hand.

"May I steal you from your friends for a time?" Dymphna asked.

"As long as you like," said Doppelganger.

She watched until the reeve was out of sight and then smiled again at Doppelganger. She took his hand and led him quickly away. "He has notified my family!" she said back to him. "We haven't much time." Doppelganger's heart raced with excitement. What did they not have much time for? She led him to a private branch that led to another tree and the most private and ornate residence in town. The guard stations along the way were as yet unmanned. She pulled him inside with her where they found a young she-elf who stopped her cleaning and curtsied nervously.

"Is there only you here?" asked Dymphna.

"Yes, Your Highness," said the she-elf.

"Thank you. Your services are not required further today."

"Yes, ma'am," said the she-elf and she curtsied and exited.

Pulled along in Dymphna's rush, Doppelganger only got a glimpse of the house as she took him upstairs. It was well appointed but almost cartoonish in how high and narrow it was.

Dymphna took them up two flights of stairs to one of the bedrooms. She released his hand as she entered and sat alone on the bed breathlessly. This is it, thought Doppelganger. It's yours to lose now.

He removed his weapons, his shield, and his mail and set them on the floor in the corner. He sat next to her on the bed. She sat stiffly, giving no hint of her disposition but for the increasing redness of her cheeks. "You blush like a human," he said. She touched the warmth on her own face and realized her visage had signaled her increasing warmth in more intimate places. "I'm sorry if I embarrassed you. But it only makes you more beautiful."

"You have caused me to cast away a lifetime of training and protocol," she said. "But you have struck a chord in my heart that

I have had since I was in school and first saw an aspect of a human. I think you are one of those humans with great ambition."

"Right now I only have one."

Lowering her gaze she continued, "I remember wondering what it would be like to kiss one of these strange, hairy creatures. But when I was finally able to meet humans, I always found them to be brutish or fawning, and I forgot that fascination. Until now." She looked back to him with the last two words. They were spoken soft and inviting, and she let her lips remain slightly curved around the last word. Doppelganger placed his large hands around her small hips and leaned in. He watched her close her eyes before he closed his own and placed his mouth on her parted lips. They kissed, and he was relieved when his passion was reciprocated. She moved her hands up to his shoulders. They released the kiss but remained close.

"I would wrap you in my arms if I could but you are too broad," she said breathlessly. They continued to kiss before she suddenly pulled back. "Forgive me," she said. "It was a long journey." He released her as she went into the bathroom, and he could hear the sound of running water.

"You're going to take a bath?" he called after her.

"I would feel much better. Would you join me? The sun is still out, and the water will be hot." He walked into the bathroom and saw that it was a large tub that would accommodate even his frame. She came to him and removed his shirt.

LV

The reeve led Dangalf and Nerdraaage to an inn called the King Bee with signage of a bumblebee wearing a crown at a jaunty angle. He left them in the hands of the innkeeper, who led them to a room with four large beds that would comfortably accommodate everyone but Doppelganger. The room also had a small balcony with a view of pristine forest unto the horizon.

On the recommendation of the innkeeper, both Dangalf and Nerdraaage bathed while the water was still hot. Water was not heated by fire. There were no fires in Templa Taur save for those in a few kitchens that were encased entirely in stone and with other precautions.

After washing they put on clean clothes for the first time since they left Hammersmith. It was a sign of their increasing prosperity that they now had clothes to wear while they washed clothes. Their clothes were collected by the innkeeper's daughter, Ainnir, the she-elf who had just been dismissed by Dymphna in the royal house.

The King Bee had a main room with tables inside and outside on an expansive balcony. Nerdraaage took a seat near the edge of the balcony, and though it was railed by thick vines, they both felt chills as they looked to the ground far below. Dangalf imagined that a balcony on a magically engineered tree was as safe as a skyscraper built by the lowest bidder in their old universe.

Ainnir stood by the table and smiled slightly. She offered them a menu that was indecipherable to them. "What do you recommend?" asked Dangalf.

"Our mead is quite good," she said. "We have spiced mead, fruited mead—"

"Don't you have any beer?" asked Nerdraaage.

"We have dwarven beer," she answered.

"Just bring us two of the house mead," said Dangalf and, before Nerdraaage could protest, added, "It's on me. Let's give the drink of the elves a try." They lit their pipes and enjoyed the sunset.

LVI

After stopping at the tanner, who promised to stay open until he finished her garment, Ashlyn was taken to the druid trainer. She'd crossed several branches and rope bridges when she saw an arched white door built into a large tree trunk. Just before the door, she passed under a large branch, and something told her to look up, and she beheld a beautiful and terrible red-and-gold tyger. The tyger took in Ashlyn's scent in three large sniffs and, apparently not smelling anything of interest, put his head back down. The guard ignored the cat and opened the white door for her. She entered and he closed the door. She was now alone in the room with a small table, a low lamp, and two chairs. No, not alone. There was a tyger almost indiscernible on a ledge above her.

"Please sit," said an unseen she-elf. "May I touch upon your mind?"

"Yes."

"Close your eyes."

When she closed her eyes, she saw a she-elf well in the distance lit by an unknown source. Ashlyn was apprehensive to meet the druid trainer after Nerdraaage's initial rebuff by Icil. "If you see anything too terrible or just wish to be released from this joining, open your eyes," said the figure. "But try to keep them closed otherwise. Come here, child." Words echoed as if she were in a giant chamber. But she was sure from what she saw outside that no such place could fit into the tree.

Ashlyn walked toward the magnificent she-elf. She had a friendly smile and looked young, but something told Ashlyn she had an ancient soul. She was dressed in a white fur bikini with white leather knee-high boots and straps around her neck and, wrists and one on her thigh holding a dagger. She wore her dark hair up, which gave her an aristocratic look despite the bawdy outfit. Her eyes were as green as leaf, and she stood with hands on hips looking like a mighty Amazon.

"I am Ciar," said the she-elf. "I am the druid principal of Templa Taur. You seek training?"

"Yes."

"Then it shall be my pleasure to train you."

"Thank you," said Ashlyn.

Ciar walked around Ashlyn. "You will need to lose that metal dagger. And silk is too fine for our purposes. You will need to lose your clothing."

"Right now?"

"No," said Ciar with a smile. "Not right now."

"Where are we?"

"We are in my home."

"How is that possible?"

"Open your eyes."

Ashlyn was in her chair, and sitting across from her was Ciar. "This is the room that your body occupies," said Ciar. "Now close your eyes again." And then both were back in the cavernous, dark chamber. "And this area exists in the joining of our minds. It is where you will begin your training." Then they were on a frozen mountainside. They were in a deep gurgling swamp. They bobbed up and down in the cold waters of a vast ocean. They stood in a great fire-belching desert. Each venue contained all the sensations of reality. Hot, cold, motion, the smell of brimstone. They were back in the black chamber.

"When you have proven yourself in the realm of our joined minds, you will be tested in the field," continued Ciar. She took Ashlyn's face. "You are quite beautiful." Ashlyn could only blink in response. "You must use this advantage on the battlefield. Your enemies will give you quarter, even if it is slight and unconscious. Your allies will protect and aid you more than they would their own brothers.

"I will teach you naturalism. More than the innate elven naturalism but the perfectly attuned naturalism of the druid. I will teach you the healing ways. You came here with three friends. Had you given any thought to what choice you would make if you could only save one?" The question chilled Ashlyn. "Or which one you would let die so that you and the other two may live?

"No," said Ashlyn somberly.

"Hesitation may cost all of you your lives. You will learn the Hierarchy of Life. From the righteous sapiens at the top down through the sacred animals through the expendable animals and the plants to the malicious animals and finally to the unrighteous sapiens unworthy of life at all. And I will teach you metamorphosis. But I can tell already that that will not be difficult for you. You look ready to pounce even now. First you will learn some defensive skills. All other training is useless if you are killed. There is still time for a test today if you are ready."

"I am."

"There is no chance of you dying during this stage of training, but if you are careless, you will suffer pain equivalent to natural conditions." And on Ashlyn's look of apprehension, she added, "Try not to be distressed. You are very strong in mind and body, and I have every faith in you. Shall we begin?"

"Yes," said Ashlyn, forcing a smile. They stood deep in a cold, darkened cave. An ogre skinned a dead tyger. Ashlyn backed up, clattering some bones, and found her back against the rock wall. The ogre noticed her and grunted his displeasure. He stood to his full ten feet and picked up a spiked mace as large as Ashlyn. He charged her. "You cannot defeat such a monster," said Ciar. "You must evade him and escape his dwelling." The ogre raised his mace to strike her.

LVII

Dangalf and Nerdraaage smoked and drank on the inn's balcony. A few other tables were occupied by quiet elves who drank and laughed. One strummed a lute during lulls in his table's conversation. "This place is pretty cool for an elf town," said Nerdraaage. "I could live here," he said belching.

"The elves might have something to say about that," said Dangalf.

"Everyone burps."

"That one had reverb."

They were both quite buzzed when Ainnir approached and set a small clear bowl on the table with a large insect in it. "Did she just put a bug on the table?" asked Nerdraaage. Dangalf was certain it was the funniest rhetorical question he had ever heard.

Ainnir just smiled and put a leaf in the bowl. As it munched on its leaf, the insect gave off a warm, glowing light. Dangalf picked up the bowl and studied the hungry insect through the glass. "No fire in Templa Taur," said Dangalf. "Not even for candles."

"I was asked to give you a message," said Ainnir.

"Yes, my dear," said a flirty Dangalf.

"Well, I was asked to tell you that your friend is coming, and she wanted you to know that if you laughed at her, she was going to push you both from the balcony."

"Thank you," said Dangalf. And then to Nerdraaage, "Well this should be interesting."

Ainnir departed and they saw her nod to someone out of sight. That someone was Ashlyn, who now approached them with a wry smile on her face. They immediately understood what she meant by her admonishment. The tanner had prepared her a fur bikini from the dead wolf complete with ears tied onto her head like a bonnet and a wolf's tail swinging from the bikini bottom. Nerdraaage turned red with drunkenness and his heroic efforts not to laugh. "So what are we not supposed to laugh at?" Dangalf asked, and Nerdraaage burst out laughing.

"Did my warning mean nothing to you?" Ashlyn asked. "What are you drinking?" She took Dangalf's goblet and drank from it. "It's good. What is it?"

"Mead," said Dangalf as he motioned to Ainnir to return.

"It's delicious," she said. "Elves just do everything better."

Meanwhile Dymphna straddled Doppelganger on her bed and they kissed enthusiastically. "Never could I have imagined it would be like that," sighed Dymphna.

"It was great," said a mellow Doppelganger, happy not only for his brain's recent release of endorphins but happy that all of his anatomy was proportional to his large frame.

"It was like, like," she was confounded to compare it to any of her previous life events.

"Like running across water," suggested Doppelganger.

"It was even better than that," she said before kissing him again. She only broke the kiss off when another important thought came to her. "I know I will see you again," she smiled.

"How about tomorrow?"

She stopped smiling. "But the royal guards will be here soon. My time being like my unfettered sister Ashlyn will come to an end."

"How can they stop us? You're the princess."

"You would think so. I could defy them, but that would be reported to my father."

"The king?"

"Yes. I do not wish to defy my family any more than I already have," she said. She began to cry and lay on the bed next to him.

"What's wrong?" he asked, turning toward her.

"I have betrayed my people. The only reason I am alive is because my Templar sacrificed himself for a tradition I have betrayed for lust."

"I don't believe it was just lust," he said.

"There is no reason for what we did but lust or love."

"There's your answer. It was not because of lust."

She looked up at him. "Yes," she said. "I do love you." And she kissed him.

"And your vision that we would see each other again? You are not worried that you will undo this prophecy by telling me?"

"It was not a vision," she said with glistening eyes. "It was my heart that told me."

LVIII

Dangalf, Ashlyn, and Nerdraaage returned to their room for the night. Dangalf collapsed on his bed, and Ashlyn watched Nerdraaage empty his rucksack on his bed. She snatched a small picture from his bed.

"Who is this man, and why do you have his picture?" she asked.

"It's Icil. I liked it and he gave it to me. And it's not a picture, it's an aspect."

Nerdraaage took back the aspect and tilted it before Ashlyn. The ingeniously carved image looked as if Icil were turning his head as Nerdraaage tilted it.

"This is Icil?" she said taking the aspect back from Nerdraaage. "He's gorgeous!"

"He is?" said Dangalf suddenly.

"I guess," she said. "For a dude." And she tossed the aspect back onto Nerdraaage's pile.

"Too bad you didn't know he used to be good looking or maybe you would have been nicer to him," said Nerdraaage.

"I was nice to him," she defended. "It's just that he was creepy."

"Creepy?" asked Nerdraaage. "Because of what he did or because he has a messed-up face?

"The second one," she said now lying in her bed.

Dangalf stood and took the aspect. It was a photorealistic image of an unscarred Icil made by a dwarven craftsmen. Photography would not be allowed in this world. He knew that from reading about the Schism and its restrictions on invention.

LIX

The Sundering not only destroyed the world as it was known but de-stroyed the parity and friendship that had existed between the Red, White, and Blue Schools.

The Red School is always the most celebrated of schools because it was the first and most important school. If there were no Red School, then there would not have been civilization, and the preeminence of sapien life in this world would be in doubt. Though there is talk of the White School or the Blue School surpassing the Red School, it has always been the Red School that defends civilization from the periodic darkness that inflicts this world. And should it ever come to pass that the White School or the Blue School should ever permanently displace the Red School, it must al-ways be remembered that it is only because they stand upon the shoulders of the Red School heroes who have come before. Nay, it is not a question that the Red School came first, only which of their ancient traditions is older, the hunter or the warrior? And though boasts abound on both sides over which noble occupation first set sapien life on the path to civilization, it is likely that the first Red School heroes were both hunter and warrior before specialization of classes became what it is today.

Ten thousand years ago, it was the Red School that held off the forces of darkness that existed in those first three hundred days after the Sundering. And they did so at great cost. It is said nine sapiens died for every one that lived during this time.

And when the darkness lifted, it was the Blue School that built homes and towns and bridges and ports and wagons and axes and plows. It was craftsmen of that bluest race that finished the excavation of that wonder we now know as Bran Keep.

And the White School underwent the most startling transformation during this same period, when many of the priests of the now-departed gods turned to learning the secrets of their powers. And the most heretical of these ancient priests suggested that the gods were not of a superior nature but simply "those who had come before." And their powers were not manifest, only learnt by sapiens who had the advantage to exist before human, dwarf, and elf did.

And it so happens that in time the Blue School and White School did work together to create the great portal. And it also happens that Blue and White School sapiens of the otherworld Europa did also build a portal, and that when completed there became a doorway between the worlds. And there were crossings by both from one world to the other and back. But this doorway had remained open for only a short time when the Schism began over which school might become preeminent.

The seers of Acadia envisioned the unchecked progression of the Blue School as being the path to a world befouled of smoke and noise and blinding light even in the darkest night and eventually machina begetting machina leading to the purposelessness of life that comes from lack of struggle and perhaps even enslavement of sapiens by their own creations.

And the seers of Europa saw the unchecked progression of the White School as being the path to mortals unlocking the powers of the gods, and those destructive powers being wielded by those who still contained the sapien weaknesses of pettiness, jealousy, anger, and vanity, and those imperfect sapiens possessing knowledge that could kill an army in the tapping of a staff.

And the most belligerent of the White and Blue School supremacists tried to sway the Red School to their cause, each warning that if the other school were to gain supremacy, it would lead to the eventual demise of the other schools and perhaps sapien life itself. The Red School members, gifted above all else in instantly and fanatically taking sides in conflict, wisely and surprisingly remained neutral on the subject.

And so each sapien chose to live in a world dominated by the White School or the Blue School, and those who favored the Blue School chose Europa, and those who preferred the White School chose Acadia. And some who preferred the Blue School stayed in Acadia with the understanding that they would not be able to pursue machina that threatened the sapien role as Master of This World. And now the Blue School in Acadia is greatly restricted in their creations. And they are forbidden building even that for which plans already exist, and they craft with many restrictions as set forth in the Prohibitions on Invention and Reproduction. And that voluminous listing is sometimes simply abbreviated as: Wheels not Gears. Fire not Steam. Catapults not Cannons.

And there were those who preferred the White School who did choose to stay in Europa, and they did so with the understanding that they would always be viewed with suspicion and hatred and would forever be persecuted and killed when they would practice to steal magic from that world's gods. And so great was Europa's fear of the White School that it was seen that they did destroy their portal to Acadia, forever ending corporeal transport between the two worlds.

Cronica Acadia

LX

Doppelganger entered the room, and Dangalf and Nerdraaage cheered their conquering roommate. He dropped his armor and weapons and sat facing his friends. "Back so soon?" said Dangalf.

"The royal guards are coming," said Doppelganger. "So I left by the front door before I had to slip out a bedroom window a hundred feet in the air."

"So you hit that?" asked Nerdraaage excitedly.

Doppelganger opened his mouth to answer but stopped when he saw Ashlyn looking at him. "I'll tell you later," said Doppelganger. "What are you wearing, Ashlyn?"

"Go ahead and laugh," she said.

"Laugh? You look great."

"Thank you," she smiled. "At least I have one nice friend."

"Didn't I say you looked great?" asked Dangalf.

"No."

"We were too busy laughing at her," said Nerdraaage.

"You're not princess material," said Ashlyn to Doppelganger. "You should go out with my trainer. She's hot and she kicks ass."

"He's got an elf," said Nerdraaage. "Why don't you fix me up with her?"

"You're married, and that's not even my best reason."

"I'm only married once."

Doppelganger picked up the lamp and looked closely at it. "How do you turn off the bug?"

"Drape that cloth over it," said Dangalf. Doppelganger dropped his boots on the floor and settled into his own bed. Dangalf leaned toward Doppelganger. "So? What happened?"

Doppelganger leaned toward Dangalf's bed. "You wouldn't believe it," said Doppelganger. Nerdraaage lay in his bed between them and listened wide eyed. "She takes me to the royal house and kicks the maid out. And then she pulls me upstairs to one of the bedrooms, and we sit on the bed next to each other. She said ever since she was a schoolgirl and saw a schoolbook with humans in it, she'd always wondered what it would be like to kiss one. So, perfect opportunity, I lean over and start making out with her. Then she says, 'Why don't we take a bath together?' and pulls me into the bathroom and she takes off all of my clothes. And we're still making out, and we get into the tub, and she starts rubbing me down with oils and these spices..."

Ashlyn burst out laughing. "Sorry," she apologized. "I wasn't trying to listen. Elf ears."

"And what was so amusing?" asked Doppelganger.

"Nothing," she said. "I'll be quiet."

"No, please," insisted Doppelganger.

"It's just that, something I've noticed, and it's just that in the time we've been in this world I've grown increasingly sensitive to it..."

"Yes?"

"Elves don't like the way humans smell," she said. Dangalf reflexively smelled his own armpit.

"What are you saying?" asked Doppelganger. "We smell like animals?"

"No," she said. "We like the way animals smell."

"Don't listen to her," said Nerdraaage. "Elves think their shite don't stink."

Lying down in his bed, Doppelganger was glad he had been interrupted. He decided he would not tell them any more than he had. He did not want to cheapen what he had shared with Dymphna by describing it in a way that demeaned her to his friends, and that is the only way men can describe such things to other men. He was also self-conscious about telling the story in front of Ashlyn even though the Ashlyn of the old universe had more ribald stories and jokes than the other Keepers combined. Doppelganger did not have Dangalf's perfect recollection, but his memory of Dymphna was pristine, and he relived it happily as he drifted off to sleep.

LXI

Someone knocked on the room door much too early and continued to knock until Dangalf got up. "So much for elf ears," he complained.

"I hear it," said Ashlyn. "I'm just ignoring it."

Dangalf opened the door to the sight of a spiffy soldier in the oak tree tabard of the elven royal house. Suddenly Dangalf felt wretched in his slept-in clothes and bed hair. "Her Highness summons those who escorted her," said the soldier. The others were rising quickly behind Dangalf.

"When?" asked Doppelganger.

"She awaits."

They dressed quickly, and the soldier led them to the elevator basket. Dymphna and her entourage stood by the basket waiting to depart. There were other soldiers, but one stood out from the rest: bigger, blonder, and with magnificent white armor. "Who is that with the princess?" Dangalf asked.

"Her Highness's personal guard. A Templar."

"Look at that armor," said Nerdraaage.

"You must be quiet now."

The soldier delivered the four to Dymphna, bowed, and stepped aside. The Keepers also bowed or curtsied. Dymphna's bearing was now very formal. Her Templar glowered at Doppelganger like a jealous boyfriend.

"I will send each of you a gift when I am returned home. And I will spread word of your noble deed. Please call upon my house if I can someday assist you."

"Thank you, Your Highness," said Dangalf.

She turned to leave but turned back. "One other thing," she said. "I had a vision of you all. It was so vague that I thought not to tell you. But I sense it forebodes great danger, and I will tell you as it may mean something to you. It may be an answer to your mystery. I see an outsider living among strangers. He was drawn to this world as you were, and he in turn summoned you. Forgive me because I must leave you with one final riddle. You will meet this outsider where the sky touches the center of the earth. Good luck and farewell." The princess and her entourage entered the basket and were lowered to the earth.

Doppelganger and Dangalf stood together by the railing as they looked down upon Dymphna. The Templar assisted her onto a unicorn. The procession of Dymphna and her Templar on unicorns and six others on horses rode away from Templa Taur.

Doppelganger stewed. Not once during Dymphna's farewell did she look at him. He tried to explain away her behavior as a requirement of her position, but that required empathy and the more warrior he became, the less empathy he had. He could only imagine grabbing her delicate wrists and yelling at her about how she had shamed him.

They went back to the inn and had breakfast. For the first time, Ashlyn was enjoying real elf cooking, the preparation of which involved very little cooking. The cook did not prepare portions that filled Doppelganger or Nerdraaage, but they filled up on basket after basket of bread.

Between bites or, to Ashlyn's disgust, sometimes during bites, they discussed the princess's vision. They were all quite excited to be part of a prophecy by a real seer, even such a vague one. In fact, the vagueness only made it more appealing. How less exotic a prophecy it would have been if she said, 'Go to Wyrmhold Castle and see Nil the Stormbringer.' (Which is not where their prophecy would lead. It's just an example.)

Ashlyn finally had to excuse herself to go to her training. Dangalf was happy that Ashlyn was excited about her training even if he couldn't help but notice she had not brought back to the room any books. After all, she was apprenticing for his White School!

She had described her training as a manipulation of the trainee's mind by the trainer to create any environment or scenario. Dangalf understood perfectly. It was his internal library but created and manipulated by another and much more expansive and fluid. She enthused about her training's superiority to the training gotten by the others. Doppelganger objected. To be a warrior, you needed to feel real pain and taste your own blood during your training. Ashlyn insisted that signals to the brain are why pain is felt and blood is tasted, so those elements could in fact be duplicated through mind manipulation. She agreed there were limits to how far this virtual training could take you. It was beneficial for muscle memory but less so for muscle conditioning. But Doppelganger stubbornly refused to agree even to that compromise statement.

Lastly they told her that they intended do some hunting that day. It would keep their skills sharpened, and also the cook had said that he would cook anything they brought back. The Blue School did not recognize cooks as craftsmen, but still, like the other workers they had met across Acadia, they took pride in their work.

LXII

The three went back to the room, and Doppelganger and Nerdraaage began packing their rucksacks for a day away from Templa Taur. When Nerdraaage saw Dangalf not packing, he asked him why. Dangalf said he thought he might instead go to the town library, which he had heard contained a great collection of magic books, even if they were in Elvish. "You don't speak Elvish," said Nerdraaage.

"No," answered Dangalf. "But that won't stop me from capturing the books to my memory until I learn Elvish."

"You're going," said Doppelganger, and Dangalf did not argue the point. He packed his own rucksack and started to head out before he thought to take Clay with them. Dangalf had been quite the bookworm lately and did not want to be an armchair wizard. It would benefit him to have a day out. He had almost died by battlepig because his practical experience had been lacking. And gods help them if Doppelganger or Nerdraaage violated the Lonelywood Concordance in elven lands. And Dangalf was the only one of the Keepers who had read it.

LXIII

The Acadian Concordance on Sapien and Animal Coexistence, oft times referred to as the Lonelywood Concordance for its place of signing, is the ancient document governing the righteous treatment and allowable harvesting of animals by its human, dwarven, and elven signers. The dwarves in all their cleverness had learned that animal husbandry allowed for a much greater production of animal product than traditional hunting and gathering. The elves, however, with their especial connection to the flora and fauna, found it completely unacceptable that animals would be born into captivity for the sole purpose of slaughter. Humans also found it particularly unsporting to kill an animal in a cage or pen when that animal had no reasonable chance to kill or escape its attacker. And so did representatives of the three great races early on in their alliance meet at Lonelywood in Nemetia to once and for all settle on the proper sapien treatment of their fellow ambulatory inhabitants of this world. And though many dwarves who were invested in animal husbandry objected, as noble as farming is, they were not of the Blue School and had no great body advocating for them. But the hunters seeing animal husbandry as a debasement of their great class, and likely a threat to their own prosperity, fully supported the elimination of the slaughter of captive animals, and it was so that the Red School did support the Concordance. The dwarves themselves were sympathetic to those of their clever race invested in animal farming and might not have agreed at all except that at the last minute a passionate plea on behalf of the White School was made by Grand Templar Bardrick, who told the attendees that to know the right thing to do they had only to look at their unrighteous opposites. And they all did know the terrible crimes of the trolls, goblins, and orcs, and that they sacrificed animals and killed more animals for only bloodlust and leaving their corpses to ravens and worms, and did fight one animal against another in cruel sport, and did monstrous experiments on animals. And from this they degraded into sapien sacrifice and wanton murder and forced mortal combat as entertainment and even experimented on living sapiens. And as the righteous magician bends the very elements of the universe, and as the elven naturalist reshapes himself and the forest, the wicked trolls learned to twist animal flesh into wargs and battlepigs. And this gave rise to the new witchcraft of necromancy and slavery even beyond death and so forth even unto creating that abomination Dimmuborgir, that monument of depravity, the great mound of living flesh, living but not life, where their unfortunate prisoners do go. And so with the support of the Red and White Schools and without the objection of the Blue School, the Concordance was signed by representatives of the three great races. And though it is too great a document to recreate here, we can touch upon some of its important elements affecting sapiens even today: There is nothing about the concordance that would inhibit a sapien from killing an animal to defend himself or another. Animal husbandry for purposes other than slaughter is acceptable when done without cruelty. Working animals are to be treated without cruelty. No animal is to be kept for only the vanity or amusement of its keeper. Familiars and other animals seeking the company of sapiens are permitted such that the animal's departure is not restricted when it finds sapien companionship no longer desirable. Hunters are responsible for taking prey quicker and more painlessly than if that prey were taken by a pack of wolves. Trapping or any method of capture or killing likely to cause extreme and prolonged pain is forbidden. Hunters will shoot birds in the sky and not those upon the ground. Fishers mush fish by hand or spear and are not to use nets excepting upon great bodies of water. No animal or fishes are to be taken in excess of what can be used without waste. Animal sacrifice is forbidden. Animal experimentation is forbidden. And so on and so forth. One jester was able to sum up the entirety of the Lonelywood Concordance in just six words: When in doubt, ask an elf. And that sect of fearsome elven rangers known as the Horns of Cernunnos was charged with enforcement of the Concordance for those crimes rising to the penalty of death.

Cronica Acadia

LXIV

Nerdraaage followed Doppelganger down the first ladder they came to, but Dangalf kept walking until he reached a lift. Just because they were going on a he-man hunting trip didn't mean he was about to be shamed into climbing down a thirty-foot rope ladder when there was a basket lift on the next tree.

They walked deep into the woods. Doppelganger led the way, purposefully, like he had a specific destination in mind. They passed many animals that Dangalf thought would provide the Red School's recommended daily allowance of bloodlust, but Doppelganger pressed on.

Nerdraaage seemed unconcerned that the alleged hunt had turned into a forced march. And they marched and they marched. It was all Dangalf could do to keep up with them. A bright red snake suddenly appeared within striking distance of Dangalf before slithering off.

"Whoa," said Dangalf. "I just came this close to a red snake."

"So?" asked Doppelganger not changing his stride.

"They're probably deadly poisonous. Red is a universal warning."

"I thought we were in a new universe," said Doppelganger.

"I still think red is a natural warning."

"Like that?" asked Doppelganger. And as Dangalf pressed through the greenery to where Doppelganger had stopped, the sky before him turned red. No, it wasn't the sky. It was a great red wall thirty feet into the air and as wide as could be seen. The Crimson Wall. The elven contribution to the three pillars of the Legion defeat (with the sinking of the Trollish Armada and the Battle of Nemetia) during the last Great War. A wall not constructed but grown from this world's deadliest plant, gravewhisper. It had stopped the Legion dead, literally for many, in its tracks before they had conquered all the elven lands.

LXV

For Princess Dymphna was the first righteous sapien ever killed with malice. And for this first murder to be committed against the purest of spirit, Dymphna, and by the foulest of beings, Kejavik the Naught, was too much for even the gods to bear. And so did Woden command that Sulis grow a new flower that would cover Dymphna's Rest. And that flower would be so poisonous as to kill all who would disturb her rest instantly and without antidote. And then Woden sundered this world so that elf and dwarf and human and troll and goblin and orc should be each separate and alone forever. And this we know through the oral tradition, as the Sundering did follow with three hundred days of darkness when all wisdom not precious enough to be carved into stone did perish. And in time did the sundered world drift back together so that elf and dwarf and human and troll and goblin and orc did again discover the other sapiens. And as is so often the history of sapiens, the trolls did undo Woden's will and after countless deaths they learnt to cull gravewhisper and use its poison as a great weapon to make many righteous sapiens dead. And for ten thousand years did gravewhisper grow only in Sylvania and only on Dymphna's Rest. And the noble Sirona, supreme among all elven naturalists, the creator of the elves' secret Hierarchy of Life, in answer to this threat made the perilous journey into Sylvania. And Sirona, who was wise among all others and ancient even in that time, did know what the plant whispered as it was in the first tongue that all sapiens spoke before the Sundering and the other languages were born. And it is supposed that the plant whispers in the voice of Dymphna herself. And the gravewhisper did tell its secrets to Sirona and gave up itself to Sirona, who brought back cuttings of the plant to the elves. And during the Great War, when amassed Legion forces threatened to slash and burn their way straight to the heart of Oira Nomo, it was Sirona who, in only three days' time, was able to cultivate gravewhisper into the Crimson Wall, a great wall of thirty feet in height and three hundred leagues in length, in the path of the invaders. And she had told the king of the elves that once grown the Crimson Wall could not be undone, but he did consent so long as the gravewhisper was grown so that the precious flower grew only on the elven side. As the Legion hordes approached the red wall, they scoffed at the flora as they had lain waste to many forests and ancient trunks, and they were not wise enough to see the foe they now faced. The troll witches and lycans and necromancers who rode at the back of the army with the generals too late realized that they were march- ing upon a heretofore-unseen growth of gravewhisper. And as the orcs cut and burned through the red vines, the vines did grab and entwine, and great poisons were released, and the invaders fell one hundred times one hundred and sent many more to retreat in fear and confusion and not wanting to tempt elven magic evermore. And this great Crimson Wall stands as impenetrable today as it was then, and it is recorded by the sages who record such things as the only example of both a crafted Great Wonder and a natural Great Wonder.

LXVI

"You idiot," said Dangalf to Doppelganger. "You've marched us all the way to enemy lines."

"How do you know that?"

"That's the Crimson Wall."

"Gravewhisper," said Doppelganger. "That's worth a lot of gold."

"There's a reason for that," said Dangalf. "None of us could harvest it without dying."

"Vines," sneered Nerdraaage. "We can cut them off."

"Cut gravewhisper?" asked Dangalf. "Didn't you read your poison books?"

"Some of them."

"Let's just take a closer look," said Doppelganger as he moved forward.

"You bastard!" whisper-shouted Dangalf. "You'll get us all killed!"

"Mayhap," said Doppelganger laughing. "Mayhap." Dangalf sat down and wrote a quick note before releasing Clay. He feared they would not be back in time for dinner. Or at all.

They approached within about twenty feet of the wall with Dangalf standing well behind the hulking warrior. Doppelganger noticed her first. A she-troll's body lying five feet from the wall. And her head eight feet from the wall. He nodded to the others. "Let's get out of here," said Dangalf.

"Why?" asked Doppelganger as he readied his axe.

"She looks like a witch," said Dangalf. "Maybe a necromancer. Whoever killed her can snuff us out without blinking."

"If he killed a troll, he must be on our side."

"You think trolls wouldn't kill each other for a wealth of gravewhisper!" Doppelganger moved closer to the body, and the others followed him. Dangalf couldn't turn away from the gruesome sight. She wore a black cloak that covered most of her body and gave him no clues to her class or rank. He looked to her head, and the two white points of her fangs barely showed below her upper lip. Dangalf tilted her head under his boot to make sure it was actually detached and not attached to a body hidden underground to lure them in. "Look here," said Nerdraaage as he unappeared.

Doppelganger and Dangalf walked to the spot where Nerdraaage had vanished. "Where did you go?" asked Doppelganger.

"I'm right here," said Nerdraaage's disembodied voice.

"Did you hide for a reason?" asked Dangalf.

"Two more bodies," said Nerdraaage.

Not far from the witch were two trolls in armor. They had been attacked mercilessly by the looks of their wounds, and their blood had spilled on the ground. "They put up quite a fight," said Nerdraaage.

"They didn't land a blow," said Doppelganger. "Look at their weapons." Now even Doppelganger was apprehensive. These trolls were not mercenaries or even soldiers but full-blown warriors. The three of them wouldn't stand a chance against one let alone two first-class warriors. "They stood back to back to protect themselves from their attacker."

"Attackers?" asked Dangalf.

"It's hard to say," said Doppelganger. "There's no footprints. Maybe we should go."

Suddenly Doppelganger's axe was plucked from his hand and tossed away. Dangalf raised his wand, only to have that also snatched away from him. Nerdraaage, still unappeared, was kicked in the ass. He appeared when he hit the ground. "What the—" he blurted.

They heard him laughing before they saw him, and it was a familiar laugh. Icil appeared sitting on the ground and still laughing. It was a great relief for the Keepers. "Where is my she-elf?" demanded Icil. "Is she ready to pounce on me from the trees? For the life of me, I could not find her."

"Icil!" shouted Nerdraaage as he ran over and embraced him.

"Where is she!" shouted Icil.

"Ashlyn didn't come," said Dangalf.

"More's the pity."

"This," said Doppelganger referring to the corpses. "This is nice work."

"Did you think I made assassin just on my good looks?" asked Icil. "But the witch was the real problem. A deathspeaker. Can kill with just one word. So I had to kill her first."

"What are you doing here?" asked Nerdraaage.

"I came to harvest some gravewhisper."

"I didn't think there was a human who could harvest gravewhisper," said Dangalf.

"Let me rephrase that," said Icil. "I came to harvest those who harvest gravewhisper." Nerdraaage laughed and patted his trainer on the back. Icil removed a package from his satchel and carefully unwrapped the white flower. "I watched that troll bitch for hours while she talked the plant into giving up a blossom. And when she snatched the flower, I snatched her head."

"Sweet!" cheered Nerdraaage. "How's your vendetta?"

"Things are afoot," said Icil. "I may be ready to strike soon. That's why I needed the gravewhisper, having given my last one away."

Icil looted his kills and told the Keepers to take what they liked. He removed each corpse's signet and copied the identifying marks onto a scroll. He then dispatched a pigeon to Vinland so that the sages could close the books on three more enemies. Icil gave a warrior signet each to Doppelganger and Nerdraaage.

"White School," he called to Dangalf. "You take the witch's ring. Do not wear it. And sell it only to someone who can disenchant evil things."

Dangalf handled the ring with supreme care. He read the engraving with his limited Trollish. Narrarkbringa. That made no sense, and he figured that was her name. He was pleasantly surprised to read another word as "house." Trolls identified themselves by houses as did elves. It was not unlike the dwarven clan. The third word would be the name of her house, which had entirely too many consonants in it to pronounce.

"Where is your mount?" asked Nerdraaage.

"She is nearby," said Icil. "I would call her, but I am not ready to draw attention to our presence."

"Wait till you see her," Nerdraaage promised his friends.

Icil kicked the corpses and the severed head to the wall of gravewhisper vines. The bodies disappeared in a cocoon of living red vines.

"Need some help with your vendetta?" asked Nerdraaage.

"But you are all too inexperienced to go where I need to go," said Icil. "Even as a group. I might even suggest that you are too unskilled yet to be loitering at the Crimson Wall. Why are you here?"

They looked to Doppelganger to answer. "I don't know," he said.

"I know sure enough," said Icil. "You are a warrior, and you thirst for blood. And not that of a dumb beast. Have any of you slain a sapien?" Their silence answered his question. "Then it is high time," said Icil. "I will take you to our enemies, and you shall have your blood. You do not know true killing until you kill something that is begging for its life."

"But the Legion doesn't speak our tongue," said Dangalf.

"Begging for one's life sounds the same in all tongues." To varying degrees they all desired to strike at the enemy. Even Dangalf was ready to use his fire and ice on sapiens. Weyd had spent no little time on instructing Dangalf on the enemy's history of atrocity and incorrigible wickedness. Weyd even presented him one last time before his commissioning with the choice between aspiring to the pacifistic sages or the martial mages, and Dangalf had chosen combat, just like the wizened wizard had done many decades before. Weyd had reassured him that when he actually encountered the unrighteous sapiens in combat, Dangalf would know what to do.

Icil led them away with the promise that they would that day send many Legion scum to their daevas. He examined Nerdraaage's commission and was distressed to see that Nerdraaage had not completed any of the steps required for further training. Nerdraaage explained the Keepers had an agreement to stay together during their initial training, and now they awaited Ashlyn to complete hers. "I cannot blame you for waiting on that one," agreed Icil. "But nonetheless, today we will attack a troll camp, and I will be able to sign off on many of your requirements."

Icil sprinkled the Crimson Wall with liquid from a small bottle, and the wall shrieked and retreated, creating a human-size gap. Icil ducked through. "Quickly now," he urged. And they followed apprehensively through the dripping and moaning arch.

Dangalf knew that gravewhisper was impervious even to flame. "What is that mixture?" he asked of the bottle.

"Ah," said Icil. "It is a forbidden potion." And he placed it back into his murder kit.

"Forbidden?" asked Dangalf. And then he remembered: "It is made of unicorn blood."

"You know many things, White School," said Icil. "As you should. But be assured that the wall will heal itself before our enemies find the gap." As if on cue, the Crimson Wall began to grow into its hole. "And there you go," said Icil. "Now you see why the less reverent among us call it the Crimson Weed."

"Crimson Weed," said Nerdraaage with a chuckle.

And they moved on. Dangalf noticed that as soon as they entered the lost lands, the sky was darker, it was cooler, and the natural forest colors were muted. Perhaps it was just the passing of day, he thought. "What is that smell?" he asked.

"Fires," said Icil. "The smell of the bestial orcs perhaps."

"I thought we were fighting trolls," said Doppelganger.

"I thought we were fighting sapiens," said Nerdraaage.

"We're all sapiens," said Dangalf.

"The camp flies a troll banner, but the guards will be orcs," said Icil. "The officers, trolls. Ready your ranged attacks. We may meet patrols, and we will want to silence them quickly." The smell grew stronger as they crept through the woods, and the glow of fire and the howl of wicked tongues joined it. Icil stopped them and kneeled in the woods just before a clearing that surrounded the camp. There were many wood buildings, the largest of which appeared to be a barracks. They were all one story but for the tower near the center of the camp, which was at least three stories high. From that hung a troll banner (a gravewhisper flower and a skull, an orc skull according to Icil, separated by a gold stripe, a bend sinister, on a black background). A circle of fire burned around the camp even in daylight.

"See how the wood of the buildings warp?" asked Icil. "How shabby they look? These were sacred elven groves. The trees even in death defy this black occupation."

Two guards lazily walked the inside of the circle of flame. Orcs. The first enemy sapiens they had seen. There were two of them, red as blistering sunburns, as boiled lobsters. They had an animal gait and seemed as strong as bulls. Orcs were the most mesomorphic of the Legion's races. Their mouths protruded from the rest of their faces to hold large, sharp teeth. As they drew closer, the Keepers could see black veins swelling under the orcs' skin. Dangalf had not seen Doppelganger's bloodwarp, but he had read about it and recognized it in these orcs. Orcs were thought to be the only sapiens devoid of the white bile of reason and serenity. What a cursed race they must be to live in a constant state of the bloodwarp, he thought.

The Keepers knew to be quiet as the guards passed near their position during their circle around the perimeter. One guard howled at the other, who grunted in return. It did not even seem a language to Dangalf. Dangalf hated them for how they looked and was somewhat surprised at his eagerness to kill them. Orc hatred must be a race memory in humans, he supposed. He remembered Earc, the victim of the Legion battlepig, and he found he had no mercy for these red wretches. If he felt this way, he wondered what sort of bloodlust burned inside of his Red School comrades.

Doppelganger was eager to have at the bipedal beasts. He was excited and not intimidated by the fierce-looking orcs. He knew he would be just as fierce looking to them when the bloodwarp took him. But for now he waited until Icil gave the command.

Icil instructed Nerdraaage to complete many of the tasks required for him to promote. He was to stealthily enter the camp and proceed to the tower. There he would quietly kill the tower guard, who would normally be a good archer and as such posed significant risk to the rest of them when they attacked the camp. After this he was to find and enter the headquarters building, where he was to retrieve correspondence, maps, keys, and other items of import as he had been previously trained. When he collected all that he could reasonably steal without detection, he was to return to Icil at this same spot. "Do you have any questions?" asked Icil.

"You want me to go in there?" asked Nerdraaage.

"Yes."

"Are you coming with me?"

"No. You must complete these tasks with knowledge that failure can lead to death. You would not have such concern with me along, and your mettle would not be tested. What is the first rule of the blackguard?"

"There are no rules?"

"No. That's the first rule of combat. The first rule of the blackguard is 'I know I cannot be killed and therefore I cannot be killed.'" And turning to Doppelganger and Dangalf, he said, "You two didn't hear that."

They helped Nerdraaage take off his buckskin pants and jacket so he was in his blacks only. He had worn them and slept in them constantly, and they no longer squeaked. "You have your tools?" asked Icil.

"Yes," Nerdraaage said softly.

"Packed to be silent?"

"Yes."

"Move slowly. What do we know about the type of ground in the camp?"

"Footprints."

"Only incidental. What is the bigger concern?"

"Dust."

Icil nodded. "Then go to it."

Nerdraaage unappeared, and the three watched his foot-prints as he left the grassy ground of the tree line and crossed the fifty feet or so to the ring of fire. Nerdraaage had vanished completely and at will. Doppelganger felt a flash of jealousy as he could still not summon his bloodwarp at will. He had experienced it only involuntarily after being struck in combat. But as Alfred had warned him, the bloodwarp must be summoned before your opponent's first blow because the first one could be the killing blow. He wondered if he could summon it by punching himself in the face, but he decided that would look bad in front of the others.

"When he has returned, we will attack the camp," said Icil. Icil watched Nerdraaage with an eye that easily picked up the unappeared mercenary. Nerdraaage walked slowly. Too slowly. Icil regretted emphasizing to Nerdraaage to move slowly. Too slowly also posed risks.

Nerdraaage wished he didn't have to do this until he had mastered walk without footprints, but he would have to wait until his next training for that feat. He quickly crossed the fire barrier, where motion or burning smell could betray him.

The two guards in the lazy circle approached his direction, and he began to sweat. Damn! Why did he not wait until the guards were passed before he approached the circle of fire. Now he did not know what to do. If he moved quickly, dust or sound could give him away. If he remained still, one of them could easily step wide and walk right into him. The guards continued toward him, and their approach made his decision for him. They were too close not to notice his movement, so he stayed in place. He hoped the herb he had added to his diet was up to the task of masking his body odor even under his present duress.

The red monsters approached Nerdraaage. Now they did not even speak, denying him the cover of their own noise. Instead, they sniffed at the air with flared, bull nostrils. He put his hands to daggers, held his breath, and remained motionless as they approached. They passed so closely that Nerdraaage could see the color of their irises. They were red.

When the orcs were well ahead, Nerdraaage continued toward the camp. He strained to remember his training and Icil's stories of death-defying experiences. He looked for traps, both blue and white, that the enemy would set for blackguards. He looked nervously for beasts that were sensitive to unappear, especially a lowly mercenary such as himself. And then he saw it, his worst fear in its armored flesh: an orc walked a five-hundred-pound battlepig on a ten-foot pole. Its sensitive nose was no match for Nerdraaage's rudimentary unappear. The guard walked the pig away from Nerdraaage, but its very presence worried him and jeopardized everything he wanted to do.

Nerdraaage made it to the center of the camp but in surrounding himself with buildings, he had lost sight of the pig. He pressed on to the nearby tower. He climbed the tower ladder halfway, high enough to see over the other buildings, until he caught sight of the battlepig again. It was near the two perimeter guards who were having an animated discussion with the pigmaster. Had the guards sensed his presence and called for the battlepig? Had his poor timing in crossing the ring of fire turned an hourglass on his own life? How many times as a lonely, bullied youth had he had the fantasy of being able to turn invisible? But this world had taught him that invisibility alone was not enough! He continued his climb up the tower.

Near the top, Nerdraaage looked up and over the floor of the tower. There was the sentry, bow in hand. He stood opposite and looked out into the woods. Nerdraaage did not move. He stood on the ladder and thought back to Icil's lectures on the discipline and patience of the blackguard. And while he waited patiently, he hoped that no one would come up or down the ladder. Most of all he hoped that battlepigs could not climb ladders.

Nerdraaage studied the floor of the tower. He observed the grain of the wood and where the nails were placed and picked a landing spot that would least announce him when he moved into the tower from the ladder. He recalled his instruction on unappear: breathing, joint creaking, heartbeat, body odors, body heat, and even blinking were clues to the unappeared body's presence. And it was known that these otherwise barely discernible traits became magnified, sometimes three hundred fold, even to the untrained, when there was apparently no body present to produce them.

So he waited, and his patience was rewarded when the sentry grunted quickly to another orc below, and Nerdraaage used the moment of that utterance to climb up onto the platform. The sentry turned around quickly and looked Nerdraaage straight in the eye.

Nerdraaage flashed back to his attempt to spy on Ashlyn as she bathed alone in their room. He entered the room silently. He was sure of it. He had just bathed himself and was as unscented as any dwarf ever was. He was just inside the door and had only spotted her in the tub when she looked right at him, cocked her head, and suddenly screamed for him to get out. He immediately appeared and demanded to know how she knew he was there. "I could feel you looking at me!"

It was a real-life example of what Icil had explained to him this way: "Unappear is an unspoken agreement between the blackguard and his victim. The blackguard agrees to be unseen and the victim agrees not to see. If you look your victim in the eye, you can void that agreement."

"So don't look at your victim," Nerdraaage had said.

"For fuck's sake. You have to look at your victim! Look at his nose. If he has no nose, look at his pizzle." And Nerdraaage stopped looking the tower orc in the eye and looked instead at his nose. When the orc turned back to his watch, Nerdraaage moved quickly. First he sapped the back of the orc's head, and then he took his stunned victim gently to the ground. This was not compassion but for noise suppression. He looked at his vile victim now prone on his back and readied his dagger. He hesitated only slightly before striking his first-ever killing blow. He slit the monster's throat ear to ear and restrained him until he bled out.

Nerdraaage unappeared again and lowered himself off the platform but stayed at the top of the ladder looking for the battlepig. He had orc blood on his hands now, but that should not alert a pig trained to sniff out the righteous races. Horrified, he saw the battlepig nearby sniffing the ground. It snorted on a scent it didn't like and screamed its displeasure. Fortune smiled on him as the battlepig followed Nerdraaage's scent back the way he had entered the camp.

Nerdraaage trusted that Icil and his friends could handle the pig and pigmaster if they made it that far, but he felt he was now pressed for time. He wished that he had not rushed off without asking Icil's opinion on which of the buildings was the headquarters. From the ladder, he surveyed the grounds. He decided that the building with a guard and a small troll banner was the best choice.

The guard was distracted simply enough when Nerdraaage tossed a stone at the side of the building. Icil would be proud of the simplicity. The door was open and Nerdraaage slipped into the front office. It was unoccupied. The captain's door was ajar, and Nerdraaage passed through it without any more disturbance than a breeze would cause.

He found the troll captain sleeping at a desk. He was tall and slender, trolls being an ectomorphic race. His skin was a dark blue, and he had obvious long fangs, even with his mouth closed, and large, pointed ears that were so big as to curl down at the top. Nerdraaage knew these exaggerated features meant he was of a low caste. Icil had warned him that high-caste trolls were of such a pale blue as to be almost white and had such modest ears and fangs that they nearly resembled the elves. And they would bob their tails and wear elf scalps, the trolls being completely hairless, to complete the elf illusion.

Nerdraaage took papers from tabletops and maps posted on the wall. He picked a locked chest and took from it a coin purse and scrolls. Emboldened by his success, he even looted the desk at which the captain slept and picked his pockets. Finally he removed the captain's sword from his scabbard and hid it behind a cabinet. He would have killed the captain but there was still the guard outside. He had killed and stolen. Now it was important that he escape.

Nerdraaage exited the door without even attempting to distract the guard. He simply stepped softly past him and looked about for the battlepig. He did not see it, and he went back to his friends in the woods.

LXVII

The battlepig departed from the camp, snorting and kicking up a dust storm. He had abandoned the faint dwarf trail for the overwhelming stench of human. The perimeter guards grunted to the pigmaster, but he was twice foolish and waved them off. (His first foolish was allowing the pig to trace Nerdraaage's scent to where he had been instead of where he was going.)

Dangalf and Doppelganger had backed up at the approach of the battlepig, but the battlepig and pigmaster were moving forward more rapidly than they could covertly retreat. They wanted instructions from Icil, but he had unappeared soon after Nerdraaage had left.

Flight was not an option against the battlepig (when and if he was unleashed) so fight it was. Doppelganger charged the pigmaster once they had entered the cover of the tree line. The orc released the pig from its pole, but Dangalf encased it in a block of ice. It was a stunning success not only to hit the charging battlepig with his spell but to bring its immense force to a complete stop. (Fortunately it had not reached full velocity.)

Doppelganger was upon the pigmaster a second later and brought his battleaxe down on his head. It struck the orc's helmet solidly before sliding off the metal and continuing down through the flesh and bone at the shoulder. Foolish three times, the pigmaster was lightly armored. Doppelganger finished him by bringing the axe down solidly across his exposed neck, but it was a poorly angled blow, and Doppelganger had to settle for almost decapitating the pigmaster as his head bobbled at the end of some skin and tendons. Icil reappeared, his daggers drawn for action. "Good work," he said.

"Have you been here all along?" asked Dangalf.

"For the most part," said Icil.

It was agreed that Dangalf would not fireball the pig because the pyrotechnics would alert the camp to their presence. Instead, he undid the ice spell, and before the freed pig could attack, Icil forced poisoned daggers into where the pig was not armored. Almost instantly the pig lay down on its side and died quietly. Clearly Icil was a master of porcine anatomy as well. "Did you kill the tower guard?" Icil asked.

"What?" said Dangalf.

And suddenly Nerdraaage appeared from thin air. "Yes," he said.

"Good. I was able to scout the camp. Not a White School or blackguard among them. They are only guards and mercenaries. The captain appears to be the only soldier rank of the bunch. But the three of you working together, I think you can clear the camp."

"All of them?" asked Dangalf apprehensively.

"All of them," said Icil. "But I won't be far away." And he and Nerdraaage unappeared.

The orc perimeter guards, drawn perhaps by the disappearance of the battlepig and pigmaster, approached the position of Doppelganger and Dangalf. Dangalf froze one into a block of ice. Another grand success! Doppelganger charged the other, but the alert guard deflected his attack. Doppelganger felt a chill as the orc smiled wickedly at him as they stood locked together. Doppelganger pushed the smaller orc off, but he rebounded like a spring, swinging viciously at the human.

Dangalf couldn't cast a spell since Doppelganger and the orc fought too closely and fluidly. Instead he watched carefully and let his electroplasm regenerate. He still only had the conjurer's small pool of electroplasm, and he did not know how many spells he would be called upon to cast if they were to do what in the game was called a "full clear": the killing of all enemies at a particular location.

Doppelganger found himself retreating straight back from every wild blow before remembering the fundamentals of his training. He stepped aside, and his opponent clumsily charged past him. But not before spearing Doppelganger's leg. His leg bled profusely, but it was not life threatening. In fact it was a lifesaver as it brought on Doppelganger's bloodwarp. The three martial humors pumped furiously into his body. He took on the angry tint of the orc. He grew in size and strength. Fear and pain were banished and replaced with the warrior's madness. The orc recovered and bore down again on Doppelganger. But this time, he was struck with an explosive fireball from Dangalf that seared his flesh and brought him to his knees. He did not long inhale the stench of his own burning flesh before Doppelganger removed his head.

The explosive fireball brought the attention of the whole camp. The troll captain exited the command office fastening his belt. He screamed to the lowly orcs in Trollish. Nerdraaage appeared behind the captain and whistled at him. The troll captain spun to him and sneered at the pathetic dwarf. He marched forward, determined to make quick work of the arrogant mercenary, but when he reached for his sword, he discovered that it was missing from his scabbard. Nerdraaage plunged a dagger into the captain's unarmored groin. When the captain doubled over, he plunged another dagger into his eye. Nerdraaage unappeared to seek out another victim.

Icil did not unappear and instead met the clumsy orc guards face to face as they charged him. He slew three in a row before the others halted and grouped up. Now three attacked Icil simultaneously and met the same fate as the three solo attackers. Icil's skill was such that compared to lowly guards, he was virtually invincible. The same could not be said for Dangalf and Doppelganger, who now had several of the orc guards charging them.

Icil shouted at the guards in challenge. Some turned from Dangalf and Doppelganger to charge the blackguard, but four still bore down on the two humans. This was especially troublesome for Dangalf, who had used a considerable amount of electroplasm. Unlike the warrior class, which became stronger as the battle raged on, the wizard class became weaker as electroplasm was expended and one-use spells became unlearned.

Doppelganger was attacked first and found himself trading heavy metal with an axe-wielding orc. He was enjoying the give and take, almost toying with his opponent, when he saw that the other three orcs were pursuing Dangalf. He suddenly remembered what his role was: just like in the game, he had to protect the squishy. Dangalf was in peril, and they had no healer and no healing potions. Doppelganger stopped toying with the orc guard and killed him.

Doppelganger charged after Dangalf and his pursuers. Dangalf could not outrun the mesomorphs, and he quickly looked back to see the speediest of the three orcs right at his back and ready to spear him. He did not know if the spell was ready again, but he had no choice but to cast it. He had never before known such relief when the orc immediately behind him was cast in a block of ice. But there was no celebration or even let up as two pursuers remained.

Dangalf saw Doppelganger coming to his rescue and was able to curve his retreat toward him. The angle allowed Doppelganger to catch up with the last pursuer. He struck at his leg, and the orc fell painfully to the ground. Doppelganger gained on Dangalf's final pursuer, who realized he would not kill the little human before the big human was upon him. He stopped his pursuit and turned to fight Doppelganger.

Doppelganger's defense of Dangalf had worked. Perhaps it worked too well, as the first orc limped quickly toward Doppelganger, and he found himself fighting both of them. Realizing he was safe from pursuit, Dangalf turned back to see Doppelganger furiously defending himself from the two orcs. He summoned his electroplasm to cast a spell, but he found he was completely drained. He had no spells to cast without rest. And then he did something no one of the Red School would understand in these circumstances: he lay down and slumbered.

Doppelganger saw Dangalf lying on the ground and knew that no massive fireball was going to bail him out of this fight. Not anytime soon anyway. The wounded orc, slowed by blood loss and severed tendons, could not defend himself adequately as Doppelganger charged. Doppelganger killed him but only after turning his back on the healthy orc. And the healthy orc was a mercenary, the same class as Doppelganger. He was ferocious and clever, and he placed his sword under the arm of Doppelganger's armor. Doppelganger shrugged off the attack before his heart or lungs were pierced but not before serious damage was done. His left arm fell limply to his side. It was all he could do to parry his healthy opponent while he retreated. Then with a crash, the final orc was released from the crumbling remains of Dangalf's ice block and charged toward the wounded Doppelganger.

And Dangalf slumbered. His electroplasm was replenishing only slowly. He feared that Doppelganger would soon be dead and couldn't help but selfishly think that this meant he would be dead soon after.

Just as the second orc guard reached Doppelganger, he let out a sharp cry and fell dead to the ground. Standing behind him was Nerdraaage with his blade stained with stinking orc blood.

Nerdraaage flanked the final orc menacing Doppelganger. The orc turned on the dwarf furiously but suddenly a black raccoon mask covered his eyes and he was blind. Nerdraaage stepped behind the wildly swinging orc and placed both his blades in his back. The orc went down, and Nerdraaage finished him off.

Doppelganger and Nerdraaage, bloodied and panting, collapsed to the ground. They watched wearily as Dangalf limped over to them. "I think I pulled a muscle running away," he said. Nerdraaage laughed first. Doppelganger joined in even though as the bloodwarp faded, laughter racked pain through his dead arm. Dangalf was so overcome with emotion that they had survived the frenetic combat that he could have laughed or cried. But since his friends had chosen laughter, he joined them.

They made their way to the troll camp. The compound was littered with a dozen orc bodies and the troll captain. The buildings were just now catching fire. Icil greeted them with a torch that he tossed into the last building.

"How does it feel to finally bust those hymens?" he challenged them.

They laughed again. They were overcome with the rush of victory and the pride of facing death with honor. It was exhilarating, a glorious release, when locked in a battle to the death to see your opponent finally fall dead before you. Gentle, scholarly Weyd Salint himself had impressed upon Dangalf the importance of ridding this world of the bastard races of the Legion, and now that he had met the enemy face to monstrous face, Dangalf knew it was true.

Suddenly dark shadows appeared overhead, and a great whooshing sound overtook them. "Run," said Icil, who looked worried. It was a frightening thing for the others to see such a man as Icil look worried. They looked up, but the creatures came from out of the sunset and were silhouetted. "Run!" shouted Icil furiously.

Dangalf, slowed by his limp, ran alongside Doppelganger, who was slowed by his dead arm. "What about Nerdraaage?" he asked.

"He can unappear," said Doppelganger. They looked back at a fearsome sight as they ran. It was wyvern riders, the Legion's answer to the dragoons. The very best warriors of the Legion Warrior class. Masters of murder. Icil also was a master, but there were four of them and only one of him. Still he remained visible and stood his ground as the giant wyverns landed around him. He wanted to buy the others time to escape.

The orcs landed in a circle around Icil, their wyverns trotting to a stop before they dismounted. They dwarfed Icil, who stood fearlessly visible to them. These were not like the orc guards and mercenaries whom they had just overwhelmed. They were massive and ferocious and heavily armored. They would not be wyvern riders if they were not also battle tested a hundred times over. With a nod from the biggest orc, two of them took off after Doppelganger and Dangalf. They ran like beasts, and even if Dangalf and Doppelganger hadn't been injured, it would only be a matter of minutes before they overtook and dispatched the two humans.

Dangalf turned back long enough to cast the closest orc in a block of ice. He didn't even have a second to turn around and continue running before the monster orc smashed his way out of the ice block. Dangalf and Doppelganger both feared this failed spell was their last hope to escape alive.

They continued desperately through the bush only to stumble upon a large tyger of purple and blue. Doppelganger instinctively raised his axe. The cat stepped back and moaned. "No," said Dangalf as he pulled his wounded friend past the cat. They reached an open field and found Ciar standing before them.

"Lie down," she told them, but they hesitated. "I am a very good healer but if the orcs chop your heads off, I will not be able to put them back on." They did not know her, but they did know that she was a she-elf and that her composure was reassuring, so they lay down. Ciar whisper-sang in Elvish. The surrounding fauna grew in a few seconds to cover Doppelganger and Dangalf in a cocoon of vines and leafy plant matter. It was somewhat uncomfortable as branches and roots poked into and around their flesh, but it did seem to camouflage them well. Dangalf desperately hoped it would be enough.

Something heavy began walking on Dangalf. He dared only move his eyes, and he looked up to realize in terror that one of his orc pursuers stood right on top of him. "Go back to your stinking swamps before these woods swallow you!" Ciar said. The orcs looked at the she-elf druid, about twenty feet ahead of them and paused. Though she was no match for them in a fight, they did not like being in elven lands, even occupied elven lands, facing an elf witch.

One of the orcs shot an arrow at her that was brilliantly fast and perfectly aimed, yet she was able to sidestep it. The other immediately followed with his own shot, but she only tilted her head, and it missed her. They continued to fire in rapid succession, and she moved no more than necessary to dodge their arrows. Dangalf felt the orc step off from above him. Both charged toward Ciar, and in response she morphed into a brilliant white-and-gold tyger and speedily retreated. They stopped and she changed back to she-elf form still out of range. They understood. They could not hit her with their ranged attacks, and if they tried to pursue her, she would always remain ahead of them in her tyger form, pulling them closer to the crimson wall.

Dangalf could see their terrifying forms through the leaves over him. One of the orcs screamed at Ciar. It was a terrifying bestial sound that would have caused Dangalf to flee uncontrollably if he had not been solidly entwined. Ciar did not speak Orcish, but she knew it was a promise of terrible things to come should they meet again. The other wyvern rider blew a kiss to Ciar, and she knew that also was a promise of terrible things to come should they meet again. And then they both ran back the way they had come, one stomping directly on Dangalf's face.

The two orcs left to deal with the assassin were in no hurry to face him. It was not fear but caution and experience that stayed their hands. They went through their gear, still keeping a close eye on the visible blackguard, to find the perfect tools for killing him. They uttered back and forth. Icil imagined that they were confused by his failure to unappear. He would try to use their confusion to his advantage.

Finally, they were prepared, and they separated so that they might approach him from different angles. The one behind Icil charged and just before he reached the assassin, Icil unappeared. Then he reappeared behind the orc and drove both of his daggers into the armor gap at the neck. Icil did everything correctly, but the beast was so ferocious, so thickly muscled, that it would not die quickly or even drop to the ground.

Icil could only hold onto his daggers and hope the beast would succumb before the other orc planted an axe between his shoulder blades. The other orc instead fired arrows, but Icil was able to use the first orc as a shield.

The orc finally gurgled and dropped heavily to the ground. Icil unappeared again. The other orc returned leisurely to his wyvern where he rummaged for more gear. He replaced his plate helmet with one of leather, which didn't make sense to Icil until he recognized it as a Serpentine Helm. It would give its wearer heat-sensing vision—the perfect foil for an unappeared opponent. Icil had faced this threat before and knew to lower his body temperature as much as he could.

The orc marched toward him with his ice-enchanted axe. If the blade touched Icil at all, it would put a deathly chill on him that would slow his movement or even freeze him in place. Either scenario meant he would be an easy kill for the ferocious wyvern rider. He wished he had processed the gravewhisper flower into poison, but there was no time now. Icil braced himself as the warrior marched forward as if he knew exactly where Icil laid in wait. He could hear the enchanted axe now. It howled like hurricane winds across a glacier.

And suddenly the orc stopped and in an instant threw his axe violently forward. Icil recognized the throwing motion before it was completed but he had also seen that it was so off the mark that he would not have to dodge it. Icil would have laughed would it not have given his position away.

But with the sound of a groan and a thud, Icil sickly realized he had not been the target. Nerdraaage lay dying in the dirt behind him with the orc blade tossed through the center of his chest. Icil knew Nerdraaage's life could be measured in a handful of sand. He needed the orc to go to Nerdraaage, to pass Icil and give him his back. But the orc seemed surprised that he had struck a dwarf and was in no hurry to go to him. The orc armed himself with a shortsword from his belt.

Finally after scanning in every direction for the assassin, the orc moved to the dying dwarf. But as soon as his first finger touched the handle of the blade in Nerdraaage's chest, Icil moved with unsurpassed quickness. He knew Nerdraaage's life hung in the balance. The impalement may kill him yet, but a twist of the blade would kill him certainly. Icil had killed deathspeakers before they could utter a word and dodged lightning cast by

Nil the Stormbringer, but could he strike quickly enough to stop this monstrous wyvern rider before he killed Nerdraaage?

Icil inserted his dagger between the orc's leg armor and angled it down to the tendon. He felt it cut loose and with that the orc lost his balance and the leverage he would need to twist his blade. The orc howled like a wounded animal. Icil pushed with all his might and moved the massive orc away from Nerdraaage.

Icil stepped in close to his opponent. He made the orc pay for his heat vision as he bashed the top of the leather helm, stunning the orc. The orc swung powerfully at where Icil used to be. It was all Icil now as he had his way with the wyvern rider. He killed the orc and enjoyed the deathblow more than he usually did. This orc had wounded his apprentice, and against his better judgment Icil had become fond of the dwarf mercenary.

But there was no time for celebration as he heard the arrow just in time to dodge it. The other two orcs had returned from their fruitless pursuit and opened fire on Icil. They fired in unison, and he dodged the headshot at the cost of taking an arrow in the leg. He unappeared, but that trick would not long delay the master warriors. The self-sealing properties of his dragon-wing leather meant that there would be no blood trail, but the poison from the arrow crippled his leg, and he could no longer walk without footprints. They could easily track him, and he did not have the speed to escape them.

He moved to the trees, taking them away from Nerdraaage. They followed him methodically and grunted in Orcish back and forth. Their pursuit was measured, which was bad for Icil. They would not take their wounded opponent lightly. He heard one of the orc words for "blood" and knew that they could smell his as it pooled in his boot.

Icil would not make the trees. He stopped and prepared for a fight. He had killed every Legion assassin sent to close his book and even escaped the Witchfinder General. He would survive this. After all, *I know I cannot be killed and therefore I cannot be killed.* (Though he had to admit his present situation was certainly testing the limits of this philosophy.)

Icil's only regret was that in his hubris he had brought along Nerdraaage and his friends into a situation that they were as of yet unfit. He had hoped to protect them from serious harm, but he had not taken into account a flight of wyvern riders descending upon them. There were only a hundred wyvern riders in the entire world.

The wyvern riders slowed as they approached where he lay in wait. They would not be surprised by him, and working together they would kill him. The fact that Icil knew he could not be killed did not matter to them. They were too careful now to stumble into Icil, so he leapt forth to meet them. He drove both of his daggers up and under the chest armor of the first orc, driving and twisting furiously toward his black heart. His back was exposed to the other orc, who immediately placed his giant axe between Icil's shoulder blades. It was a ferocious blow that seemed to Icil to almost split him in half. But he endured the pain as he continued grinding his blades into the first orc. And still he knew he could not be killed. He desperately wanted to hear the orc's death rattle before the axe chopped into his back a second time.

And then Icil felt himself whole again, filled with a lightness and strength that he had felt only a few times before and always on the battlefield. Flesh and bone knitted itself back together. He was being healed by druid magic. He did not stop to look for the source or consider it further, but his strength renewed, he plunged his daggers further into the orc until his fists entered the wounds created by his daggers. He felt the leathery heart through his blades and penetrated it. He watched the life leave the orc's red eyes as he pulled his fists and daggers out of the orc's belly.

The remaining orc also saw that Icil was healed. He paused only a second to consider abandoning his attack on the human to kill the druid, but he knew that he would never reach her before the assassin killed him. His only option was to cause more damage to Icil than the druid could heal, and he stepped up the intensity of his attacks. But Icil, having dispatched the other orc, now turned to the final orc and faced him with full strength and speed. The orc's desperate attack was sloppy, and Icil was able to avoid the massive blows before he stepped in close to the orc and killed him with a dagger to the eye. Icil had allowed himself while in the heat of battle to imagine that the druid was his beloved she-elf blackguard reborn as a guardian spirit, but he could see now that she was not his lost love reincarnated as valkyria. Before the orc had even dropped to the ground, Icil shouted for Ciar to heal Nerdraaage.

Nerdraaage, true to blackguard mythology, had believed he could not die but was dying nonetheless. He saw a tunnel with a light at the end, and he was speeding toward its fatal conclusion. But at the end of the tunnel was bliss: Morna holding a child that he knew was his son. His grandfather, the only father figure he knew, who had died only a few years ago and left Nerdraaage all alone in the other world. Not alone. He had three friends whom he had only known briefly but who had been his best friends over the last six months and between two different universes. He saw them as they looked in this universe. Doppelganger, Dangalf, and Elftrap. No, it was Ashlyn now. And she was his friend too. And Icil was there. Icil, who would not even train him at first, was now his friend. The visions were clearer than any dream or memory, as if he could reach out and touch them. He reached out and touched a she-elf. "Relax," Ciar told Nerdraaage as she cast waves of healing upon him.

Nerdraaage felt himself becoming whole again. His sight returned to him just in time to see Ciar removing the axe from his chest. She whisper-sang more Elvish words and laid her hands upon him. And he could hear and feel the crunch of bones and the squish of organs as they knitted themselves back together. He felt the energy of the earth pulsing through his body. In a great circle around his body, plants withered and died as Ciar stole their protoplasm to make Nerdraaage whole again. Great tentacles of brown grass stretched out in every direction to trees that shed their leaves as they gave up their lives to the dwarf. Ciar was sworn to protect the Hierarchy of Life, and it was necessary to sacrifice even beneficial flora to preserve dwarves and other righteous sapiens. For righteous sapiens were the protectors of this world and all the flora and fauna.

Nerdraaage raised himself up on his elbows to the sight of Icil, Doppelganger, and Dangalf watching him anxiously. They sighed and smiled and laughed and cried each in his own way at the sight of a reborn Nerdraaage. "You are lucky, Master Dwarf, to belong to the sturdiest of the races," said Ciar. "That axe pierced all three of your hearts."

"Three hearts?" asked Nerdraaage, surprised as much as the rest of the Keepers. *Because the world itself sets upon three pillars.*

Ciar rose from kneeling and turned to Icil with a reproachful smile. "You must take your charges from this place now. I have not the magic to heal even a water sprite. I will be slumbering for two days now because of your folly."

"The wyvern riders were unanticipated," explained Icil. "Before that, my charges attacked and destroyed an entire Legion camp. Before you leave see for yourself what is left of it. Smoldering ruins and orc corpses. All done without a healer or healing potion."

"You're welcome," said Ciar.

"Forgive me," said Icil bowing. "I owe you my life."

"So do I," said Nerdraaage.

"And I," said Doppelganger.

"We all do," said Dangalf.

"And I thank you," said Ciar. "We are grateful for your efforts. Each attack on the Legion occupiers helps hasten the return of our lands. Who knows? Maybe someday even Master Icil may salvage his reputation with the elves."

Nerdraaage was astonished. "Why wouldn't you have a good reputation with the elves?" he asked.

"Long story," said Icil. "Just remember, reputations can be lost as well as earned."

"I did not think it possible for one blackguard to kill four wyvern riders," marveled Ciar.

"I could not have done it without you."

"I was only there as you battled the last two. I will tell my people of this battle today." Icil nodded. The purple-and-blue tyger walked into the middle of the group and sat down. Nerdraaage eyed it suspiciously, but otherwise its extraordinary presence went unmentioned. They all assumed it was with the druid.

Clay returned to Dangalf, and he understood. "Ashlyn got my message. You're her trainer, Ciar!" he said.

"Yes, Dangalf. She was concerned about your well-being."

"We really need to thank her when we get back."

"Thank her now," said Ciar, nodding to the tyger, which stopped panting and took on a more dignified look.

"Ashlyn!" said Dangalf in pleasant surprise. "You've morphed!" Metamorphosis was the foundation talent of the druid. And Ashlyn had already learned it.

"I liked the bipedal version better," said Icil.

"This is wonderful," said Dangalf. "Can you turn back?"

"She has not mastered the reverse transformation," said Ciar.

"You mean she's stuck like that!" shouted Nerdraaage gleefully.

"Metamorphosis is never permanent, but she will need to increase her own pool of electroplasm before change is easy for her," explained Ciar. "I taught her advanced techniques out of order so that we could move quickly to find you."

"Why is she purple?" asked Doppelganger.

"Isn't she beautiful?" said Ciar. "Tyger colors are unique to the individual druid, determined by aura, environment, even emotional state."

"Like a hairy mood ring!" said Nerdraaage.

It was agreed they needed to depart these lands quickly, and they followed Icil to the tied-off wyverns. It was believed that no human, dwarf, or elf could sit peacefully upon these imports from Oceania (just as no gryphon would allow orc, troll, or goblin upon his back) so it was customary to kill them and deny their use to the enemy. But Ciar forbade their murder as Sirona had not yet placed wyverns in the Hierarchy of Life, and to kill them might be a crime. And so Icil clipped their wings instead. He said this would allow them to fly but never again allow them to bear the weight of armored orc warriors. As proof, he spurred the wyverns to flight, and they each flew off. One made an angry and threatening swoop at the party before realizing he was alone in his attack and flew after his fleeing mates.

Dangalf and Doppelganger affectionately stroked tyger Ashlyn. Even Nerdraaage found himself touching her beautiful coat. Ashlyn enjoyed the affection like an oversized housecat. Ciar bid the humans and dwarf farewell and morphed into her white-and-gold tyger form. She ran back toward free elven lands with tyger Ashlyn following.

Icil led the males back the way they had come. He was effusive with his praise and told them how he would write his report to the sages. Icil credited them all with the razing of the camp. He signed off on Nerdraaage's pilfering of the troll intelligence and his killing of the troll captain. He additionally credited Dangalf and Nerdraaage with four orc kills each and Doppelganger with eight. No one disputed Icil's accounting—ascribing kills was subjective work after all, and Dangalf and Nerdraaage did not resent the advantage being given to Doppelganger. His class required the highest enemy body count before he could train further. Dangalf was required only once to kill an enemy sapien in honorable combat. (Honorable in this case being defined as combat in which he himself faced a reasonable chance of death or serious injury.)

Icil reported Doppelganger and Nerdraaage for the additional honor of sustaining grave injury during combat. Doppelganger told Nerdraaage there was a badge awarded for that. Nerdraaage was quite excited about the thought of getting a badge until Icil told him that blackguards don't wear badges.

"Let's not forget Dangalf," said Doppelganger.

"What did I do?"

"You pulled a muscle in your ass running away." And they all laughed at Dangalf.

"It was a muscle in my leg," he said flatly.

They spent one last night together in the woods after crossing back through the Crimson Wall to the safety of elven lands. By the fire they drank and smoked, and Icil regaled them with stories of assassination and assignation. He had fucked she-dwarves and she-elves and mermaids! More than one thousand females of various stripes (including striped ones). Even a she-troll! Nerdraaage had nerd-lusted for she-trolls ever since he had lain eyes on their wickedly sexy avatars in the game. Many lonely nights he had spent in front of his computer looking at explicit fan art of the blue devils. "A she-troll!" he said excitedly.

"Dangerous but a good lay," answered Icil. "You must hold her tail tightly so its passionate swishing does not dismember your member."

"Angus said she-trolls have teeth in their minges," said Nerdraaage.

"I can not say for certain," said Icil. "I have been with only one, and she was all gums down there." The Keepers laughed, and Icil found himself unable to resist joining in. And with that, their relationship changed forever. It was a bonding experience second only to that bonding that takes place in combat. And they had already undergone that. The Keepers knew that they could now call Icil a friend and he felt the same of the three.

There was something eminently irresistible about Icil. This supreme life-taker was also an unrepentant life-liver. Dangalf imagined Icil in their old world, before his disfigurement. He supposed that Icil would slip right into his new world without missing a beat. He would be a war hero or a rock star or a billionaire or perhaps the first to be all three. And of course a lady-killer. But even these imagined versions of an ubersuccessful Icil in a world that Dangalf despised (and that had despised him first) could not diminish the fondness that he had for the rakish rogue. Icil would not be an NPC in any world.

They went to bed, and Icil slept while unappeared. Nerdraaage marveled at the discipline that allowed Icil to remain unappeared while he slept. Dangalf picked up a rolled aspect that Icil had held in his hand all night as he had regaled them. It was of a beautiful, innocent-looking she-elf. Dangalf suspected correctly that she was Icil's lost love. And now it was the avenging of her death that was his sole driving purpose.

LXVIII

I cil woke the three Keepers at first light the next morning. "I would like to show you something before I take my leave," he said. He stepped out into a clearing and looked up into the bright morning sky. He put a small metal tube to his mouth and blew into it. He shielded his lens-covered eyes from the sun as he looked expectantly to the sky.

A great shadow appeared first and a moment later a great bird. But it was not bird as it had the body of a cat. The Keepers looked on with amazement as they recognized the massive creature as it settled on the ground near Icil. It was a griffin. They stepped hesitantly toward the beast until Icil took it by its muzzle and waved them over. "This is Siobahn."

The griffin kept her wings partially outstretched as if prepared for flight as the Keepers approached. Though she was not as menacing looking as the wyverns, it was clear that the large beak and claws and muscular body could do great damage to a sapien if the griffin was so inclined. But this one just watched them carefully as Icil stroked her feathered head. Dangalf could smell her, but it was not foul like an orc. It was natural and musky, not unlike the family dog he remembered as a child.

They reached out and touched her body. Her hair was shorter than a tyger, more like a textured skin. The feathers were soft in one direction but razor sharp against the grain. It was a magical moment as the sun shone down sporadically between fast-moving clouds. "Can I ride it?" asked Nerdraaage.

"I have almost killed you once these last twenty-four hours," answered Icil. "But when you are an expert rider, I will give you your first griffin lesson. All of you." Icil mounted the griffin, and the others stepped clear.

"I'll write you," said Nerdraaage.

"Write me care of the sages," said Icil. "I'm afraid that even the most skilled and persistent bird would find it difficult to track me." They all felt melancholy about the parting. They were blood brothers now after all. Icil reached into an inside chest pocket and pulled out two attached silver tubes. "I want you to have this," he said, presenting it to Nerdraaage. "Open it."

Nerdraaage pulled apart the tubes revealing a parchment. "A map," he said. "Of elven lands."

"Not quite," said Icil. "It is a map of wherever you are. The work of a goblin artisan."

Dangalf knew the term artisan. As much prestige as there was being a member of the Red, White, or Blue Schools, there were certain hyphenates of this world with the special accomplishment of being recognized in two schools. There were the Purples, like Angus the Young, recognized by the Red and Blue Schools; the Templars, recognized by both Red and White Schools; and the Artisans, recognized by both White and Blue. But for the Artisans, it was not a matter of being an expert craftsman and magician independently as a Purple could be independently talented as a warrior and a craftsman. Artisan instead was a title reserved only for those creators that could imbue their crafted items with magic. "Won't you need this?" protested Nerdraaage.

"It might save me some aimless wandering," said Icil. "But for you, it might save your lives." Doppelganger and Dangalf also marveled at the gift. They recognized its game counterpart: an onscreen minimap that showed the area surrounding a player. Where the player had not yet journeyed, the map would appear blank until discovered. It was another amazing realization of a game concept. But since this map was owned by Icil, lands well beyond their experience already appeared. "You will forgive me," said Icil to Dangalf and Doppelganger. "For presenting my gift to just one, but knowing what brothers you are, I know this gift will be of benefit to all including my fair she-elf. Farewell to you, Keepers of the Broken Blade!" And with that Icil trotted off toward an opening in the trees and spurred Siobahn into the air. Icil made one pass over them and saluted. The griffin made a thunderous squawk. The Keepers saluted back until Icil disappeared into the clouds.

LXIX

Their magical map led the three Keepers back to Templa Taur an hour quicker than their original journey. Dangalf let Doppelganger and Nerdraaage argue over who would bathe first and slumbered on his bed. Nerdraaage took second bath while Doppelganger rested on his bed.

They all owed a great deal to Icil, for in one afternoon they made significant steps in completing their journeymen levels—steps that would have taken them months without his guidance and help and conceivably years if they had been cast into this world alone. Successful completion of the next step of training meant going from a per diem pay to a monthly salary. Future training would also be paid for, and they would receive gear allowances. Each would become an associate member of their respective schools when they were only sponsored members now. School facilities at larger cities were complexes with dormitories, dining halls, libraries, training areas, and social clubs. Access was based on membership status, and associate members had access to all but the most inner sanctums of their campuses. The most extravagant example of each school was found in that school's racial capital: Red in Vinland, White in Oira Nomo, and Blue in Bran Keep.

Dangalf warned that with their next promotions came the increased possibility of "orders from Vinland." One or more of them could be sidetracked from their own ambitions for a special mission or even to go to war. Missions may not hinder them much, and they could even offer significant rewards, but war would put all their plans on hold indefinitely. Hopefully they would all have advanced rank before open war began so that they were not treated as mere catapult fodder. "Tub's all yours," said Nerdraaage.

Dangalf looked at the opaque water. "Can I get some clean water?" asked Dangalf.

"And why is that?" challenged Nerdraaage.

"It's murky," explained Dangalf.

"It was murky when I got in," said Nerdraaage.

"But you just had Doppel's filth. Now it has the filth of both of you."

"Three is a sacred number!" said Nerdraaage.

"Not when it comes to bathing!" said Dangalf. "I'm going to order some more hot water."

"If it was Ashlyn's bath water, you'd chug it like a beer!" said Nerdraaage.

"What is that supposed to mean!" demanded Dangalf.

Doppelganger turned away with an expression that said he couldn't believe what Nerdraaage had just said. "Go on," commanded Nerdraaage, arms folded in indignation and nodding to the tub.

Dangalf was finally shamed into taking the third bath. He stuck his toe in the murky water. It was still warm, so it offered at least some comfort. He lowered himself into the tub, and it wasn't too bad. Nerdraaage burst out in laughter. "What?" asked Dangalf.

"You wouldn't see me taking the third bath! Rub a dub dub!" Dangalf ignored their laughter. It was good to wash away the blood, sweat, and dirt from the past few days, even in used bath water. And the only reminder that he was taking third bath was a fine layer of grit under his backside. And he fretted a little about Nerdraaage's vulgar suggestion. Was his attraction to Ashlyn so obvious?

LXX

When Dangalf, Doppelganger, and Nerdraaage took their usual table at the King Bee, they were surprised to be celebrated by all the gathered elves, who for the most part had ignored them during their stay. Word had spread of their heroic deeds just beyond the Crimson Wall. Dangalf found the praise intoxicating and wished he had done great deeds in the other world. But then he thought, in his old world, he might not have gotten any praise. He thought the Keepers might have been criticized or even charged with a crime for acting with such autonomy and decisiveness and lethality. Best not to think back about the other world, he thought finally.

The three were already drunk with praise and were well on their way to being the other kind of drunk when Ashlyn arrived. She headed for their table only to be stopped at the bar by an elf with whom she exchanged pleasantries. And then other elves, male of course, exuberantly celebrated her arrival. She was dressed in her usual barely there leather, so that wasn't the difference. It was all in her attitude. Ashlyn touched the elf's arm

(*What a flirt!*) as she excused herself and walked to her friends' table. "Where's your dagger?" Nerdraaage demanded.

"In the room."

"Why aren't you wearing it?"

"Metal is a problem. It will drop off when I morph. And when I change back, I have to remember where it is and hope no one's taken it."

"Can I have your dagger?" asked Nerdraaage.

"You already have yours and Dangalf's."

"You can never have too many daggers," said Nerdraaage. "What about your clothes?"

"What about them?"

"Do they fall off when you morph?"

"Leather and fur clothing will stay on me during metamorphosis," said Ashlyn. "Cloth would fall right off me, leaving me naked when I changed back." Ashlyn looked at Dangalf as she said this. He swallowed, convinced his Adam's apple had taken on the size of a plum. "Stone, metal, paper—it all drops off when I morph," she continued.

"That could be a problem," said Doppelganger. "Not being able to carry any gear."

"We don't need a lot of gear. Plus, I always have you guys to carry my gear," she smiled.

They excitedly told her stories of the Crimson Wall, where elves and trolls harvest the deadly blossom when not in mortal combat with each other. And the troll forward camp that no longer existed because of the sabotage and slaughter they had wrought. And the promise of Icil to teach them griffin riding when they were ready. Oh, and the enchanted map that he bestowed on Nerdraaage.

Ashlyn politely listened to their stories and then told them of her own exciting adventures. She could now shapeshift at will but only into tyger form or *felis sapien*. And just today she had journeyed to a nearby infirmary with Ciar, where she had practiced healing minor injuries with major success.

Doppelganger thought of Dymphna, downed his mead, and ordered another. He took Dangalf's pipe and puffed on it, which was unusual for him.

An elf dressed in hunters' buckskin entered the inn and greeted his party. Before he sat, he recognized Ashlyn and approached her. Doppelganger bristled that he would approach a female sitting with him but waited to hear the elf's words. "Ashlyn," he bowed. "My good fortune to see you two nights in a row."

"Hello, Fionn," she smiled.

Fionn stood tall and confident with shoulder-length black hair. His paleness suggested he did not hunt during the day. Dangalf wondered if he aspired to the Horns of Cernunnos, an elven-only force of rangers that operated almost exclusively at night. He was strong, but more ectomorphic than Doppelganger. He wore a large hunting knife at the front of his belt in what Dangalf found to be a sexually vulgar manner.

"Fionn has just begun his pathfinder training," said Ashlyn by way of introduction. "These are my friends, Dangalf, Doppelganger, and the rest."

"Pathfinder," said Doppelganger. "That makes you a second-class ranger?"

"Third class," corrected Dangalf. "Just like us. He won't be second class until he completes his training."

"Your gray friend is correct," said Fionn. Gray friend! thought Dangalf as he absently stroked his beard. "I don't mean to interrupt," continued Fionn. "But I have spoken to my trainer, and he has permitted you to heal for me during my warg hunt. Provided it is allowed by your trainer."

"She said it was cool."

"More of your foreign tongue," laughed Fionn.

"She said it was fine," said Ashlyn. Was she blushing, she wondered? Conversing with Fionn had been much easier yesterday without her friends watching her.

"So charming. Very good then. I shall leave you to your friends until a time when we may speak alone."

"Good night," said Ashlyn smiling. Fionn bowed to Ashlyn and nodded to her companions before departing.

"A new friend?" asked Dangalf.

"He and I were the last ones when the tavern closed last night," said Ashlyn.

"You came here alone," said Dangalf.

"He will need to kill a warg to complete his training, and those are usually found in Legion territory. He's allowed to bring a healer, and that would also fulfill one of my own requirements."

"Sounds dangerous," said Doppelganger jealously.

"You two gonna sleep in the woods together?" asked Nerdraaage with a mischievous grin.

"We will be in the woods, and I suspect sleeping will take place at some point," she said.

"Boy, is he in for a big surprise," said Nerdraaage.

"Why?" said Ashlyn.

"I'm just saying, looks can be deceiving," said Nerdraaage.

"What do you mean?" she pressed.

"Everybody calm down," said Dangalf.

"I just think that it might be kind of embarrassing. I mean, what happens if you two share the same tent and you need to cuddle together because it's so cold. I mean, he thinks he's cuddling up to Liv Tyler and all of a sudden he finds Orlando's bloom."

"What the fuck!" said Ashlyn as she stood angrily. She raised a fist, and it was a cute little fist, but not at all suitable for hurting a dwarf. Her outrage only made Nerdraaage laugh harder. "In case you haven't noticed," she continued. "I'm she-elf all over.

And if anyone should know that, it should be you, you little peeping pervert."

"I was just practicing my unappear!"

"I'm sorry you're an ugly little dwarf, but don't take it out on me." Ashlyn's sincere outrage only made Nerdraaage laugh harder. He enjoyed this moment. In one fell swoop, he had avenged all of Elftrap's previous cruelty, and it felt good. As Ashlyn looked at the laughing dwarf, she was suddenly overcome. She squeezed her eyes tight, but it was too late. A flood of tears streamed down her face. She walked away but only got as far as Fionn, who stopped her. She shielded her face from him as he spoke to her.

Dangalf stood up angrily and scolded Nerdraaage. "Now look what you did!"

"What?" said Nerdraaage. "She's always calling me short and ugly and stupid."

"And smelly," added Doppelganger.

"And smelly," said Nerdraaage, laughing harder.

Ashlyn left the inn, and Fionn started to follow her, but Dangalf intercepted him. "Sit your ass back down!" he commanded Fionn.

Dangalf found Ashlyn in the room. She could have gone elsewhere, but she had hoped someone would pursue her and she wanted to be found. Now, she lay face down on her bed and told Dangalf to go away but not wanting him to go away. He sat on her bed and studied her fine elven form from the back. She truly was all she-elf, and he wanted her more than anything. Nerdraaage had been right. Dangalf would chug her bathwater.

Dangalf said words that he thought would comfort her, and she allowed herself to be coaxed into turning over, though she kept a forearm across her face to shield her crying eyes. He asked her to take her arm from her face, and she protested about how ugly she was. He persisted, and she removed her arm but turned her eyes away so as not to look at him. He took the liberty of touching her face to turn it toward him. Her face was warm and lightly streaked with tears. She looked up at him with moist eyes, and he had to swallow his plum again. She told him her eyes must be all red from crying.

"Your nose too," he added.

More tears came, and she tried to turn away from him, but he stopped her. He told her about how beautiful she was, and she stopped struggling and turned back to him. She was the most beautiful creature he had ever seen, could even imagine, and her crying did nothing to diminish that. She hugged him close and cried and shuddered against him. He imagined her shuddering would feel like that also if she were to climax.

She was a she-elf, a female, she insisted. In body, in brain, in temperament, in any other aspect. Dangalf said he had known that all along as he luxuriated in the heat of her body against his.

Dangalf imagined how they would make love: She would tell him that she was completely female and offer to prove it to him. He would say it was not necessary, but it was too late as she stripped out of her furkini. She would insist that he look at her and he would run his eyes up and down her hairless, lithe body. They would hug more and begin kissing passionately. She would lie back on the bed and tell him to make love to her. And he would oblige. He was not an otherworld virgin like Nerdraaage, but it had been a long time nonetheless. And he had never had anything close to Ashlyn.

While Ashlyn tearfully poured her heart out to him, Dangalf ran the scenario of him and her making love through his mind over and over. The fantasies varied slightly, but all revolved around the idea of her commanding him to make love to her and his ultimate compliance to preserve their friendship.

He hugged and reassured her for hours before Doppelganger and Nerdraaage noisily returned. (They did not want to catch Dangalf and Ashlyn *in flagrante*.) Dangalf rose and was standing by Ashlyn's bed when they entered. Nerdraaage shuffled over to Ashlyn's bed. "Ashlyn, I just wanted to say…" And suddenly Ashlyn sprung from her bed and planted a big kiss on the side of the dwarf's face, which made him groan and wipe his face. "I thought you said I had to apologize!" Nerdraaage shouted at Doppelganger, who shrugged in response.

Ashlyn sat back on her bed, laughing but with tears still streaming down her face. All these males had caused so many confusing thoughts and feelings for her, but it was Nerdraaage who was finally the catalyst. He made her cry. And it had been a very therapeutic cry. She had given up the last vestiges of her former self. There would be no more shame or doubt or hesitation. She was a she-elf now. She had always been a she-elf.

For his part, Dangalf thought he had laid down a solid foundation for what would soon be his and Ashlyn's white-hot lovemaking. But in *The Great Book of Unhappenings*, that secret and magical journal that follows each life, it was recorded this night that, with the slightest masculine assertiveness, Dangalf would have made love to his beloved Ashlyn. But he did not, and he never would.

LXXI

The next morning they ate breakfast at their usual table. They were unusually quiet even for an early-morning occasion after a night of smoking and drinking. A pigeon fluttered down next to Ashlyn. She took the note and fed the bird some seeds. "It's from Fionn," she said. "He has to postpone his warg hunt. He does not need me at this time. We're staying in the same inn, and he sends me a message by bird." This news would have shaken Ashlyn's fragile ego only a day ago. But she had been reborn again in a baptism of feminine emotion. "I must have made a real ass of myself last night," she laughed.

"It didn't help when Dangalf told Fionn to sit his ass down," said Nerdraaage.

Ashlyn glowered at Dangalf, who didn't look back as he attempted to conceal his satisfaction that Fionn was out of the picture.

"Now I know why elves hang with elves," she said.

"And dwarves with dwarves," said Nerdraaage. When neither of the humans spoke up, Nerdraaage turned to Doppelganger and said, "You're supposed to say, 'That's why humans hang with humans.'"

"Why?" said Doppelganger. "I didn't make an ass of myself."

An elf wearing the tabard of the elven royal family entered and spoke to the innkeeper, who pointed to the Keepers' table. "Now what?" said Nerdraaage.

The elf approached them with a large rucksack. "I am a courier to the House of Oira. I bring word of His Majesty's gratitude for your service to his ninth daughter. And I bear gifts chosen by the princess herself." He removed four packages, read the names on the packages, and presented them. "Farewell," he said, bowing before he departed.

"Were we supposed to tip him?" asked Dangalf.

Nerdraaage had not received many gifts in his previous life and tore into his without delay or ceremony. Inside the wrapping was an ornate box and inside that a more ornate smoking pipe.

"Nice," said Dangalf.

"Nice?" said Nerdraaage. "Do you know what this is?"

"A pipe?"

"This is a garrote pipe," said Nerdraaage. He snapped the pipe stem from the bowl, and a wire uncoiled between the two pieces. "Icil taught me about these during my weapons training, but I never imagined I would have my own." On closer examination he read a marking. "Rumpelstilzchen! That's the best goblin weapons maker there is! The princess must have gone to a border town for this."

"I don't think the princess was tramping around a border town," said Ashlyn.

"It's a working pipe, too," continued Nerdraaage. Dangalf marveled at the craftsmanship and was reminded that the foul goblins were renowned also for their Blue School. The dwarves inadvertently paid tribute to them in their boast that *the goblins build toys and the dwarves build monuments.* But what toys the goblins did build!

"What are you waiting for?" asked Nerdraaage. "Who's next?"

Ashlyn looked at Dangalf excitedly. "Go ahead," he said.

Ashlyn opened her box and took out a white bone-like dagger. She marveled at it before looking at the enclosed scroll for confirmation. "A dagger," said Nerdraaage. "You said you can't use daggers."

"This is a kraken tooth," said Ashlyn. "It's what druids call 'of the flesh.' Bones, teeth, leather—they're all 'of the flesh' and will stay with a druid even during metamorphosis."

Nerdraaage took it from her and cut his hand in the process. "Damn, it's sharp."

"Haven't you ever handled a kraken tooth before?" scolded Dangalf.

Ashlyn removed the leather scabbard from the box and wrapped it around her thigh. She slipped the dagger into the scabbard and proffered her leg to the other Keepers. "Isn't this gorgeous?"

"Yes, it is," said Dangalf dreamily.

"I shouldn't have this yet. It's too good."

"Same with my pipe."

"Open yours," she told Dangalf.

Dangalf opened his box and took out a heavy, folded garment. "I think this is," he started. He looked at the label to be sure. "Emperor's New Clothes LTD Vinland. It is. It's a flying cloak."

"No way," said Nerdraaage, fearing that his own gift was diminishing. "Just like in the game." Dangalf slipped into the cloak, which was entirely too nice for the rest of his wardrobe. He fastened some leather straps. "So you can fly now?" asked Nerdraaage.

"If by flying you mean like a flying squirrel," said Dangalf. "This is made just for a wizard. A wand pocket. A staff strap. Now I need to buy a staff."

"Jump off the balcony," suggested Nerdraaage.

"I don't know," said Ashlyn. "Emperor's New Clothes? It's like they're telling you it won't work. Like they're in on the joke."

"It works in the game," said Nerdraaage.

"I don't think Dymphna would buy me a phony flying cloak," Dangalf asserted weakly. He looked at the ground far below. Jumping did not appeal to him even in his luxurious flying cloak. He read the scroll he found in a pocket.

"That's the whole point of the story about the emperor's new clothes," said Ashlyn. "No one dared acknowledge the fraud."

"I say jump," said Nerdraaage. "We have a healer right here."

"I can't heal splats," said Ashlyn.

"Oh sorry," said Dangalf. "It says right here: 'After use return for repair and repacking.'"

"Okay, you have a fake flying cloak," said Nerdraaage. "Good. I still have the best gift."

"I don't know," said Ashlyn. "Doppel hasn't opened his."

"Oh, right," said Nerdraaage. "Biggest and best gift last!"

"I'll open it later," Doppelganger said.

"Go on," insisted Ashlyn.

Doppelganger lifted his gift onto the table. He unpacked boxes within boxes and unwound wrapping after wrapping.

"I'll laugh so hard if there's nothing in there," said Nerdraaage. Finally Doppelganger uncovered a shining, silvery-white breast-plate. He set it on the table standing upright. The others marveled at it. Dangalf could find no parallel for its color other than the Acadian moon itself.

Nerdraaage picked it up. "It's so light."

"It's adamantine," said Doppelganger, and off the looks of his friends explained: "It was not all skirmishing and verbal abuse with Alfred. I also learned about different armor."

"It would be worth more than gold," said Nerdraaage.

"Is there anything with it?" asked Ashlyn.

"Nothing," said Doppelganger feeling again through the wrapping. "Not even a note." He had thought that maybe Dymphna ignored him on her departure for the sake of decorum. But he had hoped that she would send him a note when she had the chance, and this had been a chance. *I see a time when we are parted. And during that time look for me close to your heart.*

"You'll have to wear something over that," said Dangalf. "We would all be killed for that." Doppelganger nodded but did not touch the armor as Nerdraaage set it back down on the table.

"Okay," conceded Nerdraaage. "You have the best gift."

"Don't be an ingrate," said Ashlyn.

"I wasn't being an ingrate," he insisted. "I have the second-best gift."

"I think the best gift she gave to all of us," said Dangalf. "Her prophecy."

"Oh, yeah," said Nerdraaage. "The prophecy. How did that go again?"

"She saw a vision of our summoner," said Dangalf impatiently. "An outsider living among strangers. And we would meet him where the sky touches the center of the earth. Has no one else considered this riddle?"

"I've been busy," said Nerdraaage.

"I thought about it a little bit," said Ashlyn.

"You're the White School," said Nerdraaage. "We just expected you to figure it out. You have the divination deck."

"Yes," said Dangalf. "We should use the divination deck. Out in the woods away from Templa Taur."

"Why out in the woods?" asked Nerdraaage.

"We must escape the safety and light of the town," said Dangalf.

"How do you know that?" asked Ashlyn.

Dangalf recalled a line from *How the Dead Lie*, one of the divination books borrowed from Weyd: "He can not penetrate the darkness who looks from a lighted room and the edge of the precipice provides the best view of the abyss."

"When?" asked Ashlyn.

"The last day of the month. At thirteen o'clock."

"I'm pretty sure there's no such hour."

"There is that night. Acadian days are not exactly twenty-four hours, so they have a periodic thirteenth hour, which is a very black time. Celebrated by all sorts of wicked creatures. It will be perfect for our purposes."

Ashlyn excused herself for her training. Nerdraaage gathered the boxes and wrapping and said he would sell it, with the coin going to the communal fund. Doppelganger and Dangalf were alone for a moment, which didn't happen much anymore. Doppelganger studied the armor without touching it. "She said she would write me," he said. "I would rather have had a letter than the adamantine."

"Well, you got adamantine," reasoned Dangalf. "Look, she's a princess. She's busy."

"She's eighteenth in line to the throne. What could she be doing?"

"Opening shopping malls? She may still write you. There's no reason you can't write her."

"Dear Princess. Remember me? I'm the mercenary who smelled so bad you had to give me a bath."

"Stop obsessing over her," said Dangalf. "If you must obsess on something, obsess on the riddle she gave us!"

"I no longer have the patience for that. For study or learning. I have no interest in it, and I don't think I'd be very good at it if I tried." Doppelganger spoke words that Dangalf knew to be true but had been hesitant to admit even to himself. The funny, curious, and educated Doppelganger had changed since coming to this world. They all had changed, but he feared that Doppelganger had lost something of himself that the others had not despite their transformations. Making Doppelganger's retreat into his lizard brain all the more jarring was the expansion of Dangalf's own brain. The interaction between memory, analysis, and creativity was faster and freer than it had been for him in the old world, even though his brain mass was unchanged. He has always enjoyed learning, but now it was intoxicating because he learned easily and recalled effortlessly. He reveled in the release of dopamine and white bile as he tackled and solved problems. But his thrilling intellect could only comprehend sadness for Doppelganger's diminished capacity even as he was determined not to make his pity obvious.

LXXII

On the last day of the month, the three male Keepers sat at their usual table and drank. Dangalf's eyes were closed in semislumber. His companions found his companionship lacking, even annoying.

"Wake up!" said Doppelganger.

"Sorry," said Dangalf. "I was reading about a horrific massacre."

"We could tell by your smile."

"Oh, no. I was happy because it was not far from here. A perfect place for our séance." Before Dangalf could go into detail, his companions looked to the entrance of the inn. Dangalf as well turned to see a magnificent, knightly figure just entered and looking about. A fierce warrior he appeared but for the perfection of his armor and the cleanness of his face. He wore a tabard of pristine white, bordered by a red-and-white checkerboard pattern with a windmill in the center.

The knight seemed to recognize the Keepers on sight and approached them. They were too in awe to even stand in respect. "Doppelganger of Hempshire?" asked the knight.

"Yes."

"I am Osbert, son of Wilfrid," said the knight.

Doppelganger stood and saluted. Osbert was clearly his superior, but what exactly he was still escaped him. He did not appear to be a warrior though he wore their armor. "This is Dangalf of Hempshire," said Doppelganger. "And Nerdraaage of Clan Stonefist." His friends stood and saluted, and Osbert returned their salutes.

"So it is true," said Osbert with a smile. "Red School and White School, human and dwarf, acting in concert. There is an elf also?"

"She's training," said Doppelganger.

"Ah," nodded Osbert. "I was wondering if I might speak to you alone, Doppelganger."

"Of course," said Doppelganger, looking quickly to his friends before leaving with the knight.

"What does it mean when he says he's Osbert, son of so and so, and you guys are just of Hempshire?" asked Nerdraaage.

"That's a little bit of class snobbery. It means he knows who his father is."

"Don't you know who your father is?"

"Yes. But unfortunately he's in another universe. In this world, I'm a bastard." Nerdraaage thought to take his Clan Stonefist scarf from inside his jacket and wrap it around his neck. He did not want to be mistaken for a dwarf of low birth.

Parentage in Acadia was only an issue for humans, and it manifested itself in honorifics such as "son of" when fathers were known and the even more prestigious surname when lineage was from a fine family that could be traced back generations.

"Fanciest warrior I ever saw," said Nerdraaage.

"That was no warrior," said Dangalf.

LXXIII

Doppelganger and Osbert walked about the deserted branches and bridges of Templa Taur. Doppelganger was eager to hear what Osbert had to say, but he would let the knight speak first. They had not walked far before Osbert spoke. "You have already gained the notice of the Temple, Doppelganger."

"The Temple," said Doppelganger. "You're a Templar!"

"You're familiar with our order?"

"The Temple of the White Rose," said Doppelganger just as he spotted the small white rose on the left side of the tabard.

"Alas, the only order of Templars since the corruption of the Red Temple."

"The Witchfinder General," said Doppelganger, remembering game mythology and their early and violent introduction to the general's minions when they had first come to this world.

"Grand Templar Aelfweard was appointed as Witchfinder General to root out and destroy the human covens that had taken up the practice of black magic," said Osbert. "Instead he became a zealot who found all magic to be criminal and began murdering druids and wizards, among others. Now he is holed up in his temple over a thousand years corrupted by the same black magic that he was charged with eradicating." And after a moment: "But enough of our great tragedy. I bring glad tidings! You and your deeds have come to the attention of Grand Templar Wilfrid. He invites you to the Temple and to test yourself to see if you would be among those few who are chosen to be called Templar."

"I'm honored," said Doppelganger. "But I have completed my apprenticeship. I am a mercenary, and I'm almost ready to train for soldier."

"Of the first two Templars, one was a warrior," said Osbert. "We only call those who are experienced combatants. All of our novitiates were apprenticed in other classes. Few are invited to train. Fewer still are successful in joining our ancient order. Only one in nine."

"I don't know what to say," said Doppelganger. "I hope to become a dragoon."

"Dragoons are fine warriors. But it is the mount that makes a dragoon, not the man. I would say that most Templars fight as well as a dragoon, but no dragoon could ever join our order."

"Why not?"

"Warriors are fueled by rage. Every dragoon is guilty of one great sin. History's greatest warriors are remembered as much for their great sins times three. They do not love their lives. And that is what makes them so formidable. A Templar must be a warrior without sin."

Osbert told how the Templars was an order where commoner and noble alike were brothers. In fact, Templars were also said each to be prince of the Temple under the king of the Temple, the Grand Templar. And he spoke of many other great things that could be told without the divulging of secrets that could only be known by Templars. Their walk ended at the stables. "But say nothing for now," said Osbert. "This invitation once given is never revoked. But it comes with a warning. Remain pure of heart, or you will forever disqualify yourself from our order."

"You make it sound like a great thing that I would consider it even for a moment when all I have ever wanted is to be a dragoon. When my entire group is dependent on me being a warrior."

Osbert introduced his great white steed, Shadowless, which impressed Doppelganger mightily. "Stay good, Doppelganger of Hempshire, and perhaps we will meet again," said Osbert.

"Farewell, Osbert son of Wilfrid."

Doppelganger returned to his friends. "You have been invited to the Temple?" asked Dangalf.

"You knew he was a Templar?"

"The windmill on his tabard," explained Dangalf.

Doppelganger told his friends that Osbert had invited him to novitiate as a Templar. They were impressed but they were also concerned. They were all proceeding nicely in their chosen classes and thought it would be disharmonious for one to change classes now. There were no Templar trainers in any town, only at the Temple of the White Rose itself. And they all knew that few players chose to play Templars in *Cronica* because you could play for months in the class only to be randomly rejected at the end of your apprenticeship (most players were), and even the player successful at becoming a Templar could not accumulate wealth. And the accumulation of virtual gold was a measure of success and a driving force for most players.

Doppelganger assured them that he had no intention of becoming a Templar. He was a warrior and would not deviate from that path until he was a dragoon. "Besides," Doppelganger said. "They have a terrible training requirement that I can not imagine suffering through."

"What is that?" asked Dangalf.

"Reading."

LXXIV

When Ashlyn joined them later, they told her of what had transpired. And though Doppelganger reiterated that he was not interested in becoming what he called a warrior-light, Ashlyn was concerned. A Templar who specialized in protection would duplicate many of her healing talents. But she shrugged it off. Could you really have too many healers in a world where you could die for real? Dangalf told them how it honored the Keepers that Doppelganger was even asked. Obviously, they were gaining significant reputation if they had been heard of in the Temple of the White Rose, far removed geographically and politically from Vinland.

They ate dinner, and Dangalf described to them the location for their séance. It was called Blackened Hollow, where the Witchfinder General himself led a party of Templars to massacre a coven of witches. So disturbed was the land that Sirona herself said it could not be consecrated, and it remained wicked and forbidden. It was here that Dangalf thought they should have their séance: the perfect site for a black rite. "Why the site of a massacre?" asked Ashlyn.

"You want a place where many died," answered Dangalf. "So as to increase your chances of contacting a spirit. A battlefield doesn't work as well because combatants tend to final matters in anticipation of death. But massacres are of the unprepared. And their spirits linger because of unfinished business. If my study is true, I will summon one of these spirits and make her give up her knowledge."

Ashlyn was skeptical, but Doppelganger and Nerdraaage seemed eager. They had met orcs and trolls and had survived the encounter, even come out ahead. Now they would be summoning a specter (and hopefully only a specter) on its own corrupt and dangerous ground. And at the thirteenth hour nonetheless.

They began the journey timed to reach the Blackened Grove before the wicked hour. The magical map was very helpful for that purpose and could be read even in the darkness. They were well armed as Dangalf warned them that other parties, unfriendly parties, might seek out the grove for wicked purposes that night especially.

Ashlyn transformed into tyger. It was the first time they had seen her morph, and it was a miracle. But they had seen so many miracles and each had performed his own, and so it passed without comment. But still it was very nice, and they smiled and nodded back and forth. They followed her into the moonless dark woods lit by a canopy of stars and a softly glowing magical map.

The ground was smooth and the trees spread so as to make passage comfortable, and in no time they had walked for several hours. Their destination finally appeared to them unmistakably ahead. It was a pitch blackness against the ordinary blackness of the surrounding woods. It was the unreflecting and unforgiving noir of the Blackened Grove. Tyger Ashlyn became she-elf again and stood just outside the circle of black that delineated the wicked site. The others stopped with her and allowed Dangalf to enter the circle first. It was his séance after all. The circle felt different upon entering. The air was colder, and the springiness of life underfoot was replaced with the softness of ash. They followed Dangalf deep into the Blackened Grove until they were surrounded by charred and crumbling trunks and the living forest was out of sight.

"Watch out for that—" said Ashlyn as Dangalf stumbled into a stone table. "Stone table." At least Ashlyn's eyes were sensitive enough to differentiate the shades of black that comprised the Blackened Grove at night. Dangalf felt around the table and found it to be suitable for his purposes. He took out three black candles, lit them, and set them upon the table. It was enough light to lead the others to the table, and they sat on the block stools surrounding it.

"Are we sure we want to do this?" asked Ashlyn.

Dangalf set the divination deck upon the table. "There's still time to back out," he said.

"What are we doing exactly?" asked Nerdraaage.

"Spirits are caught in shadow, in planes between worlds, and they see things from a perspective not available to the living. I will ask it questions about why we are here. But the dead are confused at best and deceivers at worst, so it will not be a simple interrogation. The first step is to find a spirit. But that should not be difficult here. Our warmth and light, our conversation and respiration will be like beacons to specters and spirits and phantoms and geists. Like moths to the flame. I hope we get only one." He looked about for any further objections, and none was said.

Dangalf laid out nine cards from the divination deck, six chosen by him according to his books: the Wheel of Fortune, the Precipice, the Carpenter, the Hanged Man, the Lighthouse, and Charon. The other three were chosen by the spirits: the Virgin, the Tower, and finally the Keepers.

"What is that card?" asked Ashlyn of the card with the warrior, the mage, the dwarf, and she-elf and clearly entitled the Keepers.

"That's our card," said Dangalf.

"We have a card?" demanded Nerdraaage.

"I just found out about it myself. It's one of the deck's sympathy cards only recently developed."

"I don't look like that," complained Ashlyn of the she-elf spritely balanced on one tiptoe.

"You look exactly like that," said Nerdraaage.

"Oh, well have a look at your big, fat face," she countered.

"I'm not fat. I'm endomorphic."

Dangalf dripped wax on the corners of the cards to hold them down against the breeze. And so they waited. And winds whipped around them sounding like the whispers of the dead, and the dead whispered like the sounding of the wind, and so ironically the Keepers worried when the winds blew and relaxed when the dead spoke. The candles burned through a third of their life, but that said more about the quality of the candles than it did about how long they waited. An especially gusty whisper blew out their candles, and they were in a darkness made even more black by the memory of the candles. When Dangalf relit the first candle, another party had joined them sitting at the table. She was a delicate-looking girl on the cusp of womanhood. She wore a red hood and cape with a white blouse. But even her girlish appearance was so startling in its suddenness as to momentarily terrify all of them. Even Dangalf, who thought he knew what he was doing, knocked over the unlit candles. He righted them and lit them quickly. She removed her hood to reveal braided blond locks. She had pouty red lips and blue eyes wide with innocence. None of the Keepers yet dared speak, so it was up to Red Riding Hood.

"Where am I?"

"You're in the Blackened Grove," said Dangalf. "Not far from Templa Taur."

"Yes," said Red. "I remember being brought to the elven lands. What happened? Where is my mother!"

"You don't know?" asked Ashlyn gently.

"I remember the men coming. They were dressed as knights, but they attacked us."

"The Witchfinder General," said Dangalf. "There was a great massacre on this spot."

"I remember him," said Red, growing more anxious. "They said they were Templars, but they were murderers. We were just women and children."

"Were you a witch?" asked Ashlyn.

"I am only a child," she said, weeping. "My mother is a naturalist. We were humans who wanted to live as the elves do." Dangalf remembered the divination deck and began to lay out cards as she spoke. "We were not witches anymore than you druids are." She looked about curiously. "Where is my mother?" Ashlyn looked to Dangalf, but he was flipping his cards. "How long have I been asleep?" It was an uncomfortable silence for the others. And Dangalf was just playing with his cards.

When he did speak, it was not what anyone wanted to hear from him. But it was as he read in the cards, and he spoke it, surprising himself as well as the others. "You're lying," said Dangalf.

"Sire?" said the girl through a sorrow-choked throat.

"Dangalf!" said Ashlyn.

"You know you're dead," he continued to read his cards. "You play at deceit. It must be very boring to have died so young and to be trapped on this desolate circle of ash with no playmates."

"Please," cried Red. "Help me find my mother!"

"You are daevayasna," Dangalf said while reading his cards. "Demon worshiper. Necromancer. You have made blood sacrifices." Dangalf paused over one especially troubling card before looking at Red. "You have sacrificed sapiens." Red shot him a wicked look that none thought this innocent face was capable of before seeing it. "Show us your true face," commanded Dangalf as he laid the Looking Glass card before her. And then she showed her true form, and it was that of a black, charred skeleton with just enough flesh attached to indicate a very violent and painful death. The black flesh glowed red in spots like burning charcoal. And she screamed the sound of the tortured deaths of a legion, and all before her were frightened so that their lizard brains took over and commanded fight or flight. Doppelganger stood up and readied his axe. Nerdraaage unappeared with his daggers ready. Ashlyn morphed and retreated, climbing as high as she could on a charred and branchless tree. Only Dangalf was able to react from the bigger and comfortably appointed part of the sapien brain. Before the séance he had readied his repair dwarves, and now they emptied barrels of white bile into the river of his blood to keep Dangalf phlegmatic. And so he sat there impassively, holding his cards against her wind, until she finished screaming.

"You cannot harm us," challenged Dangalf. "Bellow your cacophony, release your foul odors, vomit your sickening bile…" And with that Red unleashed a torrent of ectoplasmic bile into Dangalf's face. He had time only to close his eyes before he was covered in an unctuous and stinking soup of bile. He wiped the vile liquid and even viler squishy bits from his hands and face. "I guess I should have expected that," he sighed. The others returned cautiously to their seats.

Red laughed like a schoolgirl juxtaposed against her grisly appearance. "What are your names?" she asked.

"Don't tell her!" shouted Dangalf.

"But I know your name," she said with a broad smile that caused charred skin to crumble from where her face creased. "Dangalf."

"I'm sorry," said Ashlyn.

"It's not your fault," said Dangalf, wiping out bile that had somehow splashed into his ear. "I didn't mention it. I didn't think my séance was going to be such a rousing success."

Red looked at Ashlyn jealously. "She is your beloved, Dangalf?"

"No," said Ashlyn quickly. She didn't have to deny it that quickly, thought Dangalf.

"Righteous you play at but it was men just like you who drowned me and hanged me and finally burned me!"

"It was a triple killing," said Dangalf academically. "Customary for killing witches. And your presence tonight suggests even this was not entirely successful."

"Do you think me pretty, Dangalf?" she asked gently. "Before, when you saw my original self?"

"We are not here to answer your questions, witch," he said. "You are here to answer ours."

"I require a blood sacrifice."

"We will not kill to satisfy your blood lust," said Dangalf.

"Just a little something," she pleaded. "A coney. A field mouse. A leach ripe with human blood."

"No."

"I require an offering!" she shouted supernaturally. And then quietly: "A prick of your finger, Dangalf. So that I may have just a taste."

"You would like that, wouldn't you?" said Dangalf. "My name and my blood."

"Yes," said Red, smiling and crumbling some more.

"This is your offering," said Dangalf setting a balled cloth on the table and unwrapping it. It was the ring taken from the troll necromancer slain by Icil. Doppelganger was perturbed. Dangalf had not mentioned keeping the ring. What other secrets was the conjurer hiding? Why were they even here at this wicked place with this foul creature? How deeply had Dangalf delved into the Black School?

Red's eyes widened. She knew this was the ring of a great troll necromancer, and she wanted it. "I will answer you one question," she offered.

"Three," said Dangalf.

"Very well," she said. "Two questions."

"Three," insisted Dangalf. Red hissed at him. Curse him, she thought. This black dilettante knew that she was compelled to answer one of his three questions truthfully. But perhaps she could still deceive him.

"What are your questions!" she shouted. She remained angry so as to let him believe he had outwitted her.

Dangalf hesitated. Perhaps he should have thought this out beforehand. Honestly, he had not expected to get this far. "Who summoned us to this world?" he asked.

"Your summoner can be followed by the footprints he leaves beneath the waves," said Red. Dangalf turned a card. It was the Dagger.

"What does that mean?" asked Nerdraaage.

"Treachery," said Dangalf. "She is lying. I ask you again, who summoned us to this world."

"Your summoner no longer lives," said Red. Dangalf turned another card. The Scrivener.

"Now she tells the truth," said Dangalf.

"Our summoner is dead?" asked Nerdraaage.

"I think her answer was pretty clear," said Dangalf dejectedly. "And the Scrivener card couldn't be a more reliable sign that she is telling the truth."

"Why would she say he is not alive?" asked Ashlyn. "I mean instead of saying he's dead." Red remained with the same look of distaste she had on her face when the questioning began.

"There are many ways to say the same thing," said Dangalf.

"Yeah," agreed Nerdraaage. "Everyone here talks like they're writing a poem."

"Ask her another question," said Ashlyn. "You have one more, right?"

"It wouldn't matter," said Dangalf. "She has given us her truthful answer."

"Isn't there anything we can learn from an untruthful answer?" asked Ashlyn.

Dangalf understood finally. A yes-or-no question at this point would give them a truthful answer when Red's answer was reversed. "Is our summoner dead?"

"No," said Red.

"Which means 'yes,'" said Dangalf. "When her untruthful answer is reversed. Whoever summoned us to this world is dead. And they may have taken the secret of our purpose with them."

"You didn't turn over a card," said Ashlyn. Red held her ashen tongue, but it was all she could do to not vomit on the she-elf.

"It doesn't matter," said Dangalf. "She has given her truthful answer and confirmed it with her final lie." Ashlyn stood and turned over the next card. It was the sword. Another weapon, but not like the dagger. It was the weapon of truth and justice and divine appointment.

"She told the truth," said Dangalf. "She was compelled to tell the truth once but she did it twice to deceive me. And it almost worked had it not been for you," he said humbly to Ashlyn.

"Stupid bitch," hissed Red. She vomited her remaining bile up, but it was not enough to project at the she-elf and instead dribbled down her own chin. Dangalf was impressed. Clearly Ashlyn had an impressive intellect even if not a full ectomorph.

"Our summoner is not dead and he's not alive?" asked Nerdraaage. "What does that mean?"

"He is a lich," said Dangalf.

"Undead," said Nerdraaage solemnly.

"You have your answers," screeched Red. "Now give me my ring!"

"Don't give it to her," said Doppelganger. "We have our answers. Let her rot. We can still sell it."

"No," said Dangalf. "We are righteous. Lawful good. Only trouble can come from misdeeds. Even against a wretch such as this."

"Put it on my finger," she said raising her left hand. Dangalf picked up the ring and stood to reach across the table. He slid it on her digit gingerly hoping that her finger would not crumble away during the process. "Dangalf," she crumble-smiled. "My betrothed!"

"Go back from whence you came," pronounced Dangalf, and as he did so he slapped down the Graveyard card to compel her. But it was in fact not the Graveyard card that appeared on the table but the Black Wedding card. He started fanning through the deck for the Graveyard card. He should have known things had gone too smoothly.

"Yes, Dangalf," said Red. "I will be your black bride!" She rose and limped one-footed around the table toward Dangalf.

"Let's just go," said Dangalf to the others as he scooped up his cards.

"Don't you have to complete the ceremony?" asked Ashlyn.

"Ceremony's over," said Dangalf. "Let's go."

Dangalf hustled off the way they had entered Blackened Grove, and the others followed. "She's still following us," said Nerdraaage.

"Just ignore her!"

"We shall be together forever until death do us join," Red called after Dangalf.

Dangalf stopped outside the border of the Blackened Grove and caught his breath. "Don't worry," said Dangalf. "She will not be able to leave her ashen domain."

"You will never walk alone, dearest Dangalf," said Red as she left her ashen domain.

"I've had enough of this," said Doppelganger. He charged the burnt corpse and hacked it to pieces until it could no longer walk. And then he hacked it to smaller pieces until it could no longer call to Dangalf. And then just as Dangalf sighed in relief, she rematerialized as Red Riding Hood but this time wearing a blood-red wedding dress and carrying a bouquet of black roses. Doppelganger swiped through her with his axe, but she was only a specter and immune to his worldly axe.

"You gave me your ring and name, Dangalf," said Red. "We are bound forever." And she floated toward him.

"Okay, run," said Dangalf. They all ran until Red could no longer be seen or heard. And they kept running. And Dangalf being the least mesomorphic felt as though he would die from exhaustion, but he kept on because he had the most reason to run. And they kept running all the way back to Templa Taur.

When they returned to the safety of the town in the trees, they all climbed into their respective beds just as light was coming up. All except for Ashlyn, who said she had to go to training. Dangalf felt bad and suggested she could miss one day of training, but she insisted she was fine. She had run all the way back to town in tyger form and had used only a fraction of the energy that the others had.

They discussed briefly their new knowledge that their summoner was a lich. And apparently a lich with free will. These were some of the most rare and powerful monsters in the game. They possessed both the secrets of the grave and the strength of those who felt no pain or fatigue. If the Keepers did not know before that they faced a formidable foe, they now knew it with certainty.

LXXV

They entered without the clanking and squealing that should accompany the opening of the dungeon's ancient door. In fact, to the untrained eye, it would appear that they entered the dungeon without opening the door at all. But then that illusion came easily to the assassins. Troll sisters who moved as one. The sister assassins were so inseparable that the sages of Vinland kept only one book on them.

The she-trolls saw the new sign in large Acadish letters that read, "Welcome to the Dungeon." They understood it was motivated by this human foible called "humor." In Trollish, humor referred only to the bodily fluids that dictated temperament. Likewise they had no word for laughter, the closest being *hasa*, the involuntary sound and shudder that overcame one after seeing another wounded or killed in an especially dishonorable way. And smile? Well that in Trollish was a cut of the throat that ran from ear to ear.

The she-trolls were drawn breathlessly to the screams, which had now ended and were replaced with the sound of feasting. It pleased them to see their master eat. They had been drawn irresistibly to him since he first confided in them his true nature. So seduced had they been that they allied with him to imprison their own mistress while he ascended to her throne. "Get out!" he bellowed at them angrily when he saw them.

"We have done as you commanded," said a sister.

"I will have your heads!" he shouted, and they were gone as quickly and quietly as they had entered. His anger at them was a reflection of his own shame at what he had become. Nothing drove that point home more than when he fed. He had become a loathsome creature. But lichs did not generate protoplasm and had to get it secondhand. And there was no source riper with that than living brains. He had made himself a lich willingly and not without purpose. *The path to divinity*, the ancient grimoire had promised.

LXXVI

The she-trolls approached their master again as he sat on his throne, only months before vacated unwillingly by their former mistress. They crawled across the expansive floor to his place, but they were blackguards and trolls and they covered the distance quickly. They kept their eyes averted and hoped that this sign of subservience would please him. They both knew that he would kill them without hesitation, and that excited them. There was so little left in this world for them to fear.

They stopped before him, and one chanced a glance at him. He looked down on her sternly, but their subservience did please him, and he smiled. He had washed his face after his meal, but his teeth were still stained crimson. She nodded excitedly, and the other dared look. They flicked their forked tongues gratefully at being back in his good graces.

The armored lich stepped to the first she-troll and brought his sword down across her chest. Even her blackguard reflexes were not quick enough to avert the blow. But it was clearly not his intention to kill her and only her leather tunic was separated.

Exposed now was a strange bloody wound between her blue breasts heaving with excited breaths. He turned to her sister and tore open her tunic. She also bore the mark, the wound that would never heal: a scarlet letter in the shape of a unicorn *bloodrune.*

He spoke to them in their own language. He had split his tongue at the tip so that he could speak even the ancient Trollish words. This self-mutilation was not an extravagant commitment. After all he could no longer feel pain, and if he wanted it whole again, he needed only to sew it up. "You have done something that not even I can protect you from."

"You will take us to Oceania," said a sister. "Where we will all be reborn of the flesh."

"Perhaps," he said. And then, "What of Princess Dymphna?"

"She had a Templar with her," hissed the other. He understood what that meant.

"Bring in Kaldmunnr," he said.

Kaldmunnr entered as the she-trolls held open the throne room doors for him. He could not see if they meant to kill him. Fear was clouding his vision. It had for some time. He wished he had never taken on his new master. The goblins had paid him well enough, and he knew he would have lived long in their service if not richly. He saw the lich sitting in Gykoja's throne. There was not even the pretense anymore that he was doing her bidding! Certainly the royal seers must have seen this and informed the queen of this affront. As Kaldmunnr approached his master, the she-trolls unappeared. He could not tell if they had left the room, only that he could not see them.

"Come," said the master, rising and taking a lone cup from a nearby tray. "Drink."

The troll picked up his robes and walked quickly toward the lich. He nodded as he took the cup. "Will you not join me, sire?"

"I," hesitated the lich. "I eat and drink only in solitude. Drink up. I would not kill you with poison." The troll took a drink. It was warm and unpleasant, but it was not poison. "You said Princess Dymphna would be without guard. Perhaps with a guard of low rank. She was instead escorted by her Templar."

"There was a unicorn in my vision," he explained nervously. "Perhaps I lost the Templar in the unicorn's aura." Suddenly he saw that this same unicorn had gone dark, murdered by the she-trolls who had brought him here tonight. He shuddered despite the effects of the drink.

"Now the princess and her family have been alerted, and we will not again have such an opportunity because of your corrupted vision," said the armored lich. "Drink up. It will numb the pain." The seer looked wide eyed. "Yes," said the lich. "The pain is coming."

The troll gulped down the last of his drink. "Sire, my vision was good! Free will is the enemy of all seers!"

"Free will is a bitch," said the man in his strange vernacular, laughing. "But still your vision is lacking. Henceforth you will move in to the tower. The slaves will see to your needs." The lich took the cup and saw that it was empty. "Especially until you adjust to your new circumstances. But your vision will be purer than ever before. Girls, help Kaldmunnr with his sight." And with that his twin minions appeared behind the seer, and each plucked out one of his eyes with a fingertip hook designed just for that purpose.

Kaldmunnr fell to his knees screaming and covering his new skull holes. It was not from pain—the drink had seen to that; but the horror of knowing that his eyes were gone and could not be repaired. The fresh eyes were ripe with nourishing electroplasm, and the trolls handed them over to their master. "The royal seers are blinded at birth so that they are not confused by worldly sights," said the lich. "You will serve me all the better now, and in return I will make you rich. You will live here and enjoy our hospitality." Trollish also had no word for irony.

Kaldmunnr rose up on his knees and uncovered his face. Blood ran from his empty eye sockets. In haunted voice he pronounced, "The otherworlders that you summoned are arrived."

LXXVII

Several weeks passed, and Ashlyn was close to completing her training. They all looked forward to her joining the other Keepers, no longer a neophyte, but as a metamorph, a third-class druid, ready to quest and explore and, most importantly, to heal her comrades. With their healer in place, they felt that they would be a formidable force.

And then the Legion Pangaea attacked Templa Taur.

Dangalf saw them first. As he watched from the comfort of their usual table at the King Bee, and being considerably buzzed, the three hundred warg riders bearing torches against the night looked just unreal enough to give him pause as they rode up on the town.

Elf horns sounded, and Ainnir went to their table, took their glowing bug, and told them that the four might want to return to their rooms.

The rope ladders had already been pulled up for the night, but there was a basket of elves that had just left the ground and were being pulled up to the town. The orc attackers concentrated on this target and barraged it with arrows. Multiple arrows hit each of the elves. "I'm going to get my bow," said Doppelganger as he ran off.

"Me too," said Nerdraaage.

"I'm going to help heal," said Ashlyn. She morphed, and all her coins fell to the floor as she ran off.

"Wait for me," said Dangalf as he absently picked up her coins.

These warg riders were orc archers. They shot flaming arrows up into Templa Taur. Soon small fires broke out in dozens of places across the town.

Rainmakers took their perches high in the trees and spoke their ancient words to the sky. The sky obliged with light rain. The town's falcons were dispatched to allies in all directions.

Nerdraaage returned to the King Bee because of its panoramic view of the enemy and because that's where the beer was. Short, strong, and well trained, Nerdraaage was deadly accurate. However the warg riders were accompanied by lycans, the trolls' bastardized version of the druid. Users of black magic, they were not true metamorphs, instead changing into a corrupted lycan form, a trollwolf. Still, they were able healers and they healed Nerdraaage's victims who returned fire at him en masse. Nerdraaage retreated behind the bar where he had a beer. He could not think of a better way to spend the evening.

Doppelganger, impatient for combat, fired at the orcs from the Keepers' room. He hit one orc and knocked him off of his warg. He saw a nearby lycan casting a healing spell over the orc and shot her through the neck. She crumbled to the ground and, despite all the carnage going on, an especially angry call arose over the killed lycan and soon spread among all the attackers. Doppelganger found himself the target of hundreds of arrows fired over a few seconds. He crawled out of the room as ricocheting arrows tore at his body. Only his chest and back were unscathed as he had had the foresight to put his adamantine on.

Doppelganger, now taken by his bloodwarp, was a frightening sight when he came upon Dangalf and Ashlyn. With some Elvish words and flourishing gestures, Ashlyn healed his wounds. Dangalf shot fireballs at the enemy below, but they were small blasts as the enemy archers did not give him time to cast the larger ones before he was targeted.

The Keepers all drew the wrath of the warg riders by specifically targeting their healers. The lycans congregated so that they could heal each other. This only meant more orcs died due to their unattended injuries. The Keepers were forced to move constantly along the protected walls against the heavy volleys they attracted.

The rain soon poured forth, and the fires were all extinguished, and no new ones took hold. The wargs bogged down in mud meant the orcs were easy targets, and many died. The lycans hissed back and forth to each other about the human warrior and mage, the dwarf hunter, and the she-elf druid who appeared to work in concert. A troll horn sounded, and the warg riders and lycans, once free of the mud, left as quickly as they had come.

The other Keepers were happy to find Nerdraaage unharmed. For some reason he seemed even drunker than when the battle had begun. Ciar joined them and told them that they had lost three elves versus "dozens more" orcs dispatched that night. She said this raid, with so many lycans present and with no real hope of taking Templa Taur, appeared to be designed as a training exercise for new healers. She figured that they got more exercise than they intended with the Keepers specifically targeting them. The orcs were little more than fodder in this exercise as they had been throughout their long history with their troll masters.

Of the three fatalities, only one had been captured by the enemy: an archer who had fallen to the ground. It was not her death alone that was troubling but that the raiders took the elf corpse with them. "For their black ceremonies," Ciar supposed quietly.

"How long was the battle?" asked **Dangalf**.

"Just under an hour."

"Seemed longer. I'm exhausted."

"Longer?" said Doppelganger, his bloodwarp subsided. "It seemed only a few minutes!"

"And how would you know?" challenged Dangalf. "You weren't even here. It was your doppelganger. Your id monster."

"There was still a little of me in there," said Doppelganger smiling.

Ciar took their scrolls and certified their defense of Templa Taur and authorized payment to the Keepers who were per diem. They thanked her, and she bid them farewell, but the Keepers stayed where they were talking about the battle. The excitement of combat and the thrill of victory wired them all up, and reliving the battle in words seemed to be the only way to unwind.

It was daylight when a sudden cracking and whooshing startled the Keepers. They looked about on the ground for another attack even more terrifying than the last. But Ashlyn saw it first, and she pointed to the sky. It was a flight of dragoons and astonishing to behold. There were only about twelve, but they seemed to cover all of the sky, so enormous were the dragons and with such great wingspans. The dragons were gold or green or black or red in brilliant, glistening scales. "They're beautiful," said Nerdraaage. And then almost angrily, "Why are they beautiful?"

"They're males," said Ashlyn. "You want ugly and about ten times bigger? Those are the females. No one rides a female dragon."

"Then where do little dragons come from?" asked Nerdraaage.

The dragoons themselves, some of the largest mesomorphs in this world, seemed insignificant on the backs of these beasts.

The elves waved and cheered each as they passed in pursuit of the raiders.

One human dragoon passed closest of all, rocking gently with every great whoosh of wings. He blew a kiss to Ashlyn in passing. Dangalf turned to share a laugh about it only to see her blowing a kiss back to him. "They're going after our lost sister," she enthused.

And for Doppelganger it was settled. He was not locking himself away in some temple with a pile of books and a vow of poverty. He wanted to be a dragoon floating past the admiring women and she-elves blowing him kisses, Princess Dymphna among them wishing that she had written to him as she promised. He was still daydreaming when he followed the others back to their room and was caught off guard by their angry looks. Then he looked in at the room and their belongings scarred by a hundred orc arrows. "I'll get the maid," he said.

LXXVIII

When Ashlyn completed her training, there was a ceremony celebrating the occasion. Since it was held in a white hall, only Dangalf could join her. Doppelganger and Nerdraaage were not allowed past the white archway. And though the black-guard's ability to unappear, the ranger's ability to command animals, and the warrior's bloodwarp drew upon the magic of this world, they were all classified as being of the blood school and not the magical school.

Dangalf had been excited all day to attend his first ceremony in a white hall. He had had no such ceremony for he had trained in a human town that had only a small red hall. So Dangalf told Doppelganger and Nerdraaage that he thought it "sucked" that they couldn't attend, but he really didn't mean it. He enjoyed the air of exclusivity especially since he was one of the exclusive. He liked that Ashlyn had only him to share this special moment.

Earlier he had gone out shopping and bought the best hat he could find. He chose a large, brimmed floppy hat. The new hat was more Gandalf and less Merlin. He then spent more modestly on a new robe and boots. But he was satisfied that the expensive hat and his flying cloak made him look like an esteemed member of the White School as long as he kept his cloak closed.

Inside, the white hall was not very white and wasn't much like a hall. Grass, flowers, and moss grew on the floor as if it were the ground and not fifty feet in the air. Pristine white birch trees served as the hall's columns, and it was lit by shafts of sunlight.

Other druids had come to celebrate their new comrade, and many assumed various animal shapes. There were sea lions and tygers and bears. Dangalf wandered about them, smiling joyfully at the sight. He stopped and spoke to a unicorn. "Pardon me," said Dangalf. "I did not know that druids could take on the unicorn form."

"That is a unicorn," whispered Ashlyn from behind.

Dangalf nodded to the unicorn before turning to Ashlyn. She looked lovelier than ever. She wore her same furkini but her hair was up and adorned with white feathers. Streaks of blue and purple paint, her tyger colors, decorated her face. "New hat?" she asked.

"I treated myself on your occasion," he said. He wasn't sure if the hall counted as indoors or outdoors, so he carried his hat in his hands.

"I like it." Ashlyn extended her arms and he obliged her with a hug. He had not been this close to her since the unhappening they shared on her bed after Nerdraaage had insulted her. He was probably lingering on the hug more than she had intended, but what the hell? "I only wish Doppelganger and Nerdraaage could be here," she said.

"Mmph," he breathed into her neck.

"I have to work the room," she smiled as she undid the hug and stepped away.

Still, Dangalf stood by the unicorn, drawn by its spirit. He slowly raised his hand and gently stroked its white coat. He could feel his own protoplasm surging at this thrilling connection. Just to touch such a creature rejuvenated him. He remembered what the *Cronica Acadia* had said of unicorns: *Sexless and immortal...a hundred times a hundred did the great crafter make...now less than half that number...an hourglass on this world...and when the last is gone, so shall the magic of this world be undone.* He was humbled as he realized that he was touching a warm, living being as old as the world itself. He shuddered as he thought of the troll blackguards that had killed Princess Dymphna's unicorn and finally understood how that was a crime against this world.

Another druid in sapien form approached the unicorn, said elven words, and touched its coat. Dangalf moved along so as not to monopolize the unicorn.

Most of the attendees were she-elves, but there were a few elf druids. The male druids were better fighters than the females—they were bigger and stronger in animal form—but the females were the better healers. And since druids were primarily valued as a healing class, belligerent elves tended to pursue the wizard or ranger classes, which also suited the ectomorphic race.

From the entrance a large, glorious bird flew in and in a fiery flash turned into a stunning she-elf. Dangalf watched her in awe as he realized she was a fenix, the druid master class.

Cronica Acadia, among its many mysteries, provided clues to the uncovering of its ancient predecessor, the *Cronica Oceania.* Where the *Acadia* was thought to number 1,200 copies, the *Oceania* was thought to exist as only 120 copies. Each volume was written by the same hand and untranscribable. (The most learned sages of Vinland who had tried to copy one of the *Cronicas* found that they had only written gibberish.) It was clear that the author(s) meant that if you were to benefit from the wisdom of the *Cronicas*, you must first come into actual contact with one.

Upon studying the *Cronica Oceania*, scholars found reference to the lost land of the same name. This led brave humans to the island continent lost for ten thousand years when the sundering of the world had sent it off beyond the edges of the map.

Those same first explorers found dragons and griffons and wyverns and other flying creatures no longer extant in Acadia, where they had been hunted to extinction during the three hundred days of darkness following the Sundering, when sapiens battled with the creatures of the sky to remain at the top of the food chain.

As these flying beasts were returned to Acadia, members of each school's master class were provided a flying mount as they became available. Among the rarest of the flying creatures, the dragons were appropriated by the master warriors, who named themselves dragoons. The other master classes appropriated griffons for their flying mounts, smaller and tamer than the dragons.

The Sundering had also destroyed writing not cherished enough to be carved into stone. And now ancient monoliths of wisdom in the form of broken tablets or rubbings from Oceania were presented to the greatest minds of the White School. Among these ancient runic carvings was the lost secret of druidic transformation to flight form. The druid masters learned to metamorphose into flying creatures, and they named themselves after the indestructible fenix. Where other masters would ride upon flying creatures brought back from Oceania, Oceania provided to the druids the ancient secrets to again become flying creatures.

The fenix was a sight with her great mane of hair, adorned in feathers and ivory and other treasures "of the flesh." He bowed royally as she strode past, and she smiled at him. She was a powerfully magical creature. He could tell that just by her brief passing. He had not before been in the presence of a sapien who exuded such a pure and overwhelming magical aura. No, wait, he had been. But his senses were too coarse to identify it when he had encountered it. But it was not only electroplasm that stirred in him as he watched the she-elf strut by in her fur loincloth. He watched the fenix go to the unicorn, speak old Elvish, and touch it. The unicorn stepped lively as if the fenix's touch had also stirred something in it.

The druids, now all in sapien form, lined up, and the fenix took her spot at the top of white stone steps at the front of the hall. Dangalf stood with the druids thinking that the elves certainly know how to do things right. His and Doppelganger's graduation ceremonies were basically handshakes, and he was not sure that Doppelganger got even a handshake. Nerdraaage had at least gotten a commencement address when Icil placed his hand on his shoulder and told him, "Kill. Steal. Escape."

The fenix spoke in Elvish, and Dangalf wished he had studied the language. He was studying Trollish because he thought that would benefit the group most since they already had party members who spoke Dwarvish and Elvish. And Trollish was the common language of the Legion. He studied modern Trollish as spoken by all the members of the Legion Pangaea and Olde Trollish, the Trollish of black rites, the Trollish that had no vowels and was spoken properly only with a forked tongue.

The fenix called Ciar before her, and Ciar curtsied. She also presented Ashlyn, who stepped forward and curtsied. Dangalf struggled to understand. He recognized "elves" of course and a few other words: "sister," "druid," "nature," and "learning." He ascertained that Ciar was formally swearing to Ashlyn's training and proficiency, that Ashlyn was now, or would soon be, an associate member of the White School under Ciar's auspices.

Ashlyn, who like Ciar stood a step below the fenix, was about to speak when the fenix said, "You have a guest here. Perhaps you would like to speak Acadish."

Ashlyn confidently recited: "I move through the forest stepping from falling leaf to falling leaf. I nurse the righteous, for they make the world good. I smite the unrighteous put here to test my resolve. I am of divine symmetry, begotten of the stardust that made adamantine and the feather. I was animal before I was elf, and I know how to be animal again. I will be humble before the smallest life and bold before the gods. This I pledge to the druids of the sacred grove of Nemetia."

The fenix tied a leather collar around Ashlyn's neck. "I welcome you to the School of White, Ashlyn," she said. "Show us your colors."

And Ashlyn turned into her tyger form, and afterward all the druids took animal shapes, including the fenix, who became a bright white tyger, adorned with rune symbols in the shape of stripes. And there was great howling and roaring and screeching, and even the unicorn was moved to rise up on hind legs and cry out. Dangalf clapped.

The druids returned to bipedal form, and Ashlyn humbly accepted their well-wishes. Dangalf kept to himself until Ashlyn went to him. "Grats," he said.

"Thanks."

The fenix approached and smiled at Dangalf, who bowed again. "And who is this?" asked the fenix.

"Your Highness," said Ashlyn. "I would like you to meet Dangalf of Hempshire."

Of course, thought Dangalf. She had obvious royal bearing, but he was misled by her druidic scanties and the whole bird thing. But the immortal elves did expect all to answer a calling, even the royals, and to many elves the druid calling was the most honorable. "I present Princess Grian."

"Another one of the four who saved the royal sister," said Grian smiling.

"Your Highness?" said Dangalf. "Princess Dymphna is your sister? You're both elf princesses. Of course you're sisters," he said with a laugh. "Our other friend Doppelganger thinks very highly of your sister," he said.

"Is that so?" said Grian. "You speak of the human mercenary?"

"Uh, yes, ma'am," said Dangalf.

"Dymphna has had an infatuation with humans since she was a child. I hope she was not unduly familiar with your friend. She was thirteenth born after all, and you know what they say about the thirteenth born."

"I'm sorry, ma'am. I do not."

After a moment Grian said, "You see, my sister is very—special. She applied to the Guild of Sages and Seers at only nine years old. She received a perfect twenty-four on their exam."

"Ma'am, I've read of that test. I thought twelve was a perfect score."

"A perfect score was twelve. But you see, my sister answered all of their questions before they were asked. They created a new scale because of her. Not that anyone else has ever scored above twelve since."

"Ma'am, she told us of an ancestor visiting her," said Dangalf. "With a warning and bloodstained room left behind."

"It was quite a colorful story she told," said Grian. "And it had all of the household in an uproar. That is, until it was discovered that it was my own sister's blood in the room. Quite a bit of it as well."

Dangalf nodded solemnly, and just as Grian was turning away, he asked, "Ma'am, did your sister have any wounds that would have produced the quantity of blood that was found?"

"She did not. But the fact remains that it was her blood. And there was no other evidence to support her story of the bleeding butterfly."

"Are you without guards today, Your Highness?" asked Ciar.

"I fly too high and too fast for escort, sister," said Grian smiling. After a few more pleasantries, Grian bid them farewell. In a fiery flash she became a fenix and departed in flight. Now the others were free to depart, and in short order they did.

Ashlyn took Dangalf's hand as they left the hall. She was pleased to find Doppelganger and Nerdraaage waiting outside the white arch waiting for her. She hugged them both. "Grats on becoming…what are you?" asked Doppelganger.

"I am a metamorph," she said beaming.

"Keep it simple. She's a wannabe druid," said Nerdraaage as he presented to her a bouquet of tyger roses.

Ashlyn thanked him and bit the head off of one of the roses. She looked at her friends staring at her. "I'm sorry," she said. "I haven't eaten all day."

The unicorn departed the white hall. "So how come a horse gets to go to your ceremony and we don't?" asked Nerdraaage.

"Horse?" asked Dangalf. "You mean the unicorn?"

"Whatever," said Nerdraaage. "At least you wouldn't have to worry about me taking a dump in the middle of the ceremony."

"If only I could have been certain," said Ashlyn.

"Who was that big bird who left here?" asked Doppelganger.

Horses! Big birds! Now Dangalf understood perfectly why there were white halls and red halls. "That was Princess Grian," said Ashlyn.

"Princess, huh?" said Doppelganger. "How far from the throne is she?"

"Tenth in line," said Ashlyn.

"Oh," said Doppelganger. Dangalf resisted the urge to tell him what was said about Dymphna.

A hawk presented itself to Ashlyn, and she took the message. She smiled as she announced it was congratulations from Fionn. Dangalf frowned. "Thank God," she said. "I was afraid he thought I was a psycho after that night in the King Bee."

There were no other gifts for Ashlyn as it had been previously decided each would take her shopping to get something she liked instead of something they thought she'd like. That had been her idea.

LXXIX

After lunch they went to the town hall, where they checked the board for quest postings. As in Hempshire and Hammersmith, there was a large, faded poster advertising ten thousand gold for the head of the Witchfinder General, but they reasoned that they were still far from being able to kill the Grand Templar Aelfweard. "How many kills do you need to move on to your next level of training?" Doppelganger asked Ashlyn.

"None," she said.

"None?" asked Dangalf. "Even I had to kill one sapien."

"Healing class," she explained. "But I need to do a lot of healing, so you guys feel free to get wounded a lot."

It was Ashlyn who found their next quest: a plea to return children stolen by goblin slave traders. It was not the richest quest they had considered, but it was within their operational range (being near river transport on the Mor Duin), and the paltry reward (barely enough to cover their anticipated expenses) meant that it would meet the altruism requirements of three of the Keepers' commissions. (Blackguard candidates were not required to demonstrate altruism.) The two humans also found themselves surprisingly eager to be on a quest that would take them out on the water. Ashlyn was relieved that her first combat healing experience would be against the weak, unimposing goblins.

It was this weakness that drove goblins to kidnap children. They were more manageable than adult slaves, and when they grew unmanageable in size and strength and will, they could be sold to the trolls. The trolls were expert slavers and for eons had enslaved the ferocious orcs. It was only post-Sundering, when the worlds collided again, that the trolls gave up enslaving orcs, for the most part, to make them allies against the righteous races.

They made arrangements to set out the next day for their first quest with the Keepers all per diem members of their respective classes. With the help of Doppelganger's back, Dangalf was able to return all of his library books in one trip. Ashlyn said good-bye to Ciar, who kissed her on both cheeks.

That night while Dangalf slumbered, a knock came at the door of his imagined library. All the dwarves had already entered and were busy repairing his body, so he was very curious. He looked through the peephole to see Red Riding Hood in her red wedding gown. He woke with a start but there was no relief in waking—in fact his terror increased, as he saw Red sitting on his bed. She was projecting her pretty visage which was just as well. If it had been her charred and mutilated form, Dangalf's heart might have just given out altogether. "Good morning, Dangalf," she said brightly. She sat with her legs tightly folded under her body as only children and elves can do. "Were you dreaming of me?"

Dangalf's intellect resumed control, and he relaxed. She was just a specter after all. He had nothing to fear from her in a room full of his friends in a town protected by elven magic. "I think you know the answer to that," he said softly. Could his friends see and hear her? Would they awake to think he was talking to himself? He was almost certain he was not. "Why are you here?"

"Silly! I am your black bride. Your blood bride. We are bound forever!"

"That is not true by any measure, and you know it. Your kind are tricksters, and your game does not frighten or amuse me."

"Ah! But it amuses me, and it has been so long since I have had any amusement, beloved. And now we are man and wife. I have your ring!" and she displayed the oversized ring on her small pale hand.

"I may be a stranger to your lands," said Dangalf, "but I know that there is no custom or law by which we are married."

Red laughed. "Custom or law!" And then Red took on a seriously spooky smile. "Your customs and laws are bleating to my ears. I am a witch. Daevayasna. You are my betrothed Dangalf because I will it. I WILL IT." Then Red looked fearfully to the door. "Now I must leave you, but before I go," and Red moved her rosy red lips toward Dangalf, and he did not move away from her quickly enough.

Ashlyn awoke even before the pounding on the door. She smelled smoke. She opened the door, and Ciar stepped in. She was followed by an elf in robes she had not seen before and two guards carrying torches. Torches in Templa Taur! "You have brought great evil here," said Ciar.

"What do you mean?" asked Ashlyn and she looked around. Doppelganger and Nerdraaage sat up in bed. And beyond them she saw Dangalf in the torchlight. He was covered with ectoplasmic bile.

"She is gone," said the robed elf. "The witchmistress from the Blackened Grove. Abigail is her name," he divined.

"Abigail," said Dangalf thoughtfully. Now he had *her* name. Ciar gently chastised the human conjurer for his dabbling in the black arts but had little to offer them in the way of a solution. "They have unfinished business, those who will not depart," said Ciar. "They can haunt a place or an object or a person. It seems you have detached this ghost from her place and attached her to yourself."

"How do we attach her to something else?" asked Ashlyn.

"Often they may be satisfied by the simplest of closure," said Ciar. "One famous story tells of a violent ghost who departed with the shuttering of her house against the coming winter. Other times it is more ceremonial."

And then Nerdraaage came up with the perfect solution. He said that they should hold an actual wedding where Dangalf married Abigail. All the others agreed that this was the worst idea ever.

But whatever the long-term solution, the immediate solution was to leave and draw the entity away from the town. Since they were already packed, the only change was eating breakfast on the road instead of one last meal at the King Bee. They left a handful of silver coins and a note for Ainnir. Nerdraaage said that they were overtipping, but he was reminded that they had not paid for anything since they arrived.

Doppelganger carried provisions and the communal coin, which was only gold now, as the odd silver and copper pieces were divvied up among the party. He wore his breastplate, but beneath a hemp shirt with an ordinary-looking mail shirt over that to disguise the wealth of adamantine.

Ashlyn's rucksack contained more clothes than the other three carried combined. But what she wore did not weigh much or take up much room. She also traveled without provisions as she had the least need and was now a naturalist trained to live off the land.

Nerdraaage assumed the appearance of an ordinary hunter. (Only the keenest observer would recognize him puffing away on a garrote pipe.) He carried the largest weight of provisions which was mostly beer.

Dangalf, without armor or weapons and with his books tucked away in his imaginary library, traveled light as well. He had only a small appetite, and Ashlyn had promised she would find enough food and water for them both.

The Keepers had a hearty breakfast in the woods by daylight. Afterward they studied the map, even though they generally knew where they were going. Doppelganger pointed to a point of interest and dragged his finger across the map. To everyone's amazement, the map scrolled along with his finger. He had accidentally uncovered another secret of the map. Even though the default setting was to center the map on the location of the bearer, you could actively scroll the map in any direction. An enchanted map would only display places that the bearer had already visited, but since Icil was the previous bearer, this map provided them a nearly complete map of Acadia. Dangalf scrolled about looking for Oceania, but the map was unfinished outside the borders of Acadia. And on those unexplored margins it was ominously written, *Here Do Be Monsters.*

LXXX

The Keepers' immediate destination was Portsmouth, a well-fortified town just across the Mor Duin River as they traveled west from Templa Taur. Technically part of Hybernia, the town was founded and administered by humans, the dwarves wanting no part of a port town on the wrong side of their towering, defensible mountain ranges. Over time it was fortified as a naval base, but it retained its civilian populace. There they would charter a boat to take them to within striking distance of the goblin slave camp.

When they first arrived in this world, they were blissfully unaware of the grave dangers they faced. As they learned of these dangers, their skills and mettle rose to keep their fears in check so that it always remained just as an undercurrent—which was good because it kept them alert. And now confidently, with just the proper amount of fear, they headed off to Portsmouth, the first town they would encounter that had no companion in the game that introduced them to this world.

They walked for hours and as usual it was without burden or boredom. They talked genially, and sometimes Dangalf would tell them stories from the *Cronica Acadia*. And even when they were silent, Dangalf was still fascinated by what in their old world would have been a monotonous dirt road through woods and rocks. But he marveled at every oddly bent tree and the occasional gigantic boulder and knew that for each one there was a story behind its posture and placement.

Even before they had sighted town, the humans had smelled the river, and it filled them with gladness. Doppelganger's mesomorphic lungs filled like a billowing sail. "Smell that," he said.

"I know," said Dangalf. "It's intoxicating."

"What?" Nerdraaage asked.

"The river."

Nerdraaage sniffed at the air futilely.

"Water doesn't have a smell," said Ashlyn.

"It does," insisted Doppelganger.

Dangalf had never been a water person, or even a beachgoer, and had even gotten seasick on a Disney cruise, and so he didn't entirely understand this new fondness. He chalked it up to race memory and something he had read in *Cronica Acadia*: *The elves have their trees and the dwarves have their rocks, but humans have the great vast ocean and all that lies beyond.* The Mor Duin River was fresh water, but the prospect of traveling on it excited Dangalf and made him glad *Huckleberry Finn* was among the books he had captured in the other world.

Portsmouth came into view as much larger than Hempshire, and the guards at their stone gates were better garbed and stood straighter. They sported shields of red, white, and blue, but the design was the Vinlandian ensign, an anchor, and not the Great Lighthouse. The port town was teeming with all sorts, and the guards did not stop any of them for papers. But Dangalf stopped anyway to ask them for directions.

They met with the scrivener, and he examined their commissions. He copied their achievements for dispatch to Vinland should their original scrolls be lost. He also recommended to them a Captain Longfellow. He was an old man, but the scrivener believed him to be in port with a craft to rent at a fair price.

Longfellow was not a charming sort. Dangalf thought "old sea dog" was an appropriately nautical description of him. He puffed a pipe and wore britches with knee socks, a puffy, mostly white shirt, and an eye patch. He barely spoke, and what words he managed to utter were clearly of secondary importance to the work he did about his ship. Or was it a boat? Dangalf didn't dare ask. It was small with sails and oars tucked away. There was no cabin.

Longfellow took a cursory look at their commissions and muttered that dwarves and elves were bad news onboard but to sail with a she-elf was just begging to be scuttled by Icanus. (*Cronica Acadia* identified Icanus as a minor river deity of interest only to "sailors and drowning people.")

The Keepers were adamant that Ashlyn was going. Longfellow puffed on his pipe, sewed some canvas, and grumbled in Trollish about she-elves being only useful when clutching their ankles. Dangalf warned Longfellow, also in Trollish, that Ashlyn could appear behind the door as either the lady or the tyger.

"And why would a wizard speak Trollish?" demanded Longfellow. "There'll be no witchcraft on my boat."

"But you spoke Trollish," sputtered Dangalf.

"All sailors speak some Trollish," shrugged Longfellow. "They have the best curses." They all laughed, even Dangalf a beat later (for all his intellect, the others still got some things quicker than him), and Longfellow winked at Ashlyn. Or at least she thought he winked at her, but it was difficult to tell since he had only the one eye.

And the laughter mollified the old salt, though he did not actually laugh, and he even puffed out a chanty for them as they took to the sea:

Toes on her feet
Toes on her hands
Has enough toes
For a marching band

They sailed against current, Longfellow zigzagging the breadth of the river to do so. He also told Doppelganger to grab a set of oars and begin rowing. Dangalf asked if he should grab a set of oars as well. Longfellow looked him up and down and barely shook his head.

Longfellow's craft appeared to be able to hold a dozen children should they be so successful in their rescue. They hoped to rescue at least one and didn't know what they would do if they rescued too many to fit into the small craft.

Dangalf watched their progression on their magical map. Each of Doppelganger's strokes rushed them forward in the water. Both humans were in their element on the open water. Ashlyn and Nerdraaage were not so fortunate, both being separated from the earth, which metaphorically and literally kept them grounded. Nerdraaage sat in the very bottom of the boat drinking heavily. Dangalf understood just how out of sorts he was when he refused lunch. Dangalf knew that no elf or dwarf had visited Oceania because of the weeks-long journey by sea. The trolls had done so only by burying themselves alive in soil from Sylvania. That method of sleeping in dirt had not tested well for either elf or dwarf.

It was just about sunset when Longfellow announced, "We be coming up on your Dragonfly."

"Not according to the map," protested Dangalf.

"Your map be wrong."

"The map is never wrong," insisted Dangalf. Longfellow didn't bother to argue with Dangalf as Dragonfly came into view in rebut. "The map has just changed," said Dangalf as the name Dragonfly was erased on one spot and reappeared at the correct location.

The town was comprised entirely of boats and ships. Residences, merchants, and government offices were all ship-board so that when threatened they could haul in their anchors and docks and depart en masse like a dragonfly skittering across the water. As such they occupied no permanent spot on the map but instead rotated through a trio of locations. Dangalf figured the map must have first indicated where Dragonfly was located when Icil had last visited.

"Finally," said a wan Nerdraaage. They had only stepped onto the dock when they were greeted by the port-reeve, who was also the town scrivener. Portsmouth had sent word that the Keepers would be arriving. He welcomed them with genuine excitement, which flattered the Keepers, and introduced them to the ser-geant of the guards and the smithy. Dragonfly was so small a town that the smithy was on the short list of village dignitaries.

They asked about lodgings and the port-reeve walked them down to the commercial dock. On the way, the port-reeve proud-ly pointed out the landmarks of his town, which where in fact not landmarks in the traditional sense. Keeping the town on boats was thought to be more practical than installing the substantial defenses necessary for a river town so close to enemy lands.

The tour ended at the tavern and inn, two sister ships oppo-site one from the other on the same dock. The tavern was called the Astrolabe after the ancient navigation instrument. Painted on the side of the tavern was the promise "Where the longitude meets the labitude!" Already the tavern was full and boisterous, sailors being the same in every universe.

They thanked the port-reeve and went first to the inn, the Anchor Watch. The rooms were small and oddly shaped and without portholes. This required that they each take their own room, but the cost was not much. They offered a room to Longfellow, but he asked for the coin instead and slept on his boat.

The inn and tavern were both owned by Captain Gordon, who ran the tavern and left his widowed sister in charge of the inn. The Keepers put their things away in their rooms and met back on the bow. Nerdraaage announced that he had had enough of this rocking ship and was heading to the Astrolabe. He did not stop or even respond when Ashlyn said the tavern was also a rocking ship. The others followed.

As the Keepers were about to push into the Astrolabe, two rough dwarves limped out, each with one boot on and the other boot full to the brim with beer. And all along Dangalf had thought Donald had been speaking euphemistically: *There comes a time when every dwarf must stop drinking beer from his boot.*

The Astrolabe was crowded with human sailors and fisherman and travelers, but there were also a few women who will be charitably described as entrepreneurial. Dangalf noticed how the ruffians leered at Ashlyn, and he stood close to her.

Doppelganger pushed his way up to the bar. The patrons he bumped turned to him angrily, looked at his size, and begrudgingly made room for him and the Keepers. Dangalf apologized to one relocated human, but that just seemed to make the man angrier. Dangalf moved quickly to put Doppelganger between him and the crazy-eyed man.

Captain Gordon was well decorated with ink and was very fit. Dangalf was glad to see him smile. The customers looked rough, but at least the owner was kindly. Dangalf was already missing the quiet civility of Templa Taur.

"What's your poison?" Gordon asked. He was a great talker especially with people just hearing his stories for a first time. He told them he had gotten lucky as a privateer and decided to take his substantial booty, buy a couple of old whaling ships, and retire to a safer profession before he got unlucky.

Behind him was the largest and most explicit portrait of a mermaid that any of them had ever seen and seemed to answer the ancient riddle of how a human could have intercourse with the legless beauties. "I like your painting," said Nerdraaage when Gordon returned with the beers.

"Thank you, master dwarf," said Gordon. "That is Vaylana, the only lass I ever loved."

Dangalf laughed and then on Gordon's hurt look said, "Oh, you're serious." Gordon turned his back and moved down the bar. "I'm such an idiot," Dangalf said to his friends. "Mermaids are real here."

"Everything is real here," added Ashlyn.

And the drinking began in earnest.

Doppelganger and Nerdraaage stood at the bar. Dangalf and Ashlyn sat at the first table that became available. Ashlyn had become quite the tease since she had come to terms with her sex while sobbing on Dangalf's shoulder. She could not imagine hiding her long legs under the table, so she sat on the table with her feet resting on a chair.

They kept drinking until even the drunks had tired of drinking and moved on. Gordon snoozed behind the bar. The Keepers and only a few diehards remained in the tavern. "The more I drink, the steadier this boat becomes," said Nerdraaage with a laugh. "Maybe I will set to sea with you after all," he told Doppelganger, following up on a topic introduced by Gordon a few hours ago. "Kraken don't scare me!"

But Doppelganger was fixated on an elf at the other end of the bar. "How did an elf merchant get a sword like that?" he grumbled.

"Walmart," said Nerdraaage laughing.

"Elf," he shouted in the otherwise subdued bar. "I like your sword. Where did you buy it?"

Dangalf and Ashlyn turned from their own conversation. Dangalf's expression said, *What now?* He knew sword buying was a Red School insult. Weapons were handed down, awarded, captured, or made with your own hands. Gordon's tavern keeper's sense caused him to blink awake, and the stragglers in the bar, despite their drunkenness, quieted and turned to the elf for his response.

"If you would like it, come and take it," said the elf without looking. His dispassionate response would have been a sober man's first warning.

But Doppelganger was drunk. And he had faced many opponents, and none had bested him. And he had killed now, and he was good at it. "I will duel you," said Doppelganger. "And I will take your sword when I win."

"A wager," said the elf, finally looking up to Doppelganger. "And what do you wager in return?"

"I have nothing as valuable as your sword. Only some gold coins."

"Keep your coins," said the elf. "If I should win, I will take the she-elf for the night," he said turning to Ashlyn.

"No!" Dangalf said as he rose.

"We are not slavers, elf," said Doppelganger. "She is not mine to wager."

"You sport such confidence," said the elf. "I thought your companion might share it. My sword against a night with your she-elf."

"We accept!" shouted Nerdraaage.

"No we don't!" shouted Dangalf.

"I hear so many voices, but not the one that matters," said the elf, fixing his gaze on Ashlyn.

"She's off the table," said Dangalf. "Well, I mean she's on the table. But she's off the table as far as any wager is concerned." And then he said angrily, "Doppel, you're drunk."

"Listen to your friend, Doppel." And the elf turned back to his drink.

"I don't need to be sober to beat your likes," said Doppelganger.

"Then just duel him and forget the sword," said Dangalf.

"I won't insult my friend," said Doppelganger. "What else can I wager?"

"As you said, nothing of the value of this sword," said the elf.

"What of this?" said Doppelganger, and he exposed his adamantine breastplate.

The dwarf turned to him, for the first time not looking dispassionate. "And how would you come by adamantine?" said the elf softly, almost to himself.

"No," said Ashlyn standing. "Not that. If you win, I will spend the night with you."

"No," protested Dangalf, but the wager was set, and no one wanted to hear his protests.

"It's a sure thing," announced Nerdraaage. They walked out to the dock.

"Here or on land?" asked Doppelganger.

The elf removed his cloak and looked down the forty feet of pier. "Here. I do not want the walk to last longer than the duel." Ashlyn had never seen such a mesomorphic elf before. He was packed with bulging muscles. "You are a healer?" he asked her.

Ashlyn hesitated before answering. She nervously clutched her druid collar and realized how he had guessed. "Yes."

"Be ready to help your friend."

Nerdraaage approached Ashlyn urgently. "Don't heal Doppelganger until the duel's over," he said. "That's cheating."

"You said the elf didn't stand a chance," whispered Dangalf.

"He might get lucky," said Nerdraaage.

Doppelganger took his axe from his sheath and crouched for combat. He had six inches and a hundred pounds on the elf. "Take out your sword, elf!" he commanded.

"I am ready," said the elf.

"I won't tell you again," shouted Doppelganger. This elf mocked him, and it was good. His rage was overtaking his drunkenness.

"I am ready." Doppelganger did not like attacking an un-armed opponent, not of a righteous race anyhow. But this elf mocked him and needed to be punished. It would be up to Ashlyn to heal him.

Doppelganger raised the axe to strike the elf with the bottom of the handle. Before he could move the axe forward, the elf stepped in close to Doppelganger and also took hold of the axe handle. Doppelganger saw the elf's muscular upper body. It was as if an elf head had been planted on a human body. A powerful human body. And the elf now had a better grip and more leverage on the axe than Doppelganger had. Doppelganger was in jeopardy of being knocked backward to the ground unless he released his own axe.

The elf struck his palm to Doppelganger's nose and in the same movement pulled Doppelganger's axe away from him and held it, laughing. This infuriated Doppelganger. Though logic dictated that he concede at this point, the bloodwarp had begun and would not let him. He grabbed and took the elf's sword from its scabbard. The cocky elf grabbed quickly for his sword but was too late. Doppelganger took it and thrust it at the elf's chest. The elf, however, was too fast and turned what could have been a deathblow into a flesh wound across his chest.

The elf cried out more in rage than in pain. And then it happened almost instantly. The elf was overtaken by his own bloodwarp. If it hadn't been apparent before, all now knew that

Doppelganger fought another of his own class. And one much better. They faced off now as warped human and warped elf, with reddened skin and blackened veins pulled tight over bulging muscle and bone.

The elf was expert, though, and had experienced many bloodwarps both involuntary such as now or at will when battle required it. And to a certain extent he had the ability to sublimate the bloodwarp when outside of true and frenetic combat. He heard in the background, over the coursing humors that pounded in his ears, the plea of the she-elf but he couldn't immediately understand her. And so he abated his instinct and desire to behead Doppelganger. It would have been easy for him to do but he was all too aware of the consequences of killing a duelist so much below his own rank. Murder, the lawful good called it. And he had known too many of his elite brotherhood felled by that charge. But this human was so stubborn and strong that he might not allow the duel to end until he was mortally wounded.

With blazing speed, the elf struck Doppelganger with the axe, blade sideways, so it bashed him like a mace. He next relieved Doppelganger of his sword and sliced it across his belly so that the beer he had drunk but not yet digested poured out onto the pier. Let the smell of his beer and blood and belly juice let him know what a terrible mistake he has made tonight, thought the Elf.

Doppelganger, dazed from the bash, fell backward. He had enough sense to hold his sliced belly with his hands to keep his guts from exploding out when he crashed back onto the dock. And he was mostly successful at that as he landed with a bang and a squishy sound.

The elf now registered Ashlyn's cries that her healing was "not good enough." He felt a bitter chill pass through his body, and he spun around looking for the source. The mage of the group stood holding a wand, wide eyed with terror. But all of those of the elf's kind were warded against such low-level spells. "Put that wand away," he commanded.

Ashlyn kneeled beside Doppelganger to heal him. He was still taken by the bloodwarp, which was good. He would not feel pain, and his clotting would be rapid. First she cast a healing spell to stop his bleeding. It did not work. He was losing the redness of the bloodwarp, and even the normal tan of his face turned pale as his humors poured from his belly. She had seen enough in her training to recognize that his very life was draining away, and she was not good enough to prevent it.

"Ashlyn," said Dangalf dumbly.

"He's over water!" shouted Ashlyn. "I can't heal him away from the land! Drag him to the shore!"

"He'll die first," said the elf. "Use your well!"

Her well of electroplasm. "I haven't enough," she cried.

Suddenly, Captain Gordon pushed his way past the gathered bystanders and kneeled next to Doppelganger. He lifted his head and held a potion in an ornate bottle to his lips. The Keepers had seen that bottle before. Doppelganger's eyes were rolled back in his head and he could not drink.

"You must heal him!" said Gordon. "Bring him back enough so that he can drink!" So she cast her best healing, and without being able to draw on the protoplasm of the living land, it took all of her small electroplasm pool. She fell forward on her palms, almost fainting.

Doppelganger blinked back to consciousness, and Gordon poured the potion into his mouth. Doppelganger swallowed. The bleeding stopped. Organs repaired themselves and were drawn back into his body's cavity. New pink flesh stitched up his gaping wounds. "That tastes terrible," complained Doppelganger.

Dangalf recognized the signs of electroplasm depletion in Ashlyn. He kneeled to her, but she waved him off. He checked on Doppelganger, who was still recovering but would clearly live. Then he went to Gordon. "Can we pay you for that potion?"

"You cannot just buy these," said Gordon. "And what of the next fool dying on my pier? Will I just throw your coins at him? You'll replace it, you will."

"I have a gravewhisper flower," said Ashlyn weakly. "You can have it."

"There you go, Captain," said the elf. "A master alchemist can make three healing potions from a flower. He'll keep one for himself, and you will have two."

"I suppose that will do."

"It will do tomorrow," said the elf. "She has other obligations tonight." He stepped to Ashlyn. "Heal me."

"I cannot," she said without looking at him. "I am empty."

"I will fix that soon enough." And then he turned to Doppelganger, who was getting off the ground with the help of Nerdraaage and Dangalf. "Because I am ever magnanimous, I will say this to you stranger: You are not the disgrace that you originally presented. You fight well enough for your station. You may even have a trace of honor when you are sober. May this defeat make you a better fighter." Doppelganger turned away from the elf wordlessly with the help of his friends. The memory of his rage and near death and his present humbled state would not allow him to be magnanimous.

Dangalf and Nerdraaage helped Doppelganger onto the Anchor Watch. Dangalf looked back to Ashlyn and was distressed to see that she was remaining behind, limply, on the dock. He would drop Doppelganger in his room and rush back to her.

The elf turned back to Ashlyn and smiled down at her. "I have traveled this world for many days without fair haven," he said. "And I can not imagine that any is as fair as yours." Ashlyn then realized that, despite the violence of the night, the elf still intended to collect on his wager. She looked up at him angrily for what he had just done to her friend, but there were other emotions that began to rise in her as well. She ran her hands across his chest and was able to stop the bleeding. "What is your name?"

"Ashlyn."

"Dream," he smiled. "Tonight you are my dream. My name is Niall. Do you have a room here?"

She thought this is how every female should be taken, as the prize in a battle between two dashing warriors. But how to act? She did not want Niall to think of her as a coney. (A drunken dwarf had called her that in Hammersmith. To her immense pleasure, Nerdraaage had risen and punched his brother dwarf to the ground. She teased him mercilessly about it, but she was flattered that he had risen to her defense while Dangalf had closed his eyes in semislumber and researched what a coney was. After all the violence was done, Dangalf opened his eyes and announced that a coney was a rabbit but it was also used to describe a promiscuous female. And then he asked why there was a dwarf on the floor.)

Ashlyn had felt sexual desire before in this world, especially since coming to terms with her sex, but nothing like her desire for this Niall. But she was also fearful of this strange elf with supreme confidence and violent prowess. And this fear only fed into her desire. And the desire fed into her fear. It was intoxicating. She looked up at him with the innocent expression of a virgin on the cusp, because in this world, in this gender, she was just that. "I have a room," she said. Niall took her hand and took her to her room, and then he took her.

LXXXI

When Niall awoke at daybreak, he found a large tyger in bed next to him. He understood the message and dressed quickly. He smiled at her before leaving.

When Nerdraaage made his morning visit to the tavern, he was surprised to see Dangalf already at a table and drinking. He joined his friend and ordered a beer. Dangalf nodded to him but was otherwise silent. Nerdraaage could see that his friend was hurting, and it was up to him to make everything better. "Everyone's gotten laid except you," he said.

"Are you casting aspersions on our innocent Ashlyn?" asked Dangalf.

"Didn't you hear them fucking all night?"

"I thought it was just the boat creaking."

"No," said Nerdraaage. "They were fucking all night." Dangalf realized subtlety was wasted on a dwarf. And he remembered how Nerdraaage didn't necessarily get subtlety even before he was a dwarf. "I say we stay another night and you get one of those tarts that was in here last night," said Nerdraaage. "And maybe I'll get one too."

"Didn't you just get married?"

"Angus said it's the bucket that taints the well. The well doesn't taint the bucket."

"And what would a dwarf know about water?"

"Well, it's just an expression. It means—"

"I know what it means."

With Niall gone, Ashlyn returned to bipedal form. It wasn't that she hadn't enjoyed what happened last night—no, it certainly wasn't that—but the daylight made her self-conscious so close to her friends' quarters, and she thought that tyger form was the best way to get him to depart before there were any other happenings.

"What?" was the only response Ashlyn got when she knocked on Doppelganger's door, but she entered anyway. He was shirtless and still in bed and looked at her impassively. She smiled and sat on the bed next to him. She touched the long pink scar on his stomach, and he quivered.

"I can put some extracts on this. There would be no scar."

"No."

She took her hand away. Ciar had told her Red Schoolers would want to keep their scars. "How do you feel?"

"Fine."

"You look good," she said. "I wanted to tell you about last night."

"Please don't."

She glared at him, and he turned away. "I wanted to tell you about his tattoo."

"Why?"

"It was a rune. A dragon bloodrune he called it. Burned into his skin orc style with a hot iron."

"What does that mean?"

"He was a dragoon," she said. "1337." The numbers stood for "leet": elite in game jargon. She hoped this old reference would humor him a bit. "You dueled a dragoon. He thought you did very well for your rank."

"For my rank," muttered Doppelganger.

"And you're only going to get better. He told me." She put her hand on his chest. His breathing grew heavy, and his heart pounded.

"You should leave," he said. And she did. She was apprehensive when she joined her friends in the tavern, but she smiled bravely and her friends greeted her without judgment or ridicule. Everything seemed perfectly normal, but she was distressed to see Dangalf already drinking. (It was not unusual or of concern for Nerdraaage to drink in the morning.)

For his part Dangalf only had to look at the shining Ashlyn to forgive her. After all, she likely didn't know that she had betrayed him. He also had the small consolation of knowing that two more of his divinations had been realized: Ashlyn had taken a lover, and his own heart had been broken. He kept these revelations to himself. He wanted to use his divination deck further, but he was still chilled by the memory of his ghostly pursuer. There was no reason to believe she was out of the picture. Just lagging behind them. Abigail the elf seer had called her.

It wasn't long before Doppelganger joined them. They ordered breakfast from a wench of about thirteen but, like all the young workers they had met, mature beyond her years. It was a revelation to see clever and polite children after coming from a world where most of the adults were not. After finishing breakfast they ordered extra food to take for lunch and the rescued children and in case Longfellow was hungry.

Ashlyn presented a small package to Gordon, and he gingerly unwrapped the gravewhisper flower. "One healing potion for me," said Gordon. "Another for the alchemist who makes them, and the third I will send off to you."

"That's not necessary," she said.

"I don't want more than what is coming to me," he insisted. "Besides, you adventurers will likely need it before I do." And so they bid farewell to Captain Gordon, the port-reeve, the smithy, and some drunk who wandered into the line of town dignitaries.

Longfellow refused the food with a shake of his head, and they launched. It was pleasant enough sailing, and after several hours they could see the sky before them getting red too early and in the wrong direction for sunset. Longfellow said it was Brimstone, the goblin lands, where smoking craters colored the sky. Ashlyn could smell the sulfur. But they would not travel that far. The goblin slave camp was known to be on the coast of elven-occupied lands, and Longfellow said he thought he knew where it was.

The enchanted map changed to show their slow progress toward their destination, a ruined temple for Sirona. Longfellow pulled into a hidden cove and grounded his boat. It was agreed that they would approach the camp from the woods. Once they had the children, they would either return to the ship or Dangalf would signal with a fireball for a pickup on the run. "The sky is full of fire in these parts," puffed Longfellow. "How will I know yours?"

"Mine will be green," said Dangalf.

"Can you do that?" asked Ashlyn.

"Give me a farthing."

"For doubting you?"

"I can make copper burn green." And Ashlyn smiled and demanded a farthing from Nerdraaage, and he gave it without protest because Ashlyn was their healer and they were going into combat.

The four stepped from the boat onto the ground, and Doppelganger pushed the ship back until it was floating free again, and Longfellow dropped anchor. Nerdraaage made himself unappear and took point.

After a few hours, Ashlyn stopped them as Nerdraaage returned and became visible again. He had found the slave camp up ahead. He saw half a dozen human children and at least one each of dwarfling and elfling in cages. There were a dozen goblins, but they didn't seem to be guarding their captives so much as they were gambling and eating and sleeping. They pressed on with Nerdraaage still unappeared and on point but not so far ahead of his friends. They met with him again in the cover of trees just outside the goblin camp.

The goblins were green-skinned endomorphs with a variety of displeasing characteristics: short, bow legged, hunchbacked, potbellied, wrinkled, beady eyed, and cloven hoofed. They all had at least one gold tooth and some a mouthful. Doppelganger saw one especially repugnant goblin poking a stick into a cage, teasing a small red-haired girl, and decided he would kill him first.

The goblins were in fact using the ruins of an old temple. Dangalf thought it was clear evidence that if the gods ever did walk upon this world, they had since departed. What just god could allow one of his or her temples to be used for such an abomination?

It was decided that Doppelganger would charge the camp and just start killing. The goblins didn't seem to pose much of a threat to him, and he would have Dangalf's firepower and Ashlyn's healing from the trees to support him. Nerdraaage would watch his back, striking and unappearing as needed. Dangalf initiated a ready check. Doppelganger and Nerdraaage answered in the affirmative. Ashlyn answered in the affirmative as well, only not as quickly or confidently.

"Okay," said Dangalf with a nod. Doppelganger charged the temple grounds and let rip a horrendous war cry just before he split the skull of the goblin girl-teaser. He killed another startled goblin with one blow before the goblins even knew what was happening. When they realized they were under attack, strange Gobspeak cries sounded through the camp.

A readied goblin appeared before Doppelganger. Doppelganger charged, and the goblin threw a weighted net that wrapped around Doppelganger's legs and brought him tumbling down. Other goblins appeared and started pelting the fallen giant with stones from slings and small arrows from wrist-mounted crossbows. Ashlyn was furiously healing Doppelganger. His wounds brought on his bloodwarp, and he tore through the net that entwined him.

Nerdraaage killed the goblin who netted Doppelganger. Now that he was visible, the goblins targeted him also. Doppelganger charged his attackers on the temple altar. He swung his axe horizontally and beheaded one and bisected another goblin with one blow. By the time Dangalf got off his first fireball—an enormous blast that incinerated one, killed two others, and knocked back half a dozen—the goblins had had enough. Doppelganger had to chase after them to kill two more. When he returned to camp, Nerdraaage was already picking at the cage locks to free the children.

"That was some nice healing," Dangalf told Ashlyn.

"Thanks," said Ashlyn. "There's a lot of magic on these grounds to draw upon. Nice fireball by the way." But before they could congratulate each other further, a second wave of attackers appeared. Four armored and oversized goblins charged at them. Doppelganger parried and pushed back one of the attackers, who lost his helmet. They were not oversized goblins; they were dwarves!

Dangalf managed to freeze one in an ice block and flee. Ashlyn morphed in tyger form and escaped back to the trees.

Doppelganger battered at one of the dwarves, but he was strong and well armored and would not die easily like the goblins did. Ashlyn morphed back to elf form and healed Doppelganger from a hidden position as he battled three dwarves. Nerdraaage struck and unappeared as he fought his sturdy racial brothers.

From the woods, Dangalf blasted a dwarf with a quick fireball. The battle seemed to belong to the Keepers when a dwarf blackguard appeared behind Ashlyn. Dangalf saw him, but the dwarf struck even before he could yell. He stabbed Ashlyn with a dagger, and she dropped silently to the ground. The blackguard saw Dangalf preparing a fireball to strike him, but he just smiled a black-toothed grin and unappeared. Dangalf hesitated. He wanted to run to Ashlyn, but if the blackguard was still there, he could easily kill Dangalf. "Help!" Dangalf shouted. "A blackguard has stabbed Ashlyn." And then he spun around fearfully. Was that a blackguard stepping behind him?

Both Doppelganger and Nerdraaage ran to Ashlyn, and Dangalf joined them. Ashlyn looked glassy eyed and was barely breathing. Nerdraaage felt behind her. "Good cut," said Nerdraaage. Nerdraaage tasted his bloodied hand. "Teatwhisker," he said.

"What!" said an exasperated Dangalf. But before Nerdraaage could answer, Dangalf recalled the blackguard poison books he had read. The blackguards had vulgar sexual names for their poisonous plants. It helped the less literate members of their class learn their herbology.

"This blackguard is a baddie. It's a terrible poison to use on elves."

"What do you mean terrible!" cried Dangalf.

"Well," said Nerdraaage calmly, "good for her." Nerdraaage produced a small glass vial and poured it into Ashlyn's mouth. "Try to swallow that," he said. Ashlyn, still glassy eyed, appeared to swallow, or twitch. They watched her for some time. Ashlyn tried to speak. They leaned in more closely. Finally and hoarsely she said, "Idiots, go get the kids!"

"I'll go," said Doppelganger.

"There is still a blackguard about," warned Dangalf. His eyes teared up as Nerdraaage fussed over Ashlyn. Nerdraaage, who had seemed the most unfit for his race and class and this world, had stepped up to become a brave dwarf and a skilled blackguard. And he saved Ashlyn. Soon she was sitting. She felt ill, but she smiled to comfort Dangalf, who looked sick with worry. She cast healing spells upon herself when she was able.

They found Doppelganger, who had freed and collected all the children. Ten there were: eight humans, a she-elfling, and a male dwarfling. The children who surrounded Doppelganger excitedly ran to the newcomers. They were still young enough, and rescued early enough, so that their ordeals had not compromised their innate exuberance.

Nerdraaage looted the last of the corpses, and then he and Ashlyn led the children into the woods. Doppelganger pointed to the dwarf still blinking but otherwise frozen in a block of ice. "That was quite a spell you cast," said Doppelganger. "Counter it and I will kill him."

"No," said Dangalf. He began to cast an unnecessarily large fireball, the biggest he had ever cast, and shot it at the dwarf trapped in the ice block. The dwarf and ice exploded in a shower of ice shards and blood. It was overkill, and even Doppelganger thought so. And he smiled and patted Dangalf on the back. They caught up to the others, and the children marveled as Doppelganger's bloodwarp faded and he returned to normal.

Dangalf, reflecting on his vulgar display of power, worried now that his pyrotechnics might have signaled wyvern riders or some other monstrous response. He told the others of his concerns, and they agreed he should signal for Longfellow. He took a farthing and blasted it into the air in a great, streaming, green fireball. They hunkered down near the shore until Longfellow sailed up after an eternity of twelve minutes. They rushed the children onto the boat, and Doppelganger pushed them back into the river before climbing aboard.

The stoic Longfellow counted the children and pronounced it was a "good catch." He turned the craft back the way they had come, this time traveling with the current. They would sail straight through to Portsmouth.

The dwarfling sat with Nerdraaage, who was going through his loot. The dwarfling's eyes, already recognizing fine jewelry, marveled at a solid silver ring. "Can I have that?" he asked.

"No," said Nerdraaage, quickly putting the ring away. "But you can have a farthing." And he handed the dwarfling a copper coin, which meant he had to give one to each of the youngsters who rushed to him with their hands out.

"Did we get any good loot?" asked Ashlyn.

"A little," said Doppelganger. "Mostly junk."

"Those goblin teeth will set you up just fine," said Longfellow with a one-eyed wink.

"Goblin teeth?" asked Ashlyn.

"The gobbies," Longfellow said between puffs. "Puts all their wealth in their heads. Silver, gold, gems." The Keepers looked back and forth between themselves in varying degrees of distress. "Killed gobbies and didn't take the teeth," muttered Longfellow. "You don't like gold?"

"Let's go back!" demanded Nerdraaage.

"With those fireworks you set off?" scoffed Longfellow.

Dangalf stewed. He was angry that they had forgotten the goblin teeth. He especially should have known better. He had read how goblins had even healthy teeth pulled and replaced with ones of precious metals and stones. As the *Cronica Acadia* said, goblin mouths were "the only place that thieving race could protect their treasure one from another." Dangalf was also angry at himself for not having a better strategy against the goblins. And he was furious that they were attacked by dwarves. Dwarves didn't attack the Acadian Alliance of Righteous Races in the game. They were a righteous race!

He was angry about the attack on Ashlyn. She could have been killed. And he was furious that her attacker escaped unscathed. Could he be on the boat with them now? How long would Dangalf see that black-toothed grin out of the corner of his eye? He stewed further as the children recounted their experiences. Some had been taken while they slept. Still others stolen off the roads or from farms. A few had checked into closets or under beds to look for monsters only to find them. Someone mentioned parents, and soon all the children were crying.

"What kind of shite world is this where everyone knows that the goblins have a camp full of slave children and they don't do anything about it?" demanded Dangalf. The others looked at him in surprise.

"We just did something about it," answered Doppelganger.

"We are only four," shot back Dangalf. "Where are the other heroes?"

"There are a lot of fires to put out in this world," said Longfellow, tapping the dottle out of his pipe.

"I don't see how you people can go about fishing and drinking and buying things with the world like this."

"We have had war and we have had peace. And right now we be in a moment of peace for the most part. You might forget how close we came to losing the last war and putting an end to good deeds evermore. And who knows. Maybe it is your deed today that sparks the next. And there are few who think the next war won't be the last, that things will be decided once and for all. Or maybe they will just attack the folks at Dragonfly. Whatever comes of it, your good deeds will not go unanswered. The folks at Dragonfly all knew this, but none spoke to stop you." Dangalf fell silent. Would their quest today bring retribution on their hosts? He hated to even consider it. What would be the point of any heroism then if it would be met with an equal and opposite reaction?

In time, Dangalf's spirit buoyed as they moved swiftly on the great river. The children's resilience was amazing, and they again reverted to boisterous laughter and play. Dangalf watched with amusement as the children attached themselves to the others. The two girls and the she-elfling gravitated to Ashlyn, who did her best to entertain them. Ashlyn had her own miniature in the she-elfling. She was a rarity, the she-elfling, permitted to be born only because another elf had died. That was how the immortal elves dealt with population control. The frightened doe had latched onto Ashlyn's hand since she first set eyes on her. The she-elfling's fear was gone, but she still held the hand of her big sister and looked at her adoringly. "Do you think I will be as beautiful as you when I am grown?" she asked. Ashlyn thought a moment and said, "You have a much better start than I did at your age."

The six human boys were fascinated by Doppelganger, and his disinterest did nothing to dissuade them. The dwarfling was naturally attracted to Nerdraaage. He played with Nerdraaage's beard, and Nerdraaage tugged gently on the child's modest beard. "It's a fine beard," said Nerdraaage. "It will be ready for braiding in no time." The others looked at each other with growing admiration for Nerdraaage. It was their first sign that the new husband would also make a good father. And then he gave the dwarfling some beer.

"Beer," scoffed Longfellow. "At sea we drink bumbo!" It was the most animated they had seen him. He went to a cask and filled two cups. He handed one to Nerdraaage and kept the second.

Nerdraaage took a drink. He stopped tasting it, licked his lips, and returned to drink more. "Bumbo is good!" he finally announced. The dwarfling reached plaintively for the bumbo and was granted a swig. Doppelganger was next.

"Can we have bumbo!" cried the boys.

"When you have beards," said Dangalf.

"Let them have some," said Doppelganger, choking it down. "Then they won't ever want it again."

At sea we drink bumbo! The cup was passed about, and all the Keepers drank some and made a pronouncement afterward because moments were good but a ceremony was even better.

The children finally wore out, and they lay under blankets on the deck. Longfellow had Doppelganger place a lantern at the front of the boat. The Keepers were also worn out and found comfortable places. But the children would not sleep, so Longfellow told tales of the rediscovery of Oceania when he was still young enough to sail on the great ocean. He spoke of krakens and an alabaster whale large enough to swallow the biggest human ship. He told of mermaids and their wicked sisters, the sirens. He told of the great flying creatures of Oceania, which he helped bring back to this land. He told how Acadians had to again learn to ride flying beasts because they had killed off the native ones when the world was dark. He told how good and wise men had said that flying creatures were things of mythology until they were brought trembling before a full-grown dragon. He told of how the trolls were desperate to share in the riches of Oceania but were not sea-hearty creatures like humans and orcs. And so the trolls buried themselves in crates of dirt until they could be unboxed at journey's end. And to this day only humans, orcs, and trolls have ever made the trip to Oceania, where they have carved out their two competing colonies but still are only two mere specs on the rediscovered continent. And the part colonized by trolls and orcs had wyverns, which they sent back so their armies could fly against us. But the human colony was near griffins and dragons, and the griffin was superior in every way to the wyvern, and the dragon was the rarest and most impressive of all flying creatures, and dragoons could slay a dozen enemies before they even dismounted just by using the dragon's great swishing tail. And though now sailors brought back dragon eggs for hatching by the elves, so desperate was the Alliance for air superiority that they brought back full-grown dragons at the beginning. And he said solemnly that for every dragon they brought back, Oceania took three men, the dragon took three, and the sea another three—all so the dragoon could be carried aloft and descend in complete surprise on the enemy at any place on the map. And he wondered if the dragoons ever thought about the men who went to the bottom of the sea so that other men might fly.

The children slept now, and Longfellow fell silent, occasionally puffing on his pipe and looking to the stars for guidance. Dangalf was the last of the Keepers still awake and wondered where the old man got his stamina. He blinked a few times before he fell asleep himself, knowing that they were in good hands under a blanket of stars and with Longfellow at the wheel.

LXXXII

The children assured that the Keepers woke up early the next day. They found Longfellow still at the wheel, and he told them they were two hours to Portsmouth. When they landed, the children unloaded excitedly onto the dock before they were even tied off. Dangalf quietly asked Doppelganger for the captain's fee.

As the others herded the children over to the Pale Whale for breakfast, Dangalf paid Longfellow, who accepted without thanks. He then bid farewell to Longfellow, who nodded in return and then went back to his work. Dangalf did not know what to make of the captain's stoicism. Did he not like the Keepers? Perhaps he just didn't like Dangalf. Or maybe "like" wasn't something that Longfellow injected into the equation, and Dangalf figured he probably shouldn't either. Longfellow had provided the services they had contracted for and executed his duties perfectly. Maybe Longfellow felt that that was enough, and Dangalf realized it was asking too much to also want to win over the old sea dog, to change him into a joking and back-slapping best friend forever. It made Longfellow all the more genuine that he was not any different to the Keepers when they left him than when they had found him. With a grizzled jack like Longfellow, it was compliment enough just to stay even with him.

The children were excited to enter the whale's mouth that served as a door to the Pale Whale and made quite the moment of it. Despite their hunger, the children ate and drank slowly. Dangalf realized later he probably shouldn't have told them they would be going to the orphanage when they were done. Eventually Doppelganger, as the de facto leader of the party—the children both idolized him and were terrified of him—roused them from the table and marched them all over to the orphanage.

The orphanage's matron seemed like a kindly human (or more accurately, she was definitely human and seemed kindly). A staff of five females (three humans, a she-elf, and a she-dwarf) appeared immediately. The staff told the children to say good-bye, and the children said good-bye without a hint that they would never see their four rescuers again. The staff was especially exuberant and rushed the children out of the office as if to get the separation over quickly for the children (and perhaps for the Keepers as well) as you might quickly peel off a bandage that had attached itself to skin. "They will be fine," said the matron with a practiced smile.

"And the dwarfling?" asked Nerdraaage.

"Well, it depends on his tartan," she said. "The better clans will have him home in a few days."

His clan! thought Nerdraaage. He never inquired about his clan. Some dwarf he was. He had been fighting it for some time, but his eyes finally began to water. "I assure you, master dwarf, that he will always have a home with the humans if no other claims him."

"What kind of life is that for a dwarf! Surrounded by humans."

"Are you crying?" asked Dangalf, regretting it as soon as he asked it.

"I'm not crying," said Nerdraaage. "The tears haven't broken the plain of the eyelid." This last was said as he pointed to his moist eyes. "And what if I did cry? I'm not some cold-blooded elf that only cries when a tree is cut down."

"What did I do!" said Ashlyn.

"We will do our best to send them all to family. If that is not possible, they will be sent to the orphanage that can best keep them."

"Sad that any child would have to be in an orphanage," said Dangalf.

The matron puffed up slightly about this. "I grew up in an orphanage. All of our children have their own beds, clean and warm clothes, three meals a day, and are kept until they can apprentice or take husband. The pity is not every child has it this well."

"I'm sorry," said Dangalf. "I meant no offense."

"He does that a lot," explained Ashlyn.

"May I have your commissions?" said the matron, resetting her smile. The matron took her seat and began recording the deed on each of their scrolls. She returned the scrolls as she completed each. "It is a pity that public service does not pay better," she said, taking out a small chest from the desk and opening it. "But I trust the appreciation of the children was also reward." She made four stacks of farthings.

"I want to donate my reward back to the orphanage," Ashlyn declared suddenly. A chill ran down Nerdraaage's spine. Was he going to be shamed into giving up his own payment? Fortunately, Doppelganger and Dangalf were not making any motions as to refuse payment.

"My dear," said the matron, "If you had ridden up here on unicorns in Vinlandian finery, I would gladly accept. But it would not do for our per diem to be sleeping in stables." The best sleep I ever had was in a stable, thought Doppelganger. The matron pushed the little stacks forward, and they all took one, Ashlyn lastly and only after Nerdraaage motioned to take her stack as well.

The Keepers next went to the town scrivener so that their deeds were recorded and reported to Vinland. Outside the scrivener's office, they glanced over the quest postings. There was an advertisement for opportunities in Oceania that excited the two humans still exhilarated by their aquatic journey, but it was only for sailors or those who had achieved principal status in their classes, so it was not necessary for Nerdraaage and Ashlyn to voice their objections.

As if in answer to the question of what to do next, a great white owl alighted upon Ashlyn's shoulder. She removed the message from his leg and tossed some seeds onto the ground. The owl looked down at the motionless seeds and back to Ashlyn. "Sorry, I don't have any mice," said Ashlyn, and when the owl looked at Clay, she told him, "He is not for eating," and the owl flew off. Ashlyn read, "Please meet me at Portsmouth. It is of the utmost import. I will be there by noon of the third. I will await you at the Pale Whale if you have not yet arrived or have departed and must return. Theodore the Wise, Guild of Sages and Seers."

"Guild of Sages and Seers!" enthused Dangalf. "Well that is an unexpected honor. All the way from Vinland!"

"Oh, great honor," mocked Nerdraaage. "Unless we did something wrong!"

"They don't send sages to arrest people," said Dangalf.

"How do you know he's a sage and not a seer?"

"The wise," said Dangalf. "The equivalent title for a seer would be the lucid. Sages and seers have four levels of honorific titles..."

"When is the third?" interrupted Doppelganger.

"It's today," said Dangalf.

It was close to noon, and they headed back to the Pale Whale to wait. They sat at a corner table where they could see everyone who entered. Dangalf had suggested that everyone remain sober for their honored guest, but Doppelganger and Nerdraaage wordlessly declined. Within an hour there was a commotion outside the door. One excited young woman entered the Whale and pulled the serving wench back out with her. The only word that Dangalf heard was "carriage." Well that sealed it. Their guest had arrived and by no lesser means of transport than carriage! Horses were themselves a symbol of prosperity, but never before had the Keepers beheld a carriage!

They all turned to watch as a guard wearing a Vinland tabard opened the door and glanced around the inn before Theodore entered. Suddenly they all understood what the matron had meant by Vinlandian finery. He was garbed in rich and colorful silks, including his chaperone hat, a flat, round hat much larger than his head with a scarf-like tail. He held his nose in the air, which made him seem a snob, but he did make the effort to smile when he saw Dangalf waving to him.

"What a hat," said Dangalf softly. The other Keepers followed his lead by standing in honor of their guest and remaining so until he took the seat that Dangalf had reserved next to him.

After a cursory glance at his tablemates, Theodore waved off his guard with the back of his hand. "See that the horses are changed," he ordered.

Doppelganger's cheeks flushed at Theodore's treatment of the guard. Or maybe it was just the wine. Either way he was glad he was no longer a lowly guard and on his way to becoming a warrior. Maybe then, titles and honors heaped upon him, he would feel confident to march into the elven royal house and demand to speak to Dymphna. His attention returned to the present as he was introduced by Dangalf, as they all were in turn.

"Some wine, sire?" asked Dangalf already waving down the wench.

"No," said Theodore. "Wine makes you forget."

"Which is exactly why we do it," said Doppelganger, raising his cup.

"Nevertheless," said Theodore. "My calling is to remember." After a pause, Theodore continued: "Well you four are the cause of much hand cramping for our scriveners. They must document all of your accomplishments as well as the growing body of opinion about your ragtag group of humans, dwarf, and she-elf of White and Red Schools. The scrolls are piling up, and already there is talk about opening a book on each of you. Others think that we should open one book on the four of you, but then the question becomes what do we call that book?"

"*Keepers of the Broken Blade*," suggested Nerdraaage.

"Fascinating! And what is this broken blade?"

The Keepers looked back and forth to each other. Dangalf, who knew, did not want to admit to Theodore or the other Keepers that the name came from a Hardy Boys mystery. "It doesn't mean anything," Dangalf said softly.

Theodore nodded politely. "Well, I'll mention it at the next guild meeting."

"There are times I think I would be better suited to being a sage," said Dangalf.

"Is that so? You know we are pacifists?"

"I wouldn't mind being a pacifist."

"Your accomplishments say otherwise. A brutal narrative of carnage in a very short period of time."

"That's mostly them," said Dangalf, pointing at the red schoolers.

"I suppose it's easier being a pacifist when you travel with armed guard," said Doppelganger.

"So this mercenary cuts with words as well," said Theodore.

A mortified Dangalf laughed too hard at Theodore's remark before turning on Doppelganger. "Theodore is our guest all they way from Vinland," he said.

"I am a repository of Alliance wisdom," said Theodore. "Outside the confines of Vinland, my guard is a requirement of my order and not a personal vanity."

"I apologize for my friend," said Dangalf.

"It is not necessary," said Theodore. "It is the curse of his class to always be seeking battle. All the more odd, though, that a pacifist-inclined mage would seek his company. But to the purpose of this gathering." Theodore removed a tube from his pocket and some scrolls from within the tube. "I have here your four bloodrunes. What if anything do you know of bloodrunes?" Dangalf began to speak, but Ashlyn shot him a glance that he read as, *Let Theodore give the lecture.* "Each sapien, each living creature, or at least those that bleed, has a bloodrune," explained Theodore. "From a drop of blood or even a speck of dried blood, a skilled humorist can project that blood's rune on parchment or other medium."

"A humorist!" said Nerdraaage guffawing.

"Alchemists," said Theodore. "They specialize in the four humors. Those humors that make the warrior's bloodwarp or keep the mage phlegmatic. They are blood and biles white, yellow, and black. But today our only interest is blood. All blood can be distilled into a bloodrune unique to the individual. As unique as a snowflake."

"Or a fingerprint," said Dangalf.

"A fingerprint," said Theodore curiously before turning his hands over to study his own. "Why that's brilliant!" Dangalf sank in his chair. After impressing upon Nerdraaage to cease his stream of otherworld colloquialisms, now it was Dangalf introducing fingerprinting to the new world! "You know where fingerprints could be utilized," said Theodore still contemplating his own. "Crime scenes where no blood was spilled." Theodore took Nerdraaage's cup and applied his fingerprints to the outer surface and studied them.

"Ah," said Dangalf. "Please tell us about the bloodrunes."

"Oh, of course," said Theodore. He unrolled a scroll, which he held down with Nerdraaage's cup to Nerdraaage's growing annoyance. "This," said Theodore. "Is my bloodrune. The rune shape is the same for all humans. The uniqueness of the bloodrune can be found in the smaller patterns imprinted upon the racial rune. We are still unlocking the secrets contained in all of these patterns, but there are some things we know to be certain. For example, this marking is called the appendage because of course I am male. A female would have no such marking."

Ashlyn could feel Nerdraaage staring at her and grinning. "Can we see Ashlyn's?" asked Nerdraaage.

"Of course," said Theodore removing another scroll from the tube and spreading it out. Nerdraaage leaned excitedly over it.

"Ashlyn of course has the elven bloodrune," said Theodore.

Suddenly Nerdraaage pointed frantically to a mark on the rune. "What is that!" he cried. "Is that a male appendage!"

"That," said Theodore flicking the object off the scroll, "Appears to be a leaf fragment."

"Oh," said Nerdraaage, putting his pipe into his pocket.

"As you can plainly see, your lovely Ashlyn is a perfect example of the she-elf specimen," Theodore leered at Ashlyn, and she smiled politely. She had learned being female meant a lot of creepy looks from unexpected sources, and she was dealing with it.

"Dangalf next," said Theodore, unrolling another scroll. "As you can see, it is a human bloodrune not unlike my own."

"Why is it so faded?" asked Dangalf.

"Ah, very good. It is faded because this is not your bloodrune," said Theodore turning the scroll over. "This is. You do not have a human bloodrune. You have the mirror image of a human bloodrune. Borrowing from the lexicon of heraldry, we call this type of bloodrune a bend sinister."

"What does that mean?"

"Simply put, you are not of this world." Theodore leaned back and waved to the serving wench. "Poisonberry tea," he ordered as the Keepers looked back and forth to each other in varying degrees of worry.

"We are not of this world," Dangalf finally said.

"I know. I just said that."

"What are you going to do with us?" asked Ashlyn.

"I am a sage," answered Theodore. "I do not do anything. At least not as you mean it. I make reports and recommendations."

"Then what will you recommend?" pressed Doppelganger.

"Further study. There have been otherworlders before, and I do not believe there is a consensus on what if any harm they pose. After all it could be that your presence here will continue to be beneficent. If so, it would seem best to allow you to fulfill your purpose and not lock you away in a tower."

Dangalf and Ashlyn examined their scrolls. Theodore handed Doppelganger and Nerdraaage their own. "Feel free to keep these," he said. "There are secrets locked away in all of our bloodrunes."

"Can you tell us about travel between these worlds?" asked Ashlyn. "I mean, we still, when we have a quiet moment, can't believe we're here."

"Legends say that in ancient times sapiens moved freely between this world and another. It was a world very similar to Acadia. Mayhap yours?"

"Mayhap," said Doppelganger.

"At least they could have been similar in ancient times," added Dangalf.

"That all ended with the Schism," said Theodore. "The near-war between the white and blue Schools. It is said that the other world destroyed their portal to our world."

"How did people move between the worlds?"

"Quite easily, I understand. There was a portal at both worlds. It is unknown if some communication existed between worlds to devise these portals or if it was pure chance that they would be made complementary. One would step through as through a doorway."

"That's not how it happened for us," said Ashlyn.

"No, I don't suppose it was. The other portal was apparently destroyed. And you need a functioning portal at both worlds. But there are claims of other contact with this sister world. The more common and simplest is called bleed-through. It is the most ephemeral contact. Seers and other gifted sapiens say they touch the other world with their minds, but the contact is typically during slumber or trance states and is as fleeting as a dream. Ancient texts describe a more complicated process called a soul crossing or journey. It requires a great deal of magic, and parties on both worlds must cooperate to achieve it. In this case the soul alone crosses the barrier between worlds. I believe that is what you experienced."

"But these bodies," said Dangalf. "These are not our bodies. They come from a...I don't know how to describe it in terms you would recognize," said Dangalf.

"These bodies come from a game," said Ashlyn.

"It is only your soul that transferred to this world," said Theodore. "The manifestation of the body was the expression of the soul. Some believe the bloodrune is the foundation of the being, that it is all about the blood. Others, and I include myself, believe the blood and by extension the bloodrune is the manifestation of the soul. As such the bloodrune is also called a soul pattern. Since you did not bring your blood to this world, only your soul, it is an argument in favor of saying your blood, by extension your bodies, are the manifestation of your souls. These bodies probably represent you better than the bodies that you discarded."

"Discarded?" said Ashlyn.

"Discarded is inexact, and I apologize for my coarseness," said Theodore. "I do not know what happened to your old bodies other than to pronounce that they are no longer occupied by your souls."

"What was that schism you mentioned?" asked Ashlyn.

"The Great Schism. It erupted between Acadia and Europa, the legendary other world. It was a battle over the preeminence of the White or Blue School. Magic or machina."

"Machine," Dangalf explained to his friends.

"Our ancients believed magic to be the better school for our world while the other world chose machina, and each world and every sapien separated along those lines. The Blue School remains an important element of Acadia, but our craftsmen build to complement sapiens not replace them. And there are restrictions on the practice of the Blue School so as to prevent their excesses. And it is said that those that chose Europa, the world of machina, destroyed their own portal, so great was their fear and hatred of magic. Does this Europa, the world of machina, sound like the world you came from?"

The Keepers nodded. "But there are some good things about the other world too," Nerdraaage defended. "Our world."

"Spoken like a true member of the bluest race. I'm sure both worlds have their advantages," agreed Theodore. "Different roads they took, but they are not dissimilar. You would not have been able to travel here if there was not still some magic left in your world." And that last comment made the Keepers feel a little better. If they should make their way back to the world they started in, willingly or not, it was nice to know that it was a place not devoid of magic. And the drinking began in earnest.

And though they sat at the same table, they were two different parties. Doppelganger, Ashlyn, and Nerdraaage drank and smoked and sang and joked. Theodore and Dangalf drank poisonberry tea and talked about hats. But occasionally the parties intersected. "You're drinking something called poisonberry!" demanded Doppelganger of Dangalf.

But Ashlyn answered, "Poisonberry is one of the most beneficial plants ever discovered. It was purposely misnamed by a human witch who hoped to keep the secret all to herself."

"Good show," cheered Theodore. "However, it was an elven witch."

"There are no elven witches," challenged Ashlyn.

"My dearest Ashlyn," said Theodore smiling. "Not a witch and yet bewitching. I should have ultimate knowledge and still have to surrender to you in argument."

"That's the wisest thing you've said tonight, Theodore," said Ashlyn with just a trace of flirtation. Dangalf tried to turn the conversation back to hats.

Nerdraaage, not interested in conversation with another sap making goo-goo eyes at Ashlyn, took his looted ring from his pocket and tried to bounce it into his cup. It immediately caught the eye of Theodore, who was an inquisitor first and a flirt much further down that list. "What is that?" asked Theodore.

"That's my loot!" shouted Nerdraaage because he was drunk.

"May I see it?"

"You can see it from there!" Ashlyn took the ring from Nerdraaage and gave it to Theodore.

"Clan Ghostbeard," read Theodore. "Where did you get this?"

"I took it off a lesser dwarf than myself after I killed him," said Nerdraaage.

"Killed another dwarf?"

"That's right!"

"As an otherworlder mayhap you didn't know that killing a fellow dwarf will get you estranged from the dwarven family."

"Wha?" said a suddenly sober Nerdraaage.

"I know all of the dwarven clans including the one-dwarf clans. Even the legendary lost clans. There is no Ghostbeard. In fact, only the five founding clans may reference beards in their clan names. This clan is an obvious affront to the royal families. And these are goblin tool marks. This just gets more curious. What were the Keepers of the Broken Blade's plans in the coming days?"

"I think that we should go back to that slave camp and see if there are more children we can rescue," said Ashlyn.

Theodore waved dismissively. "There will always be more stolen children," he said. "This is important. But I suppose only one of you needs go. Nerdraaage would be the obvious choice."

"We stay together," insisted Doppelganger.

"Very well, all of you then. And if it will ease your consciences, I will impress you. Let me see your commissions." Dangalf handed his over first, and Theodore took out an extravagant plumed pen that wrote without being dipped in ink. This magical pen was only slightly less magical because of the blue stain it left on the pocket of Theodore's Vinlandian finery.

Theodore finished Dangalf's scroll and began writing on the next. Dangalf excitedly read to the others what was writ on his: "By my authority as an officer in the Guild of Sages and Seers, you are ordered to report to Bran Keep expeditiously."

Bran Keep! The dwarven capital! The twenty-thousand-year-old mountain fortress overlooking enemy lands! They were eager to visit all of the great cities of Acadia, but now they were actually commanded to visit one! And they were going there not as tourists but as heroes, seekers, mercenaries, and adventurers!

"Seek out Loremaster Fearghas," said Theodore when done writing. "He is my dwarven counterpart. A stout bird could fly the ring to Bran Keep, but he will have questions for you, so it's best to bring it yourself. Something tells me this ring could be of utmost import. I suggest you ride at first light."

"But we have no mounts," said Dangalf.

"Then you should leave now."

LXXXIII

Theodore's carriage was magnificent. The horses were adorned with white plumes on their heads, and the carriage was festooned with banners of the White School and of the Guild of Sages and Seers. A brilliant Vinlandian shield was on the carriage doors.

Inside it was appointed better than any space the Keepers had seen except for Doppelganger, who had visited Dymphna's royal quarters. Each facet bore intricate details: a gold dragon head's door handle, an aspect on the inside door depicting the Great Lighthouse such that the light spun around as you opened and closed the door, a gold rune inlaid in highly polished wood on the ceiling that depicted what they now recognized as the human bloodrune. The window shades bore the crest of the Guild of Sages and Seers.

Theodore apologized to the Keepers for not being able to take them all the way to Bran Keep, but he was sailing for Oceania, and the ship would not wait. He expounded on his explanation as was typical of the White School. Human seafarers had rediscovered the long-lost land, but the trolls were quick to set up a competing settlement. It appeared this would be the next front in the war against the Legion and, if so, they needed to master the secrets of this mysterious land to be victorious. If the unthinkable happened and the Alliance was defeated in Acadia, then Oceania would be their last refuge.

Dangalf mentioned how the map of Acadia that existed in their old world showed a parity between the Alliance and the Legion and how startled they were to arrive here and see a map depicting the neutral Nemetia and half of the elven lands under the control of the Legion.

Theodore told them how close humans had come to annihilation when the Trollish Armada appeared just off the coast of Vinland. And the destruction of humans would have meant the eventual destruction of the other righteous races.

LXXXIV

The Trollish Armada sailed under the command of Kejavik the Eleventh, the troll prince and necromancer and a high priest in the Uroboros Cult and the Eleventh incarnation of Kejavik the Naught. And he was Kejavik the Devout, and as the officially recognized reincarnation of Kejavik the Naught, he was entitled to all of the titles of his previous lives: the Impaler, the Black Tongued, the Elf Eater, the Shaper, of the Leather Apron (a dandy who would signal his murderous rampages by donning a leather apron over his silk raiment), the Collector, the Unmentionable, and so on. And each incarnation of Kejavik was blacker than the previous. Kejavik the Devout was an especially powerful witch most learned of the Black School, the Legion bastardization of the White School. A prince was he by their own black bloodlines, who might have become king of the trolls if he was so inclined but instead shunned the royal path for priesthood in the Uroboros. And so it was that Kejavik's display of black piety moved thousands of trolls to the Uroboros, and it did surpass all of the lesser death cults in numbers and influence and became a threat to the royal family itself for rule of the trolls and by extension the Legion.

410

His Trollish Armada that day did carry six thousand orc marines, one for each man, woman, and child in Vinland. And the trolls are not seaworthy creatures, and the orcs were not disciplined or intelligent sailors, and Kejavik devised the method where the trolls would sleep encased in Sylvanian dirt, twelve sleeping for every one that commanded. And by this rotation did they sail to Vinland despite the great nautical distance, all the while hidden in great plumes of fog, and while keeping the orcs on course and prepared, and it is now this same method they use to sail to Oceania and bring troll wickedness to another world.

And near Vinland the devious fog was lifted. And Kejavik and all the troll officers were awakened from their temporary graves, and they did take their place of command over the armed and ready orc marines.

And know that with Vinland crushed, the Legion would sweep through human lands, and would flank the elves who would be trapped against their own impenetrable Crimson Wall. With human and elf conquered, the Legion would sweep through the dwarven lands, and though that land is dug deep with many redoubts, none more formidable than Bran Keep, none of these fortresses would withstand a siege of more than a few years.

But humans, unprepared as they were against such a force, still did sound the city's alarm. And the mage Ozymandias, who already before this was a recluse, left his tower and went down to the shore, where were gathered a paltry number of defenders and many more common people. And it had been many years since any common man was allowed to behold Ozymandias. And so one half of the people did beg Ozymandias to save the city while the other half despaired that the force of enemies was too great for any one man to matter and sent up a great cry of woe. And only Ozymandias's personal guards kept the masses from pulling on his robes and falling at his feet, and still did the old mage just stand at the shore and watch the encroachment.

And with no fleet to challenge them, the human ships almost all off to Oceania, Kejavik sailed his armada into the great bay. And then when each ship was in the bay did Ozymandias touch his staff upon the water, causing it to freeze. And no wizard had ever frozen such a great body of water before and certainly not of seawater, which freezes so much colder than fresh. And it is said by those who were witness that Ozymandias, already ancient, aged one hundred years in that moment. And aboard the flagship of the Armada, Kejavik, a great magician himself, was aghast and impressed, and he knew such a powerful spell could not be held long by mortal human, and he ordered his officers and marines to hold. And the spell did hold, and the waiting took its toll, and the ships began to crack and shatter under the weight of the ice, and Kejavik's captains warned that the ships would sink when the ice vanished and pleaded that they be allowed to release the marines, and Kejavik relented. And the furious orc marines charged across the frozen ice to the dozens of human soldiers and militia that were still gathering on the shore. And with all the orcs disembarked and away from their ships, Ozymandias touched his staff upon the ice and returned it to water, and those who witnessed this say he aged another one hundred years and collapsed on the rocky shore. And at the same time, six thousand orcs, weighted down with armor, disappeared under the waves. And Ozymandias was carried back to his tower.

All lost and with his cracked ship sinking under him, Kejavik did utter a death curse and plunge himself into the water and doing so created a great living wave that picked up the shattered ships and drowned orcs and crashed them against the city of Vinland, killing nearly all her soldiers and others who had gathered on the shore and leveling the docks and homes and buildings and all that was not made of stone. For three days did the living wave pound at Vinland as if an angry giant, and even some in stone buildings were pulled out by great fists of water and drowned. And all were drowned of the city's prisoners in the dungeon, and still their evil spirits linger there.

And ever since Kejavik's death curse did end his life, the sages of Vinland have been watching for his next reincarnation. And though he would be Kejavik the Naught's twelfth reincarnation, he would be his thirteenth incarnation, and thirteen is the most special number to the trolls. It is known that this Kejavik would be raised to outdo all his pre-decessors in brutality and belligerence, and it is supposed he would be the troll to lead the Legion in their final battle to destroy the Righteous Races. This monster may yet be already born, but if so he remains unknown and unseen to the Guild of Sages and Seers. But they have already opened a book on him, sitting on a shelf in the most secure place at their white library, next to the closed books on his previous incarnations, and blank except for the title Kejavik the Twelfth.

Cronica Acadia

LXXXV

W hile the other Keepers slept, Dangalf marveled over the story of Ozymandias freezing and then unfreezing the Great Bay of Vinland. No wonder Ozymandias had been unseen for so long. He was probably still slumbering from that feat. It was a master example of an *electroplasm debt*. Weyd had touched on the subject only casually as it was such an advanced technique. At the highest level, a mage, or more likely an archmage, could continue to cast magic even when his body and his staff and his wand were depleted of their electroplasm store. Later the mage would create that electroplasm while slumbering, paying his electroplasm debt, but at a much slower rate than when replacing his innate pool of electroplasm. Dangalf found the idea of using electroplasm before it was created to be magic's answer to some of the more unseemly theories of quantum physics.

Dangalf looked out the carriage window at the darkness outside and suddenly missed the bent trees and impossibly large boulders that seemed so significant when they were walking. He wondered how many stories outside the carriage he was missing as they galloped along through the night. Progress, he thought, drifting off to sleep.

As the carriage slowed, everyone was awakened by the changing sounds and momentum. The carriage stopped, and Theodore gave them complicated directions for the relatively simple journey. The guard gave them each a week's per diem in advance and made them sign for it. They all saluted Theodore, and he returned their salute awkwardly, pacifists not being good at saluting. The carriage sped off, and the Keepers walked toward the great mountains ahead that dominated the horizon, six peaks in all and the tallest being Mount Bran but more commonly known by the dwarven capital it housed, Bran Keep.

Precisely where and when Theodore said they would, they came upon a sign featuring three blue hearts, and they were certain that this was the House of Hearts Inn. It was at a busy crossroads and river port, and with nightfall approaching the inn was filling to capacity even though it was the largest inn they had encountered yet. There were even nine horses kept at the stables, more than they had ever seen in one place before.

They were lucky to get the last table even though twenty souls and rising stood at the bar. Nerdraaage wondered aloud why anyone would stand and drink when they could sit and drink. His friends had all noticed this phenomenon in the old universe, but they could not explain it.

They were now in Hybernia proper, and the inn was mostly dwarves but with a fair amount of human travelers as well. The Keepers ate and drank and smoked and otherwise enjoyed the night as had become their custom. They worked hard in this world and faced great peril at times, and even though they enjoyed their new adventurous ways, they also liked to unwind with food and drink and leaf and good conversation. Tonight Ashlyn and Nerdraaage argued the finer points of dwarven culture: "Dwarves love farts," she said.

"I think you love farts," he countered.

"Listen," she said. "They named the inn at Hammersmith A Farting Away."

"It's A Farthing Away."

"Everyone called it A Farting Away."

"That was just in the game."

"It wasn't just in the game," she said. "And this inn wasn't even in the game and it's called House of Farts."

"It's called House of Hearts!"

"It sounds just like House of Farts!"

"House of Hearts doesn't sound anything like House of Farts," he said. "How can you say dwarves love farts?"

"Uh, because I have a nose." As ridiculous as their argument was, it was the elf's and dwarf's earnestness that made Dangalf and Doppelganger think this was the funniest conversation they had ever heard.

The busty human serving wench told them the rooms were filling fast, so they asked her to reserve one for them. "With a window!" insisted Ashlyn.

The wench said she would make it up for them, and as she turned to leave, Doppelganger spun her back to face him. "I'll help you," he smiled.

"Yes, you look very helpful," she said back to him in such a way that everyone at the table knew Doppelganger was going to get laid and no one had to say it.

"He's going to get laid!" said Nerdraaage.

It wasn't long before a cocky, human male, a hunter carrying a large tankard with some military markings on it, sat next to Ashlyn and chatted her up. She barely looked at him, and every time he asked her a question, she gave him a curt or sarcastic answer or just plain ignored him. Dangalf almost felt sorry for the man. He was coming at Ashlyn with every pickup line in the universe and a few he recognized from the old universe. He almost expected to hear him ask her, "What's your bloodrune?"

Dangalf and Nerdraaage looked at each other and laughed quietly every time Ashlyn shot down one of the man's clumsy come-ons. Dangalf was trying to think of a gentle way to tell the clueless Romeo to leave when Ashlyn stood and left the table under the clueless Romeo's thick arm. Well at least Dangalf wasn't alone. He still had Nerdraaage, and the more estranged he became from Doppelganger and Ashlyn, the more he liked Nerdraaage's company. He raised his glass to Nerdraaage. They were alone together. "I'm going to go write a letter to my wife," said Nerdraaage, and he left. Yes, Dangalf thought, I can always count on Nerdraaage!

And suddenly alone at his table, he became aware of the covetous eyes of what were now forty souls gathered around the large bar. Clearly some of those standing and drinking were of the school that preferred sitting and drinking. In what he felt was a complete lack of respect, three dwarves approached and sat at one end of Dangalf's table with their backs turned to him. Dangalf went outside and sat on a bench. He angrily imagined that these pushy dwarves would never have dared to sit down at a table where Doppelganger was sitting alone. But the cold air was chilling his anger, and he wondered if Doppelganger was done with the wench because he was ready to climb into a warm bed.

He stood to leave when a mewling caught his attention. He looked around to find a black cat under a nearby bush. It did not seem scared but would not come out and mewled again. He retreated to the lost table and found that the dwarves had completely overtaken it but the Keepers' plates were not yet removed. (Apparently Doppelganger was not finished with the wench.) He took a chunk of venison from the tray and went back to the bush.

Dangalf tore pieces of the meat and tossed it in the direction of the cat. The cat pounced on it and ate it quickly. Dangalf tossed the meat so as to lure the cat from under the bush and close to where he sat on his bench. He could see it wore a collar but was emaciated. When the meat was gone, the cat let Dangalf pet it and even began purring. Dangalf felt sorry for the wretched thing, but it did have a fur coat and he did not, so he eventually said good night.

Dangalf entered the House of Hearts and went upstairs to the rooms and wondered which was theirs when suddenly the serving wench was expelled from one of the rooms still undressed. That must be it, he thought. She saw him and pulled her dress over her front, which provided her no cover as she ran down the hall from Dangalf. Dangalf knocked on the door, and Doppelganger answered it. "What just happened?" he asked on entering.

"Oh, I was done with her," said Doppelganger.

"Doesn't look like she was done."

"When I'm done, I'm done," said Doppelganger, lying down on the floor. There were only two beds, and Doppelganger had used one, but now he was lying on the floor, which better accommodated his size.

"I see," said Dangalf, not seeing at all, but then he was tired. He got into the unmussed bed. Doppelganger had been getting coarser ever since their arrival in this world but for a brief respite when he was with Princess Dymphna. Dangalf wondered if his sudden burst of misogyny wasn't Doppelganger's way of dealing with what he felt was her rejection of him. Or maybe that was just the Red School way. Hadn't that dragoon found it appropriate to take Ashlyn as a prize in a contest? The brutes of this world didn't seem to suffer a lack of female company.

Nerdraaage came in next. He undressed and got into the used bed. He had just lain down when he shot back up, crying out. He rearranged the bedding violently before lying back down. Dangalf smiled to himself as he blew out the bedside lamp. He may not have gotten laid, but at least he wasn't sleeping in someone else's wet spot.

And so Dangalf began his slumber to be followed by hopefully another three hours of sleep. He found this was the optimum amount of sleep under ordinary circumstances. Weyd had impressed upon him that slumber meant a hyperwakefulness of the mind, and it was important to also sleep and grant the mind its down time to dream and otherwise unwind. He put himself in his virtual library and took down a handsome new grimoire, Ozymandias's *Instantaneous Relocation of Living Beings by Well and Other Water-Based Mediums.* He cracked it open in his favorite leather chair. Yes, the archmage was discussing spells well beyond Dangalf's rank, but what harm could there be in reading ahead?

After an hour or so, Branan, the velvet-loving dwarf, entered quietly from the door Dangalf had created for his repair dwarves and sat down at a desk to eat his lunch. "Don't mind me," he said. Dangalf smiled and continued with his reading. About fifteen minutes later, another knock came at the front door. "Now who do you suppose that is?" asked Branan.

"I have a bad feeling," answered Dangalf. He rose and went to the door and opened the peephole carefully only to see Ashlyn smiling on the steps.

"May I come in?" she asked.

"Of course, of course!" said Dangalf opening the door.

"How is this possible?"

"It's that druidic mind connection I told you about," she answered as she entered. "This is my first time trying it. Hello," she said upon seeing the dwarf.'

"This is Branan," said Dangalf. "From the crew I told you about that repairs my body during slumber. Branan, this is my friend Ashlyn."

"Hello."

"And where is the rest of the crew?" she asked.

"Having lunch in the colon," said Branan.

"You don't eat with them?"

"Perhaps you did not hear me," said Branan. "They are having *lunch* in the *colon*."

"Branan is a little more…particular than the others in his crew," explained Dangalf.

"This is so amazing," gushed Ashlyn. "It's like he's real."

"And what do you mean by that?" demanded Branan.

"I'm sorry," she said. "I'm just very impressed with your personality and how you look and the fact that we can converse like this when in reality you're just a figment of Dangalf's imagination."

"And of whose imagination are you a figment?"

"I didn't mean to offend you," said Ashlyn.

"She misspoke, Branan," interjected Dangalf.

"Aye, I should leave. It will take the rest of my lunch to get back to the colon. At least it's all downhill."

"Nice meeting—" Ashlyn managed before the door closed. "You. Well, he was a little aggressive."

"Oh, he's a good sort once you get to know him."

"But he's you. Was he voicing some anger you have toward me?"

"No, I'm not angry. But I am a little surprised. So you can just enter my slumber like this?"

"Druids don't do that without permission. That would be black magic. Speaking of which, you might want to think about bars on those windows."

"That's a good idea. But not bars. They don't fit the motif. Maybe some sturdy shutters." Dangalf studied his large, beautiful windows for a moment but turned back to his guest. "There will be time for that later. So tell me, where are you now?"

"I am slumbering on the floor just next to your bed." And the unease between them soon lifted and they talked and laughed.

And Dangalf forgot all about her leaving him for the Red School lothario. (Hm, perhaps Branan was voicing Dangalf's anger.) And Dangalf gave her the deluxe tour, which was pretty easy as there was just the one room. He didn't eat during slumber, so there was no need for a kitchen. (He didn't know where the dwarf repairmen got their lunches. Some inn in a dwarven town down the road just beyond his imagination, he imagined.) There were no grounds to show Ashlyn as he hadn't bothered with landscaping beyond what he could see out of his windows. Weyd had warned him not to let obsessive designing and building of his imaginary library distract him from the primary reason for slumber. "It is a grave threat to apprentice mages, getting lost in your mind," Weyd had warned.

"Losing your mind?" Dangalf had asked.

"No. Getting lost in your mind. Being seduced by the limitless boundaries of your imagination and losing touch with the real world. Ignoring even the basic requirements for self-preservation. It is the second most common accidental death for apprentice mages."

Dangalf nodded, but another question came to him, "What is the first most common cause of accidental death?"

"Spontaneous combustion."

Ashlyn declined a visit to his colon to see the dwarves at work, so they sat next to each other laughing and talking like they did those first weeks in this world. Their literal meeting of the minds was very recuperative and restored them to the simpatico they had developed in Hempshire. And even though Ashlyn was distracting him from study, he was sorry to see her go when she finally left. She left by the front door, both of them agreeing that it was more symmetrical than her just disappearing from the library like a light switching off.

During breakfast the next morning, Ashlyn noticed Dangalf pocketing some sausage as they prepared to leave. "I fed this cat last night, and I'm going to see if he's still around before we leave." The cat was under its same bush and came out expectantly even before Dangalf showed it the food. It ate hungrily, and Dangalf patted it. In the daylight he could see soot lifting off of the cat and saw that it was not black but tortoiseshell. Dangalf said good-bye to the cat, but it was not to be. The cat followed closely behind Dangalf, more like a dog than a cat it seemed, as they headed down the road.

"Looks like you have a pet," said Nerdraaage.

"A familiar," said Ashlyn. "Mages don't have pets."

"Maybe I should name him," said Dangalf.

"Her," said Ashlyn.

"You should name that cat Dirty because he's so dirty," said Nerdraaage.

"Dusty," said Dangalf. "She's dusty not dirty."

"Come on, Dusty," said Ashlyn to the cat.

"No," said Dangalf. "I said she is dusty, literally."

Nerdraaage took out some venison jerky and kneeled down. "Com'ere, Dusty!" he said, and she ran over to him.

"I'm not naming my familiar Dusty," said Dangalf.

"Come on, Dusty," Doppelganger joined in. "We're going to Bran Keep!"

They walked not south on the well-traveled road that would eventually lead to Bran Keep but west to the River Gorm. There they sought out the large flatboats that sailed down the swift river toward Bran Keep. These boats were large and built without luxury, for when the journey ended near Gorm Falls, the boats would be broken apart, and the human crew would travel for days back to their starting point and build a new flatboat once again for the southern journey.

They found one large flatboat readying for the journey downriver. It was about fifty feet long and flat, as the name would indicate, but for a shelter in the shape of a triangle at the middle of the deck.

Dusty seemed apprehensive about getting on the flatboat, but Dangalf carried her aboard, and she looked about curiously. She trotted into the boat's shelter and jumped up into a large sand-box. "That's not for you!" hissed one of the sailors, and Dusty ran from the sandbox just as he dumped firewood on top of it. She didn't stop running until she reached the reclining Dangalf, and she burrowed her way into one of his large robe pockets.

Dangalf, when he handed over his ten-crown fare, now with some gold coins of his own in reserve, felt as though he was cheating the sailors for their hard work. He knew the crew would spend two days sailing south, weeks walking back, and then, well he had no idea how much time it would take them to build an-other flatboat. But the sailors set their own prices, and there were multiple flatboats to choose from, so who was he to argue with the free market? Besides, in their quest browsing, they had seen how much even a journeyman mariner—jacks they were called—could earn on one voyage to Oceania if they were dissat-isfied with their river work. And then, as they waited and waited, he realized that they weren't about to set off until the boat was full of paying passengers and cargo so the crew was probably do-ing all right for their investment in time.

There were no dwarves among the passengers, which was odd since they were in dwarven lands going to the dwarven capi-tal, but understandable due to dwarven water intolerance. But dwarves did deliver most of the cargo that filled the flatboat. There were even horses, three of them, that were loaded inside the shelter. Perhaps the sailors rode these horses back to speed their return to the headwaters.

Soon a dozen more people were aboard, and the crew of three sailors must have made their quota because they gave a final call, jumped onboard themselves, and cut loose. The current took the boat with such a force that the Keepers found themselves nearly tipping over even as they sat. Dangalf had read about this river and now told the other Keepers about it over the roar of the water. It was crafted by the dwarves to be the fastest river in this world. More miraculous was that the Dwarves had carved out or built up the land around the river over the millennia so that it actually flowed the opposite direction from how it began. This testament to their craftsmanship was recorded when they named it the River Gorm, or the blue river, not because of the color of the water—in fact, the water churned white wherever you looked—but in honor of their great racial school. And now the Keepers were racing toward the Great Wonder of Bran Keep on the Great Wonder of River Gorm.

Nerdraaage had fortified himself with liquor to make this waterborne journey, and he was the first to fall asleep. Dangalf could have slept too, but he was enjoying the ride—a great flume ride it would be in the other world if amusement parks were four hundred leagues long and there were no lawyers.

The sailors would rise occasionally at a bend in the river and stand at the ready with great wooden poles, but from what Dangalf could see, they did little more than dip their poles in the raging waters. He knew the river was constructed by the dwarves to be able to transport cargo without any crew. But he supposed any cargo that included passengers would also require a crew to counter the unpredictability of sapiens.

Ashlyn sat motionless with a look of discomfort on her face and her arms wrapped tightly around herself. It wasn't long before the sailors started chatting her up. "We don't get many elves on the Gorm," said the sailor whom Dangalf hated the most and who was also the best looking of the sailors. She glared at him impassively, but he was not one to be dissuaded. "Not feeling well?" The handsome sailor convinced Ashlyn to follow him and had her hold his pole, while he held her, around one of the bends because, he said, "It feels better to steer the boat than to have the boat steer you." It wasn't long before they were sitting next to each other and running their toes through the water. All three sailors vied for Ashlyn's attention, and the handsome sailor, Billy he said, was repeatedly frustrated by the senior sailor, who found a multitude of odd jobs for Billy just when it seemed he was getting somewhere with Ashlyn. Dangalf liked the senior sailor, and not just because he was the ugliest of the sailors. As the sun went down, the senior sailor had Billy light a fire in the sandbox. Dangalf found a spot under the shelter, and all the Keepers slept close to each other and the fire.

The next day was more of the same: water rushing through high rock walls topped by evergreen trees. For those who were not asleep, the sailors drew their attention to a formidable dwarven fortress, and the sailors waved to the lookouts as they passed. The sailors explained that the fortress contained a lever that if released would send tons of earth and rock into the river and send the rushing waters over a nearby cliff. It was designed to prevent enemies from using the Gorm to launch their own attack on Bran Keep.

Nerdraaage and Ashlyn slept and slumbered their way through most of the day and the next night. Dangalf and Doppelganger played goat with the sailors, and Dangalf no longer felt guilty about the paltry sum he had paid for the journey after being the big loser and losing most of that to the ugly sailor, whom he no longer liked most among the sailors.

On the final day, they packed up bedding and food stores and other things that had been unpacked during the trip. Nerdraaage and Ashlyn awoke, but both were lethargic. Neither had eaten during the journey, but they would be back on solid ground soon.

About a mile before Gorm Falls, the river took a steep bend for the sole purpose of running flatboats aground. They were all told to brace themselves, but the grounding on a bed of sand was rather anticlimactic. The passengers unloaded first, and then the sailors unloaded their cargo quickly. Billy only had time for a quick "farewell" with Ashlyn, and he was summoned back to the boat as the sailors began their energetic demolition of the flatboat before the next one would arrive.

The Keepers stopped to admire the Ten Thousand Steps (technically 10,002 steps) going straight up for about a mile inside of the cliff. But as only Doppelganger was eager to make the celebrated climb, they instead paid to have themselves lifted by basket with the rest of the cargo to the road above.

They exited the basket and began again on the road to Bran Keep, of which only the peak was visible on the winding mountain road. Smoke could be seen coming from vents in the mountain. It was chilly now, and it would get colder as they climbed. They didn't have winter clothes per se, but they all wore layers, and the physical exertion of the climb upward kept them all warm enough. Nerdraaaage was actually sweating as he had the thickest blood and wore two layers of leather.

The other travelers were mostly dwarves now, and their glances revealed that they regarded the Keepers as a motley and suspicious group, but they responded politely when any of the Keepers greeted them. It began snowing, and that was a concern for all. The road obliterated, they feared that, even at walking speed, snow blindness would lead them off one of the sheer drops that were occasionally exposed by the winding road. Doppelganger fearlessly pressed on in the lead.

Dangalf saw Dusty jumping through the snow, picked her up, and placed her in what had become her usual pocket. She poked her head out to watch their progress up the mountain. Ashlyn morphed into tyger form with a noticeably thicker coat than the others had seen before.

Still a few hours from Bran Keep, they enjoyed the most spectacular view of the marvel that could be had. As with a skyscraper of the other world, they would lose perspective on its immensity as they got closer. The mountain had windows carved into it on lower levels. Immense banners hung over the carved front of the mountain, one for each of the royal clans.

"That's my banner!" Nerdraaage said excitedly. "Clan Stonefist!" They all nodded in appreciation as Nerdraaage fastened his tartan scarf into a hood.

The Clan Bluebeard banner was elevated one-third above the others to signify that the current king was of their clan. They were similar to human banners in their shield design, but human banners were of Iberian shape, and these were heater shaped.

Below the founding clan banners were other large banners, including the Blue School (though school banners were unmarked by default, they were typically adorned with special markings, and this banner was adorned with hammer and anvil); another banner was for the Red School, adorned with the dwarven bloodrune (it was male), and still another was a red, white, and blue banner of the Acadian Alliance of Righteous Races.

Two stout guards in Bran Keep tabards and kilts of Stonefist tartan met the Keepers coming the opposite way. "And who might you be to wear those colors?" asked one of the guards of Nerdraaage.

"Nerdraaage," he answered.

"Oh, Morna's husband!" said the second guard, who promptly gave Nerdraaage a dwarven hug, which involved clasping each other's arms.

"Welcome. I am Odhran and this is Cormag." And Cormag also hugged him. "What brings you to the keep?"

"We have orders from Vinland," said Dangalf, and Nerdraaage introduced the other Keepers to the guards.

"Well, we won't keep you," said Odhran. They bid farewell, and each group went opposite directions. Dangalf looked back to see the guards release a pigeon that flew over their heads toward the keep.

As they neared, the marvel only inspired more awe. There were grand staircases, columns and doorways, watchtowers, and giant dwarves in relief, recreating great moments in dwarven history, all carved out of the face of the mountain.

The wonder of the computer game faded each time they made a new discovery like this. Though knowledge of Cronica was better than being thrust into this world with no knowledge, the game was a poor substitute for the real thing.

They found more guards stationed in towers at the great drawbridge before the keep entrance. The drawbridge was massive with inversely impressive railings. An inattentive sapien could trip over or slip under them. It was dwarven Darwinism at its most precarious. It tested their nerves to even cross the bridge when they saw the gaping chasm below. Of the four, Dangalf kept most perfectly to the exact center of the bridge.

And still they walked and walked. As their perspective changed, some great things vanished from sight while other great things appeared. Statues that had looked ordinary from a distance now towered overhead. Each held torches of real flame to light the way, literally and metaphorically, for other dwarves.

"The Path of Giants," said Nerdraaage reverently.

"Giant dwarves," laughed Ashlyn.

They approached a hole in the side of the mountain. They might well have missed it had it not been for the dozen heavily armed guards standing around it. So incongruous was the sight that Dangalf had to detour his friends from the road to the guards of the hole. "Excuse me," he said to the guard who seemed the least annoyed by their arrival. "What is this place?"

"Why, this is the Profundity!" boasted the guard.

"The Profundity!" echoed Dangalf. And then to his friends, "According to legend, this dwarven tunnel goes to the center of the world."

"It is no legend!"

"Of course," bowed Dangalf slightly and then said to his friends, "I meant to say it is absolutely a tunnel to the center of the world," and then back to the guard, "Are we not allowed to enter?"

The guards found that amusing. "Heroes are you!" said the guard. "We are not here to keep heroes out! Only to keep in things from the deep!" They bid the guards farewell and returned to the road and kept walking and walking. Finally they reached the great staircase that would, in only about five more minutes of walking, take them into Bran Keep.

Wagons came and went from ground-level entrances on either side of the massive staircase, but they took the majestic route up the stairs. At the top of the stairs, there were three great arches at least sixty feet in the air with open doors of iron. As they entered they passed blue pyres, and the embers from those danced around the Keepers, outlining them each in uncountable tiny lights that burned out without harm. It was Nerdraaage who recognized it: "Dragonsbreath. Antiblackguard fires."

They entered the keep and were awestruck again. An entire city spread out before them. Great pillars reached up to the top in support of the hollowed-out mountain. At the misty top was the inn, accessible by mining cars on a twisting track of metal. They watched a train of mining cars click click click up the track.

More banners and carvings decorated the interior walls. Directly across from the entrance on the far side of the keep and built up to tower over the rest of the city was the façade of the royal palace, with great columns and statues and Clan Stonefist guards decked out in dress regalia of fur and precious metals. On the right side were great skylights that lit the city with daylight. Opposite of that was a crashing waterfall from vents in the ceiling.

The engineering feat was unimaginable. Each building, from the merchants that lined main street to the private residences built up along the walls to the grand palace at the back, were all carved into the original stone. A perfect execution of a master plan from twenty thousand years ago. (And work was well underway hollowing out an adjoining peak.) Nerdraaage was the first to speak. "Have you ever seen anything so awesome before!"

"Never," said Ashlyn. "I bet we have to exit through the gift shop." They walked down the main street, and it bustled with hundreds of she-dwarves. Half the dwarven population lived in the keep or just outside its gates. This was a much higher than the percentage of humans or elves that lived in their respective capitals.

The Keepers grew hungry as they passed a variety of the fresh foods being offered for sale on carts. Even Ashlyn marveled at the fruits and vegetables available for purchase in the dwarven capital. After all, her people regarded dwarves as carnivores. And though it was hard to imagine a dwarf eating raw fruits and vegetables, they did have a love for pies and jellies and stews.

They passed the butcher, the baker, and the chandler and dozens of other merchants offering every conceivable service. "Beard washing!" said Nerdraaage. "I want to do that before we leave!"

"Me too," said Dangalf scratching his beard.

"Do you supposed I could get a shave?" asked Doppelganger.

"No," scoffed Nerdraaage. They stopped at a tattoo parlor and browsed the hundreds of runic designs displayed on squares of red, blue, and green skin. In front of the shop was a well-inked dwarf who looked like he had personally harvested each of those squares of RGB skin. He was only slightly less terrifying because he bobbed slowly in a rocking chair. "You sell magic runes?" asked Nerdraaage.

"I create skin runes," said the dwarf. "You must supply your own magic." He told them some prices, and the Keepers started to realize that the big city was full of luxury that they could ill afford.

They walked all the way to the stairs of the royal palace. There was no great gate around this palace as the entire city was considered impenetrable. Either way, there were plenty of guards and more dragonsbreath. Nerdraaage approached one of his royally garbed clan-kin, and after some pleasantries, he returned to his friends with directions to the White School and Loremaster Fearghas.

They left Bran Keep and journeyed through a torchlit tunnel to the second hollowed-out mountain peak. It was full of industrious dwarves carving and lifting and shouting. And dust everywhere. But even as work continued, some of the grand buildings were already occupied. "Leave it to the dwarves to put the White School in the ghetto," remarked Ashlyn.

"And there's the elven embassy," added Dangalf. They found the White School and had to admit that whatever bias the dwarves had against the White School, their Blue School vanity would not allow it to be housed in anything but a grand complex of elegantly carved buildings. They took stairs up to a columned entrance. An arched door with a dwarf-high peephole stopped their progress. Nerdraaage knocked on the door. "Yes?" asked the dwarf behind the great nose that filled the peephole.

"I would like to see Loremaster Fearghas," said Nerdraaage.

"I'm sorry," said the nose. "Only those of the White School may enter."

"I am of the White School," said Dangalf, and the nose cocked in his direction.

"So am I," said Ashlyn, and the nose cocked in her direction.

The door opened, and a yellow-haired dwarf stepped out. He seemed nervous. "Your commissions please," he said. Dangalf carried both their commissions and handed them over for inspection. "I am Lorekeeper Camran. I will take you to the Loremaster." He ushered them into the White School and closed the door.

"I'm glad I walked all the way here," said Doppelganger, dropping heavily on the stairs before stretching out.

"He has a cat in his pocket!" Nerdraaage shouted after them through the still-ajar peephole. And then, dropping down next to Doppelganger, said, "Oh, well. They'll be back."

"How do you know?" asked Doppelganger.

"'Cause I have the ring."

The Lorekeeper led Dangalf and Ashlyn through a series of hallways past aspects of famous magical people. The most prominent of those was Ozymandias, looking especially heroic as his aspect depicted him freezing the bay at Vinland. "Forgive me," said Dangalf. "But I notice your beard is unbraided, in the human fashion."

"Oh," said Camran playing with his beard. "It was braided, but I unbraided it. Nervous habit." Dangalf and Ashlyn smiled. They liked this nervous dwarf. They were led to a well-appointed library, where Camran motioned for them to sit. I'm sorry," said Camran. "You'll have to wait here. I would give you a tour of our school here, but I am so close!"

"Close to what?" asked Dangalf.

"Only the greatest ambition of every alchemist since time immemorial."

"Turning lead into gold?" Dangalf asked excitedly.

"Oh," said Camran. "Perhaps I should have qualified that. The greatest ambition of every dwarven alchemist." He looked back and forth between the human and elf. "Powdered beer," he said excitedly.

"Powdered beer?" said Dangalf less excitedly.

"Oh yes," insisted Camran. "Why, the greatest burden borne by dwarven troops is beer weight. That and the perishable nature of liquid beer significantly impacts on the duration and range of our forces." Camran excused himself, and Dangalf couldn't help but wonder what powdered beer would do to that great body of dwarven wisdom, beer no longer being wet.

"I like yours better," said Ashlyn looking about.

"My what?"

"Your library," she said smiling.

Ashlyn sat while Dangalf perused the library. It was so quiet, so well insulated from the work outside that he wondered if Camran and Fearghas were the only two in the complex of buildings. Fearghas appeared, and he was as sturdy and confident as any dwarf and would have seemed of the Red or Blue School but for his fine robes. "You have something to show me?" Ashlyn and Dangalf looked at each other dumbly.

The front door of the school opened, and Fearghas charged out, followed by Ashlyn and Dangalf. "Would you mind if we went to the inn?" Fearghas asked between Doppelganger and Nerdraaage.

"Mind?" asked Doppelganger. "We insist."

Fearghas led them through the hollow mountain toward Bran Keep. "No pillars," said Fearghas motioning about.

"That's right," said Dangalf. "No wonder why it's so much more open."

"See those ribs upon the walls?" asked Fearghas. There were great ribs of stone around the inside of the mountain that extended all the way up to the top. "That was my idea. Instead of pillars. It caused the builders some consternation, to be out-crafted by a satin wearer, but they couldn't argue with the advantages. Still some said it wouldn't work, so I told them to relocate my school underneath my design. And in the arrangement, I secured a new White School three times the size of the last." Fearghas laughed. "Of course if it all comes tumbling down on me, I suppose that they will have the last laugh." And off the apprehensive look of the Keepers, he added, "That was a joke. It will never come down."

They came to signage for The Wee Hours Inn with an arrow pointing straight up. There was a line to take the mining cars up to the inn in the sky, but the operators ushered Fearghas and his party to the front of the line. There the Keepers saw their first gnome and stared and whispered to each other excitedly about him. They knew he was a gnome because he wore a red cap. He was so small as to be dwarfed by dwarves. "I hope he's tall enough to get on the ride," Ashlyn gushed to Dangalf.

Doppelganger said he wouldn't fit in the small seats of the mining car, and the operators told him he'd have to take the stairs. He looked at the stairs curving all the way up around the inside of the mountain and forced his frame into a mining car after all. He was too thirsty to make that long walk. It was a magnificent view of the keep in all directions as they click click clicked up the track. "Look," said Nerdraaage, waving at a mist with his hand. "A cloud inside!"

"Sometimes it even snows," said Fearghas.

Nerdraaage leaned back toward Ashlyn. "The Wee Hours," he said pointing to the inn still above them. "That's not a fart joke."

"No, that's a pee pee joke," she answered. They reached the landing, and Fearghas spoke to the innkeeper, who ushered them to a table against the wall. Dangalf told the innkeeper they would need a room, and the innkeeper asked if they wanted an outside view or an inside view. "Outside," said Dangalf without much thought.

Dangalf placed his rucksack on the ledge of the window before realizing that there were no glass or bars to prevent his belongings from crashing down to the floor of Bran Keep below, so he relocated his bag to the floor. The view was terrific with all the grandness of the keep now in miniature below.

A she-dwarf approached and took their orders. The gnome they had seen below entered. "Gnome!" cried the inn regulars.

"Many a sprite and gnome and other creatures came to the keep seeking protection with the fall of Nemetia," explained Fearghas. The she-dwarf returned with a cart and placed a firkin of beer on the table and then a cooked chicken next to that. She pulled a blue privacy curtain across the table as she departed.

Fearghas tore off a leg and began eating. When the others hesitated, he said, "Eat. It's The Wee Hours. A chicken with every firkin." When only Ashlyn still hadn't touched the chicken, he assured her, "Concordance compliant."

"I love this place," said Nerdraaage, pulling off the other leg. And they all ate chicken, even Ashlyn, who was mostly vegetarian now. But this was their first chicken since arriving in the new universe, and it looked and smelled delicious. And apparently the dwarves had figured out how to farm the domesticated bird without violating the Lonelywood Concordance.

Done eating and after varying degrees of beer intake, Fearghas signaled it was time to smoke by taking out his pipe and lighting up. The others joined him. Fearghas inhaled deeply and then exhaled until he seemed to melt into the upholstered bench back. "Theodore is a wise and serious human," said Fearghas. "Perhaps you should show me what you have brought." Nerdraaage slid the silver ring to him. Theodore turned pale. "I do not think I want to touch it," he said.

"Is it cursed!" said Nerdraaage worriedly.

Fearghas picked up the ring and examined it. "These are goblin tool marks," he said.

"That's what Theodore said!" said Dangalf.

"Where did you get this?"

"From a dwarf that was working for goblin slavers," said Nerdraaage.

"Did you kill him?"

Nerdraaage paused. "Yes," he said.

"Good," pronounced Fearghas. "This world is a wicked place, filled with many wicked things. That is why dwarves choose to know of only dwarven things. But ignorance of a wicked thing is no protection against it. That is why we have lorekeepers. We know the wicked things so that dwarves be protected from them.

"We do not lock up criminals. When a dwarf commits a crime that cannot be forgiven, such as the murder of a dwarf, he is judged to be no longer of the dwarves. The process is called estrangement."

"Strange dwarves!" interjected Dangalf.

"No!" shot back Fearghas. "A human misnomer. Strange, yes, but in every legal and moral sense no longer a dwarf. An un-dwarf. His name is stricken from the clan archives as if never born. But his name and bloodrune goes into a book that the lorekeepers maintain for reasons I have already explained.

"As part of the estrangement, his face is shaved as cleanly as a she-dwarf's. And then he is banished from all dwarven lands. But because there is no record of this estrangement but for the decree of horning and the lorekeepers' secret books, his shaved face is to alert all dwarves that this wretch is no longer of the dwarves. It is believed before he can grow a full, dwarven beard again, that all three corners of the world will have seen or heard that he is estranged.

"Unwelcome in human or elven lands, these undwarves make their ways to wilderness or border towns, where they can live among the other wretches and support themselves through scrounging and criminality. Sometimes these newly estranged are taken into criminal gangs of other undwarves. And the veterans, who have by now regrown their beards, call their new barefaced initiates *ghostbeards*." Fearghas turned the Clan Ghostbeard signet ring around to face the others.

"The goblins have long employed undwarves as mercenaries," continued Fearghas. "And we have tolerated this arrangement for centuries. There was never a concentrated use of undwarves that we could attack with any certainty, and finally because we hear whispers that the trolls are unhappy with the alliance between goblins and undwarves. And generally speaking, anything the trolls don't like is good for the Alliance.

"But lately there have been ominous whispers, talk of widespread recruitment and organizing of the strange under one banner. These undwarves know our fighting methods and the secrets of our cities. They are bloodthirsty and ruthless, which is why most of them were estranged in the first place. They are angry and resentful of a dwarven family that has turned its back on them. There could be as many as six thousand undwarves."

"Six thousand?" said Dangalf.

"Aye," continued Fearghas. "But these undwarves are cowards also. And where the dwarven race rejects their immortality, these undwarves find no shame in living a thousand years or longer—well past the accepted limits on an honorable lifespan. We could be talking about a force of every undwarf since the process began before the great Schism. A force like that could tip the course of battle in favor of the Legion, especially if they were applied specifically to dwarven targets.

"You four have brought us the first concrete proof that undwarves supported by goblin gold are organizing themselves into a paramilitary force mimicking the very dwarven system that excommunicated them. It is a terrible warning. Let us hope we have not received it too late." Fearghas told Nerdraaage he must keep the ring to present to others as evidence, but it would be returned to him in time. He signed all of their commissions for "meritorious service" and authorized payment to them.

Fearghas had some questions for the Keepers regarding their origins. As an honored and learned dwarf, they trusted him with their tale. He was fascinated to hear about the other world. How the contact between both worlds was ever made was one of the great mysteries, he said. "What is known," said Fearghas. "Is the great balance that exists between the two worlds. Twenty-four hours in each day. Twelve months in a year. The trinity of the sun, the world, and the moon. A system of nine planets."

"Our system only has eight planets," said Ashlyn.

"What?"

"We did have nine," she said. "But they decided that we only have eight planets."

"There are ominous signs wherever we turn," Fearghas said somberly before bidding farewell.

LXXXVI

"What a day," cheered Dangalf. "We've performed meritorious service to the Alliance, we have more gold then we've ever had, and we're in one of the greatest cities in the world."

"The greatest," said Nerdraaage.

"What do you want to do?"

"Beard wash!" shouted Nerdraaage.

"I'm in!" said Dangalf. And though they could have found cheaper accommodations, they stayed at The Wee Hours at the top of Bran Keep under the highest peak in the known world. It was a large, windowless room with a fireplace and four beds big enough for the largest humans. Tapestries of battle scenes covered the stone walls.

Doppelganger opened a small iron door opposite the entrance, and the wind that swept in was such that it almost snuffed out the fire. They did have to relight their lamps. They ducked through the doorway and stood close together in a small room open to the elements.

Their view should have been of the unmolested homeland of the gnomes and unicorns and other magical creatures, some not yet catalogued. Instead it was now Legion-occupied Nemetia. Fires of unnatural colors burned across the landscape, but these were not the comforting flames of hearth or camp. Wicked creatures howled in unseen wickedness. Directly below them they could see three more floors of rooms and, below that, sheer rock face down to the tree line.

Dangalf could only bear a minute of the howling wind before all four retreated back into the room, locking the door behind them. The Keepers slept briefly but were too excited to stay in bed, and they all awoke within thirty minutes of each other.

They rode the speeding mining cars down to the keep floor. It was a chattering, gravity-driven thrill ride that only stopped near the very end with the screeching of metal brakes and a celebration of sparks.

They explored the expansive capital. They found the Stonefist Inn, where Nerdraaaage learned he could stay for free. They passed the great hourglass that was thirty feet high and turned over once a day in a very precise and formal ceremony, and they all agreed that they had to return some midnight to watch it.

They visited the human corner of the keep and were surprised to the see the Vinlandian Mint, which in the game was located in Vinland. The minting of coins was a human invention accepted by even the dwarves, who saw its superiority to sacks of ore previously in use for currency. But the Trollish Armada had been seen as a dire warning about the vulnerability of Vinland and its wealthy mint, and so it was relocated.

Dangalf impressed Doppelganger to go with him and pay their respects at the human embassy. In the other world, both would have forgone such formalities. Schmoozing or networking, ass-kissing even, is how they would have dismissed it. But Dangalf at least viewed it as worthy endeavor in this world, an obligation even, and they were greeted by a deputy of the ambassador who recalled reading dispatches about them. They chatted briefly over Aged Vinlandian while the deputy sized them up. Dangalf was quite pleased when the deputy found it proper to invite the humans and the rest of the Keepers to dinner when it could be arranged. How well into the Triangle of Achievement's recognition level they would be to be invited to dine with the ambassador! "I'll need a new hat," said Dangalf.

Doppelganger and Nerdraaage checked in to the Red School. It was a large complex of buildings and walled-off "outside" areas. There were entrances to this most human of schools in both the human corner and on the dwarven side. There each met and presented his commission to dwarven trainers. The typical dwarven skepticism to unknown commodities was somewhat alleviated by their documented achievements. And though the red dwarves viewed with suspicion Nerdraaage's friendship with Doppelganger (they were fortunately unaware of his White School and elf friends), they viewed Doppelganger's friendship with Nerdraaage as a sign of the human's noble character.

Ashlyn and Dangalf paid their respects to the elven ambassador. And though they were admitted to the ambassador himself and the meeting was cordial, no dinner invitation was forthcoming. They returned to the Red School not long after Doppelganger and Nerdraaage had exited. Doppelganger stated he was going to stay at the Red School as the warrior trainer had been summoned to meet him. Ashlyn decided to visit the hospital because Dangalf and Nerdraaage were intent on pampering themselves.

There were several fine-looking establishments that advertised beard washing. Dangalf and Nerdraaage finally settled on the Wash and Brush-Up Company, which coincidentally had the cutest she-dwarves standing out front. The beard wash was a glorious experience. Dangalf and Nerdraaage sat in adjoining chairs. Both she-dwarves smiled and spoke softly throughout the process. Dangalf noticed them nodding to Nerdraaage's arm, which reflected in tattoo that he had only taken one wife. In addition to the pleasant beard treatment, Dangalf felt the breast of his washer against his arm as she leaned over him. She smelled nice, and he covered his lap with his hands as his arousal was unrestrained by any garments beneath his robe.

The beards were combed out and powdered. Who knew the dwarves capable of inventing such luxury? Nerdraaage agreed to braiding. Dangalf declined. "Beard spikes?" asked Dangalf's she-dwarf.

"What's that?"

She showed him a book of aspects, each featuring a belligerent dwarf with different types of ferocious spikes protruding from his beard.

"It prevents the enemy from clasping your beard," she explained.

"Oh, I want that!" said Nerdraaage.

"Gold or silver?" asked his she-dwarf.

"Gold!"

"Excuse me," interrupted Dangalf. "How much is that?"

"Thirty sovereign per foot."

They both realized that was more gold than the four of them had combined. "I'd better not," said Dangalf. "Sometimes I sleep on my stomach."

"Do you have anything cheaper?" Nerdraaage asked.

"There is silver and bronze as well."

"How much is silver?"

"Er," interjected Dangalf leaning over to Nerdraaage, "isn't your class supposed to appear unassuming?"

"I forgot," said Nerdraaage. "Sometimes I sleep on my stomach too," he explained to the she-dwarf.

Dangalf's beard was finished. He paid and told Nerdraaage he would see him back in the room or at the tavern.

"Tavern," said Nerdraaage.

Dangalf went outside, where he collected Dusty and went forth feeling better than he had in a long time. He had come to love Acadia—the simplicity of life, the companionship of his honorable and gifted friends, the purposefulness of his labors, and the sheer pleasure of learning. And now he felt especially good because of some indulgent grooming provided by a sweet and pleasant-smelling she-dwarf. But perhaps the biggest reason for his good feeling was the lifting of a burden of which he was previously unaware. The sprawling keep, impenetrable from outside forces (even those that could swoop down from the air) and guarded inside by plentiful and stout dwarven guards, finally allowed him to relax completely for the first time since they had arrived in this world. Even the self-medication of drink and smoke had not completely banished the worry of being stabbed in the back by an invisible and black-toothed assailant or snatched up by a passing dragon as a quick snack. But there were no such fears here.

He stopped by the keep's waterfall, and using a water cup, put there purely for ceremonial purposes he suspected, he drank of the crystal-clear and ice-cold water. When he was sure no dwarf was looking, he let Dusty have her fill from the cup.

Dangalf returned to the Keepers' room, which was dark. Even the fireplace was out, and there was an unpleasant chill in the air. He lit the first lamp he could find in the darkness and looked about. On the other side of the room was a chair with a hoodie sweatshirt draped over it. He thought that was very odd because, even though he loved hoodies, he did not expect to find one in a twenty-thousand-year-old dwarven fortress carved into a mountain in an alternate universe.

His mind flashed back to his childhood when in his darkened bedroom he saw his chair occupied by a bloodthirsty monster with murderous intent. He had been frozen in fear until he screwed up enough courage to shine a light on the monster, and it was proved to be only a hoodie draped over a chair. And that was the thought going through his mind as he approached this hoodie draped over a chair only to discover in the lamplight that it was actually a bloodthirsty monster with murderous intent.

LXXXVII

He was definitely in a sack. It had happened very fast, but now Dangalf could feel the cold wind penetrating the cloth as he was dragged through the doorway to the outside mountain wall. Then he was hoisted into the air, which gave him quite a fright because he knew how high off the ground the room had been. The sack moaned like demonic corduroy as it was pulled upward against the rock face.

Once at the top, he was dragged through the soft and chilly snow, and he first heard his abductors. He knew they were black-guards because this was the first sound they had made. The one he had seen in his room was a she-troll, but he did not recognize the language they spoke. It was a Trollish dialect that Evenson had not discussed. He then realized it was twin-speak, and his brain made the terrifying connection that he was taken by the deadly sister blackguards that Icil had described as "moving as one." He screwed up his courage. "Why did you take me?" he asked in his best Trollish.

"Ah!" cried the first she-troll as the dragging came to a sudden stop. "Release him before he curses us!" Dangalf cried out as he felt the sack moving suddenly downward before it was stopped.

"Fool!" said the second she-troll. "Master said he is an elementalist!"

"He speaks Trollish!"

"Yes, but he screams like a human," said the second she-troll.

And Dangalf and the sack continued the soft but cold ride through the snow. He decided to save his Trollish for a time after he was released from the sack and hoped that time would be soon.

He felt himself go up and down several hills of snow and around unknown obstacles, but they never strayed far from the sheer mountain face. Eventually they stopped, and the sack was released. He felt he could open the limp sack, but now his fear of being in the sack had turned to a fear of facing what was outside of the sack.

"Come out, Dangalf," said a familiar voice.

Dangalf found the sack closure down by his feet and carefully spread it open. He kicked his legs out first and removed the sack like a nightshirt. The first thing he saw was crimson snow that led to the bodies of two dwarven guards.

He then looked up to the twin blackguard she-trolls a dozen feet ahead of him. They watched him with slightly bared fangs and hands on hips. They were clearly malevolent, and he wondered what it said about himself that he also found them to be incredibly seductive. He hoped he would live long enough to look back on his capture by these two wicked and lithe creatures as the erotic fantasy it could be if he wasn't so afraid of being killed. Behind them were three black wyverns huddled against the cold.

And then finally, as if he did not want to reveal the sight to himself, Dangalf looked to a knight standing fearlessly at the precipice. He was huge, larger than Doppelganger, and he was covered in black armor that looked like it was cursed by the sun never to reflect light. It looked like the accounts Dangalf had read of black adamantine. And if so, it would be impervious to any of Dangalf's fire spells. Things just kept getting better.

The black knight wore swords at each hip, and both were enchanted. One burned with flame, the other a vaporous frost. Akimbo the warriors called fighting with a sword in each hand. Even his cloak blew majestically in the harsh wind.

Not so majestically, Dangalf's robe blew high, exposing his skinny legs. He held his crotch lest the harsh wind expose his frozen manhood to the unforgiving she-trolls. He did not know what was worse: the fear shivering or the cold shivering. He stood there dumbly until his hat blew off. "My hat," he said, grabbing his head too late to hold his hat to it. He watched it skitter down the mountain face.

"He is worried about his hat," the knight with the familiar voice said in Trollish.

"He speaks Trollish, Master," said one of the sisters.

"Of course he does," said the knight, again in Acadish. "I knew you would take to this place, Dangalf."

The voice. Why hadn't Dangalf made the connection yet? What was the point of his great mind and memory if he could not? But then he realized his error. It was not a voice of this world as he had expected. It was a voice from the old world. And not a live voice but a digitized voice from the Internet—from the team chat feature of Cronica. "Regicide?"

"You remember."

"It's only been six months."

"Six months?" said Regicide solemnly. "Six months off the calendar in the old world, and I have been in this world almost twenty years."

"Twenty years!" said Dangalf in disbelief, though it gave him comfort. They could conceivably return to their home world without having missed much.

"The two worlds are parallel rivers that speed up and slow down independently," said Regicide. "Presently this world must be moving faster."

"Then time travel would be possible between the worlds if you could map these changes."

"What a great mind you have already. I am glad I did not wait longer for our reunion."

"Who are those she-trolls?"

"My minions," said Regicide. "Porsche and Mercedes. Their true names are impossible to pronounce without a forked tongue and nearly impossible with one. So I named them after a couple of strippers I knew in the other world. Though to be honest, those strippers were much crueler than my she-trolls."

"Master, why do you insult us?" asked Mercedes. Or Porsche. It was impossible to tell.

"Why are you with trolls?" said Dangalf. "You're human." Mercedes and Porsche sneered at him.

"About that," said Regicide as he removed his helm. "There was a little accident." His head was a pattern of mismatched and ragged skin held together with dark stitches. Dangalf was horrified but understood that Regicide was now a lich.

"Undead!" said Dangalf, remembering Dymphna's prophecy. "You were the one who summoned us here!"

"I did."

"How? How did you even get here?"

"I willed myself here. I knew that Cronica was more than a game, and so I immersed myself in it. I would dream about it at night. And I began seeing this world, and I found a great she-troll necromancer who was seeing our world. Our minds found each other, and we communed. It was she who brought me to this world."

"You were the human captain who sacrificed himself to Gykoja! Our friend lost his arm because of your scheming."

"The lucky ones lost limbs. The unfortunate ones died. And the most unfortunate were raised up again to serve. But we won't go into that now. Suffice to say it was for the grandest of reasons: my deification." Regicide went to one of the wyverns and removed a book from a saddlebag. He returned to Dangalf, eager to share with another who would appreciate the ancient tome. "It is a burden that I can not carry my library around in my head as you do," said Regicide.

"*Cronica Oceania,*" said Dangalf, releasing his crotch to take the book. "You have it."

"Oceania is rediscovered. A primordial land that holds the very pool of life itself. An ancient ceremony performed at that site will restore life to me. And it will be a life that can never again be confined to the grave. I'm sorry to say that you will be part of that transformation."

"What do you mean?"

"The ceremony requires human blood. Unfortunately, I did not realize that the human blood rune of this world would be the mirror image of my own and would not work for the ceremony. Before I displaced Gykoja, I was able to have her summon your group to this world. I knew if your group came here, there would be at least two humans who would match the pattern of my own bloodrune." Regicide took back the *Cronica Oceania* and returned it to his saddlebags. One of the she-trolls retrieved an obviously goblin device of hoses and jars and metal teeth from another wyvern. "There is so much more I would like to share with you, but these guards will be missed at some point. So now I must take your blood."

"My blood? How much of my blood?"

"All of it. The ceremony is uncompromising. And you would become a most formidable foe if left alive." Regicide was cold and final. The she-troll with the goblin blood-remover approached. Dangalf thought about attack, but the creatures were far greater at combat than he and outnumbered him. It was a fight-or-flight situation, and fight was not an option. "But first, we must remove your ward," said Regicide. "It was foreseen that you would be warded against physical harm."

"I've been warded against physical harm?"

"It was also foreseen that you would be unaware of that warding." And instantly the other she-troll was roughly upon Dangalf and in his pocket. With a supreme look of terror, she withdrew her hand, but not before Dusty howled at her and gashed deeply into her hand. She backed up terror stricken and unappeared.

Dusty leapt from Dangalf's pocket and charged at the other she-troll. "A cat!" screamed the other she-troll in her black tongue. She dropped the goblin device and unappeared herself. They escaped without even footprints in the snow.

Regicide stood there somewhat chagrined by the retreat of his fearsome she-trolls. "You might have known that trolls have an irrational fear of housecats," Regicide said. "But then that still wouldn't explain why you carry one around in your pocket." Dusty stood in front of Dangalf, howling and hissing at Regicide. "Come back, girls," commanded Regicide. "I will slay the kitty for you." Regicide drew a sword and took a step toward Dusty.

"Hurry, Dusty!" Dangalf shouted, and Dusty ran back to him and leapt into the pocket he held open for her. Dangalf ran to the edge of the mountain and jumped. The two she-trolls reappeared by Regicide as he stepped onto Dangalf's last footprints. They watched Dangalf fall and disappear into the mist, his last words echoing back up the cliff.

"He has death cursed us!" said a she-troll.

"Fool, I told you he is an elementalist," said the other. "What did he say, Master?"

Regicide paused over the confounding words. Words in the old tongue, from the other world, the other universe. A language rarely spoken in this world and in a phrase never before uttered here: *Goodbye, Mr. Chips!*

LXXXVIII

Doppelganger was next to enter the room, and he was in no condition to notice the subtle erasure of Dangalf's sacking and removal. As he relit lamps and the fireplace, he was stoking his own warrior fire with beer. The dwarves at the Red School had all taken turns bashing and mocking Doppelganger, and as his frustration had grown, his skills seemed to fail him.

Yes, they were soldiers and warriors, and they were supposed to be superior to his mercenary rank, but his pride would not let go of his repeated failures. And how dare they add insult to injury by mocking him!

The warrior trainer cursed out Doppelganger when he couldn't summon his bloodwarp. It was as fundamental as unappear to the blackguard and metamorphism to the druid, and like those it had to be summoned on command. It had only been coaxed out of him before and then only when his own blood stained the ground. To summon it after he was wounded might be too late. The trainer told him what he already knew: he would not become a soldier until he could summon the bloodwarp on command. And the fact that he could not yet do so meant that he might never make warrior, let alone become a dragoon.

Filthy little bastards, thought Doppelganger as he drank. Short, gold digging, farting and belching, hair-braiding, beard soup-making foreigners. And he fell onto his bed and kept drinking.

Ashlyn entered the room unfortunately too late to interrupt Doppelganger getting drunk but too soon for him to be passed out. She closed the door but rested her back against it rather than enter further. Something was wrong about the room, but the minutiae of the wrongness was overpowered by the drunken angry warrior dominating the room. "You and Dangalf didn't come to the tavern."

"Come here!" he barked to her from his bed.

That was a new! She had never before been commanded so roughly. She sauntered over to his bed but remained standing.

"Sit down." She sat on the bed next to him. "Drink." He handed her his bottle but she hesitated.

"Why don't we go to the tavern?"

"Because if I never see another stinking dwarf it will be too soon!"

"Wow," said Ashlyn. "I've thought that to myself so many times. And now that I hear someone else say it, it just sounds so... ignorant."

Doppelganger sat up angrily. "Are you saying I'm ignorant?"

"No. But you're losing yourself."

"What?"

"Well, we've all changed. I mean, look at this," said Ashlyn with a hand flourish across her body. "But we've all kept our basic personalities. We're ourselves first and our classes second. But you, it's different. Your personality, the person I knew at least and the person Dangalf remembers, has been sublimated. You're a mercenary first and Doppel second."

"You bitch." Doppelganger pulled the bottle away from her and finished it. "You tell me I have lost myself to the warrior, and the dwarves tell me I'll never be a warrior." Doppelganger lifted the bottle to his mouth and finding it still empty, threw it crashing against the stone wall so he wouldn't make that mistake again. He looked Ashlyn up and down. "Why do she-elves dress like that?"

"Because we can."

Doppelganger sat up and grabbed one of her wrists in his iron grip. He was terrifyingly fast for a big, drunk mercenary. She remembered her training and bent like the reed into him, and his grip naturally loosened. But he did not release. "Don't you know there are consequences for dressing like that?"

"You should definitely be thinking of consequences right now."

Doppelganger pulled her close to him and kissed her pale belly. He looked up for her reaction, and she looked down at him dispassionately. He responded to this by tearing open the front of her top. And then she was a tyger and slipped out of his grip. She strode to the other side of the room, where she transformed back to elf. Doppelganger laid back down on the bed, momentarily defeated. She tried to close her top, her back turned to him. "You ripped it," she said sadly.

"So what?"

"I don't have many nice things."

"You sound like a woman," he laughed. "Buy another!" And he threw a coin purse from the nightstand at her, but it fell short of its destination as the coins dispersed across the room.

"Why did you change back?" he demanded.

"I can't talk to you while I'm morphed."

"What would you like to talk about?"

She sat in a chair, still on the far side of the room. "I just want to see how this plays out."

"What do you mean?"

"I want to see if this marks the end of the Keepers."

Nerdraaage entered boisterously and drunkenly, but he was not so drunk that he couldn't discern that a great crime had occurred. "Hey! Who threw my coin purse on the floor!" He sat on the floor and hummed a song as he placed the coins back into his purse.

"Stinking dwarves," snarled Doppelganger.

"What?" said Nerdraaage.

"You should probably leave," said Ashlyn to the dwarf.

"They have years more training than I have, but they mock me for not being as good as them! I'm twice the warrior any of them were at my level! The blue race doubts my Red School talent! Humans invented the Red School!"

"Or at least unappear," continued Ashlyn's warning.

"What?" said Nerdraaage turning in confusion between Doppelganger and Ashlyn.

Doppelganger stood menacingly. "Watch this!" First Doppelganger turned the color of his school. And then he began shaking, and black veins appeared all over his body, pumping the powerful humors to every inch of muscle, bone, and brain. Bones creaked and clothes strained as he became taller and wider. Muscles bulged as if to test the very elasticity of his skin. Brow and cheeks pushed forward. His nostrils flared with a great snort. His jaw unhinged and formed a large, ferocious mouth. His pupils dilated until his eyes appeared black. He cried out.

Doppelganger took two steps toward Nerdraaage and kicked him from the floor into the wall behind him. If Nerdraaage wasn't so drunk and a dwarf, he might have been hurt. "Son of a…" said Nerdraaage as he picked himself up off the floor. He couldn't finish his curse before Doppelganger was on him again, but the sturdy dwarf wrapped himself around Doppelganger's legs. This was of dubious advantage since it allowed Doppelganger to rain blows down on Nerdraaage's head, and he opened up bloody gashes there. The sight of blood fed Doppelganger's bloodwarp.

But the blood stopped as new pink skin grew over the wounds. The druid was healing him. He tossed Nerdraaage aside and charged at Ashlyn. She morphed into tyger and leapt out of the way. Doppelganger charged toward her again, but Nerdraaage intercepted him. He pounded his stone fists into Doppelganger's gut, but Doppelganger didn't feel anything. He kicked and punched the dwarf brutally.

"Nerdraaage!" said Ashlyn angrily. "You're a blackguard!" It took a split second, but Nerdraaage remembered that he was in fact a blackguard, and he unappeared.

Doppelganger spun around looking for his unappeared opponent. He kicked and swung at the air, but he couldn't find him. Then he took a chair to increase his wingspan and swung around the room in an attempt to strike his invisible opponent. Then he saw Ashlyn standing in the corner of the room and changed targets. He kept his arms spread wide as he approached her. She would not escape him again even in tyger form.

But Ashlyn didn't have the electroplasm to morph anymore. She had expended it all with her first morph and the healing of Nerdraaage. She was after all a very new druid, and there was no natural magic to draw upon in the stone room. So she stood defenseless, knowing that the blows that had so injured the tough dwarf would tear her flesh and crush her bones. There was only her kraken-tooth dagger on her thigh. But she would not. She could not.

And just as he approached her, Nerdraaage reappeared behind Doppelganger and placed a dagger into his back. "Say hello to my little—" Nerdraaage was in the process of a quote that he had often employed in the game when Doppelganger knocked him furiously back against the wall.

"You backstabbing coward!" cried Doppelganger. "You want to use weapons? I have weapons!" Doppelganger retrieved his axe and marched toward Nerdraaage still on the floor where he had been knocked. Doppelganger raised the axe above the wounded dwarf before he suddenly collapsed to the floor with a crash that must have been heard in the room below even through the stone floor. Ashlyn ran to Doppelganger.

"Oh my gods!" she said. "I hope you didn't kill him!"

"Nah," said Nerdraaage. "But I should have."

Doppelganger stared at Ashlyn weakly as his bloodwarp subsided. He looked as though he wished he could apologize but maybe she was just projecting. She turned him as much as she could to look at his back wound. She had generated a little bit of electroplasm and healed his back. "Hey!" yelled Nerdraaage. "What about me!" Ashlyn went to the dwarf. She kneeled next to him and examined him. She spoke the magic words and cast heals upon him as she felt her electroplasm welling inside of her. "He kicked my ass," said Nerdraaage.

"No," said Ashlyn. "It wasn't a fair fight. He was taken by the bloodwarp, and you didn't want to hurt your friend."

Nerdraaage tried to find the insult in her words but couldn't. "What do we do with him?"

"Let him sleep," said Ashlyn. And then suddenly, "Where's Dangalf?"

LXXXIX

Ashlyn stood in the guard command post before the sergeant of the guard, the ranking guard in the keep at this hour. "My friend is missing. He's a human conjurer. Dangalf of Hempshire."

"I have my own problems, she-elf. I'm missing a patrol."

"Can you at least let the guards know to be on the lookout for him?"

"Write down his description. I'll pass it along. Still it will be twenty-four hours before all the patrols and posts get the message."

"Why twenty-four hours?"

"It will take that long before they all cycle back through the keep for briefing."

"Can't you send pigeons to them?"

"Pigeons? To each patrol and post for a misplaced human?"

Nerdraaage entered, just hearing the last of the conversation. This dwarf was not of his clan. Stonefist alone had responsibility for royal protection, but the keep guards were of many clans.

Nerdraaage knew none of these clans was as prominent as his own when he said plainly to the sergeant, "Send out the birds." And they were sent.

XC

Regicide had failed. He and the she-trolls searched for Dangalf until dwarven griffin riders chased them away from the keep. Even with his assassin molls, he was not ready to take on an army of Bran Keep defenders. Not yet anyway.

Dangalf's escape was only the second failure of his otherwise brilliantly executed plan. (The first was the unforeseen difference of human bloodrunes between the two universes—the bloodrune bend sinister.) But Dangalf's escape was especially troubling. Dangalf just happened to be carrying a cat in his pocket, perhaps the one creature in this world that would terrorize the she-trolls. And then that Dangalf should be wearing a flying cloak to make his airborne escape from the mountain! Flying cloaks were impossibly expensive, and even then there was a years-long waiting list to purchase one. It was a great prize that one would not expect to be in the possession of so humble a conjurer.

Now Dangalf knew that Regicide was here and that he needed his blood. He would tell Doppelganger, the other candidate blood donor, and they would be prepared. Regicide tried to banish his doubts. This was his world after all. He had a twenty-year advantage over his former friends.

Regicide knew from an early age that he had been born in the wrong world. He had diagnosed himself as a sociopath, and that had been independently confirmed by several of his ex-girlfriends. He didn't push old ladies downstairs—he might even hold open a door for them—but his displays of kindness and gentleness were ruses. He had no problem with violence, but he considered unfocused violence to be a distraction. Those practitioners ended up in jail or asylums, and he wanted to rule the world. The problem was how? There were no summer camps for would-be world conquerors as there were for gifted athletes or musicians or computer geeks. Politics bored him. The leader of the most powerful nation had to shun, for the most part, all of the most enticing aspects of power and privilege. Only a few petty dictators in the desert or in the jungle had the kind of power he wanted to wield. And they were merely smoldering cigarette butts waiting for the monolith of civilized society to extend a foot and snuff them out.

Then one day Regicide passed a decrepit bookstore that had suddenly appeared overnight. Now in this bluest of worlds, he was not unaccustomed to a new building popping up overnight, but an old decrepit one popping up overnight bore further investigation. "Used Books" the signage read without any further ado. Seldom before had he entered a bookstore (all the combined wisdom of the world was online, was it not?), and he had never before entered a used bookstore, but something drew him to this place. He wondered how many times before he had passed without realizing a bookstore even existed in this too-small spot between the Laundromat and the Mexican restaurant.

The first thing he noticed was the clerk just inside the counter. It was as if his face was a bad drawing. It was bent in a horrendous frown, or maybe his face had begun to melt.

The shelves were mostly bare and dusty. It was one of those businesses that looked like it couldn't have existed unless it was run by a charity or a criminal front, or a gift shop during the off-season at the worst amusement park ever. But one book did draw his attention, breathed at him through the cobwebs. (Something made the cobwebs heave above it.) He wondered how many people had passed by it before. Then he thought about the incongruity of the whole situation and wondered if no one had passed by the book before, never stepped foot in the shop, never even saw it.

He liked the cover art. Some Boris Vallejo rip-off with a massive swordsman in victory pose and a chained girl on her knees next to him. (On closer inspection she wasn't human. But she wasn't bad either.) And he couldn't help but think that the triumphant swordsmen looked a bit like him, if he was to be depicted in such fashion by a second-rate Boris. The book appeared unread but still had yellowed with age the way cheap paperbacks will. *Cronica Europa* it was called, and he slipped it into his back pocket.

Regicide wasn't in the habit of shoplifting—usually too much risk for too little reward. But he wasn't against criminality and liked to keep in the practice. And there certainly weren't any security cameras in this hovel. And he seriously doubted Picasso-face was going to make an issue out of it. Could he even see out of those drooping eyeholes?

And so he looked directly at the clerk as he exited, but the clerk only displayed his inscrutable melting frown and said something unintelligible as if muffled words said by a real mouth behind the drooping and dead mouth of the false face.

That night Regicide began to read the yellowed book. And within a few pages, he was so astonished that he went back to the bookstore that very night to question the clerk before he melted away completely, only to find that the bookstore was already gone and had been replaced by an alley and a dumpster and a power pole with a hundred buzzing electric tentacles.

He went back home and continued reading the *Cronica Europa* and its magical history of this world that was known to few and forbidden to all. He learned how magic had been subjugated in this world since the Schism. And he learned about Acadia, the companion world that existed just beyond the unseen barrier.

He learned that there had been a valiant attempt in just the last century to wield ultimate power, and it had begun brilliantly. The Leader had dared to use the words and signs of magic in his pursuit of world domination and in quick fashion conquered Europa. But flush with victory, he deferred to his generals. He allowed machina to become the dominant force of his war, and magic was reduced to a ceremonial component because the generals knew machina and did not know magic, and it was not considered by them that their ancient race knew magic long before it knew machina. And so his tigers and panthers, named for the White School but built by the Blue School, ultimately failed against the overwhelming industry of the enemy. Western machina and Eastern horde bore down on his capitol, and the Leader died, never surrendering, in his underground keep. It marked the end of the last great effort for ultimate power.

Not even the ancient emperors who ruled the world and proclaimed themselves gods wielded the power that Regicide sought. For the closest example of that power, you would have to go back to the old king. Not the sanitized king of Sunday school but the unexpurgated king of forbidden history. The polytheistic, polygamous idolater. The king of supernatural lifespan, unparalleled wisdom, and unimagined wealth. The sorcerer on the magical throne who commanded demons to construct his temple. The king who wielded Sarrum Shuhadaku, the Sword of Kings, that would make its last appearance in this world as Caliburnus, in the hands of a crowned cuckold who thought himself good and would not wield the sword to its potential. The same sword that the old king, finally and completely corrupted by darkness, used to cut in half a baby that was claimed by two mothers. This story made a lot more sense to Regicide than the bowdlerized version, which only works if you believe one of the two bickering women would have been satisfied with half a baby. But the king's jealous god, who had commanded that he have no others gods before him, finally smote him.

And Regicide read further and learned about Acadia. A passageway was discovered through magical accident by ancients who carved and painted their knowledge on their own skin and any other surface that would hold a rune. That portal was finally destroyed by superstitions that would try to purge all magic from this world and would make knowledge of the other world so unreal and forbidden as to become myth and fantasy. Regicide knew that Acadia lay just behind a veil, but how to lift it?

When the game *Cronica* was introduced, Regicide was astonished. Someone else must have known about Acadia. He knew this was his key to lifting the great veil. He played it fanatically and became expert at it. He immersed himself completely in the virtual world, his avatar, game lore; and he programmed himself to dream about Acadia. In time his mind bled through to the other world, and he contacted and seduced a great troll witch, the Necromancer Princess Gykoja. The trolls now controlled the ancient sites in Nemetia, and it was she who was able to summon him to the new world. It was his first seduction, his first step into bringing about his quest for ultimate power.

And though only his soul made the crossing, he arrived to Acadia in human form. He set about making himself revered with the humans and the dwarves and the elves, and he did so by demonstrating courage and strength and wisdom. And he did all this alone, without the friends and allies that accompanied Dangalf. In time he rose to the rank of captain and devised a plan of attack against the hated witch Gykoja. He led a company of dwarves and humans that marched into Sylvania and attacked Gykoja's castle. Gykoja retreated but still struck down the humans and dwarves as they approached her in her throne room. And those she struck down she raised again as lichs and immediately set them to work against their former comrades. It was slow going, but Regicide broke through to Gykoja herself. He was close enough to cut her head off and send her lich army back to the grave. So drained was she by her own frantic spell casting that she fell back helplessly on the ground before him. And then, to the dismay of his troops, he took off his helm and kneeled before her. Gykoja understood. Her electroplasm recovered, she spoke black words that killed him, and she raised him and set him to work killing his own troops. Those that could escape did. They were few, fewer still that made it back to the free north. At least one escaping dwarf left an arm behind. It was as Regicide had planned.

Regicide allowed himself to be killed and raised from the dead, and Gykoja had agreed. But she was unaware that Regicide had tricked her and would retain his free will even during necromancy. And he knew of another ceremony that would allow him to be born again to living flesh with the infusion of human blood. And once a lich becomes again alive, he is immortal. And unlike the dilettantes before him, Regicide knew to first make himself immortal before he conquered the world. For ultimate power cannot be wielded by a mortal.

Regicide seduced Gykoja's she-troll minions, who now served him. And he stole from Gykoja her *Cronica Oceania*, which he knew contained the secret to the pool of life, where his rebirth must take place. But he would need blood from humans of his home world. He convinced Gykoja to summon the rest of the Keepers to Acadia. With that great spell expended, she was vulnerable, and he imprisoned her while she slumbered.

So what if Dangalf and Doppelganger now knew that he hunted them? He had an insurmountable advantage over them. He had rediscovered this world five thousand years after the Schism. He had accessed his race memory and, without classical training or proximity to the still-sacred sites, reached out to Acadia. He had brought himself to this world when they were still playing computer games. Dangalf and Doppelganger and Elftrap and the dwarf that had replaced him were nothing but his invited guests.

But he was concerned that they would make others aware of his ambitions, and there were some of this world that could still stop him. He knew he should not dwell on that and visualized instead his ultimate success. He would get his otherworld blood, and he would take the she-trolls to Oceania for his rebirth as an immortal. He had promised them carnal pleasures the likes of which they could not imagine when he was reborn of immortal flesh. He told them that when he ruled this world, they would be at his feet, most special among all his slaves. But he wondered if the she-trolls suspected a trap—that the ceremony for his rebirth required a sacrifice of that which he held most dear.

They did not know. But what Regicide did not know was that the murderous she-trolls would be more difficult sacrifices to make than he anticipated. For they kept a dark secret that no living creature other than they knew. For those living creatures that had known their secret—their parents, their tutors and trainers, and other unfortunates—had all been killed by the sister assassins.

XCI

Dangalf, frozen and exhausted, had finally reached civilization. He was back at the bottom of the Ten Thousand Steps, and he was met by guards who were on high alert due to recent events. After he pulled the ripcord on his flying cloak, he had coaxed it to float him as far away from Regicide and the trolls as he could. It was just as well, since he saw them at various times circling overhead as they searched for him. But unfortunately it also meant he had taken himself miles away from the entrance to the keep—miles compounded by the mountainous terrain.

The guards looked suspiciously at him as he dragged his unfurled flying cloak behind him. It would have made travel easier to cut it loose, but he did not carry a dagger with him, a mistake he vowed to correct. When he told the guards his name, they knew it and put him into a basket, and he was lifted up to the road to Bran Keep. Once he'd been unloaded from the basket, other guards saw to his transport in a delivery cart, which was fortunate because his frostbitten feet were in no condition for walking. He supposed he might have kept walking if he hadn't stopped, but once he stopped during his ride in the basket, his feet refused to carry him any further.

At the gate to Bran Keep, Dangalf was taken by stretcher to the hospital. There he made his report to the captain of the guard. Dangalf's feet were healed enough for him to walk again, and he returned to the room from which he had been kidnapped. No one was there, and he thought to do a reading with his divination deck while Dusty stretched out on a bed.

"Dangalf!" Ashlyn said upon entering. "Where's your hat!"

"Forget about my hat."

"Forget about your hat?"

"I have an important story to tell you," said Dangalf, still reading his cards. "I'll tell you on our journey to find Doppelganger."

"But Doppelganger is miss—" She paused. "You know Doppelganger is missing?"

"Gone but not missing. Could you take a look at my feet? We have a lot of walking ahead of us."

Ashlyn kneeled before Dangalf. He hissed painfully as she removed his bandages.

"Frostbite," she said, and then she began to heal him further.

"All of my initial readings from the divination deck have come true," said Dangalf. "Doppelganger was the last one. He reached the crossroads that I predicted, and he had to make a choice."

"Let me see your hands," she said standing. She healed the frostbite from his hands. "What choice?"

"Oh," said Dangalf as Ashlyn ran her finger down his nose, returning blood to the starved appendage. "Um, this," he said, holding a divination deck card featuring a knight with a white rose on his shield.

"The Order of the White Rose," she said.

"He has gone to become a Templar," said Dangalf. "Let's pray that the warrior fog is lifted from his mind and our friend is returned to us." And then casually he added, "So what happened while I was gone to make him leave?"

"Oh," said Ashlyn casually in response. "He had a big fight with Nerdraaage."

"Is Nerdraaage all right?"

"He's fine," she said smiling. "He's a sturdy little guy."

"Anything else?" asked Dangalf a little less casually.

"No," said Ashlyn, lying very well. "He left our communal gold as well."

"Well, prepare to leave and hear the story of my kidnapping by troll blackguards!"

"Kidnapping!" said Ashlyn with a gasp.

"Oh, it get's much better," promised Dangalf. "Find Nerdraaage! Doppelganger is in great danger! Meet me in the tavern. I have to feed Dusty and myself. But mostly Dusty. She saved my life." And he departed.

Ashlyn shook her head in confusion. She looked at the table where Dangalf had been reading his divination deck. Of the exposed cards, one stood out. It depicted a satyr ripping a woman's bodice. She resented that she lied so well only for Dangalf to have known the truth before he even asked.

Ashlyn found Nerdraaage and brought him to The Wee Hours, where they sat down with Dangalf and Dusty. Dangalf regaled both with the story of his kidnapping by the she-trolls and his flying escape from the *Cronica* player turned black knight, Regicide.

"Black adamantine!" enthused Nerdraaage. "That stuff's worth a fortune!"

"Hm," said Dangalf. "That's an interesting takeaway from everything I just told you." His story continued down the hall and back to their room while they packed to leave in pursuit of Doppelganger. Ashlyn and Nerdraaage had many questions, and Dangalf answered those that he could. "We should send Doppelganger a message," said Ashlyn.

"I thought of that," said Dangalf. "But Doppelganger can't read."

"He what?"

"I don't know that he always couldn't read, but I know he hasn't been able to read for several weeks. It must have been quite frustrating for him. But his brain shut down to only those direct functions that benefited the warrior class. And that apparently does not include reading." They rode the speeding mining cars down to the keep floor. It was still nerve wracking for Dangalf even after his jump from the mountain.

There was a great commotion on the main level, and even though it was their intention to leave expeditiously, they were swept up in the moment and momentum. A great crowd had gathered outside the royal palace, including many hundreds of dwarves, all wearing uniform tabards and standing in military formation. The mob was so great that the Keepers walked around to the side, where they were able to get much closer to the palace steps, even if it meant they had to watch on a sharp angle. Nearby a dwarf, who seemed in decoration and demeanor to be some sort of commander, spoke loudly with the elf and human ambassadors. "You can't unilaterally undertake such a belligerent action!" said the human ambassador. "What do I tell the Supreme Allied Commander?"

"Tell him he can come along if he wants," said the commander. "And you, elf! Do your people know we are coming through your lands?"

"They are expecting you, Marshal Uallas," said the elf ambassador. "But the Crimson Wall does not accommodate invasions in either direction."

"We'll dig under it."

"The roots of gravewhisper are as deadly as the vines, and those of the Crimson Wall grow deep."

"We dug the Profundity!" shouted Uallas. "We'll get past your shrubbery!"

The Profundity! They had walked past the heavily guarded entrance. "I am such a fool," said Dangalf.

"What?" asked Ashlyn.

"The Profundity. It's supposed to go to the very center of the earth. And Bran Mountain is the tallest peak in Acadia!"

"So?" added Nerdraaage.

"Princess Dymphna!" answered Dangalf. "She said we would find the one who summoned us where the center of the world meets the sky. Bran Keep!"

"Oh," said Ashlyn and Nerdraaage.

"I should have devoted more thought to her vision," lamented Dangalf. "She is a very good seer, even if she doesn't keep up with her studies. And Regicide must have his own seer, who led him right to me."

"He might know where Doppelganger is headed!" said Ashlyn.

"If the decision was made spontaneously, maybe not. At least not yet."

"Shite," she said. "We're no match for a lich knight and two assassins, especially if they have a seer who tells them where we're going."

"We can no longer follow the paths so clearly laid out for us," said Dangalf. "We need to add an element of randomness to our actions."

Trumpets interrupted their conversation as only trumpets can do. The chattering crowd grew silent. Even the commander and the ambassadors gave their attention. "His Majesty, the king," was announced.

A large dwarf in royal furs and silks and carrying a gold hammer adorned with goblin teeth descended the steps. He was Taog of Clan Bluebeard, midway through his reign as king. Ashlyn thought he looked trashy because his shirt was sleeveless, and she wondered if he had them tailored that way because he had big guns. She remembered what Dangalf had told them about Dwarven governance. Every thirty years the five clans put forth their best and brightest to be the next king. The contest between the five best and brightest was settled by arm wrestling, causing some skeptics to suggest that the royal clans weren't nominating their best and brightest so much as they were nominating their best arm wrestlers.

"Before the elves even climbed down from their trees," boomed the king.

"We went up into trees," said Ashlyn. Nerdraaage shushed her.

"When human killed human with no more thought than killing a warg," continued the king, "the dwarves already had a great civilization!" And suddenly the crowd came alive with a roaring approval that filled the giant keep. "And the six original clans carved this great city where before there was only solid rock. And this city, this keep and our civilization has endured for thirty thousand years." The crowd cheered again.

"We endured the Sundering and the blight of darkness. We endured the war of the schools and the Schism. We endured the Great War, when only one out of nine dwarves returned home. Not only did we endure, we triumphed! Even at the battle of Nemetia, when every defending dwarf was killed, we brought so much destruction upon the enemy that even the Legion lost their taste for war!" The crowd roared approval. "And now this effrontery!" said the king as he held up a small silver thing. "A goblin-carved clan ring!" The crowd reacted with thundering disapproval.

"That's my ring," Nerdraaage shouted.

"I believe you're right," worried Dangalf aloud.

"Those who can no longer call themselves dwarf call themselves Clan Ghostbeard!" shouted the king. The crowd's fury was overwhelming. "It is an insult and injury that challenges the very foundation of our ancient civilization, the very cornerstone of all civilizations, and it can not go unpunished like so many other attacks from the black side of the world!" The crowd roared approval. And then to the dismay of Dangalf and Ashlyn, the king began speaking in Dwarven. Dangalf asked Nerdraaage what he was saying, but the enraptured Nerdraaage waved him off.

"Aye, Nerdraaage is it?" said a red-haired dwarf wearing blackguard blacks.

"Yes—I mean, aye."

"You have gained much reputation with the ring you brought back. Your foreign friends as well. I am Assassin Bearach of Clan Warfoot. We have a mutual friend I believe? A human who goes by Icil?"

"You know Icil?" said Nerdraaage.

"There is not better a blackguard in all the world," said Bearach. "You outsiders have probably not before heard a dwarf say anything not dwarven is the best. But dwarf blackguards are few in number. Most don't make it past the bandit class, and many of those end up getting themselves estranged. Humans do not have the dwarven resistance to secrecy and solitude, and as such they have blackguards in many numbers, and great blackguards some become."

"Have you seen Icil?" asked Ashlyn. "How is he?"

"How well could he be? He's a wretched creature pining over a ghost." And then to Dangalf. "You humans would do well to form your own clans. Then when times are darkest, maybe you would not seem so alone." Then again to Nerdraaage, he said, "A handful of assassins and blackguards are going out by wagon in an hour to do some reconnoitering in Brimstone before the main force arrives. You are not experienced for such a mission, but you are trained by Icil, and you wear the colors of a great clan, so I have decided to ask you along. It is, after all, your ring that launched this war."

"Okay," Nerdraaage said softly.

"Good. We will see you at the stables in an hour."

When Bearach was out of earshot, Ashlyn said, "Did you just volunteer to go to war?"

"What are you doing?" added Dangalf. "We have to rescue Doppelganger!"

"What was I supposed to say?"

"No," suggested Ashlyn.

"That would have made me look real good."

"It would have been better than going to the stables in an hour and telling him you can't go," she continued.

"We need you, Nerd," said Dangalf.

"You do?"

"Of course."

"Look, it's my ring that started all of this," said Nerdraaage. "I think it will look bad if I don't go." Nerdraaage struggled for the right words to convince his friends. If ever he needed to express himself with concise and powerful words, it was now. "The bells of war are ringing!" he said.

"The bells of war?" asked Dangalf.

"You know," said Ashlyn. "The war bells."

A frustrated Nerdraaage said, "I can't just run away with my pride between my legs." Dangalf tried not to laugh at the mixed metaphor, but when Ashlyn laughed out loud, he couldn't prevent a broad smile from spreading across his own face. "I wouldn't expect skin-knickers to understand!" Nerdraaage said angrily.

"Nerd," said Dangalf as he composed himself. "You agreed not to break up the group. Not until we were ready."

"Doppelganger already did," said Nerdraaage. Dangalf and Ashlyn looked at each other. He had a point.

"Okay," said Dangalf.

The endomorph had won an intellectual victory against the two ectomorphs and enjoyed the moment. But when he realized he was going off to war alone, he wondered if he shouldn't have lost this argument.

"Wait," said Ashlyn. "What about the element of randomization we were going to use?" she continued.

"Good call," said Dangalf. "Nerd, are you willing to let the cards decide your path?"

"Okay," said Nerdraaage.

Dangalf spread the divination deck before Nerdraaage. "We're pressed for time, so I guess this will have to do. Pick one." Nerdraaage turned over the Red Horse.

"What does that mean?" asked Ashlyn.

"War," said Dangalf.

"Best two out of three?" she suggested, but it was not to be.

Ashlyn went to the elven ambassador, who still stood nearby. After a few minutes, she returned to her friends. The ambassador understood the war was actually to be a raid of only a few weeks at most. And it was hoped, since the primary objective was for the dwarves to kill their own kind (even though the dwarves would dispute that undwarves were "their own kind"), that this was not an AARR operation, and that the cold war would not become immediately hot again.

Dangalf and Nerdraaage were relieved to hear about the expected duration and that it was being called only a "raid." Ashlyn said that they could keep in touch by sending Clay back and forth. Nerdraaage grumbled that he would look bad to the other blackguards if a pigeon could find him. Ashlyn told him to write to them when he got the chance.

The stables were located down a winding stairway from the floor of the keep. It was enormous with a stench to match. There were myriad animals housed here, mostly ponies, which were favored because of their stature and thick coats.

They found a rogues' gallery of blackguards sitting on or standing near a cart already attached to four horses. They looked battle scarred and intimidating. They wore buckskin, presumably over their blacks, just like Nerdraaage. But that was the only sense in which he seemed to fit with them.

The blackguards looked unsympathetically on the dwarf escorted by human and elf and laden with goods. Nerdraaage carried a firkin of beer. Dangalf carried his roasted boar and Ashlyn his roasted chicken.

"Ah," said a black-haired blackguard. "The cook is here." The other blackguards laughed heartily. Even a stable hand leaned on his shovel and guffawed.

"Pull up my scarf," Nerdraaage whispered to Ashlyn.

"What?"

"Pull up my scarf. It's inside my jacket."

Ashlyn reached into Nerdraaage's jacket collar and pulled up his Clan Stonefist tartan and draped it across his shoulders. The dwarven laughter died down, and the stable hand returned to shoveling shite.

Nerdraaage placed his goods upon the open carriage. Dangalf and Ashlyn followed suit. "It's not a very glamorous mode of transport," said Dangalf after the Keepers stepped away to converse privately.

"We don't take mounts into battle because they can't unappear."

Bearach showed next and had a few parting words for the rouges. The army had already left, but they had a long march ahead of them. "Wait, wait!" cried a voice. It was Camran running up to them from a distance. He was pushing a cart with three casks on it. He ran up to the wagon and loaded one of the casks onto it.

"What's all this then?" demanded Bearach.

"This is the solution to your greatest problem," said Camran breathlessly.

"And what would that be?"

"Powdered beer!" he said proudly.

"Powdered beer?"

"You just add water!"

"Water!" protested the black-haired blackguard.

"Beer is mostly water," said Camran.

"Maybe the beer you drink in the White School!"

"No. All beer. Please. There is enough in these casks to make twelve hundred pints of beer." The promise of 1,200 pints instantly silenced the critics. "You'll find your loads much less of a burden, and you can reconstitute it with any local water source."

"Well," said the black-haired blackguard. "Looks like we won't need to carry all these supplies." And he tapped into Nerdraaage's firkin and poured himself a bootful. Other blackguards opened up Nerdraaage's roasted boar and chicken even though Camran had not delivered any powdered food.

Finally, Nerdraaage patted Dusty good-bye, and he and the blackguards climbed aboard the wagon. Nerdraaage saluted solemnly to his friends, and they saluted in return. The wagon began moving. Ashlyn felt like a mother sending her special child off for his first day of school, only this school matriculated thieves and backstabbers, and he might not be back for months. She felt a tear run down her cheek. "Nerdraaage," she yelled after him. "Did you remember your murder kit?"

"Yes," he answered over a chorus of dwarven laughter.

While still in the stables, Dangalf paid to have his flying cloak returned to Vinland for repacking. He had already purchased an inexpensive but warm hooded cloak to replace it. He thought the hood would be a nice deception for faraway pursuers looking for a wizard hat. And they were off, this time exiting from the stable doors below the grand stairway. As soon as her first paw hit snow, Dusty was up and into her pocket on Dangalf's robe with only her head poking out.

"I'm very hopeful about Doppelganger," said Dangalf. "Templars are great fighters, but they are also very learned. I think that the change will be good for him, that he will be back to his old self."

"Oh, I hope so."

"I wish I had done more to help him. Let's not forget it was his warrior mentality that got us through that first quest. None of us could have killed those dire wolves but him. And that was the foundation for everything we've achieved since then. And then when we got a little bit comfortable, his coarseness became a burden or an embarrassment. I wish I had reached out to him before he felt he had to go off on his own. I will never forgive myself if something happens to him."

She ran her arm inside his cloak and around his waist, and it did make him feel better. But she let go soon enough, as it impeded their walking speed to be standing so close. "You must be tired," Ashlyn said.

"Exhausted. I can sleep on the flatboat though. I'm glad you're still with me. I don't think I could do this alone."

"You could do it alone," she said. "You were alone on that mountain."

"Well, not exactly," he said, looking down to Dusty.

"I think you're going to be the most powerful of the four of us," she said.

"You think? Regicide said something about me becoming very powerful. Weyd Salint warned me that success as a mage meant I would be alone in a tower with only my books and telescope."

"No," said Ashlyn. "Just as we're going after Doppelganger now, we'll all come for you if you try to hide away in a tower."

"What about you? Maybe you'll want to associate more with the elves. I can't say I would blame you."

"Elves are fine," she said. "But I have a special fondness for humans. Maybe because I was one."

"Do you know what it means, the Keepers of the Broken Blade?"

"It's from a Hardy Boys mystery, right?"

"How did you know that?"

"I saw the book in your library."

"Of course," said Dangalf. "But have you seen this?" And he held out before her a card from the Divination Deck: *The Broken Blade.*

"You mean there really is a broken blade?"

"This is one of the sympathy cards. I believe it is a clue to our greater purpose in this world. The mask of chance makes destiny seem like coincidence."

"Who said that?"

"I just made it up."

"You should never say it again," she said laughing. And after a while, she added, "Does it strike you as unbelievable the adventures that we're having? I mean, I know we agreed that we weren't dreaming or having a psychotic episode, but still, it just doesn't make sense all of the great things that have been happening to us. And by great I mean good and bad. We've met elven princesses and ghosts. We found a ring that has started a war, and we were even present for the creation of powdered beer. Doppelganger was invited to train as a Templar. You bought me a spider ring that just happened to ward me when I was attacked by a giant spider. It just seems like too many important things have happened around us."

"And why shouldn't they? Why shouldn't we matter to this world reciprocal to how we didn't matter in the other world?" Dangalf thought of how he had always seemed to lose out in the other world, not for lack of intelligence or ambition, but due to inexplicable forces at work—as if he was out of synch with that universe.

When he was in high school, his eccentricities had made him an outcast. But he had compensated for that with ingenuity. Well before his prom, he had marketed himself as a tutor at the nearby girls' school, where they did not know him to be an untouchable. He had insinuated himself with several of the prettier girls and had scored the best-looking one of them to be his prom date. She was not only beautiful but she was the head cheerleader. Why a girls' school needed cheerleaders was unclear, but he found the very notion to be full of erotic potential. When his big night came, all heads turned when he entered the prom with a date who made his own school's popular elite seem plain. But it was not to be. Shortly after their arrival, his date excused herself. Thirty minutes later she returned to apologize and say she wasn't feeling well.

He offered her a ride home, but she said she thought it was the limo that had made her sick, and she turned around and left with the high school quarterback. Turn lemons into lemonades he had always been told, and so Dangalf flirted with the quarterback's jilted date, who responded that he was "fat." And that was years before he was fat. Dangalf thought he had never been sadder in his life than when he was riding home alone in the back of that limo. Worse, he had to ride around for hours and construct a pleasing story for his parents about the prom. As miserable as he felt, he could not let his parents know. They would have hurt more deeply even than him, and he could not bear being the cause of that pain.

Years ago, an unemployed Dangalf had impressed upon his parents to buy him a new suit, waited in a two-hour line, and earned the chance to sit down for an interview with his dream employer at an outdoor job fair. Dangalf gave the interview of his life, answering all of their questions with ease and confidence. He had had many job interviews in his life, and he nailed this one. This job was his to lose. And as he rose and bid farewell to his future employer, a pigeon suddenly landed on his head. It sternly resisted his gentle attempts to remove it. (Looking back he wondered if it had had an important message from Acadia.) He saw his interviewers' demeanor change right before his eyes. They were not seers or sages, and they didn't know exactly what the pigeon on Dangalf's head portended, only that it portended in part that they must not hire him. He got their "thanks but no thanks" letter in the mail two days later, postmarked the day of his interview.

Some people seemed to be living charmed lives in the other world, but Dangalf was clearly not one of them. And he guessed that was true for the other Keepers as well. Who was to say they hadn't been born in the wrong world, the wrong universe, the wrong body? He looked over to Ashlyn, who met his gaze and smiled. "It is a bit chilly," she said. "I hope you don't mind if I put my coat on."

"Not at all."

And she morphed into tyger form. Dusty, his other feline bookend, yawned and tucked her head into his pocket. Dangalf knew that, despite the danger, he could have been happier only if Doppelganger and Nerdraaage walked this snowy road with them.

Dangalf hadn't allowed himself much time to think about loved ones from the other world. There was too much exhilaration and jeopardy in this world to accommodate sentimentality, and now their party was splintered and facing unimaginable danger. But he thought back now to the last conversation he had with his mother. He had rushed her off the phone because he wanted to get back to playing *Cronica*. With mild disappointment his mother had told him, "You could do great things if you only stopped playing that game."

He hoped he could someday tell her just how right she was.

XCII

From a fragment discovered by the first Faraway expedition and dated by our most gifted seers as over thirty-thousand-years-old: *Woden did summon the two wisest elves, the two strongest dwarves, and two bravest humans to his mountain. He did give each pair the task of slaying the monster Grendil, who resided at the center of the earth, since the world was turned inside out, and who also did put the evil in the heart of Kejavik to make the first murder. The elves said Grendil was immortal and it was prophesied that he could not be killed by sapien, and Woden did send them away. The dwarves next set upon the task, and with their great strength dug the Profundity, which was a path to the underworld where Grendil lived. But the dwarves, when faced with the monster, found that their strength was no match, and they were slain. The two humans next took the path of the Profundity and faced the great monster. And Grendil did make the humans know that he was too powerful for them to kill. He showed them the corpses of the dwarves and of all the many more beings that he had killed and torn asunder. And the humans did not despair, for unlike elves and dwarves they would not live forever, and to lose their lives in an impossible struggle was a great thing to do. And this courage in the face of such certain death caused a perplex-ity to Grendil. He had not known but the terror and desperation of those that did face him, and it was of grievous concern that the humans had none. And Grendil thought this human courage could only come from their foreknowledge that they would kill him and that they knew the secret of his demise. And when the humans raised up to strike Grendil, he made himself adamantine against their swords and was alive no more.*

And the humans again did appear before Woden, and he instructed them to go out into his garden and each return with a flower. And it was so that one human was a priest, and he returned with a white rose, and the other human was a warrior who returned with a red rose. And Woden did command that they would each found a temple, one of the white rose and one of the red rose. And here they would teach a new class that would be of both the White and Red School. Templars would they be called, and they would fight with arms and with magic against all cruelty and injus-tice and unnaturalness. And they would take only the strongest warriors and wisest priests as novices, and even then very few of the novices could ever be called Templar. And the priest begged, "Great Woden, how will we know which novices are worthy of being Templars?" And Woden did answer, "You will know the chosen ones, for they shall be knighted by my own hand."

Cronica Acadia

The End

ABOUT THE AUTHOR

C. J. Deering was born in Portland, Maine, and earned a BFA in writing from the University of Southern California. He is a writer, historian, and gamer based in Los Angeles.

www.ingramcontent.com/pod-product-compliance
Lightning Source LLC
Chambersburg PA
CBHW071630260626
47170CB00001B/45